AGE OF FRENZY

AGE OF FRENZY

MAHABALESHWAR SAIL

Translated from the Konkani by
Vidya Pai

HARPERPERENNIAL

HARPERPERENNIAL

First published in India in 2017 by Harper Perennial
An imprint of HarperCollins *Publishers*

Building 10, Tower A, 4th Floor, DLF Cyber City, Phase II,
Gurugram Haryana – 122002, India
www.harpercollins.co.in

This edition published in India in 2019 by Harper Perennial

2 4 6 8 10 9 7 5 3 1

The essay 'A Saga of Choice and Faith' was published as 'A Saga of a Frenzied Age' in 50 Writers 50 Books *Eds. Pradeep Sebastian and Chandra Siddan (HarperCollins India, 2013).*

P-ISBN: 978-93-5302-489-5
E-ISBN: 978-93-5302-658-5

This is a work of fiction and all characters and incidents described in this book are the product of the author's imagination. Any resemblance to actual persons, living or dead, is entirely coincidental.

Typeset in 11.5/14.5 Adobe Garamond Pro
by Jojy Philip, New Delhi

Printed and bound at
MicroPrints India, New Delhi

It was at daybreak that Saaton Nayak led his pair of bullocks and set up the plough in his field at Khargali. It was quite cold and a thin film of mist hung about the forest which flanked the narrow strip of farmland. As he urged his bullocks on, the clamour of a troop of monkeys and the rustle of leaves as they swung from tree to tree carried to his ears. A peacock darted out of the forest and perched on a branch, shrieking raucously before darting off again.

A twinge of apprehension and fear gripped Saaton Nayak's heart. He shouted at the bullocks and the plough moved forward, cutting open the earth in neat furrows. They were quite alike, this pair of strong animals, with large humps on their backs. The tuft of hair at the tip of their tails looked like the tassels on a monarch's palanquin.

They had barely gone up and down twice when the plough's wooden peg came loose and it wobbled crookedly. Saaton Nayak tried to knock it back with his scythe but the peg split into two. He would have to whittle a new one now, and so he left the bullocks in the field and went in search of a sturdy piece of wood.

Suddenly a tiger crept out of the undergrowth and the bullocks froze, wide-eyed in terror. Roaring loudly, it pounced on the red bullock and snapped its neck. The other one, with dark patches, leapt up shattering the wooden framework of the plough but the bridle rope remained wrapped around its neck. The tiger attacked it next and brought it down. Saaton Nayak saw the tiger and began to scream, waving his scythe. The tiger stared at him for a moment, then slipped back into the undergrowth and vanished into the forest. The two bullocks lay spreadeagled on the ground. Their windpipes had snapped and the tiger's teeth and claws had dug deep into their backs.

Saaton crouched beside his animals sobbing disconsolately for a while. Then wailing loudly and beating his breast, he returned home. The villagers crowded about him, and their hearts sank when they heard him. A strange fear gnawed at their bellies. They believed that tigers wouldn't touch cattle when the bridle rope was about their necks. But this one had killed two bullocks when they were yoked to the plough. Deva, what sort of calamity is this.

The weekly puja performed every Monday at Shirvaddo, the locality where the Nayak community lived, was only four days away. The fear in people's hearts refused to subside. We must beseech the Lord to show us a way out, only He can save this village now. All the rituals must be performed properly.

That year Venku Nayak's family had been elected to perform the rituals and conduct all the festivals on behalf of the Nayak community. A stretch of farmland in which two khandis of paddy seedlings could be sown was set aside for the gods. The family that was responsible for performing the puja was allowed to cultivate this land. Every Monday the head of the household would perform the puja at the little shrines of the guardian spirits of the village. It was also his responsibility to see that all commitments to their village deity Lord Ramnath, were satisfactorily discharged during the year.

Venku Nayak arrived that evening with a platter of sweetened beaten rice in one hand and a vessel containing oil in the other. His elder son held a flaming cloth wick, and his ten-year-old granddaughter had a coconut in her hand. They moved towards the little shrine that was dedicated to Ghar Avai, the Big Mother, the wife of the founder of the settlement. Then they went to the enclosure where the khunti, the holy stake was stuck into the ground, and finally to the Barmo shrine. Venku Nayak poured some oil into the stone lamps that stood before each deity and set them alight. He placed a fistful of phov, or sweet beaten rice in each shrine and prayed loudly.

Of all the deities in the settlement only Santeri had a tiny shrine made of golden hay and dry grass with a little thatched door that was opened only on Mondays. This Santeri was an anthill, as tall as a fully grown man, with innumerable peaks and protrusions that were moist and fresh as though they had just been formed. No one knew when this anthill was formed or who had started the tradition of worshipping it. It must have existed before their forefathers settled at this spot. Yet it continued to grow and rejuvenate itself through the years. Its roots had plunged deep into the netherworld; countless ants and worms and snakes found refuge within it.

The horn was blown loudly and Venku Nayak lit the stone lamp. He placed the offering of beaten rice and prayed, 'Cereals and grains, flowers and fruits, trees and palms, tubers and roots … everything grows and bears fruit because of your benevolence. We shall place the fruit of your bounty at your feet, only then shall we take it home to feed our families. Our fields remain fertile because of your benevolence year after year. Give us good harvests, look after our fruits, our trees; don't let us starve, slake our thirst … O Mother!'

He took the coconut from his granddaughter's hand and placed it before the anthill. By the following Monday, the coconut would have disappeared into the anthill. As he turned to shut the temple door, he saw some men standing outside. The people in the settlement didn't normally attend the weekly ritual. So why were these men here, their nostrils flaring?

'Venku bhau, did you ask the deity why all this is happening? Our calves get stuck in the mud, small coconuts fall from the trees. Tigers kill our bullocks even as they stand yoked to the plough. Is there something wrong with the way you worship the deities, or have the gods withdrawn their benevolence and protection?' Mhablu Nayak demanded to know.

'If they don't protect the village what use are these gods to us? Why should we worship them or place balls of sweet beaten rice on their heads? Demand an answer, Venku … ask them!' Babuti screamed.

'Men are committing sins. The ridge gourd on the creeper at one's door is whisked away before one's eyes. Boundary stones that mark one's fields are uprooted and pushed back overnight. So many sins … punishment is bound to follow.'

'Don't change the topic, Venku bhau. If the gods are looking after us, how is it that man commits sins? The gods must show us a way out of this. Or these deities must leave this village. Tell them that.'

'Who am I to demand an answer from the gods? I'm only doing my job of performing the rituals every week. Everyone must come together to exhort the gods; the spirit of the Mulpurus, the founder of our settlement, must be awakened and must be invoked in an oracle's body. Catch hold of this avsar and ask for an answer. Why do you stand here squabbling before the holy mother Santeri? If the serpent that lives within her body is outraged nothing can save this village.'

'We'll do that. We'll demand an answer from the avsar. But be warned! If he says that the rituals are not being performed properly, you will be held responsible. You till the fields set aside for the gods and enjoy whatever they yield. You are answerable to the community.'

The men turned away. As Venku Nayak shut the door of the shrine, he grumbled loudly, 'They'll argue with the gods. And fight with their own relatives in the settlement. Why blame the gods for everything? Why don't you pick up your scythes and axes and drive the tiger away? But no. It's easier to blame the gods!'

It was well into the afternoon when a young man, eighteen or twenty years of age, trudged down the hill. Scared and tired, overcome by hunger and thirst, he crouched beneath the banyan by the temple. Two or three of the men sitting on the temple steps came up to him, 'Who are you? Which village do you hail from?'

'Are you deaf or dumb, or what? Creep into this village like a thief and now you won't open your mouth. One blow with a stick and…'

'No, no … don't beat me! I fall at your feet, don't cast me out!' the youth pleaded.

'Who are you? Where are you from?'

'I'm from Divade village. Lakhu Nayak's son, Ganaba.'

'What happened to you?'

The boy began to weep. 'I only drew a pot of water for those people and gave them directions to wherever they wanted to go. So they gave me a piece of jadd roti and some fruits soaked in sweet syrup. Just fruits, believe me. Nothing else.'

'And then?'

'People said I'd eaten their thick bread and their meat. My father threw me out of the house. My mother wouldn't come near me. They kept my wife away. Then all the villagers picked up stones and drove me out.'

'Why have you come here?'

'I went from one village to another, but no one would let me stay. My mother used to say that one of her cousins lived in Adolshi, so I came here looking for her.'

'What's your aunt's name?'

'It seems she had many moles on her skin so she was known as Tilai mavshi. I saw her when I was very young, may not recognize her today.' Still sobbing, he cried, 'I beg of you, don't drive me away.'

The people became wary. They had heard that some people who practised a strange religion had crossed the seven seas and come to Goa. He who ate what these people touched would be cast out by society, he would become impure, they were told. These villagers had never seen those strangers though.

The village headman, Khapru Nayak, was quite clear. 'Lord Ramnath presides over this village, His presence makes the region holy and pure. No one who professes another religion, no man who has been cast out from our faith can spend even one night here. To let him in would be a big sin.'

So eight or ten men with big sticks in their hands chased

the young man across the embankment and past the stream into the low lying fields, the khajan by the river.

Early the next morning, a corpse was found floating in the little pool where the deities were taken for a ceremonial dip on festive occasions. The whole village was terror stricken.

'Tie a rope around the body and drag it to the khajan. Such a corpse cannot be consigned to the holy flames, nor can any funeral rites be performed,' the village astrologer declared. But no one had the courage to move the corpse. It remained in the water all day.

As Sada Nayak stood by the hedge behind his house, the next morning, he noticed a pack of vultures circling above the pool. A gut-wrenching tremor passed through his frame. His heart thudded as he grabbed the shovel in the courtyard and rushed through the fields towards the pool.

Sada Nayak chased away the vultures and set about digging a waist-deep trench on the bank of the stream. A powerful entity seemed to possess his body. Grabbing hold of the corpse, all by himself, he dragged it into the trench and covered it with mud. He was a strong man, but by the time he finished the task, his head was swimming, and somehow he lurched home on faltering steps. He drew water from the well and poured the cold water over himself. Then, smashing the mud pot on the ground, he walked into the house in his wet loincloth.

People from the neighbourhood stood in silent groups in his courtyard. One of them was a woman whose face and neck were covered with dark moles. Her eyes swam with tears. Suddenly Phati Nayak rushed up to Sada's door. 'Sada, did you bury the corpse on this side of the stream or on the other side?' he screeched.

'On this side.'

'Sada, you've brought calamity on this village. A man who belongs to another faith cannot spend a night in this village. And you've buried him here for all time. There'll be a catastrophe when the gods come to bathe there during the temple festival, the whole village will be destroyed.'

One day a loud explosion was heard somewhere at the far end of the village. Had some huge banyan or peepal tree come crashing to the ground? Was it thunder? The sky in this month of Kartick was clear. People stared nervously in the direction of the sound, a strange sound that no one had heard before. Suddenly a cowherd rushed frantically down the hill. 'Those white-skinned devils have entered this village. They've killed a huge wild boar up in the hills, saw it with my own eyes…' he shouted.

In a short while, the whole group descended the hill. Two senior white soldiers were on horseback, six foot soldiers half-ran half-walked behind them. Of them, three were brown-skinned locals. One of the men on horseback had a gun slung on his shoulder. The white men wore tight-fitting coats and breeches, fine shoes and had caps on their heads. The locals wore knee-length dhotis one end of which was drawn up between their legs and tucked into the waist-band at the back. They had on thick shirts and sandals and a kerchief wrapped about their heads. All the constables had swords strapped to their waists and carried batons in their hands.

Lingu Nayak and Gana Nayak, who were working in the field, crouched behind the haystacks peeping at the soldiers. They were so fair, as though cast in sunlight. Surely these were the tallest and the strongest men alive!

'People say they're white-skinned, Lingu, but I think their skin is red,' Gana whispered. 'They eat the flesh of cows and drink human blood.'

'A race of red demons. Their nails and teeth must be sharp, like pointed stakes.'

'Their guns have fire inside, the spark goes right through a man and kills him.'

'He dies immediately, or he dies later when his body begins to rot. They smear snake poison on their swords, I've heard.'

The soldiers on horseback dismounted in front of the Ramnath temple, a magnificent structure with thick wooden beams and huge pillars. The oil lamp in the sanctum glowed dimly as though it were burning deep within a dark cave. The leader of the group was surprised to see no one around. He turned to one of the local soldiers who served as an interpreter. 'Where have these people gone, leaving the temple open like this?'

'They're scared, senor, must be hiding somewhere around.'

'If we enter their temple and seize their gods, will they come out?'

'Can't tell, senor.'

They drank water at the temple tank and took the path to Shirvaddo through the fields. There was no one in sight. Everything was quiet, as though the whole village and its people had vanished. The old soldier was angry. What sort of cowards were these people, taking fright and fleeing at the approach of other men.

The settlement at Shirvaddo was like a part of the forest. Mango, jambul, and tall palms stood guard before each of the thirty mud houses thatched with hay and dry fronds. There was a tiny shack beside each house in which they stored firewood and pats of dry cow dung for heating bathwater during the rainy months. The soldiers hurried through the wide open plain that lay between Shirvaddo and the Brahmin quarters at Raigali.

The Brahmin settlement at Raigali was quite different from that at Shirvaddo. All the houses stood within an extensive orchard of mango, jackfruit and orange trees, coconut and areca nut palms and pepper vines. A channel guided the water from a spring on the hill. It went through the large orchard belonging to the Kenkre family and then flowed through the orchards of the seven Shenai households before emptying into the irrigation canals of the fields below. On one side of the orchard was a spur of elevated land on which stood the temple of Ravalnath, the family deity of the Shenais.

Captain Castel Figredi had heard that the Brahmins were the real decision makers in the Goan society. They were known to be an intelligent class who could read and write. It was important, therefore, to win their confidence, to initiate a dialogue with them so that the administration of the Goan region could proceed smoothly. But the Brahmin community shut their doors and remained inside.

The captain knew that though it was three years since the Portuguese troops had set foot on Goan soil, the people in the villages still regarded them as a race of fearful demons. The use of bombs and explosives and the massacre of thousands of Moors had only reinforced this fear. Rumours that the Portuguese troops tricked people into eating cow flesh and other forbidden items so that they were cast out of Hindu society had begun to spread through the countryside.

'I am the captain in charge of this region. We have defeated Adil Shah and snatched Goa from him. You are now the King of Portugal's subjects. Come, let us talk,' he called out loudly. The interpreter rendered his words into Konkani. But everything remained still.

The fair skin on the captain's face flushed. He was a tall strapping man and his anger made him look even more intimidating. Leaping down from his horse, he drew his sword and rushed up to one of the houses. 'I'll break this down ... set fire to the house!' he screeched, kicking at the door.

Finally one of the doors opened and a woman hurled a large wooden measuring cup at the soldier, hitting him on the chest. A short, stockily built elderly woman stood in the doorway like Chandika the warrior goddess, her eyes spitting fire. 'Death be on you! May your body turn to ash!' she screamed. 'Why do you kick at the door, you wretched corpse?'

The captain stared at her, quite taken aback. He'd never seen a woman in such a rage before.

'Wretched creature! Crossed the seven seas and arrived here! This is a house where we follow rituals and practise our religion with care.'

When the interpreter translated her words, the captain turned to her with scorn and said, 'What religion are you talking about? Pack of cowards. You sit locked up in your houses, worshipping some powerless god, following worthless rituals!' He turned towards the village and said, 'A woman has the guts to come and stand at her door, and look at the men! Worthless cowards, hiding in their homes. Come out at once or we'll enter your houses with these guns in our hands!'

The woman suddenly let out a high pitched shriek that echoed through the settlement, 'Come out! All you men, young and old, come out at once or these impure, unclean wretches will enter your homes. Don't be afraid, come out.'

Fifteen or sixteen men emerged slowly from the seven houses and gathered in the courtyard. This was the first time that they set eyes on the white-skinned foreigners. These are men like us, they too have eyes and noses, hands and feet!

Everything was quiet and still for some time. As the tension began to ease, Shantu Shenai said in a low voice, 'No messenger from King has ever threatened us like this. They have always treated us with respect.'

'Don't talk of the other rulers. We are the strongest. We snatched Goa from Adil Shah. Six thousand Moors were massacred and their blood flowed all over Goa. We have come here today to get an assurance that you have accepted the King of Portugal as your sovereign. All the revenues and taxes will have to be deposited with us from now on.'

'We want nothing to do with you. You take everything by force. You killed the Moors and forced their widows to convert to your religion and marry your soldiers. You built your places of worship as soon as you arrived. And now you force Hindus to eat all sorts of things and make them join your faith,' Saptu Shenai protested.

'You are the ones who drive people to our faith. If someone eats something we offer, you disown him. He is cast out of his home, he can no longer practise your religion so he comes to us.'

'If you assure us that our gods and our religion will be protected, we may agree to do what you say,' Gharso Shenai stated.

'Viceroy Alphonso de Albuquerque has already given such an assurance to Mhala Pai, representative of the Hindus of north Goa, but it has not been ratified by the King of Portugal yet. Let me tell you this, the King has to follow the policy dictated by the Pope, who says that the King's religion is the religion of his subjects. At the moment, however, we will abide by the assurance given by the viceroy.'

The group of Brahmins seemed quite confused by the captain's words.

'I'm Appu Shenai,' said an elderly gentleman from the group. 'I am the village kulkarni. I look after the accounts and handle the taxes and revenues paid to the government. Tell us, how did Goa come under your rule?'

'Appu Shenai, remember you have been dealing with the Portuguese King for three years now. How much revenue did you collect over the last two years and where did you deposit it?'

'I paid the last instalment to Abdul Ghani, the patedar in the Adil Shah raj two years ago.'

'How much?'

'Three hundred and thirty two xerafins, three tangas and twelve reias.'

'And last year?'

'No revenue was paid last year. We didn't know who was ruling the place, no one from the new king's government came to collect it. So no money was set aside from our common village funds. The council of village elders declared that they wanted to see the corpse before they begin the mourning rituals.'

The captain was enraged. 'Kulkarni! You are dealing with the King of Portugal's regime, now. We dropped cannon balls all over Goa and conquered it. We overthrew the Moors, thousands were massacred, countless others fled in fear. And you say your village didn't know that we had come?'

'You are foreigners who've sailed across the seven seas.

We thought you'd gather all the loot and go away after one or two months. How were we to know that you would stay on?'

'Senor Albuquerque has set up this colony permanently. Our rule extends across the ocean and over this land. We will stay here and carry out our trade and business from here. We will fight wars and expand our territories. Kulkarni! How many people live in this village?'

'There are fifty-one houses. Seventy-two families live here. Six hundred and nine people in all.'

'You must give us the revenue for the last two years. Dasu Pai, the collector from Kalapur will be here in eight days to collect the money. At the same rate as before.'

'We can't give you last year's tax! All the paddy and grain set aside from that harvest was used up last year itself,' Appu Shenai said. His nervousness had ebbed a little and there was a new strength in his voice.

'Who is the mhal gaonkar?'

'Khapru Nayak of Shirvaddo.'

'Summon a meeting of the village council and decide on a higer rate of tax. Take the money from your common village fund.'

'How can we increase the rate?' old Adu Shenai interjected. 'The expenses of the annual temple festival and other rituals are drawn from that fund. Much of it goes in paying taxes anyway,' he said shrilly.

'Do whatever you want. Collector Dasu Pai will gouge the money out of this village, let me warn you. We'll set the rates from now on. And the currency in use will be the cruzado, our currency.'

'Your money can only be used in Goa. We use the reais,

tangas and xerafins to trade with outsiders, we bring bales of cloth and other items from outside.'

'All right. Both types of currency will be in use,' the captain declared. 'I expect that all of you will accept the sovereignty of our King. Henceforth your day must begin with salutations to the King of Portugal.'

Bhavani Shenai was a hot-headed young man. Hearing these words he shouted, 'You are an impure race come from across the sea. We have nothing to do with your King, we will not offer salutations to him or to any of you. Our heads will only bow before our gods.'

The captain's nose quivered in anger, his breath caught in his throat and his blue eyes turned bloodshot. He grabbed his baton and rained blow after blow on Bhavani Shenai who fell to the ground writhing in pain. 'We can bear blows of a sword. We cannot bear any insult to our King. This man deserves to be killed!' the captain announced as the horrified group looked on mutely.

'If you do not accept our rule peacefully, we shall force you by spilling blood,' he added, grabbing the handle of his sword. At once the other soldiers pulled out their swords and the Brahmins, who had never seen so many naked swords dancing before them, recoiled in fear as though confronted by poisonous serpents.

The captain leapt on to his horse. 'Have you heard of Jesus, Son of God?'

The people shook their heads

'Jesus, the Son of God came down from heaven to give us Christianity. That is the religion practised by the King of Portugal. If you were asked to give up your faith, what would you do?'

'We'd kill ourselves,' a few voices declared, fervently.

'If someone forced you to eat meat and the flesh of cows, what would you do?'

'We'd fast to death,' the same voices said with conviction.

'And if someone offered you land and wealth in exchange?'

'Even if all the wealth in the world were spread at our feet, we'd spurn it. We will not forsake our faith.'

The captain smiled wickedly. 'One last question, then. If someone comes with a sledgehammer in one hand and a naked sword in the other and sets about destroying your temples and your gods, what will you do, then?'

A chill descended on the group. They stared at each other silently. Finally someone said, 'God will see what needs to be done. He will punish the guilty.'

The captain spurred his horse and the group of soldiers rushed through the orchard towards the Ravalnath temple on the hill slope. This was a simple open structure with a sanctum, a tiled roof and a dung smeared floor. The white-skinned soldiers dismounted in front of the temple and walked in, still wearing their knee high boots.

'Senor, senor, your boots. If outsiders enter their temples they feel that they have become unclean…' the local soldiers protested, but the foreigners paid no attention. They tramped about for a while and then sat on the stone seats. There were five white-skinned foreigners in all. The two local soldiers stood outside, their faces dark with foreboding.

At this point, an old sadhu entered the temple. The hair on his head, his long flowing beard and moustache were all completely grey. Quite taken aback at the sight of the foreigners, the old man began to scream, 'Get out! Just get out! You've made the temple impure. You've sinned! You'll turn to ashes!'

The soldiers didn't move. The sadhu rushed out of the temple, 'Look what's happening here ... some unclean men have entered the temple with their shoes on. They've destroyed the sanctity of the place! Come drive them out!' But no one responded to his cries. Not one man emerged through the trees in the orchard.

The captain mounted his horse again and the group set off leaving the settlement quiet and peaceful. There was nothing to indicate that such a storm had swept over the settlement just a while ago, nor was there any turbulence left in its wake. Only the sadhu stood there waving his hands and screaming incoherently in the direction of the settlement. It seemed as if he was invoking curses on their heads.

The white-skinned soldiers had killed a huge boar in the hills that morning and had covered it with leaves and branches. One of the local soldiers went up to the Ramnath temple and addressed the priest, 'Bhatto! We've killed a wild boar on the hill slope. I know that you don't eat meat, but can you tell us who will skin and cut it up? We will give the villagers part of the meat.'

'Jivu Mesta will do that. But Shiva Mirashi has to make the first cut in the flesh. He performs the sacrifices at the Purus, the Payak and the Betaal shrines,' the priest said.

The captain dismissed the priest's statement. 'We are the ones who decide how things should be done,' he declared. 'We killed the boar. We'll make the first cut.'

The number of wild boars in the hills had increased in recent times. They trampled the crops and grazed with the cattle on the slopes. The villagers organized hunts to tackle this menace. They dug pits in the ground and covered them with leaves and branches. When a boar fell into the pit the villagers rained blows with an axe and broke its backbone. When they heard that the white-skinned foreigners had killed a boar with just a shot from a gun they were amazed and filled with admiration.

Jivu Mesta sat alone in his forge. The man who pumped the bellows and the helper who smote the hot iron had fled as the white-skinned foreigners approached them. The group stopped a short distance away and a local soldier asked Jivu to accompany them with a sharp knife.

'Has the Mirashi come?'

'No. They say they are the new rulers. They will make the first cut themselves.'

The blacksmith went inside and brought a long, sharp-edged knife. He called out to the two helpers who were hiding behind the house and the three men followed the soldiers into the hills.

'A large wild boar has been killed. If you want the meat come up to the hills,' the local soldier announced whenever he saw signs of human habitation on the way.

They pushed aside the leaves and branches that covered the animal and Jivu plunged his knife into the carcass as though possessed. He skinned the animal and removed the entrails which he tossed on one side. He cut off the legs and the snout with the help of his two men while the captain and his soldiers watched closely. 'This animal grew up wild and was sustained by the Lord, it belongs to the whole village, so everyone has a right to the meat. That's why the Mirashi performs rituals and offers the first cut,' Jivu babbled. 'I am committing a sin and will have to answer to the Lord,' he kept repeating as though he had gone mad.

The soldiers soon realized that some villagers were hiding behind the bushes and peeping at them from amongst the leaves. The soldiers wrapped the choicest pieces of meat in large leaves for themselves. Jivu hacked the rest of the flesh into twenty portions and the local soldier called out to the villagers, 'Come, take your portions away.' One by one the villagers emerged, nervous and hesitant. Each man crept up like a thief, picked up a portion and rushed away.

Captain Figredi was astonished. What a peculiar culture this was! Some of these people eat only fruits and vegetables. Others eat meat. They don't eat the flesh of the pigs they raise, cow meat is taboo and one who eats it becomes an outcaste. They worry about the caste and religion of the one who offers them food. Some things are fit to be eaten, some things are taboo. Everything is complicated! And except for the Brahmins, if you ask anyone if they're Hindus they say they don't know!

Fifty years later.

Adolshi was a small village about sixteen miles from Goapattana, the main township. Few people ventured as far as Adolshi since it was tucked away in the countryside and yet a sense of fear pervaded the village. In fact, these were troubled times and there was a feeling that danger lurked in the background. The body of the outcaste Ganaba – Tilai mavshi's nephew – still lay buried within the village. During the temple festival, the deity used to be taken to the sacred deva kọnd, for the ceremonial bath. But this time, the palanquin was placed at a distance from the pool, the idol given a quick dip and returned to the temple. There was no music, no flowers were offered, no rituals performed. Nor did cries of '*Har Har Mahadev!*' rent the air as in earlier times.

Bad news filtered in from the surrounding villages. The foreigners had barged into Kalapur and Merces, Palem and Agassaim and other villages on the Goan mainland with their religion. New rumours floated around every day ... Those people fed the villagers cow meat saying it was deer meat. The unfortunate ones who ate it became outcastes. The bones of a cow were found floating in a well in Merces. The well was emptied and purification rituals conducted at the bottom of the well. When the well filled up at night, another large bone was found in it. Soldiers with guns and whips picked up people from the wayside and drove them along the road to the place where these foreigners worshipped their gods...

Once, there was news that all the thieves in Goa's jails had been converted to Christianity and were set free. Now they were going about breaking into people's homes, and defiling them. Someone from Adolshi who had gone to Goapattana had seen men and women tied together, and driven to the market place like cattle and sold to the highest bidder. When he came back and reported this, the people of Adolshi were terrified. Each man began to keep his eyes peeled to protect his family.

One day, a white-skinned padre in a flowing white ankle length coat was seen wandering around the village. Tall and well-built, with a ruddy complexion and long golden hair on his head and in his flowing beard, the man seemed well over fifty. If one looked into his large dark eyes that seemed full of tears one felt as though one were gazing into a deep, bottomless lake. Who was this fearless stranger who had come from across the seven seas to wander about the village all by himself?

Padre Simao Peres went to every settlement each day and delivered his sermon in a loud but mellifluous voice. As he spoke he seemed to be transported to the realm of the gods. The qualities of love, pity, forgiveness and service to fellowmen infused his very being and this was reflected on his face and in his voice. He spoke fervently of the greatness of Jesus Christ, although for the first few weeks everyone ignored him. There was too much bad news trickling in from all sides to pay attention to a foreigner's sermons!

Yet the padre wandered from one part of the village to another preaching and reciting his prayers. His strong voice carried from house to house. Who has cast a spell on this man, why does he wear himself out in this way, people asked themselves.

One day four or five youths from Shirvaddo hailed Padre Simao Peres from a distance, 'Hey you! Don't come here ever again. We don't need you. If you're seen anywhere around we'll break your legs and drive you out!' they yelled.

However, the following morning the priest appeared as usual, recited the Rosary and started his sermon. 'Jesus, Son of God, born of the holy Virgin Mary, came to this world to spread compassion and bring happiness and joy. His heart overflowed with love and compassion. He said love your family, love your neighbours and most important, love your enemies too. Forgive your enemy for what evil he has done to you and he will become your dearest friend. Jesus said, if someone strikes you on one cheek turn the other towards him. Even your worst enemy will not strike you again. Spread the message of love all over this world. The love in your hearts and the tears of compassion in your eyes will bring peace and goodwill on earth … Amen.'

Just then, someone threw a stone at the priest. It hit him on the right temple and blood gushed forth. The priest fell to his knees and prayed to god to forgive the assailant. Then, without another word, he went away.

The next morning Padre Simao Peres was back at the same spot beneath the banyan, the wound on his temple still fresh. 'As Jesus was hoisted on to the cross he prayed to the Heavenly Father to forgive those who were doing this, "Lord, forgive them, they know not what they do." He is the Son of God, the Heavenly Father. Born of the virgin womb of Mother Mary. His heart is as vast as the heavens, as deep as the ocean. He is the King of the whole universe, the ruler of men's hearts…'

After a while, the padre noticed that a few men and women and some children stood huddled together on one side. He continued with his sermon, 'Accept Jesus as your Lord, believe in Him. Tell Him all your sorrows and your troubles will vanish. We commit sins in life, and we are punished for them. Have faith in Lord Jesus, open your hearts to Him and confess your sins. He will forgive you and make you good men, you will not feel the need to sin again. He brings good fortune, this Son of God. Each plant that He touches bears flowers and fruits, He makes sick men whole again. Jesus took the whole world's sorrows and the weight of man's sins upon His own shoulders. He went to the cross of His own free will, so that mankind would be free of sorrow.

Accept the Lord, He will deliver you from all problems … the gates of Heaven will open to you.'

Annu, who was standing on one side darted forward in a fit of emotion. 'Is all that you say true, O stranger?' he cried, throwing himself at the padre's feet.

The priest's eyes filled with tears, 'May Lord Jesus bless you and save you from all harm.'

Guna, who was standing behind a bush came forward angrily. 'We hear that your people are converting men forcibly in Goapattana and other villages, that the Chamundeshwara temple on Chornem island has been destroyed. Your soldiers beat up people who try to resist and throw them into prison. So what is this act that you are putting on here? They've sent you here first to win us over, that's why you are accompanied by that man with a sword in his hand.'

The veins on the priest's face throbbed as though he were in deep pain, 'No, my brother, you are wrong. Our religion teaches compassion, it spreads the message of love and brotherhood that Jesus spoke about. It is a sin to use force on anyone.'

'How can you force someone to accept your religion? We would rather batter our heads against a rock and die,' old man Phondu exclaimed.

'Those men are also men of faith. But they are following the wrong path. Let us pray to the Almighty to give them good sense. The way to Lord Jesus is through people's hearts. The use of force is against everything He stands for. Amen.'

The priest began to walk away with Annu following him. The villagers were amazed. 'Annu, turn back. You are an orphan with a lame brother at home. Don't get carried away by that outsider, you have your own religion,' they cried.

Someone rushed forward to drag him back but the others cried, 'Don't! He's touched that outsider, he's impure. He must bathe and be purified with dung and water before anyone touches him.'

Annu followed Padre Simao Peres through the fields, paying no attention to their words. The priest stopped by a fence and turned around. 'Innocent child, which way are you headed?' he asked.

'I'm going your way, ga. I want to go with you.'

'Why?'

'I want you to take me to Jesus.'

'Why? Don't you have your own god?'

'Whose god is Jesus, then? Isn't god the same?'

'You are still very young and innocent. Come with me, stay for a month, then decide. You can leave me any time you want, but once you accept Jesus and His Christian faith you won't be able to leave, ever.'

They set off again, crossing the open space before the temple, heading towards the priest's hut. The soldiers had come one day and built this tiny structure of wooden posts and beams and thatched it with plaited wild grass. A mud pot stood on the three small stones in one corner that served as a hearth. There were two small dishes and a cup of some dark, heavy metal that looked like brass. A crucifix hung on one of the posts.

A sturdy looking soldier wearing a thick loincloth and vest, crouched before the hearth. 'Tomas, this boy will stay with us for a month. He will then decide whether he wants to join our faith,' the padre said.

'He doesn't need a month, Father. One day is enough,' Tomas laughed.

'Why do you say that, Tomas?'

'There is only one route to this place. Once you come here you cannot go back, all paths are closed. Do you know what happened at Merces the other day? Some Christian cart drivers cooked their meal on a hearth. When they were done a Hindu family cooked a meal there. When other Hindus heard about this they were declared outcastes and driven away. The couple wept and pleaded for mercy. They were going to jump into the river to end their lives when a soldier took them to a Christian priest. They were baptized in three days.'

Annu went up to the soldier whose head was shaved except for a patch of short hair on the crown. The tuft of long hair that once grew out of that patch had been lopped off. His upper ear lobes had large holes in them as though the earrings had just been removed.

'What's your name?' Annu asked the man softly.

The soldier seemed lost in thought for a while. 'My name is Demu. You can call me Demu mama, if you like. Why are you here?'

'I liked what the padre said. I've heard that Jesus is a good god, that plants bear flowers when he touches them.'

'Who knows what's good and what's bad?' Tomas sighed. 'It's been two years since I was baptized. My wife and children are Hindus still, I can't go near them till they become Christians too. Only Jesus knows what will happen next.'

'Why did you become a Christian?'

'Fate. Robbed two gold cruzados from a white-skinned soldier's box. But I got caught. They said I could be free if I became a Christian. I was scared, so I agreed. They sent me to Goapattana where a priest baptized me in St Catherine's Church. They even let me keep my job.'

'What does that mean?'

'Nothing much. You bathe in a lake so that your past is washed away. Then they smear oil on your temples and give you something to eat. Don't ask what it is, just swallow it. Then they celebrate Mass and give you a Christian name.'

'What's Mass?'

'A ceremony to praise God. To pray for our well-being.'

'Don't they sing bhajans?'

'They sing something, but we can't understand those songs.'

'Are you sorry that you became a Christian, Demu mama?'

Tomas was filled with happiness when Annu addressed him thus. 'No. Not any more. I was very upset for a month or so, now I don't feel anything. I just want my wife and children to come to me. What's your name, boy?'

Padre Simao took off his thick cassock to reveal a thin, sleeveless undergarment that hung down to his knees. He knelt before the crucifix and began to pray in Latin.

Simao's father was a Portuguese sailor who had lived for some time in Spain after his ship sank off the Spanish coast. He had married a Spanish woman but soon after Simao was born, he had gone back to Portugal, never to return. Simao's mother, who worked in an orange orchard on the western coast, could barely make both ends meet. She married again, soon after this, but Simao's stepfather treated him very cruelly.

When he turned thirteen, Simao ran away to a distant village where he kept himself busy with church activities. The priest was so impressed with his dedication that he sent him to the seminary at the Vatican for theological studies. He stayed at the Vatican for seven years after which he served as a priest in Greece for seventeen years. Then, armed with a letter of permission from the Pope, he travelled to Ceylon, and then to Goa.

Since Simao had no letter of recommendation from the King, the Portuguese Viceroy in Goa was thrown into a quandary. The Jesuit priests exerted pressure on him to reject Simao's credentials, but the viceroy didn't dare go against the authority of the Pope. So Padre Simao Peres was sent to distant Adolshi village to preach his faith. He was to receive forty cruzados every six months and a soldier was deputed to look after his needs.

As required by law, Padre Simao Peres spent the first eight months of his stay in Goa at St Paul's College where he learnt the Konkani language and familiarized himself with local matters.

Before leaving for Adolshi, Simao Peres went to call on the viceroy. 'I often dream that all of Goa has been converted to Christianity and the King is congratulating me. I want to accomplish this as soon as possible. I will need your help to do it,' Viceroy Constantin Braganza said to him.

'I'm going to that village to spread the word of Jesus and to tell them that Christianity is the greatest faith in the world. But I won't go against the villagers' wishes and trick them into being baptized,' Padre Simao declared.

'You've been sent here by the Pope sayeb. Our King accepts the views of the Pope and honours his dictates. The King believes that all his subjects should follow his religion.'

'There is no doubt that this will happen, but it must not happen because of trickery or force. The people must be filled with a desire for the new faith, we must appeal to their hearts. Those who are converted by force or fraud might not turn out to be good Christians. They may besmirch our religion,' Padre Simao said.

'The King has a solution for this. The Inquisition. For Goa and all the other Portuguese colonies. The chief Inquisitor, Alex Dias Falcao, has just landed in Goa. He will ensure that no one goes against the Christian faith.'

'Is an inquisition really necessary for these simple unlettered people?' Padre Simao asked in a calm voice but Constantin Braganza flew into a rage.

'Let this be the last time you say anything against the Inquisition. Go to Adolshi and work according to your convictions, let the others work according to theirs. Don't come in their way. But let me tell you this, those who set out to win the world cannot afford to be patient. They don't have the time.'

Tomas and Annu had become good friends, they spent hours talking to each other. Tomas built a small hearth of three stones outside the shack and got Annu a new mud pot from the potter. He gave Annu a fistful of rice every morning for his breakfast and two fistfuls of parboiled rice for cooking his lunch and dinner. Annu gathered bits of firewood from the hill slope and used the water kept outside in a large clay pot.

'You're drinking water that has been touched by a Christian,' Tomas said one day.

'You're my uncle, aren't you? How can one become an outcaste because of an uncle's touch?' Annu said, with a smile.

'Will you eat something that this uncle cooks for you?'

'If you serve it to me.'

'No. I won't serve you any food till you are baptized. The one who feeds is a bigger sinner than the one who eats,' Tomas sighed deeply. 'The uncle is a Christian and the nephew a Hindu! This is what is happening all over this land, only god knows what will happen next!'

Padre Simao watched them spend hours together in affectionate conversation. These are ties of blood and faith; they spring from the same culture, the same land. Their religion might change, but the ties that bind them remain the same. If you build a dam across the water, does the nature of the water on either side change? All our efforts are useless, we strive in vain!

After a few moments, however, Padre Simao thrust such thoughts out of his mind. They were a betrayal to his cause. He decided once again that he would lead people to Jesus through love.

The government had provided Padre Simao with a bodyguard, but the priest didn't take the soldier along as he wandered through the village, morning and evening. Gradually the people began to view him with respect. They didn't come up to him, nor was he invited into the settlement, but they listened to him deliver his sermon as he stood by the edge of the colony, just as they would have listened to someone who had a story to tell or a song to sing.

One day while the priest was going past the artisan's colony, he spotted two people moving about in the undergrowth at the edge of the forest. An old man and a youth, sixteen or seventeen years of age, had dragged a dead cow out of the field and were cutting up its flesh with large, sickle-shaped knives. They had skinned the carcass and thrown the bloody scraps of skin on one side while the chunks of soft flesh were piled in a basket. A pack of vultures waited on a tree nearby. Both men's bodies were drenched in sweat and flecked with blood, their hands covered with blood and flesh.

Padre Simao went up to them, 'Do you eat cow flesh?' he asked.

The old man seemed nervous, 'Yes, we do, ga,' he said.

'Aren't you a Hindu?'

'No, ga. Priests and Brahmins are Hindus. We're low caste Mhars. We handle dead cattle. We weave reed mats and baskets. We go around the village making announcements.'

'So then what is your religion?'

'All that is for the big people, those who live in the village. We are low caste. We only go to the bhat or to the joish to ward off trouble from bad planets and ghosts or spirits. They give us charms...'

'So you have no religion?'

'Don't know. Must ask the joish.' The old man seemed confused.

'Do people eat food that you have touched?

'No, no! We're Mhars. Low caste.'

'Do they touch you?'

'No, no! We're Mhars!'

'Aren't you men?'

'Don't know. They sprinkle dung water to purify themselves if our shadows cross their path.'

'Are you worse than dung?'

'Who knows?'

'Will you leave your caste and your religion and join another faith?'

The old man seemed bewildered for a while, 'I don't know what you say, ga, how can we escape our caste? They say God came in the guise of a sadhu seeking alms at our door. One of our ancestors tossed a broken horn into his bowl. God was enraged. "Never again. Never again will anyone come to seek alms at your door. You will carry a horn and handle dead cattle all your life" God cursed us.'

The padre went up to him. 'Has anyone, other than another low caste person ever touched you?'

'No ga, never. Once, when I was returning from the forest I accidentally bumped into Biru Nayak. He thrashed me with a cane and then went home to bathe and sprinkle dung water on himself.'

The padre moved closer and gently placed a hand on his shoulder. The old man recoiled as though a scorpion had fallen on his body. Turning pale he said in a piteous voice, 'No, no ga! Don't touch me. You are a big man, white-skinned, Brahmin-like. If we touch them, the sins are upon our heads, they say. Do not add to our sins!'

The padre was deeply distressed. The butchered carcass, the bloody hide lying there, the vultures waiting on the tree and the sight of the two shunned men was more than he could bear. He stood there silently, unable to think or speak. Just then Annu appeared on the scene, probably looking for Padre Simao.

'Annu, will you touch these men?' the padre called out.

'No! No!' Annu almost screamed.

'Why? Why won't you touch them, Annu?'

'No one touches them. You'll become impure if you do.'

'How do you become impure? Does your body get soiled, or do you get cuts and wounds if you touch them?'

'I don't know, Padre bappa. The others don't go near them, so I don't go.'

'Do you touch bullocks and oxen?'

'Yes.'

'Frogs and earthworms?'

'Yes.'

'Then why won't you touch these men?'

'I don't know anything, Padre bappa. Must ask the bhat or the joish.'

Padre Simao lost his temper then. 'Cruel, wicked, barbaric! That's what you are!' he fumed. 'How wrong this is, how unfair! Imagine one human being refusing to touch another! Who wants such a religion! The lot of you should be made Christians immediately or drowned in the sea.'

The priest stomped away through the field with Annu behind him. The old Mhar and his son stood silently, like pre-historic figures from the Dandakaranya forests, human only in body and spirit, shrinking into themselves, lest their shadows fall on the 'big people'.

The priest was aghast at the way men could discriminate against other men. He had read books on the Hindu religion while he was at St Paul's college and had been very impressed with the philosophy, but he now felt that those lofty ideas were a mere sham designed to hoodwink the people.

He also realized that the Hindu priest and the astrologer exerted a great influence over the common people, so he decided to meet Narhar Joish, whose house was at the edge of the fields by the Ravalnath temple in Raigali. He had seen many strange things during the two months spent in Adolshi, and had many questions to ask the joish.

One part of the plain in front of the temple was almost encircled by the foothills and it was here that the Solankhe families lived. These four households were outsiders who had come to the village some fifty or sixty years ago. It was rumoured that while working for one of the kings in the north, they had committed treason and had fled to this village to escape his wrath. They belonged to the Khatri or warrior caste and often wore swords strapped to their waists. They carried logs down from the hills and shaped wheels for bullock carts which they sold in the surrounding villages Their houses were artistic, with white-washed walls and on either side of the main door was an image of the sun, etched with red mud, with large eyes painted on it.

Since they belonged to the warrior caste, like the Nayaks of Shirvaddo, people from these two communities would marry each other, but sometimes there was tension because the Salonkhes practised sati while the Nayaks did not. Yet the times were such that once a girl was given in marriage, her future was decided by her husband's family, whether they buried her alive or set her ablaze, no one could intervene. The Solankhe families had erected shrines to seven women who had committed sati during the last sixty years.

Padre Simon Peres was aware that Viceroy Constantin Braganza was going to introduce a strict law banning the practice of sati. So one morning when he noticed some people bustling about beneath a kadam tree, he hid behind a bush to watch what the men were doing. The men dug a deep trench and filled it with wooden logs. Soon some men arrived bearing a corpse on a bier. A young boy, fourteen or fifteen years of age, followed them with a slender pole held across his shoulders. A small earthen dish with a few flaming dung pats hung from the front end of the pole while a new mud pot filled with water was at the rear. When they reached the trench the pall bearers shouted 'Deva Mahadeva!

The path has come to an end!' and set the bier down. Some of the men cut the ropes binding the body and removed the clothes, the silver waist chain and ear rings and flung them away. They lowered the corpse on to the logs and covered it with smaller pieces of wood till only the face could be seen. They soaked large palm fronds in a pitcher of oil and poured the fuel over the corpse, scattering armfuls of dry grass all over the trench.

No one said a word through all this except for the young boy who sobbed inconsolably, often breaking into screams, 'Don't bring her here, don't make her jump into the pit.' Soon Padre Simao heard the sound of drums and cymbals as a group of people made their way towards the pit. A young girl, sixteen or seventeen years of age, was at the head of the group. She was fair and pretty, but her eyes were red and swollen as though she had been crying. As she stumbled along, someone in the group propped her up. Have these people drugged her into this stupor, the priest wondered.

The girl wore a white sari with a red border, the folds drawn between her legs and tucked in at the waist. There were dozens of red and green bangles on her arms and masses of flowers in her hair. Her forehead was smeared with kumkum. The few women in the group prostrated themselves before her at the edge of the clearing and then returned to their homes without a backward glance. 'Touch a live coal in the hearth and you can't bear the pain. Imagine throwing yourself into the fire!' they muttered amongst themselves, 'Would be far better if they wrung your neck and then threw you in. After all, who has seen heaven or hell?'

The musicians beat the huge drums that hung down to their knees and clanged the large cymbals without a pause.

The clamour of the drums and cymbals made the whole atmosphere reverberate and hearts jump.

The men made the girl stand on a flat stone at the edge of the pit. She was crying loudly and struggling to maintain her balance. Her eyes were fixed on some spot in the distance, unwilling to look into the pit where her husband's body lay. The frenzied beating of drums and cymbals continued, but people's faces showed no emotion. The young boy lifted the water pot on to his shoulder. Someone made a small hole at the back of the pot and the water seeped out in a continuous stream behind him. The youth walked around the corpse and the girl five times before smashing the pot on the ground. He held the palm fronds against the flaming dung and then lowered the torch into the pit. The wood that had been doused with oil burst into flame.

An old man went up to the girl and declared loudly, 'If all the emblems that a married woman sports are intact when you die the gates of Heaven will open before you. All your sins will burn to ashes in your husband's pyre. You will be liberated and attain salvation. This man will be your husband in your next life and for all time to come.

'You will be honoured as a goddess!

'You will always sport the emblems of marriage!

'You will be renowned for your devotion to your husband!

'Do not flinch, do not be afraid!

'Accept the flames in your husband's pyre with joy!

'Be transported to heaven, let salvation be yours!

'May your sins be burnt to ash…'

The flames were leaping out of the pit as the sound of drums reached a crescendo. The girl drew back sharply, but the old man pressed his fists against her back and pushed her in. Cries of '*Har Har Mahadev!*' tore the air. The girl's screams cut through the cacophony as she struggled to get out.

Padre Simao could bear it no longer, 'What are you doing, you sinners? Why did you throw that girl into the flames … God will never forgive you!' he screamed rushing up to the pit. Four or five men grabbed him and shoved him on to a stony patch. One of them hit him with his staff, 'This low caste wretch from another religion will defile the purity of our ritual. Go! Get away at once!'

The priest walked towards his shack with heavy footsteps. The girl's voice became fainter as her body was consumed by the flames. The sun was quite high in the sky but darkness seemed to be enmeshed in the leaves of the surrounding trees. A vile black shadow hung over the area, as though the heat of the blazing pyre had swallowed the sun's light, and an eclipse had begun.

As Padre Simao and Annu approached the astrologer's house, they saw him sitting cross-legged before a large chest. The joish stared at Padre Simao for a long time.

'I've seen you moving about the village trying to fool people, but you won't succeed. You won't convert anyone, except some innocent youngsters like him. Anyway, what brings you here?'

'I want to know why some of your people will not touch some others. You say cow dung and urine are holy, but even the shadows of some men are impure. How can that be?'

'Don't say a word about the holy cow. Thirty-three crore deities reside within her belly, cow dung and cow urine bear the essence of these gods.'

'Doesn't man bear the essence of the gods, too?'

'Not all men. Just Brahmins. They emerged from Lord Brahma's brain. The other castes emerged from his hands, his legs and his belly.'

'Brahmins should have some extra faculties, then.'

'They do.'

'What is that?'

'Intelligence.'

'Others have that, too.'

'No. That's the sort of intelligence oxen have.'

The padre remained silent for a while. This Brahmin was obviously intelligent.

'When I was at St Paul's college I read that the Hindu epic Ramayana was written by Valmiki a lowly Shudra, and the Mahabharata by Vyasa, a low caste man whose mother sold fish. And the Bhagvad Gita was narrated by Krishna, a Kshatriya, on the battlefield.'

'Wrong! All wrong! The Ramayana and the Mahabharata were not written by one man, in one day. Hundreds of intellectuals composed these books which kept growing over thousands of years. The Bhagvad Gita presents the essence of Hinduism and bears the stamp of the Brahmins, even though Krishna narrated it on the battlefield. Only Brahmins know the divine language Sanskrit. We composed the Vedas and the Puranas. Brahma and Brahmins are inseparable and one who kills a Brahmin commits a very grave sin. We know the holy chants and incantations, we can curse people and turn them into ash. We make rain fall in times of drought and barren women conceive, at our command the spirits of the dead achieve salvation and ascend to the heavens,' the joish rasped.

'You haven't told me why men discriminate between each other, why one man refuses to touch certain other men,' the priest said calmly.

'You are an uncivilized creature from across the seven seas. You won't understand all this. If all classes were allowed to interact and all restrictions on touch removed, it would lead to a loss of ritual purity and result in immoral behaviour. The duality of self would be destroyed, cross-breeding across the classes would dilute the purity of their blood. The well-defined hierarchy would be destroyed. Sin would reign. Earthquakes and floods would destroy mankind. The elaborate pujas we perform make the world move smoothly, God listens to what the Brahmins say.'

'If you say such things, the lower castes will forsake Hinduism and embrace some other religion.'

'Let them go.'

'I should be thankful to you. We've come here with the teachings of Jesus Christ. We want people to embrace our faith.'

'So many others have come and gone. Waves of Buddhist preachers came here, once. Where are they now? One day you will also go away with your face blackened.'

'Some of our people have come with swords to force you to embrace our religion. What will you do now?'

'We have faith in our gods. You don't know how powerful they are. If you meddle with them, you will die a painful death.'

Padre Simao laughed. 'When they come with swords to destroy your religion and break your gods, won't you resist them? With sticks and canes, at least?'

'Who are we to resist? God will resist them. He will destroy them.'

'Last week I saw a woman thrown into a funeral pyre. I was very upset. How does your religion allow this heinous crime?'

The joish's grey eyes blazed with anger, 'No one pushes these women into the pyre. They accept the flames of their own will, as a mark of devotion to their husbands. They atone for the sins of their previous birth which has resulted in the death of their husband. They have no right to live. They become a burden to the family and their love affairs and quarrels cause strife and degradation. Let me tell you the facts – Brahmin widows in Goa do not commit sati. We remove their ornaments and shave their hair to keep them away from temptation. They bathe in cold water twice a day, have a cold meal just once and spend their time in prayer and worship.'

All of Goa lived in fear ever since the foreigners destroyed the Chamundeshwari temple at Chornem two years ago. After Kashi, Pandhari and Gokarn this temple on Chornem island was the most revered place of worship for most Goans. The temple, which was fifty-two feet long and twenty-seven feet wide, was built of massive blocks of smooth, dark stone. The roof and floor were also made of large stone slabs. Farmlands and orchards not only on Chornem island, but also in far flung villages were owned by the temple and it was said that the deity's gold ornaments would fill half a sack.

During the temple festival in the month of Chaitra, people from all over Goa came to Chornem for the rath jatra. The magnificent temple chariot had four wooden wheels, each as tall as a man. On this frame stood a stout wooden post atop which were two thick beams fitted crosswise. Dozens of wooden pegs were nailed on to these beams and during the festival masses of flower garlands were hung from them. When the chariot was pulled forward, the crossbeams with the hanging garlands, whirled round and round.

Once the King of Portugal, Joav III, gave permission to start converting the Hindus, the officials on duty in Goa had their eyes on the Chamundeshwari temple. The temple encouraged people to worship idols and practise the Hindu faith and this was an obstacle in their path. Viceroy Francis Barrett was looking for an excuse to raze the temple to the ground. Once this seat of the Hindu faith was destroyed, all the wealth in the temple's coffers would be theirs. Besides, the task of conversion would become easier.

Disaster struck during the festival that year. As the chariot was being dragged along, one of the crossbeams broke and fell on the devotees killing three people and injuring many others. The Mahajans and other temple officials were terrified.

People began to speculate among themselves. Someone whispered, 'Rukmi kalavant, the temple dancer, performed her duties so well. When she danced before the chariot with the flaming oil lamps in her hands even the musicians couldn't keep pace with her steps! Wonder why she killed herself in the temple pond, though. No one came forward to claim her body, and it lay there on the edge of the pond till the temple authorities had some mhars drag it away. No funeral rituals were conducted. The deity must be angry about all this!'

Someone else said, 'The chariot's decorative frame was stored in the open in the backyard of the temple. The wooden beam must have got wet whenever it rained, but no one paid any attention to it, that's why it broke off.'

This incident was seized upon by the Governor and he banned the festival, declaring that everything associated with it – from the construction of the chariot to the procession itself – was a threat to public safety. The temple officials however, obtained the blessings of the deity and built a new chariot out of rosewood and sangvani teakwood that was stronger than the old one. But the old wheels of the chariot were retained.

When the viceroy heard that the festival would be held again, he sent a troop of sixty Portuguese and local soldiers to prevent it. The chariot, bearing the idol Chamundeshwar, was to go round the temple and then to the little Santeri shrine in a nearby grove. But even before the rituals started, the soldiers blocked the path with naked swords in their hands. The devotees refused to be cowed down, and defied the soldiers. Within minutes, the soldiers started to beat up the unarmed devotees, but in an instant, thousands of coconuts from the temple's store were brought out and people began flinging them at the soldiers. Then the captain fired the gun in his hand and people ran away, leaving twenty dead bodies on the ground. Of these, two were white-skinned soldiers, three were local soldiers and the rest were devotees who had come to the festival.

The viceroy was not content with this. He ordered the soldiers to spray oil on the chariot and set fire to it. Some soldiers armed with rods, pickaxes and sledgehammers smashed the idol of the Lord before razing the temple to the ground. They brought two cows from the village and slaughtered them in front of the temple and threw their intestines in the temple pond. All the deity's ornaments, the brass and copper vessels and all the wealth in the temple's coffers was carried away in large boats.

It took the soldiers three days to pull down the temple. All the while, two soldiers stood guard. The bhat, the pujari and the gurav who performed various priestly tasks, the devli and the kalavant who cleaned the temple and danced on ceremonial occasions, and others involved with the temple's activities remained in their homes. Every blow from the sledgehammer seemed like it was falling on their heads.

One day the viceroy sent a newly converted Christian to Chornem island with a proclamation: 'The four hundred and fifty acres of farmland and orchards that belonged to the temple now belong to the church. All your duties and obligations will now be directed towards the church. The gaonki and gaonkari system of village administration will continue as before. Those who worked for the temple can continue in the service of the church if they convert to Christianity. Those who farm the temple's land can continue doing so if they become Christians, but all farmland and orchards owned by Hindus will be confiscated by the State.'

The people of Goa were shaken. They waited with their hearts in their mouths to see what new developments the next day would bring. The slightest noise made them jump, they were scared to talk loudly. If a soldier or a foreigner happened to pass through the village, people drew back in alarm.

'They're planning to hold a feast, it seems. They will tie us up and drag us there and then force us to eat what they've cooked … cow's meat, maybe…'

'They'll take away the land and orchards of those who don't become Christians and drive them out of Goa, it seems…'

'They lock people up in rooms. Soldiers with guns stand outside. Inside, they make you accept their faith. If you don't, they burn you alive…'

Mhablu Nayak of Shirvaddo had married off his daughter to a man from Divade. After the incident at Chornem, he and his wife were worried about their daughter. The girl had last come to visit them three months ago. So one day Mhablu said to his son, 'Shambhu, my boy, there's been no news from your sister for three months. Go and see how she and her two little ones are.'

Shambhu had been wanting to go to Bai's house for quite some time, so when his father gave him permission, the boy seemed to sprout wings. Ever since his bai Vitha had got married six years ago, he used to trek all the way to her house at least twice a year. Shambhu ate some payz, or rice gruel, and set out early the next morning. He'd just turned sixteen and was young and strong and full of excitement at the thought of seeing his sister.

The route to Divade was lined with large trees and bushes, a number of streams and rivulets cut across the path. Shambhu walked along the embankments of fields where the autumn crop had just been sown. In other parts the summer crop had been harvested and the fields lay bare. The tinkling of bells around the necks of grazing cattle and the voices of cowherds calling filled him with joy.

As he passed five or six houses set in a shallow valley a little away from the track, he noticed four cattle sheds and a group of people huddled before one of them. Shambhu wrapped his towel about his head and went up to see what they were doing. An ox was lying on the ground with blood and pus oozing out of a gash on its flank. One of the men crushed some leaves with a stone and spread the paste on the wound. Immediately, maggots began to crawl out. The ox struggled to its feet.

'Who are you? Where are you going?' one of the men asked Shambhu.

'To my sister's house at Divade. Saw you, and stopped for a while.'

'Have some water, or something to drink,' someone offered.

'Oh no. I'll be there soon.'

'Be careful while crossing the river. A boatman drowned when his boat capsized recently. There were no strong winds, no storm ... suddenly the water went round and round and the boat and boatman were sucked into that whirlpool. Such a thing has never happened here in the last hundred years. But after the temple...'

'Don't talk of that, Hari. Not another word. Just pray that our village remains safe,' someone interjected as Shambhu set off again.

By the time he got to Panveli village the sun was overhead, but as the track wound through groves of mango and jackfruit it was quite shady and cool.

The boatman at the ferry crossing was dark and well-built and fearful to behold. He plied the oars as if he were in a frenzy and when the boat reached mid-stream, he stopped. Shambhu stared nervously at the vast expanse of water on either side and then at the boatman.

'Whose house are you going to?' someone on the boat asked Shambhu.

'To my sister's house. Shanu Desai, who lives by the well in that rocky outcrop, is my brother-in-law.'

The man seemed lost in thought for a while. A shadow of fear spread over his face, but he didn't say anything. Shambhu felt a sense of unease. Why did that man's face turn dark, like that?

Shambhu dragged his feet through the shallow water and began to climb up the muddy slope of the river bank. He walked towards Dula Mhar's large shack. Dula was burly, with shiny dark skin. His eyes were always bloodshot which made him appear quite ferocious. But he was a gentle, soft-spoken man, and Shambhu knew him well. Dula had come to Adolshi twice, once with the news that Bai's father-in-law had passed away and another time when a worried Bai had sent him to see if her father was well since she'd been having disturbing dreams. He had always greeted Shambhu effusively when he passed by his shack and would say, 'Oh, you've come! Bhavoji will certainly kill a large rooster for your meal!'

But today he turned away from Shambhu, and bent over the large bullock hide that was stretched on a frame. Shambhu stopped in order to greet him, but Dula didn't even look at him, continuing to scrape the hide vigorously. Shambhu went on his way, wondering why Dula Mhar was behaving like this.

As he neared Bai's house, Shambhu's head reeled. He was filled with dismay. The low walls of the courtyard had been broken down. The tulsi vrundavan, made of mud, lay on the ground in disarray and the courtyard looked as though it had not been swept for days. Shambhu felt a sinking sensation in his stomach as he reached the courtyard. Suddenly, Vitha rushed up crying, 'No, no my brother, don't step into this house!'

Shambhu noticed that the galsari, which indicated that she was a married woman, no longer hung about her neck, and there was no kumkum mark on her brow.

'What's the matter, Bai? Why can't I enter your house?' he asked thickly.

'Don't come in here. You are my only brother, you belong to a devout, religious family, if anyone sees you here everything will be lost!' Then she began to sob.

'At least tell me what the matter is! Why is there no kumkum on your forehead? Where's your galsari? Where is Bhavoji? Hurry up and tell me.'

'We've converted, my brother. We have accepted their religion.'

Shambhu was shocked. 'But why can't you use kumkum?'

'It's their law. We can't worship the tulsi plant, married women musn't wear the galsari. If we disobey them, we'll be punished,' she cried.

The young lad had come all this way with much excitement and anticipation, but seeing all this he began to cry like a child. Vitha couldn't bear to see him weep, she wanted to gather him in her arms and wail aloud too, but her feet seemed weighed down and rooted to the ground. She brought a strip of blanket and tossed it on to the porch.

'Stop crying, now. We couldn't change what was written in our fate. You be careful, always be on your guard,' she said.

Shambhu had calmed down by then. He spread out the blanket and settled down. 'When did all this happen? How? Why did you…' he asked.

'It has been two months now. Didn't send word to you. What could I say? That your sister was dead?'

'But why did you do it? Why was it necessary?'

'We get four khandis of paddy from fields that belong to the Chornem temple. Five generations of our family have tilled those fields and that takes care of our needs through the year. When the temple was destroyed, they came after us. "Become Christians. Or give the land to the church," they said. We continued with our work and sowed the fields. They came and threatened us again. "Convert at once or we'll take the harvest away." Some of the other villagers agreed to take their faith. Then your Bhavoji agreed too. He'd come back from the fields and begin to weep, "If this inheritance that feeds the family is snatched away, we'll have to go and jump into the river or the well." His whole life is built around those fields, if they go he won't survive.'

'Bai, why didn't you come to us? We could have seen what to do.'

'I wanted to. One day, in a fit of rage I picked up the children and decided to go home, but when I got to the edge of the courtyard your Bhavoji called out sadly, "Vithai, are you going to forsake me, too?" I couldn't bear that!' She started sobbing again. After a while, she continued, 'His mother stays with us. She didn't convert. She says, "Where my son is there I am. Cremate me or bury me, when I'm dead."'

Bai went in, put on her galsari and came back. She tried to hide it under the folds of her sari. 'It upsets me when I take it off, my heart beats nervously, so I put it on stealthily in the evening and take it off at dawn.'

Sounds of Bai's little one crying inside the house were heard. Her four-year-old son, Babuli, kept wanting come out, but each time his grandmother would drag the child in.

'Bai, have the children also been converted to their faith?'

'Yes. They were the first to be baptized.'

'Then I can't hold them?'

'No. Don't take that risk. An evil wind is blowing. Everyone is waiting to cast you out. Your own people have become your enemies. The other day some bones were found floating in a well in Ambode. The villagers decided to ostracize the family. The husband and wife got a priest to perform a purification puja at the bottom of the well after they had emptied it out. When the next day they found bits of burnt cow dung cakes, firewood and plantain stems floating on the surface everyone felt reassured, it seems.'

Shambhu was dejected at the thought that his sister and his nephews were alienated from him. It was as if his very roots had been cut off. He almost broke into tears when his brother-in-law arrived. Shanu went in silently, then came to the door and said, 'There can be no more coming and going between our houses. Assume that we are dead. Just want to say one more thing – don't get trapped into anything, don't stay back clinging to your fields and orchards. If necessary, uproot yourselves and go far away. Don't do what we have done.' Everyone remained silent after that. It seemed as though a torrent of words was building up in each one's mind, but the threads of conversation had been snapped. They were so close physically, but they had travelled so far apart. Darkness was falling and a cold breeze of the Kartick month was blowing across the courtyard. Time seemed to have been flogged out of its normal rhythm.

Bai's mother-in-law took the children inside and fed them, the others remained hungry. Vithai sat on the threshold staring at her brother. My brother sits outside my door, hungry and shivering, she thought, her eyes flooding with tears. 'Brother, wrap that kambal around yourself, it's cold,' she said.

Shambhu pulled the blanket over his head and ears. 'Bai, give me some water to drink. Water isn't defiled by touch,' he said.

Vithai sat quietly as though unable to decide. Then muttering, he is my brother after all, she picked up the water pot and rope and set off to get fresh water. Shambhu heard dry leaves crackling underfoot as she disappeared into the darkness. For a very long time everything was still. Shambu was beginning to get worried, He was about to call his bhavoji when he heard footsteps and Bai's voice calling out to him. She poured water into his cupped palms.

When he had drunk his fill, Shambu asked, 'Bai, the well is right here. Why did you take so long?'

'The villagers don't let us draw water from this well, we use the old one outside the settlement, the one that the cattle drink from. The three families in this village who have converted, all draw water from there.' As she hastened indoors she continued in broken tones, 'Don't tell anyone you drank water here. And toss that blanket inside before daybreak.'

Vithai stood by the open door and said 'You're hungry. Aren't you, Shambhu?'

'Not really. Had payz before I set out.'

'Shall I ask your Bhavoji to pluck two tender coconuts for you?'

'No, Bai. Not at night. Let it be.'

'You're shivering. And you're hungry. How can I just let you be?' She went into the house and brought a large cucumber and a knife. 'Here eat this,' she said.

Shambhu was very hungry. He sliced the cucumber and ate half of it. 'Go, have your dinner, Bai,' he said.

'My brother sits hungry at my door, how can I swallow even a morsel?' she cried, settling down by the wall just inside the house. 'Shambhu, are Avai and Bappa well? How's Bappa's foot?'

'All right. He hobbles all the way into the forest sometimes.'

'Why does he take so much trouble? And our neighbour Bhiki who fell off the roof? How's she now?'

'She's dead. Took a turn for the worse around chavoth.'

'Poor thing. How much she suffered at the end. Will Chandu be tied to the plough this year?'

'Yes. Bappa thinks he'll manage to work this year too.'

'Last year the kukumambo tree didn't bear any fruit. It will, this year. When the mangoes ripen, get me a basket full of the fruit.'

'I will.'

'Don't forget to bring me those mangoes as long as I live. What else do I have? What else can I ask for?'

'Bai, can't you come home anymore?'

'I'm always worried about you, I don't want you to suffer because of what I've done. Even if I come, I'll have to sit outside your door. Who will let a convert into the house? Do you see what happens when you give up your faith? Be very careful, Shambhu. Have they reached Adolshi yet?'

'There's just one white-skinned padre who roams about the village. He says we should join his faith of our own free will.'

'That's not true. Once the forest catches fire it doesn't matter whether the trees are wet or dry, they'll all burn. Look at us. When we tilled the fields that belonged to the church, our people shunned us and said we were like those converts. What could we do? If we stopped tilling those fields, the church would have given them to some other new converts. Either way we were doomed.'

Shambhu was very sleepy. He pulled the blanket tightly about himself and lay on the ground, drawing comfort from the fact that his sister sat so close. Vithai's husband spread a reed mat and lay down just inside the door while she sat leaning against the wall. Her eyes would grow heavy and every now and then she would begin to nod off. Suddenly, she'd wake up and stare at her brother's sleeping form, her eyes brimming with tears.

One time when she had dozed off, she dreamt of the sacred niche where the gods were placed in her parents' home. Suddenly she saw a huge lizard darting about amongst the gods. The lizard then seemed to jump on to her body and she woke up with a scream. She kept falling asleep and waking up in fear right through the night. 'Shambhu,' she exclaimed only half awake, 'when is the astabandhan ceremony at the Ramnath temple? Tell Mhalu ajja I'll be coming, I'm a married woman, I will take part in the suvashin ceremony...' as though she had taken leave of her senses. She went back to a fitful sleep, dreaming, waking up, and glancing at her brother to make sure he was all right.

Shambhu got up early and threw the folded kambal into the house. As he sat on the porch hugging his knees, an elderly woman stopped at a distance. 'So your brother came in the night, Vithai! Where did he eat? Where did he sleep? Did he drink water in your house?' she asked.

'No. He stayed hungry. Slept outside the house.'

'So what if he's your brother, he's an outsider now, of a different faith. Why make him sit on the porch? You should have sent him to our house.'

Vithai didn't say a word and the woman walked on. Turning around suddenly, she asked 'What name have they given you? I just can't pronounce it…'

Vithai didn't reply.

'Imagine! Giving up your religion just to keep your fields and orchards! One's faith is most important,' the woman muttered, walking on.

The family clustered at the door when it was time for Shambhu to leave. They didn't ask when he'd come again, nor did he ask when they would come for a visit.

It was almost three months since Annu had moved in with Padre Simao Peres, but each time the priest spoke of sending him to Goapattana to be baptized the boy would begin to cry. He would run away and hide amongst the bushes and the priest would have to bring him back. One day the padre sat him down and said, 'I promised I'd let you stay here for a month. Each time I talk of your becoming a Christian, you draw back. You have broken your word, and that's a sin. But I'll give you one last chance. Tomas will take you to Padre Gasper Dias of St Catherine's Church this Sunday. You'll get baptized. Or you'll go home.'

'Father, will I have to eat cow's meat?'

'You cannot say you won't.'

'And pig's flesh?'

'You cannot say you won't.'

'If I refuse to eat it what will happen?'

'You will be punished, like the others who go against the faith.'

Annu remained silent.

'You decide. After Sunday you cannot stay here.'

'Father, let me just stay here with you.'

'That's not possible. For various reasons. I won't let you stay.'

Annu returned home that night and lay down on the floor, next to his brother. When his brother woke up the next morning his eyes fell on Annu and he shouted in joy, 'Annu! You're home! When did you come?' Durpadi, who was going to the well, heard his voice. She saw Annu and began screaming at the top of her voice. 'Wretched corpse! Worthless fellow! Eats shit all over the village and then comes to sleep in the house … The outcaste has defiled this settlement, defiled the house. He's a blot on the name of our village!'

Hearing voices some men from the neighbourhood joined her in the courtyard. Purso pulled out a pointed piece of wood from the wood pile in front of Dattu's house and rushed inside. 'Get out! We don't want you here!' he screamed jabbing Annu with the wood, pushing him out as though he were a wild animal that had wandered into the house.

'You've been eating cow's flesh, have you?' Devu aimed a kick at the boy.

'No. No! I haven't!'

'Pig's flesh, then?'

'No, no!'

'What did you eat, then? Mud? Telling lies, after all you've done! Go away from here!' Purso prodded at Annu with the piece of wood while the others beat him with sticks.

Annu wept like a child as he made his way to Simao Peres's shack. 'Bappa, they've been beating me. I'll become a Christian. I'll go to Goapattana with Demu mama on Sunday,' he sobbed. The priest's heart went out to the boy whose bare body was swollen and covered with welts. He passed a gentle hand over the bruises and drew the boy into the shack.

Just twenty days after Annu was baptized, old man Manju Nayak arrived at the priest's shack saying he wanted to become a Christian too. Padre Simao was happy.

'Christianity has very strict rules. You must follow them. They also have the Inquisition. They will be watching you,' he warned.

'I will, Padre bappa. I will follow the rules carefully.'

'But why do you want to give up your own faith?'

'I don't know. I've been following you around for a month, now,' he said. 'I like what you say. I'm sick of life, Padre bappa. I want a new path.'

As Padre Simao wandered about the village delivering his sermons, Manju followed him with a pair of cymbals in his hand. He had a high, sweet voice and he'd burst into devotional songs in a mixture of Konkani, Kannada and Marathi, clashing the cymbals whenever the priest stopped to speak.

The sun was almost overhead and the whole area shimmered in silvery light. Padre Simao stood before his shack, immersed in the beauty of his surroundings.

Tomas, who had just returned from the village with some vegetables, said, 'Padre bappa, four people have come from Goapattana. Three soldiers and one fidalgo.'

'Why have they come?'

'Don't know. Didn't reply when I asked. Just swept past insolently.'

'Come. Give me some payz. I must go to the village.'

'Why must you go so late in the afternoon?'

'I have to.'

'Go then. Go and meet that white-skinned officer. He might be one of your relatives.'

The priest felt insulted by his words. 'You're going too far, Tomas. It's wicked to hurt people. I don't want any of your payz. I'm going.'

'Don't be angry, Padre bappa, forgive me!' Tomas rushed up to him striking his forehead with his hand. 'I talk like a mad man sometimes. Padre bappa, won't my wife become a Christian like me?'

The priest ate the payz and salted preserve in silence. Suddenly he said, 'Tomas, are you sorry that you became a Christian?'

'I was sorry at first, Padre bappa, but then I came here to live with you. Now I'm proud to call myself a Christian.'

The priest seemed disillusioned. 'It's been a year and a half since I came to this village, but I've only baptized six people in all this time. I want to touch people's hearts and inspire them to become Christians of their own free will, but it is not happening, Tomas!'

'Six people ... that's a lot, Padre bappa. Besides, these people's lives have not changed through the centuries. It's not easy for them to change. And this is a cowardly race. Things will move faster if the power of the sword is displayed.'

The priest dropped to his knees before the crucifix. 'My Lord Jesus, Son of God, let my heart always be full of love and compassion. I don't want to use force. You are my refuge, O Lord!'

As Padre Simao crossed the temple grounds, Rayanna Bhat standing at the door, began to mutter loud incantations as though he were abusing the padre. The temple priest had grown old, but he was still as sly and selfish as he had been in his youth. Padre Simao walked on towards the fields when he saw a couple of native sepoys and two foreigners driving a family of four as if they were cattle. The fidalgo, a Portuguese officer of noble birth, walked behind them silently. The young woman had an infant in her arms while the man held the four-year-old boy's hand. Padre Simao Peres was distressed to see the sepoys beating the hapless couple. 'Why do you beat these poor people?' he exclaimed. 'You go against the teachings of Jesus. Don't draw the weight of sins on to your heads!'

The fidalgo, silent until then spoke in Portuguese, each of his words striking the air like a sharp blow, 'This couple is from Hela village. The man got into a brawl with his brother, was arrested and confessed to his crime. He was forgiven when he agreed to become a Christian and the family was baptized at St Catherine's Church. Each family member received eight xerafins too. Then they fled to an aunt's house in this village and continued to live like Hindus.'

'What will you do with them now?'

'The children will go to an orphanage to be brought up as Christians. The man and woman will face the Inquisition.'

The padre felt a sinking sensation in his stomach. He knew what terror the Inquisition had unleashed in Spain and Portugal. It would now be promulgated in Goa. Anyone who went against the tenets of Christianity was sentenced to death. Perhaps this couple too would be tied to a stake and burnt.

'You force them to change their religion and when they make a mistake you burn them. That is not right,' the priest remarked.

The officer was taken aback. 'Criticizing the Inquisition might prove dangerous for you, Padre,' he said, nervously. 'Do you know how powerful they are, how high they can reach? They can drag the viceroy to their court and have him punished. They ensure that the Christian religion remains pure and holy, what they do is God's work. I am a fidalgo, but I am proud to be an officer of the Inquisition. If you speak against the system I will bear witness myself and haul you to court. You know what will happen after that.'

The priest thought it was better not to say anything, and walked on. Appa, the barber, who was coming from Raigali, was talking loudly, 'Gopika mavshi kept them in her house for three days. How was she to know that they had become Christians? Will people let me and my sons remain in the village, will we be allowed to take part in religious functions, she wails.'

For a moment the padre thought of going to Gopika's house. I can ensnare this whole family and convert them to Christianity, he thought. They will have to convert anyway. Their neighbours will not leave them in peace. But the next instant he decided that it wasn't right to take advantage of their difficult situation. Jesus wouldn't be happy. If they came of their own free will the next day, it would be different.

Ever since he heard about the Inquisition, Padre Simao's mind was in a turmoil. It was just not right. It would create more obstacles, people would be terrified and move further away. The task of building bonds between men's minds, of calling out to their hearts would become more difficult.

They set out in their wooden ships with sails unfurled. They faced storms and hurricanes in their journey across the ocean that covered such a large part of the globe. Many of them died on the high seas when food and water ran out. Some fell prey to illnesses. Sometimes the ships lost their bearings and sank to the bottom of the ocean. And yet the ships loaded with troops kept coming. What force guided these courageous spirits, what did they aim to achieve? The fleets sailed thousands of miles to Kochi and from there to Daman and Diu as they grew familiar with the coast.

They'd loot the ships of the Arab traders on the high seas and drive them away. They would attack the local people of the places where they landed. They were such audacious rogues, nothing seemed to daunt them.

But one thing was certain – they came armed with a crucifix in one hand and a sword in the other. Religious propagation was the basis of all their activities even in later years. Why did they take so much trouble? They didn't conquer territory or expand their empire significantly. They didn't gather immense wealth by establishing a flourishing trade. What they did, however, was intimidate the local people, beat them and set fire to their homes in a bid to spread Christianity, which seemed to be their only aim. It was this single-minded purpose that enabled Albuquerque and his small force to defeat Adil Shah's mammoth army and conquer Goa.

One should not be so naive as to believe that it was Mhala Pai's request to Timmayya to rid Goa of the Adil Shah reign that opened the door to the Portuguese and let them slip in. The Portuguese army was cruel and the first thing they did after setting foot in Goa was to massacre six thousand Moors. They appropriated their wealth and property, and took the widows and young women into their fold. They needed a base from which they could expand their empire, carry on trade and propagate their faith. They chose this spot with great care. Their presence was so terrifying that if the proselytizing demon had not taken control of their activities, they could have built a vast empire. Their colonies, too, were different from those of the other European powers. They made Goa their home even though it was impossible to administer Goa from distant Portugal. Storms and tempests during the perilous journey by sea ensured that one out of four soldiers died on the way. Albuquerque therefore encouraged his soldiers to marry local women, he even brought the beautiful young widows of the slain Moors into the Portuguese fold. Those who opted for such marriages were rewarded with money and land. They were freed from military service and settled in other trades.

Not only were the Portuguese bold and fearless, they were also very resolute. Though their aim, right from the start was to propagate their religion, they spent the first thirty years establishing administrative control over their surroundings. During this period, they assured the Hindus that their social and religious rights would be respected.

So when the forced conversions began, the Hindus were the ones who suffered the most. This was partly because of their innate love for their land and their religion. It was also because the taboos of caste and religion with regard to diet and social interaction kept the Hindus isolated within walls of blind faith.

The dismantling of these walls created a major upheaval in their lives. If the shadow of a low caste person or a menstruating woman fell on them, the upper-caste people felt that they had become impure. For them, the thought of forsaking their faith and taking the religion of people who ate cow flesh was catastrophic.

On the other hand, the Portuguese were remarkably adept at combining religion and administration. When the religious leaders demanded something, the administration executed it by using force. The religious leaders held crucifixes while the administrators clutched their swords and over them all loomed the shadow of the Inquisition. These committee members were all powerful, and everyone, right from the viceroy to the common soldier, the fidalgo landlord to the baker and the tenant farmer in the field was terrified of them. They even threatened the King at times.

Bishop Joav Albuquerque called a meeting of priests belonging to the different Christian sects in Goa. Only Simao Peres received no invitation.

'I am a faithful preacher of the Word of Lord Jesus. When all the other priests have been invited, why have I been left out? This is an insult to a faithful priest,' Simao said.

The Bishop was a tall, strapping figure with a complexion as ruddy as ripe fruit. His tiny eyes, reduced to mere slits by the rolls of oily flesh gleamed. 'The Jesuits out here do not consider you a priest. They do not count you as one of them,' he declared.

'And you?'

'I don't, either.'

'Why?'

'You have no letter of recommendation from the King. All the other priests were selected by the King. As was I.'

'But I have a letter of permission from the Pope.'

'You still need the King's recommendation.'

'Is the King greater than the Pope?'

'I refuse to answer that. Let me tell you, though … the King's religious policies are drawn up according to the Pope's orders. Yet, in his own country, the King has greater powers.'

Padre Simao Peres remained silent.

'Go back to Adolshi and work according to your convictions. Just don't interfere in the work of the other Jesuits. They say that you incite people against Christianity. You insist that people should become Christians of their own free will. This goes against the dictates of the King and the viceroy. You know how powerful the Inquisition is. You may be stripped of your priesthood and thrown into the dungeon for working against the faith.'

Padre Simao remained silent for a while. 'Leave Adolshi village to me. I'll serve the people with love and lead them to Jesus. I tell you again, using force is against the teaching of Jesus. One who truly follows the Bible will never do this.'

The Bishop was furious. 'Get out! Just mind your own business. The Pope has given you permission so I'll let you stay. Otherwise you'd have been deported to your own country. Or burnt at the stake as a traitor to the faith. A band of soldiers, officers and priests will soon reach Adolshi. They'll convert the whole village within a year.'

Padre Simao turned away quietly.

Barely fifteen days after this incident, a group of strangers entered the village. Led by Captain Diego Barrett, the group consisted of a shef, three cabos, two priests and eighteen soldiers. Except for seven local soldiers, all the others were white-skinned Portuguese. They were all Christians, even the local soldiers were new converts. Captain Diego Barrett was seated on one horse while another horse had stores and provisions strapped to its back. The soldiers too carried loads, balancing boxes, baskets or bundles on their heads.

It was a Monday and a large crowd of devotees were waiting in the Ramnath temple for the ceremonial bathing of the deity. The elderly priest, Rayanna Bhat, and his son, Subba, were conducting the rituals when Lingu, the temple musician, rushed in. 'Those wretched creatures have arrived in the village, forty or fifty of them. Brought horses and guns and swords,' he gasped.

The people were terrified. Rayanna Bhat kept chanting the name of the Lord over and over. Every time some bad news trickled into the village, the old priest's heart would be filled with dread. 'Lord, don't let those creatures enter this village. Strike them dead outside the borders,' he'd prayed. Lord Ramnath is the protector of this region, if they step into this village their children will die, they will be burnt to ashes – he'd assured the devotees. Earlier, even when the villagers saw two soldiers, they would hide and cower in fear. Now the foreigners had come in such a large group. All that they had dreaded over the years had come true.

The Betaal shrine stood just beyond the temple grounds. It was a large mud-walled structure with a tiled roof and a dung-smoothed floor. There was no separate sanctum to house this deity – a huge boulder with a pair of eyes carved on its surface – which stood in the centre of the shrine. It was ritually bathed with the blood of eight to ten goats and some two hundred chickens during the Jogvani festival celebrated on a moonless night in the month of Magh. Betaal protected the village from ghosts and spirits, fevers and other afflictions, but if he got angry he would kill their children, people believed.

The captain reined in his horse when he got to the Betaal shrine. 'This is where we will stay,' he said. The soldiers carried their loads into the temple and the two priests sat down to rest. Captain Diego Barrett and Shef Camil Ribeir stood by the horses surveying the village.

'Quiet place. Full of farms and orchards,' the captain remarked.

'Yes. The villagers are religious. Won't become Christians easily. But they'll wilt when they are faced with some trouble. Their temples and shrines give them strength. Once these are destroyed, their roots will be cut off.'

The captain stared intently at Shef Camil Ribeir. 'Shef Ribeir, which is your ancestral village?'

'I don't know, senor. My father came with Timmayya's troops from Honnavar. He fought against the Moors during the battle for Goapattana and was rewarded with a house and orchards and made a police chief by Viceroy Albuquerque. But he remained a Hindu till his death.'

'And then, Shef?'

'After he died, I was told to convert if I wanted to keep the house and orchards and work for the government. So I became a Christian. But my mother refused to be baptized.'

The captain stared at him shrewdly.

'Do you regret this, now?'

'No. This happened twenty-six years ago. I'm a Christian now, my wife is a Christian, and my children are Christians. We recite the Rosary every evening and we eat pork and beef. Sometimes I feel that this whole world should be converted to Christianity in a single night. If I could do something about it…'

'Be patient, Shef Camil Ribeir, this job will be yours. You are most suited for it. Your ears are pierced, like theirs. A sharp thorn can be used to dig out another that is embedded in the flesh. Do you know what that means?'

Shef Camil Ribeir was six feet three inches tall, well-built, with skin which was the colour of wheat. His black eyes, however, were clear and lent a touch of softness to his face.

The news that the white-skinned foreigners were camping in the Betaal shrine spread through the village like a fire fanned by the wind. This had never happened before. Sometimes, on a wave of high spirits, they'd enter a temple. But they'd leave almost at once and the villagers would summon the priest and perform purificatory rituals and cleanse the place. They had never come to the village loaded with provisions, nor had they set up camp in a temple before.

The Brahmins of Raigali and the Nayaks of Shirvaddo gathered under the banyan tree just beyond the settlement and spoke in low voices, 'We've heard of the terror they've caused in other places. Now this calamity has reached our village…'

'… my heart is sinking with fright!'

'… we should thrash them and drive them away. Chop off their legs!'

'… they're cruel people. Have the strength of elephants. And then they have swords and guns!'

'... they might be important people in their own country, but this is our land.'

'... their schemes won't work in our village. We are protected by the deities in eighteen temples, only those gods can help us now...'

Some men from the village hid amongst the bushes by the Betaal shrine and surveyed the scene. The soldiers had converted the shrine into a camp. They had set up two hearths and placed large cooking pots on them. They drew water from the temple pond and filled their mud pots at the sacred spring. The villagers were furious.

'Don't defile the shrine and the temple pond like this,' Demu Gurav screamed.

The captain glared at them. Then he drew his gun and pointed it at some monkeys on a nearby tree. Taking careful aim he pulled the trigger and a monkey crashed to the ground. All those who were hiding in the bushes ran for their lives. One of them later told the others that the monkey had folded its palms in prayer and uttered 'Ram' with its dying breath. And someone who was listening said, 'Of course. Monkeys have always been devotees of Ram. How could this one be any different?'

At dusk, the villagers gathered at Shirvaddo. Every one of them was terrified. A storm was brewing in their lives – it sought to sever their umbilical ties and cut off the roots that bound them to their land. Something was happening, something was about to happen ... Something new was going to burst forth, trampling upon the old established customs. There would be destruction everywhere. People called out to their gods, 'Deva! Only you can save us and protect our religion!' But who would protect the gods themselves? They didn't know whom to approach for an assurance that their gods would be left unharmed. We have to protect them ourselves, they thought. But we're not strong enough, we won't be able to withstand their might. The very thought of a confrontation made their limbs turn cold with fright.

Ghana Shenai of Raigali was the village chief. He was an elderly man and his moustache as well as the tuft on his head had turned completely grey.

'Fifty-two generations of our people have lived in this village, blessed by the gods. And now these people just enter our shrine and camp there! We must drive the wretches out. We'll have a meeting tomorrow, let the whole village decide what must be done,' he wheezed.

Damu Nayak climbed on to a branch of the onvli tree and let out a shrill cry, 'Dugga … Dugga … Dugga Mhar … Come quick! Inform the villagers that a gaonki will be held tomorrow!' he called.

Dugga lived in the Mharvaddo, the colony by the stream beyond the farmlands where the low caste villagers lived. He heard Damu Nayak's cry and set off for Shirvaddo. Dugga made the first announcement standing under the bael tree. 'A group of unknown mean-looking chandals has entered the Betaal shrine. The temple is defiled. Our religion is in danger. The chief gaonkar has called a meeting under the peepal tree tomorrow afternoon. Everyone must be present!' he cried.

It was already quite dark by now and Dugga still had to go and inform the people of Raigali and then go through the fields to Deulvaddo and the artisan's colony. Dugga asked for a staff to protect himself from the dangers lurking underfoot, but no one was willing to lend him one, so he cut a length of bamboo from someone's fence and swishing it in front and across the path and beating softly on his drum, he set off for Raigali.

The villagers cast fearful glances at the Betaal shrine as they sidled past it on their way to the meeting the next afternoon. Thirty-six gaonkars were seated on the stone platform around the peepal tree, about two hundred paces away from the Ramnath temple. Lame Bhairu Nayak was carried there on a rope basket slung across a pole, either end of which rested on the shoulders of his two strapping sons.

The village chief, Ghana Shenai, looked exhausted. 'You can see what calamity threatens our village. They've destroyed the sanctity of our gods and our shrine. We were confident our gods would protect us, why doesn't the Lord tear their limbs apart? What do we do now? We believed that they wouldn't come to this remote village. But the wretched creatures have reached here! I don't know what to do, I have no advice to give you all,' he said as he mopped his face.

Immediately, lame Bhairu Nayak flared up. 'Don't just sit here and mope. If you sit and cry like this, they'll push their way into your homes and cook beef on your hearths. Fight them, drive them out. Lay their corpses on the ground. Pick up your axes and sickles and staffs,' he cried.

Shiva Nayak seemed scared. 'Let us go and meet them, let us plead with them to let us be. We are poor people, leave our gods alone, we'll say to them.'

The other villagers burst out in anger at his words. 'Plead with them! With those wretched, impure creatures! If we act mild they'll only step up their atrocities. They should be thrashed and driven far away!'

Subrai Shenai was listening quietly all this while. 'The Nayaks of Shirvaddo should handle this job. They belong to the Khatri caste, they are the protectors of the village. Their ancestors were part of the King's army, they fought with swords, they say. Now you have only sickles strapped to your waists. All this is mere talk!' he said.

'Boasting about the exploits of our ancestors won't help us now. You talk of thrashing them and driving them away. They have guns that spit fire and swords that can cut us down. Don't you know what they've done in the other villages?' Lavu Nayak interjected in a reasonable tone.

'That's what I call cowardice! Stick your tail between your legs and run away from the village. Leave your temples and your gods to them,' Bhairu fumed.

'Getting angry won't help, Bhairu, we must think calmly and then decide. Let us appeal to the gods, first. If the village remains safe, we'll take the deity ceremoniously around the village. Lord Ramnath is our only refuge now, let us depend on Him. We'll ask Him for some sign, let Him indicate what we should do.'

'You mean you won't even pick up your scythes and knives if they start breaking down the temple? Is that what you are saying, Raya?' Bhairu asked.

'What use will those knives be? We'll lose the temples and our lives as well.'

'Such words don't suit you, Raya. You've grown as massive as an ox. Go home, borrow some of your wife's bangles and wear them on your wrists!'

'You're lame and won't be called upon to fight, that's why you say all this.'

Ghana Shenai decided to intervene. 'What are you two up to? Have you come here to fight?'

'Let us go away, then. We'll wrap the gods up in a kambli,

take our wives and children and in the middle of the night, start walking. Haven't other villages been abandoned like this?' Mhablu Nayak suggested sorrowfully.

Everyone fell silent as the gravity of the situation seemed to sink in for the first time.

'Where will we go, leaving our land? Why should we lose our way in barren places, why should our families be exiled from the homes inherited from our forefathers? Whether we live or die, let's face the calamity right here,' Mangru Shenai said.

Guna Nayak sprang to his feet all of a sudden. 'You said we should stay here and, if necessary, die. Why should we die slowly, like fish and other creatures do when the water in the lake dries up? Let us all get together, Brahmins and Khatris, priests and carpenters and everyone from the lower castes too. Let us pick up whatever weapon we can and attack them at once. Let there be a bloodbath. Even if we kill four of their people, our deaths will not go in vain.'

The villagers whispered amongst themselves and gradually the whispers became louder. 'Why should we get into fights with them? Why cause bloodshed? Won't we starve if we leave the village?'

'They are the outsiders. They'll threaten us and get drunk with power and after some time they'll go away. Let them do what they want. If they destroy the temples, we'll carry our gods out into the forest and worship them there. If they force us to become Christians we'll return home, bathe in cold water and then worship our own gods again.'

'We men seem quite ready to die. But what of our wives and children? What will they do?'

The noise made by the villagers carried to the Betaal

shrine. The captain picked up his gun and his sword and set off, followed by the shef, a constable and five soldiers. He stopped beneath the peepal tree and glared at the villagers. They stared back in shock and bewilderment, like oxen when confronted by a tiger.

'Who is the mhal gaonkar?' the captain roared.

Ghana Shenai rose from his seat.

'How many people have converted to Christianity here?'

'Four people.'

'Did they get their share of the yield from the land owned by the village council, this year?'

'No. We don't recognize them as part of our society or our village any longer,' Ghana Shenai said with conviction.

'You will have to give them their share.'

Ghana Shenai remained silent.

'How many of those new converts were gaonkars in the old days?'

'Two. Manju Nayak and Khemu Patkar.'

'Where are they today?'

'We've stripped them of their rights. They're outcastes.'

The captain stepped forward, stomping his feet. 'You can't hold a meeting without them. That is against the rules. The King of Portugal has declared that Christian converts will be the most important members of the gaonki system. Who is the village kulkarni? Let me see your list of accounts.'

Bala Shenai, who maintained the village accounts, handed over his list.

'The names of Christian villagers must be on top of the list. Their opinion must be sought first. Their houses must be re-thatched and repaired before the other houses. No Hindu may bid higher than a Christian in an auction. Only another Christian can increase the bid,' the captain declared.

Ghana Shenai was furious. 'That's impossible. This is our village, we will administer it in whichever way we choose. Who are you to interfere in our affairs? No ruler has ever interfered in village administration before.'

'Ghana Shenai, don't talk too much. It's not your village. It belongs to the King of Portugal.'

'What King? We don't recognize him.'

The captain was enraged. He shoved Ghana Shenai back with the butt of his gun and the old man almost lost his balance. Guna rushed forward in consternation, 'See! He's hit our chief! Get up, all of you. Thrash them! Drive them away!' Guna pulled the sickle out of his belt, but one of the constables hit him with his staff before he could attack. The sickle fell to the ground. The shef drew his whip and lashed at Guna's back and legs and face. Guna didn't utter a sound, merely turning this way and that in agony.

No one came to his aid. Each man stood there trembling in fear. When the lashing stopped, Rama Bhoi from the Deulvaddo rushed forward, threw his arms around Guna and dragged him away.

'Cowards! One man falls to the ground and the lot of you rush away in fright! What use do you have for God and religion?' Shef Ribeir sneered.

The captain turned to the villagers, and said sternly, 'The King of Portugal is your ruler. His God is your God. His religion is your religion. All his subjects must become Christians. Anyone who practises another religion will be regarded as a traitor and expelled from his empire. We will build a church here. Meanwhile, the two padres will set up a cross for worship and take you to the church at Kalapur to be baptized,' he said.

'No! We won't become Christians!' Ghana Shenai said angrily. A few nervous voices piped in from the back, 'We won't convert. We revere our faith!'

'If you don't convert of your own will, we'll have to use force. Become Christians. Or leave the village,' saying so the captain and his soldiers walked away.

No one said a word. Each man was concerned about his own future. A chilly silence settled on the village even at the height of noon.

Ravlu Mirashi had been sitting quietly on the stretch of broken wall during the gaonki. His family had conducted the Jogvani rituals at the Betaal, Barmo and Vagro shrines from time immemorial. Betaal protects the village, Barmo creates and nurtures life and Vagro destroys. All three are powerful deities and must be treated with respect, his grandfather used to say.

Ravlu Mirashi was filled with despair. He sprang to his feet, his frail body trembling as though some external power was drawing him towards the Betaal shrine. The captain, the shef, the priests and all the soldiers stared at him, amazed, as Ravlu Mirashi staggered into the shrine.

Only a small pit in the ground marked the spot where the Betaal image used to stand. The Mirashi's hair stood on their ends and he broke into a sweat as he stared at the pit. They had installed a cross on the temple roof and had stuck a large wooden one into the earth, but the image of Betaal was nowhere to be seen … until his eyes fell on the idol in a clump of bushes. 'Wretched sinners! Why did you lay hands on my God? Why did you tear Him out? You will come to no good!' he shrieked.

It seemed as if this weak, defenceless creature had gone insane. Then, without the thumping of drums or the shrill sound of pipes and without any invocatory rituals, an external spirit seemed to enter the Mirashi's body. He pulled the cross out of the ground and flung it away. He rushed into the thicket and hoisted the massive image of Betaal on to his shoulder. Leaping around wildly, as though in a trance, he rushed through the fields towards the stream.

Ravlu Mirashi plunged headlong with the deity into the deep pool at the bend in the stream. Nobody knew if Ravlu had meant to leave the idol on the bank and end his life in the pool. Or if he had meant to fling the idol in and save himself.

Several days passed. Fires were lit in front of the Betaal temple. Food was cooked. Sometimes the soldier would go into Goapattana and bring back fresh rottya, meat, spices and tobacco. They obtained rice from the villagers. They would throw down a cruzado and demand a khandi of rice to be delivered to their camp. The villagers preferred the smaller currency seraphim, riya or taank because they got everything on barter from the local Patkar's shop.

One day the captain was standing on the hillside staring down at the fields where some men were scooping up wet mud and building bunds. He knew that Padre Simao Peres believed that these people would not convert to Christianity on their own. In that case, he thought, strong measures will have to be used. They will need to be bullied and beaten, he mused. He turned around to look at the Ramnath temple.

What a magnificent structure this is! These people's religious fervour is deep and their faith rests on the solid foundation of this temple, built by who knows who and when. Unless the temple itself is destroyed, their faith won't be shaken. But that's not so easy to do. I saw what happened in Nevri village. The temple was desecrated, demolished and the people were threatened and even deceived into becoming Christians, but not even half the village accepted the new faith. The others gathered whatever they could carry and slipped out of Goa in the darkness of the night. So many settlements were deserted, so many fields lay fallow. That mustn't happen here. Every man must convert to Christianity, he must continue to live here, cultivate the lands and harvest his crops, just like before...

His train of thought was interrupted when he heard loud voices from the field below. Two men were shouting at each other, with spades raised. Captain Barrett was amused. They'll attack each other with their spades, he thought as he leapt on to his horse and trotted towards them. The men were taken aback to see the captain, and then one of them, who was covered with sweat and mud, began to complain, 'This man has encroached on my land. And now he says the ridge collapsed!'

The other man seemed to lose his nerve on seeing the captain. He quietly moved away to the other side of the field. 'Build that ridge wherever you want,' he muttered, 'and if you starve tomorrow take some more of my land. But you won't be able to digest what you've taken.'

The captain didn't intervene in their quarrel. After a few moments he turned and went away. But one thing he had realized. Land was everything to these people. Besides the thin loincloth they were wearing, they possessed nothing. He looked back and saw that the men had gone back to their work of slapping the wet mud in piles and patting it into bunds. They were the children of the earth and their roots went deep into the soil, and the living sap that nurtured the many trees and plants seemed to mingle with their blood and sustain them.

'There must be quite a bit of land that belongs to the village council,' the captain said to the shef that afternoon.

'Yes. These affairs are decided at the council meetings, like in other villages. Bids are placed for the right to cultivate this land. They pay their taxes regularly.'

'If we take control of the land that belongs to the village council, we can give it to those who convert.'

'That has been tried in other villages too, senor. Unless the land is surrendered voluntarily after the members hold a gaonki, we cannot take it over. It is against the law.'

'Forget the council meeting. We'll catch hold of the mhal gaonkar, Ghana Shenai, and force him to sign the papers.'

The next morning the captain sent a soldier to Goapattana to fetch the revenue clerk to the village. The following day the captain, the shef, the revenue clerk and a few soldiers made their way to Raigali. The clerk carried some papers and a pen in the pocket of his coat and an inkpot swung from his hand. He also had a sword strapped to his waist. The group stopped in front of Ghana Shenai's house and the captain sent a local soldier to summon the chief gaonkar and the kulkarni, Balu Shenai, who came bearing the ledger of village accounts. Bala Shenai went up to the captain and with his hand on his heart, bowed low before him. Ghana Shenai, however, stood erect, fuming.

The captain said, 'Ghana Shenai, you didn't show me any respect, but I'm not angry with you. You are the chief gaonkar, the head of the village. Just remember Joav III, King of Portugal, is much bigger than you. He owns this village and all this land. His law is absolute. The viceroy's soldiers massacred six thousand Moors. You know what the King of Portugal's soldiers can do.'

Ghana Shenai was uneasy. He realized that the captain was trying to intimidate him. For a moment he thought of turning around and walking away, but the soldiers had surrounded him.

The captain then turned to Bala Shenai. 'How much land belongs to the council in this village?' he asked.

Bala Shenai glanced at Ghana Shenai, then began to recite the figures as though by rote. 'There are fertile fields where thirty-six khandis of paddy seedlings can be sown, upland fields that can take forty-seven khandis. And sixteen khandis can be sown in the low lying fields by the river.'

The captain turned to Ghana Shenai and stared into his eyes. 'The King wants the fertile tract of land. The revenue clerk has come to take it over,' he said.

'No! We shall certainly not give up the land that belongs to the whole village,' Ghana Shenai declared loudly. 'Your King needs to grab our lands because he is surviving on payz? Or is he begging for alms?'

The captain pulled out his whip in anger, but Shef Camil Ribeir quickly stepped forward to stop him. The soldiers closed in and Ghana Shenai, felt as though he was trapped in a dense thorny thicket and two hundred wild boars with pointed tusks were rushing towards him. Yet he stood his ground.

'This land has belonged to the village council for fifty-six generations, how dare you try to acquire it? We will not give it away.'

Now the shef was enraged. 'You will have to give it up' he shouted. 'You have no choice. The clerk will draw up an agreement, just sign it quietly. Remember, the King has asked for that tract of land. It will be given back to your people some day.'

Ghana Shenai's head was reeling, but he remained calm. 'We will have to have a gaonki and get everyone's opinion at the meeting. The land belongs to everybody,' he said.

'The last meeting went against the rules, Ghana Shenai. From now on, primary importance will be given to the Christian villagers. Their opinion and their decision will be final. At the meeting tomorrow, if the Christian members say that the land should be given to the King, you can do nothing about it. One Christian vote is worth more than a hundred others. What they say will be accepted. Henceforth, you will have a say in the gaonki only if you become a Christian,' the captain said. He turned to the revenue clerk, 'Senor Viador de Fazde, get the agreement ready. He'll sign it. Just leave some space above his signature for a Christian member to sign it too. We need his signature only because he is the mhal gaonkar of the village.'

The shef drew out his sword. Sticking its tip into Ghana Shenai, he pushed him towards the rumada tree and made him sit by its roots. The other soldiers too had naked swords in their hands. The revenue clerk sat under the tree with one leg outstretched before him. Bala Shenai was very distressed to see his shoe resting against the little stone shrine that housed a god, a stone naga, but couldn't say a word.

The clerk kept dipping the pen into the inkwell and with scratching sounds wrote out the agreement in Portuguese, then read it out aloud. Ghana Shenai and Bala Shenai didn't understand a word, but what they did understand was that the foreigners had treacherously appropriated the land that belonged to the village.

The shef and a few other soldiers prodded Ghana Shenai with their swords. 'Sign it,' the shef said.

Ghana Shenai picked up the pen with trembling hands, and dipped it into the ink. For a moment he thought he should break the pen and risk getting pierced by their swords, but the feeling passed swiftly and he wrote his name crookedly on the sheet. Bala Shenai also signed his name as a witness.

Ghana Shenai wept uncontrollably as he turned away after signing the document.

'You elder gaonkara,' the captain said to him, 'there's nothing to be sorry about. Listen to me. We've acquired this land, no doubt, but we are going to distribute it amongst those who become Christians. You command respect in this village, no one goes against your word. Explain this to the people, persuade them to convert. Think about it, Shenai. Land where you can sow eighteen khandis of paddy will be yours if you bring fifty or hundred people to get baptized. Moreover you are free to do what you want with it.'

'I don't want that land. I will not become a Christian!' Ghana Shenai declared.

'Why? Christianity is a great religion, Ghana Shenai.'

'Every man believes his religion is the greatest.'

'But our religion is greater than yours.'

'How?'

'Because it is the religion of the King of this land, of the viceroy, of those who conquered you. The religion of those who have been vanquished, is cowardly and weak. Even their gods are powerless.'

Some men, women and children from Raigali were watching everything from behind a large mango tree. Ghana Shenai saw them and began to beat his breast and cry, 'I have tossed the wealth acquired by fifty-six generations into their hands. The village will never forgive me now, Deva!'

'Let them write whatever they want. Can they just pick up the land and walk away? The fields will still be here, of no use to anyone. Whoever sets foot in them will vomit blood and die,' Bala Shenai warned.

One night, a Portuguese soldier, who stepped out of the sleeping quarters, was bitten by a snake. The local soldiers summoned Kusta, the medicine man, who stroked the soldier's body with some leaves and twigs muttering incantations to remove the poison. His efforts were in vain. By morning, the soldier was dead. The captain had gone to Goapattana and Shef Camil Ribeir, who was in charge, was in a quandary. He himself was a local who had converted to Christianity, while the dead soldier was Portuguese. If the dead soldier was a local, the matter could have been hushed up, but now the authorities would have to be informed. Reports of the investigations would be sent to Portugal.

Kusta in the meantime was muttering, 'He should have been taken to the temple and laid beneath the large bell before the rituals were performed, but he belonged to another faith...'

'Why didn't you tell me this earlier?' Shef Ribeir shouted. 'Why the temple, I would have taken him into the sanctum itself, if necessary. Tell me, what rituals did you perform, what plants and leaves did you use? I want all the details. I must report the matter to the authorities.'

'I can't do that, hodda mansha, big man ga, the guru who taught me this told me not to reveal the names to anyone. If I do, the medicine won't be effective any more and I will lose my power,' Kusta pleaded.

'Nonsense! Tell me the names.'

'I won't. Really, I won't. It's a sin.'

The shef drew his whip and flicked it across Kusta's bare back. The man recoiled in pain, 'Stop, don't beat me, I'll tell you!'

In a frightened voice he blurted out, 'One is the sarpa muli, it grows on ant hills. You have to break the anthill to get the root. The other is the bark of the apatha tree. It removes the poison and purifies the blood.'

'And those leaves that you rubbed on the body?'

'Those were just nirmalya leaves.'

'Now tell me the mantra your guruji gave you. Whisper into my ear if you like.'

Kusta was quite afraid by now. 'No, no ga, I'll break my promise if I tell you. I'll die. My children will die…' he protested.

'You'll have to tell me.'

'No, no. I can't!'

The shef lashed at Kusta once again, drawing blood. 'Deva, Iswara, come to my aid, come help me!' Kusta repeated the prayer in a voice laden with tears.

The shef turned away. He was not really interested,

merely venting his anger on Kusta. Now he needed to get on with the investigation. He had sent a soldier on horseback to Goapattana with a message for the captain. By evening Tenent Santan Lobo, a subordinate of the captain who had recently come to Goa, arrived in the village accompanied by three other soldiers. They looked at the dead soldier, a tall and well-built man. They couldn't possibly carry the body all the way to Goapattana for the funeral. The Tenent walked around the temple grounds looking for a suitable spot to bury him.

There was a large field behind the Ramnath temple and beside it was an open space overgrown with shrubs and bushes. The Tenent ordered his men to bury the soldier there. The priest and other soldiers began to prepare for the burial.

A current of joy rushed through the village as news of the soldier's death spread. These people, who were always quick to mourn a death, rejoiced at this death of an enemy. God had appeared in the form of a serpent and bitten the soldier. They took it as a sign of deliverance, a promise of protection. Rayanna Bhat went about saying, 'God has punished them. They'll all die or they'll run away from the village. Didn't I always say God would save us?' The villagers agreed.

The corpse was laid on a broad plank and two thick pieces of wood attached to either end. Four men carried it past the temple to the grave. As they buried the man, the two priests chanted prayers in Latin. The villagers watched all this, and a strange thrill passed through them – this is the first grave they are digging in this village, it will also be the last, they thought.

The Tenent and his squad stopped before the Ramnath temple on their way back from burying the soldier. Seeing the bhat and his companions, he declared, 'That plain will now be the village cemetery where all Christians will be buried after death. No one else may set foot there. Very soon we will build a church close by.' The villagers became nervous. They were making arrangements for burying the dead even before they had converted people to their faith!

Sukhdo Nayak, who lived by the old well in Shirvaddo, sat alone in the darkness muttering to himself. Two of his sons sat in the courtyard wondering why their father was so agitated that day.

'They've taken away the fertile fields that belonged to the village council. They'll give those fields to those who convert to their faith. Let us acquire some of that land,' he said in a low voice.

'But we'll have to convert, Bappa, give up our religion…'

'Religion? God and religion are for those whose bellies are full. If I divide my land amongst the three of you, none of you will get much. We can't even bid for the village land any more.'

Sukhdo Nayak's sons were silent for a while. Though Sukhdo was short, his sons were strapping young men with broad shoulders and muscles as hard as iron. 'If we forsake our faith and take up theirs, we might regret it later,' the elder son said in a worried voice.

'There's nothing to regret, Ramkushta. We'll go to their church and say, do what you want. Feed us what you will. Then we'll come back and bathe in cold water before entering the house. They can keep their faith, we'll keep ours. People will talk for a few days, then they'll forget. You take my word, these foreigners have come from across seven seas, they won't stay here very long. They sleep on beds and eat out of golden plates. Why will they want to stay in this impoverished village?'

'But there are some locals who've become Christians. They'll stay.'

'Yes. So will we. If we don't acquire that land at once, someone else will. Everyone's waiting to see who makes the first move.'

'Let's go, then. We'll say we have many people at home, let them give us what they will,' Molu, the elder son, said.

'But Avo will definitely not agree. She says she wants to go on a pilgrimage to Pandhari this year,' Ramkushta exclaimed.

Sukhdo was angry. 'Let her be. She can stay in this house if she wants to. Or let her build a hut and live there alone. Let's go right now, while it's dark. Who knows what might happen tomorrow?'

They crossed the ridges bordering the fields and reached the temple plain. The trees on either side hid the sky and they could barely see the track before them, but they knew the area well. Molu was nervous, 'God will be angry with us. The villagers won't keep quiet, either,' he said.

His father turned around and whispered, 'If we turn back now, we'll wring our hands in regret later. They'll force us to convert anyway.' Sukhdo was a very shrewd man and was well aware of the situation that was developing around him.

They stopped a little distance from the Betaal shrine. A soldier stepped forward, sword in hand, 'Who's that? Who are you?' he demanded.

'I'm Sukhdo Nayak. These are my sons. We've come to join your religion.'

'Do all of you want to become Christians?'

'Yes.'

'Why have you come at night?'

'It's better to fix things up in the darkness of night. This is an evil village full of suspicious people. They're jealous. Don't care to see any one do anything good.'

The soldier went to the door of the shrine and called out to the shef. The shef soon emerged followed by constable Remet Noronha and Padre Colaso.

'We're Nayaks from Shirvaddo.'

'How many members are there in your family?'

'Nine members. I have three sons. The third one is young, but these two are married. The elder one has two children and the second has one child. We'll come with their wives and children.'

'And your wife?'

'Not her. She's not all right in the head.'

'Very well then. But why have you come stealthily like this, at night? What do you want to say?'

'For those surrounded by troubles, day and night are the same! We have come to the point of starvation, hodda mansha, you great man. We used to survive by bidding for the village lands, but now you've taken that away. If you could give my household enough land to sow four khandis of paddy seeds…'

'Not four khandis. The other new converts will also have to get some fields. We will make the whole village Christian soon.'

Sukhdo remained silent.

'You'll get a strip to sow two khandis. And that's because you had the courage to come here first.'

'But we're nine members … nine of us…' Sukhdo stammered.

'Not another strip! If you're not satisfied, go back. When the swords lash you tomorrow, you'll cower in fright and beg to be converted,' the shef said.

'I'll take what you give, hodda mansha, but give us fields on the lower slopes.'

'All right. Become a Christian first, then strike your pickaxe in the field.'

'And if the villagers object?'

'Our soldiers and constables will stand there with swords to protect you. Besides, the mhal gaonkar has signed away that land to the Portuguese King.'

Padre Colaso was delighted. Nine people had volunteered to become Christians in such a short time. 'You will be baptized at St Lawrence's Church next Sunday. Be here at daybreak. You will be given white garments and each of you will get four cruzados too,' he said.

'All right. I give my word,' the men said and turned away.

'Sukhdo Nayak! You've given your word. If you break it now you won't get the land. Nor will we let you keep your religion,' the shef declared in a menacing voice.

The words seemed to echo in the darkness and Sukhdo was afraid that someone would hear them. When they got home, the women and children were sitting on the ledge outside the house. The younger son, Vasu, lay on a reed mat in the hall.

'Where did you go so late at night with your sons? Better to eat mud, if your belly isn't filled. Why do something so evil and treacherous?' Sukhdo's wife demanded.

'Quiet! Just shut your mouth, wretched creature! Don't convert, if you don't want to. But if you stop the others, I'll break your head!' Sukhdo thundered.

'Who do you mean by others?' Gopika, the elder daughter-in-law asked.

Sukhdo lowered his voice at once. 'All of us, the rest of the family, elder daughter-in-law. You must take charge now, you're the older one. We go there, perform some rituals, and come back. Then we lead our lives as usual, they lead theirs. They've promised to give us as much land as we want, that too on the lower slopes.'

The atmosphere in the house remained heavy and tense during the next three days. The younger one, Parvati, was not deeply affected but Gopika, the elder daughter-in-law was worried and scared. Their mother-in-law withdrew into herself, wandering aimlessly about the house. Sometimes she'd stand by the well in the back yard.

On Saturday evening just after dusk, the elder son Molu said to his wife, 'We have to go tomorrow, at daybreak. We must take the children as well.'

Gopika began to tremble and clenching her teeth, she murmured, 'No, no! I won't go … I won't…'

Molu grabbed his wife by the arms and shook her violently, 'What's wrong with you?' he cried. He poured a pitcher of water on to her head and slowly she came out of the delirium, weeping like a child.

'A blazing fire consumes everything in its path. Wet or dry. Nothing escapes. Faith and religion are baseless issues. When they were razing all those temples in Chornem and Goapattana, what was God doing? Why didn't He grab the foreigner's hands? Why didn't He hold back those sledgehammers and crowbars? That's it. We must go early tomorrow morning,' Molu spluttered.

In a little while the house became quiet and still. Sukhdo

lay in bed worrying about the repercussions of what he had set out to do. Mother Earth! O Bountiful Goddess! It's for you that I'm selling my soul!

They woke up at dawn. The men drew on their vests and wrapped fresh loincloths about their hips. Ramkushta's wife, Parvati, seemed quite enthusiastic about everything but the elder daughter-in-law, Gopika, was nowhere to be seen. They found her sitting by a large anthill just behind the house. Her face was pale and swollen with crying.

When they were ready to depart, their mother Mhalkum picked up the box of pinar and dabbed smears of the vermilion powder on the women's foreheads. She called her youngest son, Vasu, to her side and flung a fistful of pinar over him so that his head and neck and the clothes he wore were stained red.

'Why do you sprinkle pinar? Do you think we are taking them to be sacrificed on the battle field?' Sukhdo fumed through clenched teeth.

They set out at daybreak accompanied by a priest and three soldiers. The sun was overhead by the time they reached St Lawrence's Church which was a large thatched hut, by the site of a temple that had been razed. Large stone slabs from the ruined temple were being carried to huge pits where the foundation of a new church was being laid.

The married women were asked to remove the beaded galsari from their necks and wipe the kumkum from their foreheads. Parvati, who had seemed unaffected till now, wailed aloud as she gave her galsari to her husband and passed a hand across her sweaty brow. Gopika, however, refused to let anyone near her, clutching at the beads with both hands. Finally her husband grabbed the galsari and snapped the string with his teeth. Gopika dropped to the ground and scooped up the scattered beads along with the dust, knotting them in a corner of her sari.

There was a stone platform in the hut and on it were a crucifix and wooden images of Mother Mary and Jesus, with a crown of thorns on His head. Some thirty persons from different localities had come to be baptized. Everyone was served payz in clay bowls and then sent to take a dip in the pond. The women were given white garments which covered them from their shoulders to their waists. The men were given long white coats and it was odd to see these upper garments paired with the meagre loincloths that the men normally wore.

An old padre stood at the pulpit facing the group of people who knelt before him. He recited prayers as he sprinkled holy water from an urn and daubed a spot of oil on their heads and temples. He made the sign of the cross at their breast and put the wine and wafer, representing Jesus's flesh and blood, into their mouths. Everyone bowed low before the priest. He went back to his place at the pulpit and announced the Christian names that had been given to each of the converts.

'Sukhdo Nayak. By the grace of our Lord Jesus you will now be known as Salvador Dias.

'Molu Nayak. By the grace of Lord Jesus, you are now Manuel Dias.

'Ramkushta Nayak. By the grace of Lord Jesus you are now Pedro Dias.

'Vasu Nayak. By the grace of Lord Jesus you are now Jose Dias.

'And now for the women – Gopika. By the grace of our

Lord Jesus you will now be known as Isabel, wife of Manuel Dias.

'Parvati. By the grace of Lord Jesus you are now Fatima, wife of Pedro Dias.'

The priest then read out the names of their three children. When the Christian names of all the new converts had been announced the padre's deep resonant voice rang out as he celebrated Mass.

'Lord Almighty, Son of God, Jesus Christ. We, your children, born into a new life have gathered at your feet to embrace your teachings and become one with you in body and in soul. Protect us, make us fit vessels for your faith and devotion. Let our sins be burnt to dust and the gates of Heaven open before us. We shall follow your teachings and uphold the faith with devotion. Bless us and help us become good Christians. Amen.

'When the whole Universe was steeped in darkness, He lit the lamp and shed light. Darkness and light, day and night, heaven and earth, land and water and all living creatures … He created them all. He sent His son Jesus into the world of men to spread the message of love and compassion and we, lowly creatures, were blessed by His presence. His heart, full of compassion, is as boundless as the sea. Ask, and He shall lead you to love, peace and joy. He shall deliver you from all sin. Pray to Lord Jesus, Son of God, show us the path of truth and righteousness that will lead us to You. He possessed nothing but love and compassion.

'One day a grieving mother came up to Jesus, "Son of God, born from the holy womb of Virgin Mary, my son lies dead. Save him, bring him back to life." Jesus went with her to her house and on seeing the boy said, "Your son is not dead. He is fast asleep." Upon hearing this the people who had gathered all around began to laugh and taunt Jesus. The Lord stepped forward and laid a hand on the boy. "Rise, O son of this mother," He said, and at once the boy sat up. The balm for all your pain and sorrow lies in His hands.'

Each of newly converts received four cruzados, coins they were seeing for the first time. They could buy a khandi of paddy or a hundred coconuts for one cruzado and in Goapattana, it could pay for a blanket or a woman's sari. Sukhdo was delighted. He gathered the thirty-six gold coins into the end of his loincloth and tucked it in at his waist.

The sunlight had begun to fade when they neared their village. Gopika collapsed in a heap under a tree and declared, 'I'm not setting foot in there, I'll go somewhere and kill myself.' The younger daughter-in-law, Parvati, laid a hand on her shoulder, 'Akka, let's go. We can't change what's in our fate, sister.'

'What fate are you talking about? They've turned you into a widow even while your husband is alive, but what does that matter? All you care for is the money!' Gopika snarled.

Parvati, who had walked briskly all the way was dumbstruck. Padre Colaso, who was waiting for them to come to terms with the situation, stepped forward now. 'There's no cause for complaint once you've been baptized. If you go against the Christian faith, the Inquisition will get you and burn you at the stake. You have sworn an oath that you will be good Christians. You will not be forgiven if you stray,' he said.

Sukhdo clutched the coins in his fist and turned on his daughter-in-law angrily. 'Be quiet and accept what you get, what difference does religion make? Seeds will sprout whether you worship Ishwar or whether you worship Jesus.

The belly has to be filled first of all. They've only removed a string of beads from your neck, they haven't broken your limbs, have they?'

'Let it get dark, at least. How can we face the villagers?' Gopika pleaded faintly.

'Listen, we have to live here for the rest of our lives.'

'This is something new in this village, but hundreds of women elsewhere have become Christians. They weep for two days and then everything is fine,' the priest said.

Darkness had not quite set in when they got to the village and the atmosphere seemed deceptively calm and quiet. Small groups of men stood and stared at them silently from the temple plain or the peepal or in the fields. It was as though a single word would be enough to set off a confrontation. The silence on both sides was pregnant with distrust as though people were just waiting to light that first spark.

Maybe they know that we'll get the land, Sukhdo said to himself. Suspicious fellows! If someone mistakenly eats something that has been touched by a Christian, these people cast him out. And if someone becomes a Christian of his own free will, they act suspicious and taunt him, too!

'You might, at times, use your first names as before, but the old family name must not be used. Dias is your surname now. I shall visit you tomorrow to teach you about Christianity and to bless your home,' Padre Paulo Colaso said as they parted ways.

Their mother, Mhalkum, who was sitting by the shack outside the house, wailed out loud when she caught sight of them.

'Why do you behave as though someone is dead?' her husband snapped.

Who is it that has died? And who has been born anew, Ramkushta wondered, for something as momentous as birth or death had certainly occurred in their lives. Mhalkum had taken a pot, a ladle and a plate and built a small hearth within the shack. 'I won't step into that house. It's a Christian's house, now,' she said.

The family bathed at the old broken well and returned home in wet clothes. They were scared that the villagers would attack them with sticks if they drew water from the new well.

'That old broken well is what you'll have to use, your bangles won't tinkle at the new well any more,' the mother-in-law called out to the women as they entered the house. 'Vasu, my son, I'd hoped that you would cook for me when I fell ill, but they've made a Christian of you too. You can't even cremate me when I'm dead. I'll go to Pandharpur for the festival and throw myself into the Chandrabhaga river,' she said.

Parvati lit a fire in the hearth and slumped beside it, her head in her hands. Gopika, meanwhile, was stringing the beads of her galsari on to a thread by the light of the lamp. With the kumkum freshly applied on her forehead and the strand of beads about her neck, Gopika seemed more in control. 'Why do you sit there listlessly? Don't we have to prepare food? They haven't eaten anything since morning,' she said to Parvati who stared at her blankly.

Padre Paulo Colaso and two soldiers came to their house early next morning. They brought a labourer from Shirdone, a new convert, who nailed two long branches to make a rudimentary cross which he stuck into the ground. Every devout Christian must have a cross by his front door. It protects the house, the priest explained. The labourer uprooted the tulsi plant in front of the house and Sukhdo's sons were told to flatten the low ridges at the edge of the courtyard.

Parvati lit a lamp as the priest entered the house chanting Latin prayers and sprinkling holy water to bless the household. All the members of the family, except Mhalkum, were gathered in the hall. 'This house is now the abode of Lord Jesus and His mother, the compassionate Virgin Mary who shower their blessings on you. Whenever you are in danger, call out to them and all your sorrows will vanish, your troubles will recede…' He began to pray, 'Lord Jesus, Master, these people have been born anew and have entered your fold. Bless them. Make their hearts clean and pure so that they may love each other as well as their neighbours and those less fortunate than themselves. Give them the strength to abide by your teachings and be good Christians. Amen!'

Sukhdo, meanwhile, was whispering to those around him, what does it matter whether it is this religion or that one, all of them say the same thing. Toil and eat the fruits of that toil.

When the priest reached the edge of the courtyard he paused, 'That lady, the one named Isabel … she's wearing a chain of beads and has vermilion on her forehead. This goes against the rules. You have sworn to be good Christians, remember.'

The priest turned around and stepped back onto the porch. 'The Council for Religion in Goa has drawn up strict rules for new converts. If you disobey these, the officers of the Inquisition will throw you in jail. If found guilty, you will be burnt at the stake on the Day of Judgement of the Faithful. Let me briefly run through the rules:

'You will not grow a tulsi plant at your front door. The

courtyard will not have the decorative ridges of Hindu households. Coconut and banana trees will not be grown beside the house. Women need no longer bathe and wear fresh clothes before entering the kitchen, they can add salt to the rice when it is cooked. Rituals like the thread ceremony for young Brahmin boys and the phal sobaan for pregnant women must not be conducted. Women must not wear blouses fastened by knots, men must not wrap dhotis about their waists. Men must not sport the sacred thread or tie their long hair in a knot at the back of their heads. Women must not wear the galsari or sport kumkum on their foreheads.

'Ceremonies like the satti and the barso must be stopped. You needn't invite the whole family and others who belong to the same gotra to a wedding, nor must you break a coconut on the occasion. There should be no practice of smearing turmeric, oil and coconut milk on the bride and bridegroom before the wedding. Ovis will not be sung, betel leaves will not be offered to show respect, nor will rice grains be showered on the young couple in blessing. The couple need not visit the bride's house five days after the wedding. The practice of fasting on Ekadashi and performing rituals on the night of the full moon will have to be discontinued. No worship of Ganesh on Chavoth, no dancing at the Shigmo festival, no lighting of lamps at Divali.

'When someone dies, don't throw his bedding behind the house, don't smear cow dung where the corpse was placed and don't keep a lighted lamp at the spot. Do not call the bhat to perform the twelfth and thirteenth day ceremonies after death, don't let the dead person's sons shave their heads or offer food to crows. Do not keep holy books of Hinduism in your houses or consult the vaij when ill. A Hindu midwife should not assist your women at childbirth. The joish and the ghadi should not be consulted about getting rid of evil spirits. You must not listen to devotional songs sung by the wandering Buas. In short, follow none of the practices that were sanctioned by your old religion, do nothing that goes against the rules of Christianity,' he said.

The priest and his companions moved away. Mhalkum had screamed loudly and fallen to the ground when the tulsi was uprooted and still lay on the ash-strewn floor. Ramkushta charged into the shack, 'Why do you writhe on the floor as though your sons are dead?' he screamed. He picked the old woman up and carried her into the house. 'Lie here. Die, if you must. Cremation or burial, why should you worry? We'll carry you to church and have you baptized, at least we'll get four cruzados!'

The neighbours had been staring silently from a distance all this while. How did this whole family give up their faith, were they mad, people whispered.

'You're talking like Sukhdo. Must have got a lot of money for this shameful act. To think that a family from our settlement just goes and converts to Christianity without a word to anyone! Deva, what will happen to this village!' one of the onlookers declared.

This was the first family in Shirvaddo that had converted to Christianity and people were enraged. The next morning their neighbour, Jana Nayak, emerged from his bath and watered the tulsi at his door with a great show of devotion. Chanting the names of the gods and muttering loud prayers he walked around the plant. 'It's fortunate that the breeze doesn't blow from that direction, or we'd be defiled by that outcaste's touch!' he said to his wife.

Five days after was Amaas, a day when Hindus symbolically offer food to their forefathers who, they believe, accept these offerings in the guise of crows. Jana Nayak placed a plantain leaf laden with food in his courtyard and made noises to attract the birds. Sukhdo turned away silently and went indoors. The old priest, Somanna, always said that the spirits of one's ancestors hung there in space craving the food and water that would be set out for them on Amaas and Punav. Deva, what will my parents' spirits do now? And when I die, my spirit will also wallow in misery, craving a mouthful of water, he thought. A strange fear took hold of him, and suddenly he seemed to lose interest in the strip of land that he had been given.

For the past three months, Guna Nayak's spirit had convulsed with rage every time he thought of the shef lashing him with his whip at the last gaonki. But whenever he expressed his thoughts, the others silenced him, out of fear. 'Quiet! Don't speak so loudly! Who knows where they'll appear from, the devils from across the seven seas! Not a drop of pity or kindness in them.' And then they would all fall silent.

Guna had two friends, Raya and Shabi, a few years younger than himself. They were devoted to him and listened to everything he said with full attention. Sometimes his words frightened them, but they were always loyal to him. Guna was quick to flare up whenever he thought something was wrong, but people ignored that because they knew he meant well. After all, who could forget the care and devotion with which he had tended to a crippled uncle who had fallen from a tree. Even a son born of your own womb wouldn't lavish so much care on you, they said.

The news of Sukhdo and his family's conversion, and

the reward he had received, soon spread through the village. Guna was furious. He vowed to teach the traitor a lesson. He rushed to Raigali and went straight to Ghana Shenai's house and found the chief gaonkar ill in bed. The spirit had been wrung out of the old man and he was just a skeleton.

'Why have you come here, Guna, what can I do for you now? The villagers blame me and look at me with contempt…' Ghana Shenai said wearily.

Tears sprang into Guna's eyes when he saw the emaciated Ghana's grey and unkempt hair, but his voice was firm. 'I didn't get upset when they forced you to give them the land … but now Sukhdo has become a Christian and in return accepted the community land. But I won't let him set foot in those fields,' Guna said.

'Don't get agitated, Guna. It's an ill wind blowing. Sukhdo should not have accepted the land. It should have been left fallow. We could have shown that the village was united against them.'

Guna walked away, still fuming. Not a single member of the Brahmin community could be seen anywhere around. The labourers in the orchards went about their work with bowed heads. Guna saw some movement by a window of one of the houses. 'You Brahmins demanded respect and honour at the village meetings,' he yelled out, 'but now that the village is faced with a calamity, why are you hiding?'

When Guna raised the topic with the Nayaks of Shirvaddo, they pleaded helplessness. 'The King's officials got the mhal gaonkar to sign the agreement regarding transfer of land. They have given a part of it to Sukhdo. What can we do? If we object, it will lead to unnecessary bloodshed. We can't match their strength.'

The next afternoon Guna, Raya and Shabi approached Sukhdo's house. He was in the yard twisting coir fibres into a rope.

'Sukhdya! You thief! You traitor! Took part of the council land and became a Christian, did you? We won't let you step into those fields. We'll break your legs. Strew your corpse in those fields!'

The strength seemed to ebb from Sukhdo's body as he rose to his feet and tottered out. He was aware of Guna's strength and knew that he had to make peace at once. 'Guna, you are like a brother to me. But this house is in a corner of the settlement, you don't know how they would come and threaten us at night. They would press swords into our bellies, threaten to set fire to the house or hang us from the trees if we didn't convert,' he whimpered.

'That's a lie! Why didn't you tell anyone? Why didn't you ask for a gaonki?'

'Didn't you see what happened at the last gaonki? They hit the mhal gaonkar, they beat you with their sticks. And then they said the new Christians would make decisions at the meeting.'

'Maybe they'll make you mhal gaonkar now!' Guna burst out angrily. 'Your house will be thatched first, you'll get the first cup of toddy. But Sukhdo Nayak, if you step into that field, I'll dig a grave right there and bury you and your three sons in it!'

Sukhdo's older son stood silently by his father's side, but the second son, Ramkushta, grabbed a stout stick and charged forward. 'Who are you abusing, you bastard? We're not afraid. Tomorrow we will plough that field. Let's see what you do.'

Calmly Guna walked up to him, wrenched the stick from him with one hand and slapped Ramkustha with the other. 'You want to plough that field, do you?' he asked threateningly. Sukhdo rushed to help his son, but Guna pushed him aside. The old man fell down and hurt his head. By this time, Raya and Shabi also jumped into the fray. The women of the household rushed out screaming.

'I tell you again, those fields belong to the whole community. If you step into them there will be more bloodshed.' Guna warned them and walked away.

'The village is aflame, Guna. You will be charred in that fire and reduced to ashes. You hit my brother. I curse you, you will not remain a Hindu, nor will you be a Christian. Your spirit will hang between two worlds,' Molu called out.

The neighbour, Jana Nayak, watched all this with great pleasure. But he did not come out of his house.

Sukhdo and his family spent the next day in fear and apprehension. It felt as if a clump of prickly thorns were pressing into their bodies.

Finally Sukhdo said to his sons, 'They gave us the fields. Let us fix the boundary stones and stake our claim while they protect us. Then we can start ploughing the fields.'

'The villagers will be all set to fight. Guna will instigate them,' Molu muttered.

'Let them try. I'll break their heads, every one of them. Won't let anyone go,' Ramkushta was defiant.

Hearing this, Gopika rushed out. 'What, are you talking of breaking people's heads! They've taken our galsaris and wiped the kumkum off our foreheads making us look like widows. Now someone will break your heads and we'll actually become widows!' She clutched at the strand of beads in her fist.

'Nothing of the sort will happen, child. Don't get involved in men's affairs. We will go to the fields with the soldiers,' Sukhdo tried to pacify his daughter-in-law. Then he said with resolution, 'Such fertile fields, will keep our bellies filled for six months at least. We mustn't give them up, no matter who objects. That Guna must be taught a lesson. We have become one of their faith, now. They will protect us.'

'Maavva of mine, ask them how he managed to beat us when they had promised protection. Is this what we get for becoming Christians?' Parvati asked her father-in-law.

Early the next morning Sukhdo went to the soldiers' camp. The Betaal shrine had been converted into a dwelling place with a proper wooden door.

'I want to meet the person in charge. I am one of your faith, you promised us protection,' he said to the soldier on guard.

Padre Paulo Colaso emerged from the camp. 'Good Christian, did you pray to Jesus this morning?' When Sukhdo remained silent, he made Sukhdo kneel before the cross and repeat the morning prayer.

'O God, my Father, I bow before you.
O God, my Father, I love you.
O God, my Father I thank you for all that I have received.
My Lord, fill my heart with Love for you and for all mankind.'

Shef Camil Ribeir, clad in a wet loincloth, emerged from the temple pond. 'They say that water in that pond has become impure because of us. The temple priest doesn't use it for his rituals. The deity will not take a dip in it. How can air and water be sullied, tell me,' he said, quite amused. He saw Sukhdo standing there with folded hands and went inside. A few minutes later Shef Ribeir came out dressed in his uniform. Sukhdo bowed low before him and said, 'We became Christians because we needed food in our bellies, we believed that you would protect us.'

'Our words are the King of Portugal's words, we will never go back on them. We are bound to protect the interests of all good Christians. But what happened to you? Why are you here so early in the morning?'

'We are being spurned by the villagers because we have become Christians. They will kill us if we step into those fields, they say. Yesterday Guna Nayak brought some villagers and beat us up so badly that my son lies injured in bed and see, they've broken my head,' Sukhdo complained.

'Who is Guna Nayak?'

'A very, wicked man, always ready to pick a fight. He fought with your high officers at the last gaonki. He incites people against you, says you must be beaten and driven out of here. Don't become Christians, he tells them.'

The shef was furious. 'Must teach him a lesson, I'll break that fellow's bones! He dares to lay his hands on a Christian?' He turned to Sukhdo again, 'Go home now, don't worry. You are a good Christian and no Christian needs to fear anyone in this kingdom.'

The shef summoned constable Remet Noronha and said, 'Go to Shirvaddo and arrest that wicked fellow Guna Nayak. Tie him up. Drag him here like an ox, beating him along the way so that the villagers hear his screams and know what happens to those who plot against us.'

Constable Remet Noronha and six soldiers set off for Guna's house. 'Guna Nayak, come out. No use hiding inside like this,' Noronha called out.

Guna's father, mother and younger brother emerged from the house. 'Where's Guna?' the constable asked.

'He's gone to the forest. To split palm trunks.'

'Lies! He must be hiding in the house!'

Everyone was terrified. 'No … no … he's not in there…' Guna's father stammered as the constable swung his whip. The old man recoiled from the lash.

'Where's Guna?' the constable turned to the young boy.

'Not here. He left at daybreak.'

The noise of the whip slicing through the air carried to everyone's ears. The young boy screamed.

'Beats up a follower of Jesus, a good Christian, and then goes into hiding!' Noronha directed two of his men to enter the house and look for Guna, but as they turned to do so the two women, the mother and her daughter-in-law blocked the door. 'Deva! These Christians will pollute our house. We will be ruined, we'll become outcastes!' they wailed.

Cabo Remet told his men to draw back. He turned to their neighbour Ravlu Nayak, 'Are you Hindu?' Ravlu nodded. 'Chaddo caste?' When Ravlu nodded again, the constable sent him to check if Guna was hiding inside. 'They're my enemies. How can I enter their house?'

'Just go in. They won't mind an enemy setting foot in their house, but they don't want a Christian in there. A slimy, poisonous snake will not make their house impure but a low caste Mhar will. They'll sprinkle dung water seventeen times to purify the place. Ignorant, ungrateful people! Go, look in every corner, and if you dare to lie I'll beat you to death!'

Making a great show of courage, Ravlu edged past the angry family and went inside. He came out a short while later saying, 'I looked everywhere, he's not there.'

'We want Guna. We won't spare him. We'll show him what happens if anyone dares to beat up a Christian,' the constable said to the family as the soldiers turned away.

Guna had gone to the forest to cut some bamboo to erect a canopy in the courtyard and was expected home soon. His wife Devki sent her young brother-in-law Mhadu to stop him from coming home. 'Tell him to go to the shack in the field at Sadgali, we'll take payz there,' she said.

Mhadu was a simple youth, fifteen or sixteen years old. His body was bare except for the loincloth at his waist. Two fresh welts, bloody and bluish-black in colour, where the constable's whip had landed, stood out on his back. He raced along the track till he reached the foot of the wooded slope. He waited there for a while and after some time saw Guna and Shabi emerge carrying loads of bamboo on their heads.

Mhadu told Guna all that had happened and Guna was beside himself with rage. Then his eyes fell on the bloody welts and he shouted, 'Mhadu, did they strike you with the whip? They must have whipped Bappa as well…' Guna threw down the load from his head and brandishing his sickle, rushed forth yelling, 'I'll teach them a lesson! I'll chop them down like the bamboos in the forest!'

Mhadu quickly grabbed him from behind and held him back. Shabi reasoned with him too. 'What use is that sickle before their might? Die, if you must, but teach them a lesson first,' he said.

The tiny shack where Guna was hiding stood on a low hillock just outside the village in the shade of a huge mango tree that seemed to hide the sky. Guna's father, brother and wife took turns at bringing him his meals. The soldiers had made two trips to his house in four days to look for him. The family was quite perplexed. Why were the soldiers making such a fuss about Guna beating up Sukhdo's son?

The soldiers were out to prove a point. They wanted to tell the villagers that a Christian convert was a privileged person, that he received protection from the King. If anyone dared to meddle with a convert, he would be punished, and forced to become a Christian himself.

Guna was bored, sitting in the shack all day. One day he told his wife, 'Pack some stuff and be ready, we might have to leave this village soon. We'll knock off a couple of soldiers, pick up our stuff and escape. We'll have to leave the village anyway.'

'Which barren plateau will you take us to, once we abandon this village?' his wife asked fearfully.

'Why should it be barren? A farmer can eke out a living anywhere as long as he has a plough. We can settle in any open space and till the soil. Or we can clear the undergrowth in the forest and grow some hardy crop … anything is better than living amidst these selfish cowardly villagers who are too scared to retaliate.'

The light had begun to wane and the sun was slipping behind the hillock when Devki decided to return home. 'It'll be dark soon. I'll come with you up to the tamarind grove,' her husband said.

'No further than that. They keep roaming about the village these days. Yesterday Sukhdo and his son built ridges in their new field. Two soldiers stood on guard with naked swords. The villagers watched everything from a distance, but no one stepped forward.'

As Guna turned back from the tamarind grove, he saw the last rays of the setting sun, like sharp arrows, fall on the large cross atop the hill. The newly white-washed structure stood out clearly even in the failing light. 'Tell Raya and Shabi to come and see me,' he called.

Devki's heart was heavy in her chest as she crossed the stream. By the time she reached home, it was time to light the lamps. But barely had she stepped in when her mother-in-law asked, 'Why are you so late?'

'We were talking.'

'What did he say? How long will he have to stay there? Haven't been able to sleep or rest these past four days. Deva, what will happen to us?' she wailed.

'He didn't say anything. Why are you crying? If it comes to that we will leave everything and go away.'

'He must have said that to you. Deva, what sort of fate is this! Leaveour land, abandon our temples and our gods. Forsake everything that's been ours for eighteen generations … where will we go then?'

Devki's father-in-law came up to them. 'I'd gone to Raigali to see if the Brahmins had any advice. But they're terrified. Subrai Shenai said that those people would forgive Guna if he became a Christian,' he said in a low voice.

'He'll die first,' Devki snapped at her father-in-law. 'He won't become a Christian. He has the courage to make barren land turn into fertile fields.'

'He has courage, his blood boils, we all know that. But what of us, old people? How can we climb those hilly tracts?'

'If you can't, he'll seat you in baskets and carry you on his shoulders.'

'Daughter-in-law, if you say such things he'll get more adamant. We won't leave this village, we'll die here. Take the younger boy with you. Once you settle down somewhere come and see if we're still alive.'

When Guna emerged from the shack the next day, his eyes were drawn to the cross which gleamed like silver in the morning sunlight. Though it stood on a hill about two miles away, it seemed as if it was only an arm's length away. There it stands striking a pickaxe deep into our hearts, he thought.

A little shrine dedicated to god Khetrapal stood just beyond Shirvaddo. Its roof was thatched with wild grass, not hay or palm fronds. So, when the month of Poush began, all the villagers went up into the hills to gather wild grass. Re-thatching the roof of the shrine was a community event and each man wanted to be involved in the auspicious work. Once it was done, the jagar was held over three consecutive nights.

Guna used to play the ghumot drum at the temple festival every year. So when the strains of music carried to his ears he got up and rushed towards the village as though possessed by a demon. What sort of vile celebrations are these? When these foreigners set fire to the shrine's roof in the days to come, not one man will rise to protect it. If only the tempo of the music would rise to a crescendo filling the skies, if only the villagers would come together with cries of '*Har Har Mahadev!*' and pounce upon these trespassers ... such a death would be preferable to this slow passive one, he thought.

Guna stood in the shadows trying to locate Raya and Shabi in the crowd. It was quite cold and the men were wrapped in blankets. Guna wound his kambal tightly about his face and head and moved closer to establish contact with his friends. Who knows if anyone noticed them slipping away, only one head turned as they edged into the darkness.

The three friends walked up the Gholi hillock, lit faintly by starlight carrying a large crowbar that they had stolen from mason Dhaku's porch. Dhaku had laid the bricks and built the cross on the hill. The sound of music and singing wafted up to their ears. Soon the cross loomed before them, gleaming dully. They stared at it like devils, with bloodshot eyes. Hatred and violence, the most base of human emotions, bubbled out of their hearts. The desire for revenge blew away all traces of decency and humanity from their souls.

Guna struck the first blow with the crowbar as though he were striking at the enemy's heart, but the cross didn't get dislodged. It merely shook a bit. In any case they didn't have the strength to destroy the cross, they were mere individuals spurred by an impotent fury, all they could do was to chip away bits of stone. The ones who erected the cross and the ones who sought to destroy it were guided by high moral principles. Each man believed that what he was doing was for his religion, for his God. Perhaps both sides were right. Or maybe, both were wrong. This mighty confusion had been created by that demon that goes by the name of religion. It draws power from God, and breeds injustice and cruelty as a result of that power. God, Himself, was the author of this confusion, perhaps.

They chipped away chunks of the laterite that had been used to erect the cross. 'This is where they plan to kill those who refuse to accept their faith,' Shabi said with profound relief.

'What do they need a cross for? If they want, they can hang two hundred people from the branches of this tree. All we can do is express our rage by breaking this cross like cowards! Anyway, let's get away now,' Guna declared.

The first visible emblem of Christianity in the village was thus destroyed. They flung the crowbar into a thicket and came down the hill. 'Don't tell anyone about this. We'll have to leave this village sooner or later. Talk to the elders in the settlement, tell them not to cling to their possessions, to be ready to leave…' Saying so, Guna disappeared into the darkness.

When Shef Camil Ribeir turned to pray to the cross on the horizon early the next morning he was distraught. There was no pall of smoke, the hill was bathed in bright sunlight, but where was the cross? His eyes darted about in trepidation and a deep sadness filled his soul. Then he began to tremble with rage. 'Go! Find that cross. Set fire to the village. The culprits must die! Drag the corpses here and lay them at the padre's feet!' he yelled.

The soldiers rushed towards the hillock, lashing out at people with their whips. The padre held the shef responsible for this incident. 'You are responsible for our safety in this village and for the well-being of the Christian religion. They've broken the cross today, tomorrow they might decide to kill us. We'll tell the King that you failed to protect our religion. They break the cross, they beat up new converts. Nothing of this sort has happened in any other village. Anyone who dares to go against our faith has been severely punished,' the priest declared.

The shef leapt on to his horse and galloped towards the hill. Tears flowed out of his eyes as he knelt before the broken cross and begged forgiveness. He moved down the hill towards Suba Telu's little shack.

'Are you the village watchman?' the shef asked.

'Yes, deva.'

'Did you go on your round last night?'

'Yes, I did.'

'Do you know who broke the cross on the hill?'

'No, deva, I know nothing.'

The shef pulled out his whip. Old man Suba was so terrified that words failed him at first. 'The jagar celebrations were on all night. Loud music. I was alone. Someone called out … no, no. They just passed this way. Wrapped in blankets in the darkness.'

'Who were they?'

'Don't know their names. I don't know them, deva.'

The shef cracked his whip and the old man fell to the ground, his bruised back brushing the earth. Blinded with rage and a desire for revenge, the shef ordered his men to set fire to the shack. Five or six soldiers went in and grabbed the sticks burning in the hearth. The daughter-in-law, whose tattered clothes barely covered her upper body, rushed out screaming in terror. Suba dragged himself along the ground and clung to the shef's feet, but no one paid attention. The thatched roof caught fire at once and in a few minutes, the whole shack was a mass of flames. The six khandis of paddy that Suba received as payment for his duties as village watchman, which would have lasted them the year, were reduced to ashes.

The soldiers questioned whoever they met over the next two days and if the answers were not to their liking, they beat them up. They arrested Dhaku the mason, who didn't dare tell them about the crowbar that was missing from his porch. 'If I build something, whether it's a platform for the sacred tulsi plant or a cross, it's like my child. How can I destroy it myself? This is the work of some strong, young man,' was all he chose to say. He was the only one who escaped their whips.

Padre Simao Peres kept away from controversy and continued with his work. His mission was to propagate his religion, not to work for social change. But any form of injustice filled him with sorrow and remorse. He believed that priesthood would give him a golden chance to serve the poor and the downtrodden and lead them to Jesus, but his experience in Goa had shattered this illusion. He was deeply upset, but he didn't let himself lose hope.

Dugga Mhar's son, Ghungo, came to meet the padre early one morning. Ghungo was a tall, well-built young man with large eyes that glittered brightly against his dark skin. He wore a tiny loincloth and his bare body was covered with bloody welts. The priest rose up in alarm and passed a gentle hand over the welts, 'Who did this to you, brother?' he asked.

The youth burst into tears. 'There was this cow's carcass in someone's shed in Shirvaddo. By the time they called us the stomach had bloated and it was stinking. The cow's leg would have broken off if I touched it,' he sobbed.

'So?'

'They told me to drag the carcass away. "It's your job. Go fetch your father," they said. I refused. "Dig a trench in the ground and bury it here," I told them.'

'Then?'

'They pushed a spade into my hands and told me to dig the trench. I refused. How can a low caste Mhar use these implements to strike the earth? I told them to dig the trench, and I would push the carcass in. They got very angry and three or four men grabbed sticks and beat me up.'

'You are a young man, brother. You're also very strong. Why didn't you defend yourself?'

'Oh no, Padre! They'd have set fire to our shack with us inside!'

'Why have you come here?'

'Padre bappa, I've heard that all men are equal in your faith. Everyone prays together and eats together.'

'That's right.'

'I want to join your faith. Make me a Christian.'

'I will. Are your parents alive?'

'Yes.'

'Are you married?'

'Yes.'

'Bring the other members of your family. Let me talk to them first.'

When the youth went away the priest turned to Tomas, 'Do you think he'll return?' he asked.

'Can't tell, Padre bappa, they're cowards. The poison has sunk into their bodies.'

'I want him to return with his whole family. I'm so angry with the Hindu religion, I want to convert them all.'

'I'm glad, Padre bappa. Ever since I heard the bad news I've wanted you to convert them by force.'

'What bad news, Tomas?'

Tears rushed into the man's eyes. 'My wife has taken our children and moved out of Goa with her parents. For two years, she kept saying she'd become a Christian. She lied to me. Now I'll serve you for the rest of my life. I'll even die for you, Padre bappa.'

Ghungo, his wife, his parents and two young sisters came to the priest's shack on the third day.

'Dugga, do you recognize me?' the priest asked, going up to him.

'Yes, vhadda mansha. You touched me once.'

'Did you become impure? Did you go home and bathe, sprinkling dung water over yourself?'

'How can we become impure? It's other people who become impure by our touch.'

'Would you like other people to touch you?'

'No, ga. If someone touches me accidently, I can't sleep all night.'

'Then why are you here?'

'He forced us to come. Said he'd kill himself if we didn't.'

'So you're not happy about becoming a Christian?'

'What does it matter, we'll burn if we're thrown into the fire, or boil if we're thrown into hot oil. Either way we will die.'

'So, what's the problem?'

'We have to fill our bellies. We get a portion of the harvest from the council's fields. They toss food into our baskets on festivals and give us three measures of paddy for dragging away dead cattle.'

'We have to beg at their doors and get beaten up sometimes,' Ghungo burst out angrily.

'That's our fate. No matter where you go, you'll still be a Mhar, you'll still have to handle dead cattle. You want to be treated like a Brahmin by becoming a Christian? Forget it.

All that will happen is that we'll lose our rights, we'll not get the income that our forefathers received.'

'Now look here, Dugga,' the priest tried to explain, 'no one will tamper with your caste or your work. If they don't give you a share of the harvest, they'll have to pay you for each task that you perform.'

'Do what you will, Padre bappa, I'll keep quiet. He's the one who's struck by this madness. Tomorrow, when the villagers beat us for converting, we'll just have to suffer their blows.'

'Don't be afraid, Dugga. The shef and his soldiers will protect you and your family. No one can raise a finger against a Christian in Goa. You are now protected by the King,' Simao Peres said, silently begging forgiveness from Jesus. 'Tomorrow is Sunday. Come here at daybreak. You'll be baptized at the Kalapur church.'

Just twelve days after this family was baptized the padre found himself in another difficult situation. The Solankhes were the only families that practised sati in the village and the he had witnessed first-hand how cruel and inhuman these people could be. Viceroy Constantin Braganza had tried to ban sati on humanitarian grounds, but until the King of Portugal issued such a decree the practice would continue in different parts of Goa.

It was well past midnight when someone called out softly in front of the padre's shack. A man stood there, accompanied by a young girl who seemed very scared and weighed down by some immense sorrow. The girl's manner of draping her sari showed that she was a married woman, but her face radiated a childlike innocence.

'Padre bappa, it's Marto Nayak of Shirvaddo,' Tomas said as he led the two into the shack.

'This is my daughter, Gunai, she's just turned thirteen. Two years ago she was married to Bhanvar Solankhe's son and two months back, after performing all the rituals, I took her to her husband's house. Her husband had cut his foot on a spade some time back, but the wound didn't heal. Yesterday, he had convulsions and fell to the ground foaming at the mouth. His body turned stiff and he died,' the man said, trying to hold back his tears. 'The husband's family insists that my innocent daughter should be burnt to death on her husband's pyre. Padre bappa, this is my only child, I love her very much, I will not let her die!'

The priest laid a gentle hand on the man's shoulder.

'I told my daughter that I would wait in the darkness and that she should slip out and join me late at night. She did, Padre bappa, and here, I've brought her to you. Take care of her, make her a Christian. Just don't let her die. I'd have taken her home, but they'd have killed us, her husband's people would. So would our own people at Shirvaddo. The Solankhes will not cremate a man without throwing his wife into the pyre. We, Nayaks, do not practise sati, but when a daughter is married into the Solankhe clan no one objects to the ritual.'

'Don't worry about your daughter, I'm responsible for her now. I swear on the blood that Jesus shed on the cross, your daughter will be happy. Not a hair on her head will be harmed.'

'If they ask me, I'll say I know nothing. Go look in the river or in some well, I'll say. Take her somewhere far away, Padre bappa, they say you have schools and houses in Goapattana where she'll be safe.'

'Go home, brother Marto, don't worry. I've given you my

word. Remember, everything is in God's hands. We should be ready to face all troubles, that's all.'

The girl clung to her father weeping as he rose to go. The priest drew her away as Marto set off homewards.

There was a lot of commotion in the Solankhe household as well as in Shirvaddo the next day as everyone looked for the girl. Marto's family was also in the dark about her whereabouts. That evening the family was forced to cremate the corpse. Padre Simao Peres was quite relieved. The next morning Padre Simao, Tomas and Gunai set off for Goapattana at daybreak. If they heard someone's footsteps on the way, they'd hide Gunai behind a bush and Tomas would step forward to check, calling out to them when the path was clear.

The Franciscan priests ran a convent in Goapattana where a few local women were allowed to stay. Since the convent was established for Christian women, Gunai was baptized and given the name Anarit Fernand before she could be admitted there.

Padre Simao Peres heard about the commotion Shef Camil Ribeir and his men had created after finding the broken cross. He tried to keep away from the controversy, yet three days after the incident a group of villagers came to meet him.

'The soldiers have started their wicked sinful ways. Ours was a peaceful and contented village. Now they are making our lives impossible. They won't leave us alone. Our gaonki cannot take place, our community lands have been taken away. They beat us and torture us. We don't know who damaged the cross, we are all suffering for it. You tell them to stop all this. We'll rebuild the cross, if they want,' Mungru Shenai said.

The priest was surprised, but he didn't show any emotion. 'Why didn't you go and tell them all this?' he asked.

'Do we have the guts to go to them? They only speak with a raised whip. Now their frenzy has increased. They say they're working for their religion, but there's no kindness or humanity in them,' Ventu Nayak declared.

'All right. I'll talk to them. But I can't promise anything…'

'They'll listen to you, they're your own people,' the men said dejectedly as they rose to go.

It was almost evening when the priest, dressed in his long flowing cassock with a heavy crucifix around his neck, arrived at the camp. The shef was standing outside, but he ignored Padre Simao Peres for quite some time. Then he said, 'Why are you here? What do you want?' Not waiting for his reply he called out, 'Padre Colaso, he's here to see you. Ask him what he wants. You complain about him all the time, now do what you want.'

Padre Paulo Colaso and Padre Benedit Ferrao emerged from within and stood opposite Padre Simao Peres without a word of greeting, as though ready for a fight. When the two priests first came to this village, they were timid and moved about diffidently. But within eight months, they seemed to have sprouted horns and did as they pleased. They even threatened the shef that they would complain to the viceroy or write to the King if they did not get their way. These were strange times indeed. The entire administrative machinery was being used for the propagation of religion and the King of Portugal, Joav III, and the Viceroy of Goa, Constantin Braganza, threw their entire might behind the clergy in their efforts to convert people to their religion.

Padre Simao Peres and these two priests had been involved

in a bitter quarrel some time ago. According to Portuguese law, a child was declared an orphan when both its parents were dead, and such a child could be baptized and brought into the Christian fold. Some priests in Goa, however, forcibly baptized children who had lost their fathers, but whose mothers were alive.

Daba Devli, one of the new converts, rewarded with a job and a strip of land, roamed about the village gathering information and reporting to the soldiers. When confronted by the other villagers he would say, 'We are of the Devli caste, we are illegitimate, we have no fathers in the day and look on no woman as a mother in the night. We don't worry about right and wrong. If someone offers us food, we go there.' It was Daba Devli who told the soldiers about Ghantu Kumbhar's death.

One day when Ghantu's wife was sitting with her four-year-old son in her lap, Padre Paulo Colaso and three soldiers came to take custody of the child. 'A widow has no rights. She gets no share of the property. How can she take care of a child?' they asked. Somanna Mesta, who was there, rushed to Padre Simao's shack. 'They're snatching that innocent child from his mother's arms, do something...' he pleaded. Padre Simao didn't want to intervene, but the old man was so desperate that he was forced to go along.

Padre Simao's imposing personality, his piercing gaze, the mass of grey hair that framed his face, and the aura of quiet wisdom that pervaded his whole being awed everyone who came in touch with him. When he reached Ghantu's home, the soldiers and Padre Colaso were surprised and angry to see him there. Padre Simao calmly explained the law in detail to them and every time Padre Colaso tried to interrupt, he silenced him up with his arguments. He quoted a similar case in which the upper court had ruled against the priest. Finally, Padre Colaso was forced to withdraw. He walked away quietly with his soldiers, but was seething inside. He was not ignorant of the law. He knew that when a child was baptized, the mother would embrace Christianity too. The child's siblings would follow soon enough, if only to prevent him from becoming the sole master of the family's wealth. However such cases rarely reached the courts for everyone knew that even if the judge decided in his favour, the new convert would never be accepted as a Hindu again. But Padre Simao had intervened and exposed Padre Colaso's motives that day.

And now Padre Simao was here at the camp again.

'They made a mistake, they didn't know what they were doing. They're ignorant villagers, after all. They must have thought that the cross was just a stone structure. Forgive them, in the name of the Lord. Love, compassion and forgiveness are the main tenets of the Bible. If we set these aside, what is the point of spreading our faith?' he asked.

'Do you mean that we do not follow the teachings of the Bible?'

'I didn't say that. Perhaps you misinterpret those teachings.'

Padre Colaso was seething with rage, but he was outwardly calm, trying to confuse Padre Simao with long-winded arguments.

'They destroyed the cross in your area because they knew you'd speak up on their behalf. They wouldn't have dared to do this elsewhere. And now you say that the cross was merely a stone structure!'

'That is right. Where there is no love, no compassion, a cross is but a stone structure. Without love, God or truth or faith mean nothing. You cannot spread Christianity by simply erecting a stone cross. The cross must be engraved in men's hearts. Once you touch their hearts, you can erect innumerable stone crosses without any difficulty. You know that many who have been forcibly converted, do not practise Christianity and seek to go back to their old faith. That is why we have had to fall back upon the Inquisition here in Goa.'

'That's enough, Padre Simao. You have insulted the holy cross. You have spoken against the Inquisition. Go, now.'

'I haven't spoken against anyone. I didn't mean to insult anyone. I came here with a request. Please don't punish the villagers any more for that broken cross.'

'All right. We won't ask any more questions. We won't punish anyone. We won't do anything. Just go, now.'

Padre Simao turned away. He was quite surprised. He'd expected them to pounce on him, but they'd accepted his request quietly enough.

Three men arrived early in the morning and stood by the door of the shack. One had a sword in his hand, the others held batons and a coil of rope. Tomas saw them and turned numb with fear, but he recovered immediately and grabbed his sword.

'I am an officer of the Goa Inquisition. I've been sent to fetch Padre Simao Peres,' the man with the sword declared.

Padre Simao Peres stared at him in consternation. He appeared calm but his voice was tremulous. 'Why? What are the charges?' he asked.

'I don't know. You'll be told when you stand before them in Vhadley Ghar, the Big House.'

Padre Simao knew all about the power of the Inquisition and the punishment it meted out. Padre Colaso had obviously lodged a complaint against him. There was no point in talking to these junior officials and so he remained silent.

The officer grabbed the priest's hands. 'Come on, tie them up,' he ordered. Tomas had broken into a cold sweat on hearing that they were from the Inquisition, but he was furious when they set hands on the priest.

'Let me see who dares to touch Padre bappa! Get back, Padre bappa, run away at once! Run far away. The world needs you! You are like Jesus!' he screamed, brandishing his sword.

One of the men twirled his baton and brought it down strongly on Tomas's arm, but Tomas didn't let go of his sword. He swiped at the man slicing off three of his fingers, forcing him to drop the baton. The official with the sword lunged at Tomas, striking him between his shoulder and his neck. The second blow landed on Tomas's neck and he fell to the ground. As the priest sank down on his knees, the officials bound him tightly and dragged him away.

By the time they reached Goapattana, which was sixteen miles away, the sun had begun to set. One man held the rope that bound the priest's hands and was looped about his waist. The rainy season was over, but the streams were full of water and Padre Simao's legs and robes were covered with mud and slush. The sweat had dried on his body and the long grey beard was wild and unkempt, making him fearful to behold. People recoiled and moved away when they saw him as he and the soldiers trudged down the street.

The Big House was a magnificent edifice, a hundred feet wide and over a hundred and fifty feet high. The walls were thick with huge doors and windows. When they entered through the front door, they found themselves in a large hall whose walls were lined with pictures and lists of names of people who had been burnt to death at the last Trial of Faith on the Day of Judgement. Beyond was a doorway where eighteen steps led to a large platform dominated by a massive cross. There was a huge table where the religious heads of the Inquisition would sit, meting out punishments to those accused of being traitors to the faith.

Everything was quiet and still. The guards and other officials spoke in hushed tones and crept about their duties as though some danger loomed above their heads. Each step was cast in fear, each word was measured as though it could lead to death. This was the case all over the Goan islands. A perception of fear, an unnamed threat weighing people down. No one dared point a finger at the Big House. Death did not come easily within those walls. Solitude and the huge weight of sorrow often killed an inmate long before he was sentenced to death. And even if the prisoner was finally released as being 'innocent of any crime', his mind and body were broken and he remained an invalid till the end of his days.

Padre Simao was overcome with despair when he reached the Big House. Darkness seemed to close in on him and all the trees seemed to shed their leaves. He wanted to shout at the top of his voice, asking the Chief Inquisitor what his crime was, but the desolation and despair all around overpowered his voice. All the features that marked my past, my education, my priesthood, the love I bear will just fall away and these people will bury them turning me into an ordinary criminal, he thought. I will die an ordinary man. My crime is just this, that I interpreted the teachings of the Bible in the right way, I understood what Jesus wanted to say and I tried to win men's hearts through love. As I stand on the threshold of this prison, I declare that you cannot spread this religion by using force, you will only spoil its reputation. The generations to come will not forgive you for this. You are tarnishing the image of a religion that is pure and founded on the principle of love.

A guard unlocked the door of a cell and two rats scrambled out. Several big cockroaches crawled up and down the walls and a rancid smell emanated from it. The cell was so tiny that a man could not lie down with his legs stretched out. They shoved the priest in and pulled the door shut. A heavy, foul-smelling mantle of darkness settled all around.

Tomas's body lay in a pool of blood outside the shack till late afternoon. He was a Christian and would have to be buried soon. Shef Ribeir arrived with some soldiers and noted details about the injuries on the corpse. He then made a list of the items in the shack. Much of the blood had seeped out of the corpse and it had become quite light by the time they carried it away on a plank. Padre Benedit Ferrao walked silently behind the body, not bothering to utter any prayers. They buried Tomas in the clearing beyond the temple which had now become their graveyard.

Overpowered by a momentary urge of greed, Tomas had been caught up in unfortunate circumstances that led to his becoming a Christian. Yet, a loyal, straightforward spirit lurked within him. Tomas, the man who stole the cruzado was the same Tomas who had given up his life for the padre.

Seven days had passed since the cross was demolished. The soldiers found out who the culprits were on the morning of the eighth day.

Suguna was Raya's paternal uncle. The two branches of the family were squabbling over a strip of land and were always at each other's throats. One tends to keep an eye on every move that an enemy makes, so when Shabi and Raya crept away from the festivities at the jagar that evening, Suguna's curiosity was aroused. He didn't recognize the third man who stood in the shadows, but this was the moment he'd been waiting for. They grabbed my tract of land. I'll teach them a lesson now. I'll force them out of the village, he thought.

He couldn't summon up the courage to approach those white-skinned strangers for the first few days, but the fire of hatred burning within forced him on. He went to their camp before daybreak, whispered the names to a native soldier and slipped away.

When Shef Ribeir and the soldiers got to Shirvaddo, they realized that none of the three men were at home. They'd gone out of Goa to attend a temple festival, the families said. The shef was furious. 'You're lying! They're hiding in the village after destroying the cross. Hand them over or we'll chop off your heads. We'll set your houses on fire. Not one of you will remain alive!' he roared.

Shef Ribeir sat down on the porch for a while, and when he calmed down, he summoned the elders from the three households. 'See, this is a heinous crime. If the King of Portugal hears of this, he will send a force to destroy you. But the King stands by the solemn word he has given the people of Goa. If all of you become Christians, this crime will be forgiven. If you want to save your lives, you better convert at once,' he declared.

He made a list of the members in each family. There were twenty-one people in all. 'I give you one day's time to decide. You must let me know by the day after tomorrow,' he said, and then leaping on to his horse, he rode away.

Shabi's father Jiva, Raya's father Ganesh and Guna's father Shiva rushed to the shack in the fields.

'What's the matter, why are you here all together?' Guna exclaimed.

'They came. They know that you damaged the cross. They say they'll kill us all, set fire to our houses,' Ganesh blurted out.

The three young men were silent.

'They took the priest away the other day. Killed his bodyguard, too.'

'That's wrong. They must be punished,' Guna exclaimed.

'Haven't you had enough of doling out punishments?' his father fumed. 'They want us to become Christians. Everything will be forgiven, they say. Otherwise they'll kill us and set fire to our homes. What do you say, shall we become Christians?'

'No! No!' the three men screamed.

'What shall we do then?'

'Bappa, Jiva dada, Ganesh dada, what do you say? Do you want to become Christians?' Guna asked the three old men.

They were silent for a while in deep thought. Finally Ganesh said, 'How can anyone give up his own faith and take up another's? How can one commit such a sin?'

'Exactly! Who knows what their religion is all about! What they eat, what they don't eat … the womenfolk will be inconsolable!'

'Sukhdo joined their faith, but he's a troubled man. His house isn't a home any more – no offerings, no rituals for the ancestors on Amavas or Punav. They don't allow you to observe any old customs it seems,' Jiva said in a worried tone.

'That's it, then. It's final. We'll leave the village.'

'Leave the village?' Ganesh was almost in tears. All their faces were clouded by grief.

'There's no other way, Ganesh dada. The whole village will have to convert, no one can escape that fate. Stay here and become a Christian. Or leave.'

'God knows who drove the stakes into the ground and set up this village. Who knows how many generations have lived here since then! We'll have to forsake our gods and leave…' Jiva began to weep and tears rushed from the other men's eyes too.

'It's no use crying, Jiva dada. We are the culprits. Why should you suffer because of us? We could go and give ourselves up, let them do what they will.'

'No, no! Don't do that!' the three old men exclaimed in alarm. 'We can't live without you. We'll die every day, bit by bit…'

'We'll round up the cattle tomorrow. The three of you must bring bedding and tools for field work. Each family must also carry a khandi of rice and a khandi of paddy seeds. We'll leave tomorrow at dusk.'

'Which way shall we go?'

'I've heard that there's a lot of fallow land in Antruz and Sange. Don't worry, Bappa. If we have the plough and other implements we can grow enough food to fill our bellies. Someone, somewhere, will appear, like god, and come to our aid. We must have faith and set out.'

The three elders returned home. They were in their fifties, but were strong and able-bodied and each man could erect more than ten feet of earthen ridges bordering the fields without pausing for rest. They weren't worried about setting up a new village in an unknown place. What seemed to devastate them was the thought of leaving their homes, of uprooting the deep ties that bound them to the soil and to the extended clan.

When they reached home, the men began to gather coils of rope, baskets, reed mats, farming tools, setting aside as much as they could carry on their heads. They stacked the rest neatly in their houses. The other families in the settlement realized that something was up, but no one asked any questions. Some felt that once these families moved away, their own houses and the rest of the village would be safe. It was a strange kind of selfishness that raged all around. As each bond that tied each man to the soil began to snap, an ocean of sorrow gathered in his heart.

Every one of them clung to this overwhelming hope, in the midst of all the turbulent emotions that raged like the Great Flood, within their breasts. 'We shall not stay away forever. We shall return some day. Take care of what we leave behind,' they told their kinsfolk. These were people who came to blows over a strip of land no larger than a reed mat. And now an entire village was slipping out of their grasp.

The neighbours merely nodded in silence. They had carried corpses from each other's families to the cremation ground, wept bitterly, shared grief and joy. Why didn't they fall into each other's arms as they took leave, loosening the ties that had bound them for generations? Each man was embroiled in the same set of troubles as his neighbour was, so he took care to strengthen his own defences. Like passengers, who desperately toss their belongings into the water to lighten the load in a leaking boat, each man was obsessed with saving himself.

They set off at dusk and reached the shack in the fields. The cattle that belonged to the three households had been gathered together and each one had its halter and rope looped about its neck. Twenty-one persons in all – herding thirteen heads of cattle through the darkness, to some unknown destination!

They had travelled only a short distance when Jiva's father Devu flopped down on a boulder, 'What am I doing here, how much time do I have left? Jiva, my son! Shabi, my dear grandson! I'm going back. Let them do what they will, I'm going back to my village. If I die, some family member will cremate my body, they won't let my corpse lie there and rot.' The old man rushed away at a fast pace and was soon lost amongst the trees.

It was around midnight when they descended the slope of the Palem hillock and set their bundles down. They built a small fire out of leaves and twigs and as they drew on its warmth and one by one, they fell asleep. The cattle were herded close together, for now these would be a measure of their wealth. When Raya woke in the morning, he realized that the pair of oxen that drew his plough, were missing.

'They must have set off for the village early this morning. Can't have gone very far. Let's go and get them,' Guna declared.

They were tired after travelling all night, yet they set off at a great speed. It was on the final slope that led down to the village that they caught up with the oxen. Raya called out to the animals and stopped them in their tracks. He grabbed the ropes trailing from their halters and tied them to a tree.

Guna and Raya sat there for a while gazing on the village which seemed so calm and quiet. Suddenly two soldiers emerged from the direction of the Betaal shrine and moved down the track that led to Nilu Nayak's house. Nilu was a member of the Nayak community who owned a small orchard and hired labour to work in his fields. The soldiers often visited his house to buy rice and vegetables and coconuts.

'Get up, Raya,' Guna said suddenly. 'We're going into the village.'

'Why?'

'We'll hide in that thick grove and wait for those soldiers.'

They drew their sickles out of their sheaths as they descended the slope and Guna told Raya what he planned to do.

'Let's cover our heads with our blankets,' Raya suggested.

'No. They must know that Guna is the culprit, or they'll harass the villagers yet again. Don't you remember what they did when the cross was destroyed?'

They waited there for about half an hour. A cock crowed somewhere near Nilu's house. Two men emerged. One was a white-skinned soldier and the other was a native from these parts. The foreigner dangled a pair of roosters with their legs tied together from one hand and held a couple of eggs in the other. Some vegetables, wrapped in a plantain leaf, were tucked under his arm. The native soldier carried a large basket on his head.

Raya and Guna sprang up as soon as they got to the bush and before anyone could bat an eyelid, they had struck at the soldier's legs with their sickles. The blows were so forceful that they cut through the flesh between the calf and the foot and each soldier hobbled a few steps before collapsing in pain. Guna grabbed the soldier's sword and they rushed off to untie the oxen. Raining blows on the animals, they drove them on at a terrific pace. Sweat poured from their bodies as they caught up with the rest of their group. It had taken them three hours to travel this distance the previous day. They had covered it in just an hour and a half now.

Everyone was aghast to see them in this state. 'I brought this sword with me,' Guna declared, as he recounted what they had done. 'It shall be worshipped in a shrine, once we set up a new settlement. Your old ceremonial sword is rusty with disuse.'

Hari Patkar's married daughter, Jani, came down from Chimbal with her four-year-old son. She came down the hillock and when she got to the temple, she burst into loud sobs.

'What do I do now? My husband's family will not let him into the house. Leave him at the door of some church, they say, or go and commit suicide. How can I push him into some river or well?' she sobbed, dumping the squalling child in her parents' courtyard.

The whole family gathered around her as the customers in her father's shop looked on.

'That Christian woman fed my child something … he's an outcaste now. What will I do with him?' she wailed.

Jani was married to a landlord in Chimbal village who also owned an oil mill. One day Jani set off for the market in Goapattana with a neighbour. She wanted to buy some combs, bangles and other trinkets.

It was a huge market with separate sections for clothes and trinkets and copper vessels. Some shops sold meat products, others sold bread and there were bars where liquor was on sale. People from different regions mingled in the marketplace, there were dark-skinned Siddhis and white Portuguese soldiers as well as local folk. A group of unkempt men, women and children were tied to each other with thick ropes which cut into their flesh and made them bleed.

'People will bid for them. They will strike them with their fists to see if they are strong enough. The women will have to carry large stones on their heads to show their strength, only then will they be bought as slaves,' the neighbour explained.

The two young women were on their way home when it struck Jani that she had forgotten to buy a pair of earrings for her son. 'Stay here with the child. I'll be back very soon,' Jani said to her neighbour, Subi, as she rushed back to the marketplace.

There was a seat outside a large stone house by the road, and Subi and the child sat down on it. Suddenly Subi remembered that her mother-in-law had asked for some red sandalwood paste for her swollen knees. She would be very angry if Subi returned without it, but what could she do, now? She couldn't carry the child all the way back to the market ... Suddenly, the woman of the house emerged smiling broadly. She was very fat and fair and wore a long dress.

'What are you doing here?' she asked in strangely accented Konkani.

'We'd come to the market. Let this boy sit here for a while, I'll be back very soon.' Subi ignored the child's weak protests and sped away.

The child began to cry loudly and the woman led him inside. It was lunchtime and when the child wailed even more loudly, the woman decided to feed him lunch. When the young women returned and called out to the child, he rushed out his face smeared with food. Jani was taken aback, 'What did you feed my son?' she asked.

'It's Sunday, so I'd cooked beef. He enjoyed the meal. Ate a handful of beef chunks,' the woman replied.

'What! He ate beef!'

'Why? Don't you eat meat?'

Jani was terrified. Subi was staring at them with a strange expression. She didn't touch the child, merely stood some distance away. Jani washed the boy's face and they set off home.

'What do we do now, Subi akka? I beg of you, don't say anything to anyone.'

'If you hide this fact, your whole family will be ruined. They'll be contaminated by this sin,' Subi declared.

'They can only know if you tell them.'

'Why should I drag this sin on to my head by not telling them?'

'What he has eaten today will come out tomorrow. Why should anyone be contaminated by it?'

'He has eaten cow flesh. Our house is next to yours. We worship the same tulsi and take part in each other's festivities!'

'He's just an infant. An innocent child.'

'What does it matter, child or adult! When he grows up, he will perform the religious ceremonies in your household,' Subi said and moved away.

When Jani got home, she realized that Subi had broken the news because an uneasy sense of apprehension had descended on the house. It was as though someone had died, but the inmates were too scared to give vent to their grief. Her husband stared at them intently before moving away. Her sister-in-law stood in the doorway with her three young sons, but even the children didn't approach them.

After a while Jani's father-in-law emerged from the house. 'Why did you leave him there? You should have taken him with you.' He said with tears in his eyes.

'He's an innocent child, what does it matter whether he eats food or a piece of filth?'

'No one is interested in your philosophy. We will be cast out of Hindu society and the villagers will break all ties with our family. You have seen nothing yet. Hindu families who have cooked food on the same hearth as Christians have been cast out of the village.'

Jani broke down again. People had begun to gather in courtyards and doorways, straining their ears to hear what was being said. Jani's father-in-law got dressed and set off to consult the joish on what had to be done. The child woke up and began to cry. Jani's sister-in-law set a plate of rice and some curry before them.

'Why do you dump this earthen saucer before us, as though you are feeding a dog?' Jani screeched. The sister-in-law didn't say a word. As the child's wails grew louder Jani mixed the rice and curry and began to feed him. Her hands trembled as she did so, it was as though he had become a stranger all of a sudden. Her sister-in-law asked her to bathe and come into the house for lunch, but Jani continued to sit there silently with the child on her lap.

'My aunt in Karmal has become a Christian. The whole family has converted to that faith. Let's leave the boy with them,' her husband said, after a while.

'No. I won't send him away. I can't live without him,' Jani began to cry.

Her father-in-law returned home after a long while.

'What do we do with these people and their scriptures!' he muttered to himself. 'The ancestors will not be gratified by the food he sets out for them, the gods will not accept his offerings. This house will remain unclean for the next seven generations if he remains here … The joish says he should be let loose in the forest, let him go where he will…'

Jani grabbed the child and held him close, 'O my child, my little one!' she cried.

'He's one of their's now. He must be sent to them,' her father-in-law sobbed.

'You mean he must become a Christian and worship their gods?'

'What else can be done, Daughter-in-law? It's better than letting him hang between two faiths.'

Jani had no answer to that. She lay on a reed mat on the floor with the child by her side.

The next day she declared that she was going to her parents' home.

All the grief pent up within Jani burst forth as she reached her father's village. She spent the next four days out on the porch, along with her young son. Although everyone showed that they were very concerned about the situation, in reality the atmosphere was quite strained.

Padre Paulo Colaso was delighted by the turn of events. Jani and her son were baptized at the Kalapur church and though she was very upset as she removed the galsari and wiped the kumkum off her forehead she bore it for the sake of her son. Her father, Hari Patkar, engaged four workmen to build a little shack close to their home. Jani took a mud pot, a ladle, a couple of earthen dishes and a reed mat and moved into the shack. A new convert to Christianity had set up home in the village. No one from her father's house entered her shack, they merely stood outside and asked her what she needed. They wouldn't eat what she cooked, even the parents were afraid they would be defiled by their daughter's touch.

It was the last Monday in Kartick and the temple bells had been ringing without a pause. It was the only temple that stood intact in the region. The temples in Nevre, Kalapur and Karanjali had been razed while the Palem temple had been locked up. The worshippers, who had flocked here from the surrounding villages, waited patiently to offer prayers and to participate in the ritual bathing of the Lord.

Shef Ribeir was fed up of the incessant peal of bells and the drone of prayers. He set off, with constable Noronha and three soldiers, and was soon standing on the temple steps. When the devotees noticed the soldiers, they were terrified.

'Bhat Rayanna! If there is any temple administrator in there, bring him out at once!' announced the shef, as he strode up to the priest.

Rayanna had grown old but he was still selfish and stubborn and quick to take offence. He was quaking deep inside, but he stood there, proud and haughty, before the soldiers.

'The King of Portugal, the Viceroy and the Archbishop

have declared that Hindus must not perform any rituals or worship idols in Goa. Idols are worshipped and religious ceremonies are performed in this temple. All of this must stop!' the shef declared.

'What work will we do if the temple rituals are stopped?'

'Do whatever you choose.'

'What about the gods? This is our livelihood, how will our families survive? Don't do this to us. This is an ancient temple with a very powerful deity.'

'Your god is powerful! What about the hundreds of temples in Bardez and Tiswadi that have been destroyed? Were those gods powerless or dead? There is nothing exceptional about your god, Bhatto. Look at our God. One cross was broken, so two houses got burnt. And so many people have swollen backs after being flogged.'

'Don't say such things at the threshold of the temple...' the priest protested feebly.

'I brought down the Devi temple at Panel, Bhatto,' the shef boasted. 'At first I thought the goddess would grab my crowbar and throw me on the ground, but nothing happened. The idol was smashed like any other block of stone.'

'You will suffer for this someday.'

'We've found a way out of this, Bhatto, we've become Christians. We just have to confess our sins, and at once they're burnt to ashes. We can go to Heaven.'

'So you are free to sin again.'

'Why don't you convert to Christianity, Bhatto? It'll solve your problem of earning a living.'

'What about the temple? And our god?'

'We'll turn the temple into a church. We won't destroy this idol. The villagers can take it away and dispose of it.'

The priest began slapping himself on both cheeks as a mark of atonement while muttering 'Shiva, Shiva, Shiva…'

The shef went on, raising his voice, 'The temple rituals have to stop. We will seal this building.'

The priest was ready to collapse as dark, threatening clouds seemed to hover above his head. 'The temple belongs to the villagers, I am only a priest here. They will tell you what they decide. Just let the palanquin ceremony in Kartick and the temple festival in Magh pass peacefully,' he begged.

'You have twenty-four hours to decide.' The soldiers moved away.

The priest rushed through his duties in a distracted manner that day.

'They will stop the puja and destroy the temple. Tell the villagers to call a meeting and discuss the matter,' he urged everyone who came before him. He sent his brother, Timanna Bhat, to speak to the village headman.

Timanna, who was much younger than Rayanna, was well versed in the Vedas and the Puranas and adept at chanting mantras. He went up to Ghana Shenai who was confined to his bed and told him all that had happened. His words, as serious and portentous as some ancient chant, filled Ghana Shenai with foreboding.

'Gather all the men in the village, never mind their social standing … go up to those evil wretches and tell them not to lay hands on our gods! Stop them! Let each god be honoured at the annual festival, then they can do what they want. Tell them to wait till the Shigmo festival is over, if the Holiye Naas, the terrible spirit of this festival, is enraged, all their children will die! Tell them this. What happens after this is their responsibility,' Ghana Shenai advised.

Dugga Mhar, who was now called Domingo, carried the news about the meeting to all parts of the village. Some twenty-five or thirty-men gathered at the appointed time. There were eleven Nayaks from Shirvaddo, seven Brahmins from Raigali and a few others from the village. The good news was that Nilu Nayak and Ranu Kenkre, two men who wielded some influence over the outsiders and who were treated respectfully by Shef Ribeir, were part of the group. The shef, who was lounging on his leather armchair, leapt up like a tiger and stared at them steadily. 'What's the matter? Why are you here?' he growled.

Kenkre stepped forward. 'What are you up to? Why do you want to pull the temple down?' he asked.

'Yes. What will you gain by destroying our temple? Who gave you the right, anyway?'

The shef turned his gaze on to Ventu Nayak. 'Coward! You dare ask who gave me the right? The island of Goa and all this territory belongs to the King of Portugal now. He can do what he wants. Who gave us the right to destroy temples in Tiswadi and Bardes? Did anyone stop us? The King wants to convert everyone in this territory. No Hindu can live here. And you, honourable Kenkre, it's been fifty-two years since the Portuguese conquered Goa, but no one has touched you till now. The King has been magnanimous. Senor Alphonso Albuquerque had promised the Hindus that their interests would be protected, so this process of conversion was delayed. But now, you cannot remain a Hindu on this island. Not for another day.'

Everyone was stunned. Finally, Nilu Nayak said, 'We'll see what can be done. We'll leave Goa, or we'll go and jump into the sea. Don't touch the temple, it has been revered by a hundred generations. It doesn't matter if no one is allowed to worship that deity, just let the temple remain.'

Suddenly the senior priest, Paulo Colaso, emerged from the camp. 'You talk of jumping into the sea. Why utter such evil words when Christianity, this vast kingdom of Lord Jesus, lies before you? This faith offers love and compassion and is so much greater than yours.'

'That's not true,' Jhulo Devli burst out.

'Do you worship cows?'

'Yes.'

'Snakes?'

'Yes.'

'Elephant-heads?'

'Yes.'

'You worship rats and dogs. Even stones.'

'You know nothing about our faith,' Bhadra Shenai retorted. 'Our religion does not claim that god is manifested in just one form. We see god in animals. In fire and in water. In everything that exists. This entire universe and everything in it is a manifestation of the divine. Which is why we have thirty-three crore gods.'

'Thirty-three crore!' The priest smiled scornfully. 'There is only one God. In heaven. He sent His son Jesus to earth with His message of love and compassion – that is what Christianity is all about. Our Jesus died on the cross to free men from sorrow. Embrace this faith of Jesus and earn the protection of the King.'

'We have our own gods. Do you know of the mother earth, Santeri? She has protected and nourished us for centuries. We do not look to the heavens, it is the earth that we consider divine.'

The priest was furious. 'You are a primitive, uncivilized race. We have strength. We have guns and swords. We have Jesus and His love. If you do not become Christians peacefully, we shall use force, or drive you out.'

Everyone was silent.

'A temple and a church cannot exist in the same village. Come, join the church. You can continue with your village meetings. Your fields and orchards will be safe,' the shef added.

'Wait for some time. Let the annual festivals in the Ramnath temple and the other shrines get over. This year's rituals will end with the traditional bonfire to appease the Holiye Naas after the Shigmo festival. We'll let you know what we decide by then,' Bhadra Shenai said.

'That's not possible senor Ribeir, don't agree to this,' the priest declared.

'Let us worship our gods till the Shigmo festival. Do what you want after that,' Nilu Nayak pleaded.

'Padre, let us give them three months' time. Our crowbars and pickaxes will be ready by then. I shall bring hundreds of these people to be baptized together at a single Mass after that. Or, they'll face my sword.'

The priest wasn't happy, but he had to agree. 'The temple rituals may continue for three months. But you must not ring the temple bell. You may not perform rituals in public places. There shall be no weddings outside your houses, no playing of musical instruments. No bhat or joish may conduct ceremonies. Nothing should mark this village as one with Hindu residents. If you go against these orders you will be driven out of Goa.'

It was as though a thunder bolt had fallen on the congregation, their backbones seemed to cave in and they turned away. That evening, no one lit lamps before the household deities. Their stomachs churned in fear. If the light seeped out, someone might come to punish them. The soldiers had declared that no Hindu rituals were to be performed in the village.

The festival marking the wedding of the tulsi plant was just three days away. How would they perform the rituals? A century-old tradition would be broken, the holy tulsi in their courtyard would curse them. When the groups of people gathered in courtyards, they felt that they were being watched. They stuck ceremonial twigs into the earth beside the tulsi and strung silk cotton garlands. All this was done in secret. There were no oil lamps in the courtyard, there was no beating of drums. When they returned home, they lit a lamp and ate the sweetened beaten rice as was tradition.

Sukhdo Nayak and Jana Nayak had been at each other's throats for over four years, but of late things had got worse… If one spat, the other would believe he was spitting at him; if the other one laughed or cursed, the first one was convinced that he was being mocked or sworn at.

Sukhdo and his family were a confused lot these days. They felt pangs of guilt and Sukhdo's wife, Mhalkum, took to her bed moaning and groaning all day. Jana had treated Sukhdo with great disdain after he became a Christian. He would stand at the window and abuse Sukhdo, call him an outcaste who had desecrated his family and his village and forsaken his religion.

One day, Jana's wife looked at Ramkustha's wife, Parvati, and exclaimed, 'Wretched creatures! Roaming about like widows even though their husbands are alive!' She said this in a low tone but Parvati was quick to respond. 'Yes. We roam like widows, but our husbands are beside us. Just wait. Your husband will die and you'll become a real widow.'

The men in Sukhdo's house came out and the quarrel intensified. Sukhdo was tired of listening to their taunts. 'Yes, we'll forsake our religion. We'll eat cow flesh. Another word from you and I'll summon the soldiers. They'll beat the skin off your back and leave you to die,' he raged.

'Selfish creature! Traitor to your race! Sold your faith for a strip of land. Sold your daughters-in-law … see how they roam like widows!'

Sukhdo was so furious that he lost control. Grabbing the pot of cooked rice in the kitchen, he rushed into Jana's courtyard. He stuffed some rice into his mouth, spat it back into the pot and then tossed the half-chewed grains on to the tulsi plant in Jana's courtyard. He rushed into Jana's house and scattered some more half-eaten rice on the hearth and on the gods in their shrine. Jana ran after him, but all this was done in just a few minutes. Finally, Sukhdo had smashed the earthen pot at their door.

Jana's wife, Saitri sank to the ground, wailing as though someone were dead. Jana cursed and abused Sukhdo through his tears, but there was no strength in his voice. The purity of their home had been sullied. An eerie silence of a cremation ground descended on both homes.

'It's all over. The enemy has ruined us. He'll tell everyone very proudly that we are outcastes,' Jana's wife wailed. By evening, she had swept the floor and sprinkled the purificatory mixture of cow dung and water all over the house a number of times. She had also poured ten pots of water on the tulsi in the courtyard, but she wasn't satisfied. The sanctity of the home had been ruined forever by the half-eaten rice that the filthy Christian had spat out.

The news that Jana Nayak and his family had become outcastes spread through the village. Janaki, who came every morning to grind rice flour, didn't come that day. The other Nayaks of Shirvaddo often cut through Jana's courtyard on their way to the temple, but it was evident that they had changed their route.

Jana decided to consult Narhar Joish. 'Shiva, Shiva, Shiva! This is a grievous sin! There is no remedy for it. You will have to burn to ashes to become pure again!' the joish exclaimed.

'Do you suggest that we become Christians, then?'

'I don't say that. But your family will remain suspended in sin for six generations. The seventh one will be redeemed.'

'You mean we can't perform religious ceremonies for six generations?'

'You have no choice. King Chandrashish stepped on the half eaten food of chandals so he and his family were sent into exile. He stayed there for six generations and then returned to his kingdom.'

Jana got up silently and returned home. Four days passed. No one came to their house. They did not visit anyone because they were scared of being turned away. It was obvious that they were being shunned by the other villagers. Sukhdo had converted to Christianity of his own free will, so the Hindu villagers treated him as a social outcaste. But Jana and his household had been defiled by Sukhdo's actions. It is unfortunate, but what can we do, the villagers said.

The Nayaks of Shirvaddo belonged to the warrior caste, but there was nothing particularly brave about them. They couldn't mount an attack. They didn't support Guna when he protested against the atrocities, they merely stood at a distance and watched everything. So Jana went to Raigali to seek advice from the Brahmins, but each of them had a different view.

'Wait for a few days, let's see which way the wind blows,' Indra Shenai advised.

'Leave Goa. Settle down somewhere far away as a member of the Nayak community. No one has seen what happened, who will know the difference?' Bhadra Shenai said.

'I'll feel guilty. I'll feel scared to touch the gods,' Jana protested.

'What sort of behaviour is this?' Subrai Shenai exclaimed on hearing of Sukhdo's misdeeds. 'Complain to the soldiers. Tell them he is a Christian, is this what Christians do? He is spoiling their reputation. Tell them to punish him for it.'

Jana returned home fired by the need to take revenge. Eight days passed and it was time for the wedding ceremony of the sacred tulsi plant. Jana's house was dark, but the others had to perform the rituals in darkness, too. We're all in the same predicament, he laughed to himself.

Jana stood before the Ramnath temple the next morning. He had never taken any step in life without seeking the Lord's blessings. If he wanted to buy an ox, or if he planned to journey across the hillock, he always sought divine permission first. Devotees could seek the Lord's blessings on Mondays and Saturdays, and this was a Saturday. He called the priest out of the temple and said, 'I need the Lord's permission. Must ask Him if I may convert to Christianity along with the others in my home.'

'That's madness! How can you do that?' the priest exclaimed.

'Bhatto. You've given me a flower as the Lord's blessings all these years. This is the last time. Don't refuse me, please. I belong to this faith as of now.' Jana dropped three coins into the priest's palm. The priest went into the temple and set the blossoms on the devrath waiting for an indication from the Lord. Jana squatted outside the temple, his heart full of worry. What would the Lord decree? What would he do if the Lord refused permission? That traitor Sukhdo had forced him into this unnatural situation!

The priest emerged after a while. 'The blossom on the right side has fallen. The Lord gives you permission,' he said dropping a flower into Jana's outstretched palm. Jana felt that the priest should have said, 'Jana papya, don't give up this religion and ritual to become a Christian, our religion is very special to us.' But no. This priest didn't have the slightest regret that he was losing one of his flock. And those people – they were bent on getting as many as they could into their fold.

Every year, on Kartick punav, the full moon night, the idol of Lord Ramnath was carried around the village in a palanquin. It was a time of great rejoicing with musicians playing all kinds of instruments, kalavants dancing in front of the palanquin, holding aloft tiers of oil lamps. Chants of '*Har Har Mahadev!*' filled the air. All along the route, people gathered in groups to worship the deity, affectionately called Chinna Ramnath. At break of dawn, the procession would move to the anval grove between Shirvaddo and Raigali, where the Brahmin families would perform a puja.

This year, however, there was no joy in the festival. People's voices seemed to stick in their throats and they seemed to drag their feet. Everyone who came and touched the palanquin reverently prayed, 'Lord! Keep this festival alive. We are helpless!'

When the procession passed the soldiers' camp, the musicians fell silent. No one said a word, but there was the unspoken fear that the soldiers might swoop down with naked swords and halt their progress. People had lit lamps on their doorsteps to honour the Lord in the palanquin, perhaps for the very last time, for who could say what the next year would bring…

Her name was Aprupe, but people called her Apu. Short and fair with a good figure, Apu was a prostitute. Her amber eyes were framed by thick, dark lashes. She had been symbolically married to a peepal tree and wore the black beads in its name, like a married woman. She wore her saree wrapped tightly around her hips and drawn between her legs. The choli came down to her waist and its sleeves reached the wrists. If someone said to her, 'Apu, why do you cover yourself up like this?' she would retort, 'My body is not cheap like that of your women, to expose it to everyone's gaze.' Apu lived with her mother in a house on the slope just beyond the temple. Shivanna's toddy shack was a short distance away. Apu's mother would sit at the door with a mortar and pestle and some areca nuts. Whenever a wealthy man passed by, she would call out to Apu, 'Ago Appu, come outside,' and start pounding the nuts furiously.

Demu Gurav was the only member of the gaonki who did not hail from the Brahmin or the Nayak communities. He owned extensive fields, some of which belonged to the family, others belonged to the temple, but remained in his care. 'Our family traces its roots back to when this temple's foundations were laid. The bhats and other priests came later…' he often said. 'They were brought here to work for the Lord. We were the original inhabitants of this land.'

Demu Gurav had three sons. The eldest was a simple fellow, and the youngest was a skilled artisan. But Dasu the second son had got used to a life of pleasure and was now beyond anyone's control. He'd carry off sacks of paddy from the house and sell them at Kashi's or Patkar's shop. Coconuts, areca nuts, nothing escaped him. He didn't spare even the chillies and pulses. His father would beat him at first, but this had no effect for he was tall and strong and would often charge at the old man. He was addicted to toddy and was besotted by Apu. The mother and daughter were delighted that Demu Gurav's son frequented their home.

One day, Dasu came home drunk. 'Bappa, you think you are the king of this village, but you've thrown your son out on the street. I can barely feed myself!' he slurred.

'You loot the house and go sniffing about the village, and yet you have the face to eat our food?' his father scolded while his mother remained silent.

'Avo! Aiy Avo! You too have joined him? Your heart won't melt if I die, it seems. Tell my father to throw me my share of the property. I will go where I choose, do what I will. Won't come back to your door to trouble you.'

His father spluttered with rage. 'Share of the property, he says! Whose property? Did you earn any of it?'

'It belonged to my ancestors, Bappo! The field by the banyan tree that takes four khandis of paddy seedlings, that's mine, from now on.'

'Why? To squander it on that prostitute or at that toddy shack? Demands a share of property while his father is alive! You won't get anything as long as I'm around!'

'I'll show you! I'll take my share before you die!' Dasu shrieked as the liquor took over.

The next evening, Ganpat Devli told Demu Gurav, 'Your second son was seen at the soldier's camp. No one knows what he was doing there.' Demu Gurav was filled with foreboding. He knew that if Dasu converted to Christianity, he would automatically get a share of the ancestral property even while he was alive.

There was no sign of Dasu for two days. Demu Gurav summoned all his courage and went to Apu's house that evening. 'Is Dasu here?' he asked.

'No. Haven't seen him for two days.'

'Don't let him stay here. He has ruined his life. You want to stay in this village or not?' Demu threatened.

Apu's mother was a woman of experience who had entertained men in her youth. 'We are prostitutes who serve this village. Whoever stops by for a night, is treated as a husband. We cannot refuse anyone. As for Dasu, he's the son of an important village elder,' she said.

Dasu came home drunk on the third evening. He stood by the gate and shouted, 'Bappa, give me my share. I'm a Christian, the King of Portugal's subject. All these constables and soldiers are here to protect me.'

Demu Gurav flew into such a rage that he was barely conscious of his surroundings. 'Don't you dare enter this house, Dasu!' he yelled. 'You are a Christian now. We worship our gods here, we perform rituals in this house!'

'This is my house. I'll go in and take my share.' Dasu was in a stupor. 'Let me see who will stop me, let's see who dares!'

Demu Gurav stepped forward. 'Stop. Don't come in. I won't let you in.'

Dasu's mother rushed up too, but Dasu paid no attention as he climbed the steps and stood on the porch. Demu Gurav lost all control. He grabbed the sickle that was lying on one side and pierced Dasu's chest, slicing down through his abdomen, spilling his guts. Dasu collapsed on the threshold as blood gushed out.

Demu Gurav sank to the ground. He seemed to have lost all power of speech. Dasu Gurav, newly christened Jose Barosh, lay on the floor, in a pool of blood.

Since he was a Christian, none of the villagers who had gathered there stepped forward to touch him to check whether he was still alive. The body lay on the threshold all night. Only the mother's wails broke the stillness. Demu sat with his back against the wall, motionless.

Someone informed the soldiers the next morning and a few of them arrived at Demu's house. Constable Remet Noronha sat on a bale of hay and noted down the details. One of the new converts who carried Dasu away was Sukhdo's son, Molu. Dasu was buried according to Christian rites. This was the third burial at their new cemetery.

Constable Gaspar Pinto and three soldiers took Demu Gurav to the prison at Goapattana. After eight days, Pinto accompanied Padre Colaso to Demu Gurav's house.

'If all of you convert to Christianity, your husband will be pardoned and your household will be spared. You will learn about a great religion full of love and compassion. Only Christianity has the power to pardon sins,' Padre Colaso said to Demu Gurav's wife.

The woman was filled with joy at these words. Demu Gurav's wife did not regret the fact that she would have to give up her religion. She was distressed because she could not mourn the son she had given birth to.

One day, Padre Paulo Colaso returned from Goapattana with the news that the Portuguese King had given the Viceroy of Goa the authority to formulate laws with regard to conversion. 'Viceroy Constantin Braganza is the pillar of strength behind this movement to Christianize Goa. He has passed a new law which ensures that fields which are not tilled by the landlords themselves, can be confiscated by the State. Most Hindu landowners employ workers to till their fields. Henceforth, only Christian land owners may do that. Besides, Brahmin landlords will have to pay at least a hundred xerafins as taxes every year.'

The shef was very pleased. 'These Brahmins own fields and cattle, but they employ others to do all the work. They lead an easy life!' The shef had been annoyed for a long time by the arrogance of the Brahmins who, he believed, were the force behind the village. Their influence must be curbed or they will prove to be impediments in the future. We must attack them right at the start, he thought.

While Ramnath was the gramdev, chief village deity, and the kuldev, family deity, of the Nayak and Gurav communities, it was Ravalnath the Brahmin families worshipped in the shrine at Raigali. They did not participate in the rituals and sacrifices to the lesser gods and spirits. The Shenais owned fields on the slopes below the settlement at Raigali. These were low lying fields that remained waterlogged during the rains, often resulting in the loss of standing crops at that time. So the Shenais preferred the more productive kharif crop that was harvested in autumn, and it was time now to start tilling the fields.

Shef Ribeir then turned his ire on the Shenais and their family deity Ravalnath. That temple must be destroyed along with the Ramnath shrine, he said to himself. The next day he went to Goapattanna and gathered details about the new law. It was designed to ruin the Brahmins and destroy their influence.

Shef Ribeir and his band of soldiers rode to Raigali the next morning and summoned the men of the village to the pathanshala, the place for reading scriptures near Subrai Shenai's house.

'Those of you who do not work in your own fields and orchards will lose those tracts of land. You may not employ labourers in your fields. Besides, wealthy landowners in the village will have to pay a hundred xerafins annually as land tax. This will be payable in three instalments and will be applicable to each of you,' he announced.

The blow was enough to break every back.

'What about those who are crippled and weak and cannot do any work? Should they starve to death?' Subrai Shenai asked.

'You know what they can do, Shenai.'

'You want all of us to become Christians?'

'Yes. The King has declared that only Christians will be allowed to stay on the Goan islands. Christian subjects of a Christian King.'

'Why don't you tie us all up and convert us forcibly, all at once?'

'There are laws in this land. The King has appointed judges. We abide by those laws.'

'First you pass such terrible laws, and then you talk of justice!' Mangru Shenai muttered.

'Laws are laws. We shall execute them with all our power. You may not employ a single worker in your fields. If you do, you shall be bound by ropes and thrown into jail in Goapattana. Your lands will be confiscated.'

The shef rode away.

People from the Phadti community who lived on the river bank, some Kunbis from the hills as well as people from the Gurav and Devli communities who used to work in the Brahmins' fields began to feel threatened. Would they be beaten up if they continued to do so, they wondered.

The Brahmin settlement was also steeped in worry. Their fields were still water-logged, the moss and algae that had formed on them had to be removed, ridges and bunds had to be strengthened. The fields had to be ploughed three times, the seeds set to sprout and then the exhausting process of sowing. Though the Brahmins did have people to work for them, it wasn't as if they did nothing themselves. They pulled out the weeds, watered the trees in their orchards, tended the cattle and cleaned the cowsheds. What they never did was plough the fields. There was a belief that Brahmins should not tear open the earth's belly, they should not touch the plough which was the Kshatriya's implement. Those who chose to work in the fields were taunted and looked down upon.

A cool wind was blowing in from the water-logged fields and Chintaman Shenai, who was sitting by the fire, said to his wife, 'I don't know what to do. The coconuts in the orchard are barely enough for our needs. We make some money by selling the areca nuts, but how will we manage without sowing the autumn crop? We can't depend on the monsoon crop, what if the plants rot in the fields? What shall we do?'

'We can sow the autumn crop. We'll do the work ourselves,' his wife, Durga, said in a flash.

'What do you mean, all the work?'

'We'll do what we can.'

'I'm scared of the plough. They say it is the demon's weapon. How can we pierce the earth with it?'

'It's better than becoming a Christian.'

'How can we be sure that we won't be forced to?'

'If it comes to that, we will leave this village and go away.'

'Do you think you can manage the work in the fields?' Chintaman asked.

'We'll do what we can,' Durga repeated.

Durga was slender, but her limbs were full and fleshy. Her face looked pinched, but her nose was long and sharp. Chintaman, by comparison, was quite sturdily built. The next morning, Chintaman, with a spade in hand, and Durga, carrying a hook and a scythe crossed Ghana Shenai's orchard and descended into their field. Much of the monsoon crop they had sown the previous year had rotted in the field. The hired labourers had merely harvested whatever could be saved, but had left the stalks and roots in the ground. They stuck out in clumps, covered with moss.

Chintaman tucked the cloth about his waist and between his legs and wound the sacred thread round his neck, so it wouldn't get caught in the spade handle while he was digging. Shoving the spade with all his strength into the earth, he scooped up small mounds of clay which he placed along the edge of the field to form a bund.

Durga hacked at the long grass and moss floating on

the water and dragged them to one side. Her feet sank into the soft mud as she moved back and forth piling the slimy tangled mass in a corner of the field. Every now and then Chintaman squatted on the edge of the field and let out his breath in long, loud sighs before he set to work again. Durga's back and arms ached and though she longed to rest, she hid her exhaustion from her husband.

The other Brahmins and their wives stood by the hedge staring at the couple. 'What sort of madness is this! Will all this effort yield anything?' they muttered.

By the evening, Chintaman and Durga had managed to clear two large sections of the field and build ridges around them. When they got home, Durga collapsed on a reed mat, too tired to move. Her nine-year-old daughter lit a fire in the hearth and cooked the evening meal. Her father-in-law, whose failing eyesight confined him to the house, lamented, 'Our women folk didn't step beyond the orchard, but what is this we are seeing today! The daughter-in-law of the house toiling in the fields!'

They set off again the next morning, but no one else joined them. Indra Shenai inspected the broken embankments in his field and stared at the grass and moss floating in the water. 'So much work!' he muttered as he walked away.

As the sun rose higher, Bhadra Shenai and his younger brother Madu walked past their field. 'Let us remove the moss and clean up the place. We'll do what we can' he said.

No one else came there that day. Durga and Chintaman worked hard all day. If Durga found her husband sitting for too long she would urge him on.

Krishna Shenai, his wife Satvati and their son stepped into the field on the third day. They worked very slowly, bending down and straightening up to rest every few minutes. Seeing this Durga, wondered how their fields would ever get ready for the ploughing and sowing. All the others simply watched. What were they waiting for, what was going on in their heads? No one knew. Maybe they had other plans which would be simpler to carry out, which wouldn't tax their bodies like this. Each man struggled to find a way out of this predicament. It was a matter of life and death. They owned land and orchards, yet their families would remain hungry. Anxiety and despair descended on the settlement.

On the third evening, all the Brahmins assembled in the pathanshala and the womenfolk huddled outside the door. The members of this community were quite civil to each other, they didn't let personal frustrations and bitterness affect their behaviour.

'For four generations now, the Brahmin community has not worked in the fields. They have hired labourers to do all the hard work. We cannot cope with it. And now these demons demand a hundred xerafins as land tax,' Mungru Shenai exclaimed.

'Let us do what we can…' Chintaman said in a low voice.

'What do you mean? Your wife is strong, so you can afford to say that!'

Durga, who was standing at the door, was quick to respond. 'What do you mean by "strong"? That's not why we are doing all this. If the monsoon crop fails again, what will we eat next year? Can anyone depend on the monsoon crop?' she exclaimed.

'All right. We'll toss seeds into our fields and live on hope. Or we'll beg for food. But who will pluck the coconuts and areca nuts? Each of us has ten or twenty cows in our sheds, who will tend them?' Bhadra Shenai asked.

The problem seemed to be getting even more complex. Subrai Shenai suddenly said, 'Let's become Christians. We'll go there and let them pour water on our heads. We can't perform any rituals outside our homes anyway. They're going to destroy the temples, too.'

'We won't become Christians. We'll work in our fields, even though people look down upon us. Let them destroy the temples,' Durga fumed.

Mungru Shenai was irritated by Durga's attitude. 'Chintaman, have you given your silver waist chain to your wife and exchanged them for her bangles? Why does she intrude when men are discussing important matters? Women have no place here,' he declared.

Durga didn't say another word.

'All of us have some money. Let's leave Goa and settle down somewhere else. We can buy fields and orchards, or cultivate fallow land. Each family can take a couple of labourers to carry their belongings. We'll drive our oxen along and carry whatever we can,' Mungru Shenai continued.

Krishna Shenai wanted to say something, but Mungru didn't let him utter a word. 'I tell you, they won't let us stay here if we don't convert. If the situation improves later on, we can return to our homes. Let our things remain as they are in the village. Let's just look for shelter outside in these difficult times.'

Krishna Shenai was furious. 'Let our things remain as they are in the village, he says! The moment they see us go they'll take over all our property. We won't get a clod of earth when we return. We're not going anywhere till death looms before us. We won't step out of this village!'

'Shall we spend all our savings, our money and gold coins even as we sit in the village? And after that, if we are forced to leave Goa, shall we beg? Think about this carefully – how shall we give them a hundred xerafins as land tax every year? Can we raise that much even if we sell all the coconuts and areca nuts in our orchards?' Subrai Shenai asked.

Devrai Shenai pointed to his lame foot and cried, 'A cripple like me, what am I to do? I cannot work in the fields, nor can I leave Goa and hope to set up fields and orchards all over again. Where will I get the hundred xerafins to pay the tax?'

No one had an answer. What does it matter whether this cripple belongs to this faith, or that? Let him become a Christian. At least one man will remain in the village, the others thought.

Rudra Shenai had been silent all this while. 'Subrai tato and Mungru anna are right. Let us go and set up a base outside Goa. We can move back and forth after that,' he said.

Krishna's protruding lower lip quivered in anger. 'You are placing your feet in two boats; and if they move apart you lose everything. I will remain here till I die. Whoever wants to go, can go.'

'We won't leave either,' Durga butted in again. 'If we must die, we'll die here.'

The men looked at her angrily, but no one said anything.

'We must also decide what to do with our gods,' Subrai Shenai said. 'The village deity has been given time till the Shigmo festival, after that they'll destroy the temple. Next, they'll turn their evil gaze on to our shrine. We must remove the idol from the shrine.'

Devrai, Krishna and Chintaman immediately protested, 'The deity will remain where He is, we'll look after Him. You can't just walk away with our god,' Devrai screeched.

'Devrai, if you become a Christian tomorrow, what will you do with this god?' Subrai Shenai asked.

'I'll worship both gods, their one and ours. Will I become a Christian just because they make me take a dip in a pool? I'll remain a Hindu in my mind. A Hindu Brahmin or a Christian Brahmin. They can't take my caste away.'

'You're mad, Devrai. If they hear that you are worshipping a Hindu god, they'll burn you to death. Remember how they dragged that padre away and killed his guard?'

Even after much deliberation, the assembly couldn't come to any agreement and therefore each man was left to choose his own path. But Krishna, Devrai and Durga were agitated by their decision to take the deity away. They didn't say anything at the meeting, but the very next day Krishna went about the village expressing his views. 'Whatever happens to our gods should happen right here. In this village. Let them remain here with their devotees. If there are no devotees left, what is the point in having gods? I will stand at the door of the shrine with a stick in my hand. If anyone tries to carry the idol away I shall break his head!'

A dark cloud of gloom settled over the Brahmin neighbourhood, stifling it, holding out the threat of an imminent downpour.

Mungru Shenai's daughter-in-law, Tulsi, hailed from Raibandar village and her family had become Christians three years ago. Her father visited her every month to check on her welfare. 'Everything is burning now, there is no distinction between what is wet and what is dry,' her father, who was on a visit, declared. 'Where will you go, if you leave this village? You will stop somewhere, uproot yourself and move on again, like those wandering performers who set up thirteen camps in twelve months. I know that new law targets Brahmins. I also know that they hold Brahmin converts in high esteem. Many youngsters in Raibandar have been given important government jobs.'

Mungru Shenai was sitting close by. 'It's hard to give up my faith. Just want to get up and go away.'

'Where will you go? Those who have gone away are in a wretched state. When they try to settle down somewhere, the local residents attack them and drive their cattle away. A landlord in your own village, but a wandering minstrel elsewhere…'

Indra Shenai, Mungru's son, was sitting there too. 'We can go away for some time and return when things are more settled. This can't continue for long. Things have to improve,' he said.

'Forget it. Once you leave, they'll confiscate your property and give it to the new converts. If you return, you'll find some Kshatriyas or some other lower caste in your house. He won't let you touch a single coconut on your own palm tree.'

Mungru Shenai let out a deep sigh. 'Can't decide what to do,' he said sorrowfully.

'Get baptized and lie low for some time. Don't worship Hindu gods and don't make a big show of worshipping Christian gods either. Forget religion, just concentrate on your fields.'

Devrai dragged his lame foot and met the village padre on Saturday evening. He sent a message to some labourers from the Phadti community, 'Come and sow the autumn crop in my field. Everything has been settled now.'

Devrai and his wife woke up early the next morning and Devrai's wife sprinkled water on two large baskets of paddy seeds setting them to sprout. Then, the couple and their three children accompanied Padre Bernadet Ferrao to the church at Kalapur to be baptized.

They returned as Christians that evening and quietly entered their home. A Christian household now existed right in the middle of a purely Brahmin locality. The large tulsi, worshipped by the whole community on ceremonial occasions, stood in Devrai's courtyard. The ridge in his courtyard had collapsed during the previous year's rains and he had left it alone. But what was he to do about the large stone structure bearing the tulsi plant?

Devrai's eyes fell on the tulsi as soon as he stepped out into the courtyard. If they see it he said to himself, they will punish me. But the plant belongs to the whole community, so what am I supposed to do, he wondered. Devrai removed the plank covering the baskets of paddy and checked if the seeds had begun to germinate. As he turned away, his eyes fell on the tulsi plant once more.

Devrai went to the haystack in the garden and gathered a large bundle of hay. He spread the hay all over the stone structure in his courtyard hiding the tulsi plant from sight.

'What are you doing? Why are you covering the plant?' Bhadra Shenai asked, aghast.

Devrai stared at him for a long time. 'Uproot it and take it away, then,' he said, finally.

Bhadra Shenai was surprised. How did this lame Devrai

change so quickly, he wondered. No one protested against this action, people just stopped and stared and then walked away. The Brahmin settlement seemed to be drawing its last few breaths.

Two men and three women from the colony by the river came to Devrai's house the next morning. They led the oxen out of the shed, picked up the plough and other farming tools and began to work in his field. The women cleared the moss and debris, while one man yoked the oxen to the plough and tilled the field. The other labourer strengthened the ridges and embankments.

Bhadra Shenai seemed to have lost interest in his field and Krishna Shenai was working very slowly. It was only Durga and her husband who toiled unceasingly. They had cleared the field over a period of seven days and had strengthened the ridges and embankments. On the eighth day, they led the oxen down and set the yoke upon their backs, but neither of them knew how to assemble the various parts of the plough.

Chintaman had never bothered with the tasks in the field since his father had supervised it all. Even though his eyesight was failing, the old man would stand on the embankment directing the labourers in the field. Durga knew nothing about farm work either since her father, Ghana Rao, worked in the debt recovery office at the port in Agashe. So she went up to the workers in Devrai's fields and pleaded with them to show her how to set up the plough.

'If the sharp edge keeps getting stuck in the earth, draw this part up and fix it at a higher notch. If it merely skims the surface, fix it at a lower notch,' one of the workers explained. As Durga thanked them and turned away one of the women remarked sarcastically, 'If these Brahmins hitch up their clothes and step into the fields, what will happen to us, how will we keep our bellies filled?'

Chintaman guided the plough crookedly up and down the field all morning. As the oxen rested in the shade of a tree, he ate his lunch of rice and rossa that Durga had brought him. Durga soaked three khandis of paddy seeds, placed them in baskets lined with hay, and covered them with planks of wood. That night, as Chintaman lay in bed, he began to shiver violently. Durga piled all the quilts she could find in the house on him, but the shivering didn't stop. 'Heat a sickle in the fire, plunge it into water and let him drink that,' her father-in-law said. Durga did as she was told and the shivering stopped in a while. Around midnight Chintaman's body seemed to be on fire, but after a while the fever abated. A short while later, it grew hot again. Durga sat there anxiously. I've soaked three khandis of paddy seeds for sowing, and here he lies, burning in fever! What shall we do, now, Deva! she thought.

Just two days later, Ghana Shenai, the mhal gaonkar, died.

'Good thing he's gone. He really suffered the last few days. He was filled with remorse after they forced him to sign away the community land,' a villager remarked. 'He went away, just in time!' someone else said.

It was only Mungru Shenai and his son, Indra, close relatives of Ghana Shenai, who were inconvenienced by his death. They had planned to get baptized within the next couple of days so that they could get labourers to work in their fields.

'We are going to give up this faith, why should we worry about these funeral rituals?' Indra exclaimed. 'He who is jumping into a well doesn't bother about the cold or the rain.

Besides, they don't have any such rules about mourning. Let us go tomorrow, as planned. The priest will be waiting for us. Otherwise we'll have to postpone it for thirteen days.'

They were baptized just three days after Ghana Shenai's death. Mungru's wife bound everything in the household shrine as well as the containers of kumkum in a large piece of cloth and tossed the bundle on to the loft. Tulsi, who had been quite delighted all this while, began to weep. She had goaded the family to get baptized as she was eager to do what her parents had done. Yet, now that the moment had arrived, she was shattered.

Durga sat by Chintaman's side for seven long days as the fever came and went. The roots and leaves that Tama Mirashi prescribed and the broths and potions that the medicine woman, Shevthu, prepared had had no effect. One night Chintaman broke out in a sweat and his body became so cold that Durga was scared. She quickly gathered hot ash in a rag and rubbed the bundle all over his body.

Durga was beside herself with worry. They'd toiled so hard, but they couldn't sow the three khandis of sprouted seeds sitting in the house as the field had not been ploughed. What would they eat next year? How would they pay the land tax? Who could say that the monsoon crop would not fail again? Sometimes she'd be overcome by the urge to set off on her own, to strengthen the ridges, to plough the field. But soon she'd realize that she couldn't do anything without her husband's support. All her strength and courage stemmed from his presence at her side.

The sprouted seeds were beginning to wither. Meanwhile,

there was much activity in the fields that belonged to Devrai Shenai, now known as Diego Gracias, and Mungru Shenai who was now Mingel Gracias. Workers urged the bullocks on as the fields were ploughed and spades dug into the moist earth.

Rudra Shenai's wife, Sumitra, kept herself busy with fasts and rituals all through the year. She would sing devotional songs to the rhythm of a pair of brass cymbals. There were seventeen idols of gods and goddesses in her household shrine and by the time she finished bathing and worshipping each one of them, the sun would be high overhead. Rudra Shenai was terrified that she would kill herself if he dared suggest that they become Christians.

Subrai Shenai spent most of his time in the Ravalnath temple, these days. He would repair the wooden beams on the roof and set new tiles. He always maintained that his deepest fears and misfortunes were allayed whenever he took the name of the Lord. These people say, 'If your gods were powerful, wouldn't they have struck our hands away when we destroyed them?' They also say that when their god was nailed to the cross, He forgave those who committed the deed. Deva, perhaps you will also forgive these people – perhaps the gods in the various temples they have destroyed, forgave them too. But Lord, I won't let them set hands on you. You might forgive them. I will not, he kept muttering to himself.

When Subrai Shenai got to Rudra's house, it was time for the lamps to be lit before the household gods. They sat in silence for a while, seeking strength from each other's presence.

'Can't think of what to do, Rudra. Now their eyes are on our fields. They will turn to our gods next. We won't escape their clutches if we stay here. Sometimes I think Mungru and Devrai did the right thing...'

'What do you mean?' Sumitra demanded in a shrill voice. 'Don't animals fill their bellies? Should we forsake our religion so that we can hold on to our fields and orchards? That would be a sin. A grave sin!' She remained silent for a while. 'We've decided to leave the village, bhaya.'

'Isn't it better to move away before they create problems for us? If they take away our gods and our faith, what is left? Let's take our savings and get out, we'll keep going till we find shelter somewhere,' Rudra declared.

'And what about the deity? Who'll take care of Him?'

'Come with us, Unna, don't forsake us now. We'll take the Lord with us.'

'And what will you and I do with this deity?'

'He'll stay wherever we do. If we stay in a shack, so will He.'

'When do you plan to leave?'

'Sometime this week.'

'Bhadra plans to stay at his father-in-law's place for a while. Let's ask him to join us. We'll cross the river to Dwarbhat and hire bullock carts after that.'

'The boatmen charge a lot of money to take people across the river at night, Unna.'

'What can we do, Rudra, we'll have to pay. These people demand thirty xerafins as the first instalment of the land tax. The boatmen won't ask for more than twenty xerafins.' He paused, then added, 'I don't know what Chintaman and Durga plan to do.'

'Tell them to come with us. If they stay here, they'll lose their fields as well as their faith,' Sumitra declared.

Subrai set off for Chintaman's house. Chintaman had lost so much weight that he looked like a skeleton, his skin as pale as the cream on top of milk. He needed his wife's support to sit up in bed. Durga, who had always been brave and positive, was a dejected woman now. Her ready smile had been replaced by a sorrowful look.

'How are you, Chintaman? You fell ill at the wrong time.'

'I'm going to die, Dada. Better to die than to become a Christian. God is sending me this death,' Chintaman moaned.

Durga glared at her husband angrily. 'Who's forcing you to become a Christian? You say all sorts of things and then you begin to cry!'

'Look Chintaman, Bhadra, Rudra and I plan to leave the village. Who can pay a hundred xerafins as tax? And even if we do, what guarantee is there that we won't have to convert later? You can come with us too.'

'And what about the fields?' Durga asked.

'Fields, she says! These fields have taken control of her life!' Durga's husband spluttered in rage. 'Do you know what a hundred xerafins means? You can buy four oxen for a hundred xerafins. You won't get so much even if you sell all the grain that you harvest in your field!'

'But we can pay that in three instalments, can't we?'

'She's mad, Unna.'

Durga fell silent for a while. 'Bhaya, this man can't stand erect for a moment. Who knows what problems we'll face once we set out! Can't take two steps on his own and he wants to tramp from village to village! We'll see how it is for a week or two. If you can wait for us, very well.'

'There's danger on all sides, my dear. I'll speak to Rudra and see.'

Shef Camil Ribeir summoned Ranu Kenkre to the soldier's camp and explained the new law in detail. 'You may not employ a single worker in your field. You'll also have to pay a thousand xerafins as land tax every year.'

'A thousand xerafins!' Kenkre was aghast.

Kenkre was a tall, fair man with a thick moustache on his round face. He wore a dhoti and a shirt beneath a long coat and had a turban on his head. There was a smear of sandalwood paste on his brow.

'How much tax do you pay now?'

'Eighty xerafins.'

'The Brahmins of Raigali, who paid seven xerafins all these years, have to pay a hundred under the new law. You can afford a thousand xerafins,' the shef said.

'I employ twenty workers in my fields and orchards. I look after them and their families throughout the year. I can't afford a thousand xerafins,' Kenkre protested.

'Don't worry. You won't have to bother about those workers any more.'

'How will we manage our fields and orchards, then?'

'This law has been formulated for Hindu land owners alone. You know that.'

'I'm a Hindu. I want to remain one.'

'You'll have to follow the law then. The viceroy is sending a strong message to Hindus – Convert to Christianity or leave Goa. I'm saying this for your benefit … become a Christian at once. You'll have no more problems. You can pay land tax at the old rate.'

Padre Paulo Colaso was standing close by. 'We believe that anyone who stays in Goa without becoming a Christian is insulting our faith. Hindu sinners like you continue to stay in Adolshi only because we are governed by cowardly officials like Shef Ribeir. Go home and decide what you want to do. A new set of brave officials will move into this village to take everyone to Jesus. We will not let you stay here if you insult Lord Jesus and the Christian faith.'

Ranu Kenkre was intelligent and well-educated, with a warm, open disposition. To this was added the sophistication that comes with wealth. He was hurt and angered by Padre Colaso's accusation. 'You know nothing about Hindu philosophy. Hinduism and Christianity teach the same principles, there's very little difference between the two. You go down on your knees before statues of Jesus, Mother Mary and other saints. We worship idols of our gods. We believe that the body and the soul are separate entities, that the soul is immortal and imbued with divine grace, just like you do. Good deeds take man to heaven and bad deeds lead to hell – we believe this too. There's just one difference. Our religion does not pardon us when we commit sins so each man has to suffer the fruits of his evil actions. You believe that Jesus is a prophet, who brings the Word of God. We have prophets in our religion too, not one or two, we have ten. Each one came down to earth when the world was full of sin. They came to protect truth and righteousness, to destroy all evil, just like Jesus did. Jesus was an ocean of love and forgiveness and compassion. He could conquer people's hearts with love.

This is why I have faith in Him, I respect Him with all my heart. Padre Simao Peres would talk about Jesus, his words would bring tears to our eyes.'

Padre Colaso was irritated by this reference to Simao Peres. 'Enough of your nonsense! Christianity is the religion of the King of Portugal. We have crossed the seven seas with the blessings of the Holy Pope to convert our subjects and spread the Christian faith.'

Kenkre realized that these people were not interested in tenets or philosophy. They had come here with a mission to increase the number of people who subscribed to Christianity; they were not too concerned about spreading the tenets of their faith. He got up quietly and walked away.

The undercurrent of tension that had existed between Padre Colaso and Shef Ribeir had become an open dispute in recent times. Padre Colaso believed that it was the shef's duty to wield the sword on his behalf and enforce his dictates. A padre couldn't wield the sword as a man of God, but he could issue orders and it was the shef's duty to execute them, he felt. The shef was a devout Christian, but he didn't believe in using ruthless means to force people to be baptized. He knew that it would be necessary to use force at some point of time, but the padre wanted to start with using force.

Ranu Kenkre returned home and lay down listlessly on his bed. His mind was in a turmoil. After a while he summoned his younger brother, 'Will you become a Christian, Puru?' he asked.

Puru stared at his brother's anxious face. 'What's more important, one's fields and orchards? Or one's faith, Tato?'

'One's belly is more important, my brother.'

'Do you really believe that is the truth?'

'What one feels when one is in grave danger, that's the truth, Puru.'

'In that case, I'll become a Christian.'

'And your wife?'

'She'll do whatever you say.'

'Ask her, anyway.'

Ranu and his wife were carried to the Ramnath temple in their palanquin the next day. After performing the puja, they sat down to talk to the bhat and the other devotees. One of the labourers who often came to work in their house was praying with great devotion. 'What did you ask for, a male child for your son or a good groom for your daughter?' Ranu teased.

'I don't want anything for myself, Dhanaya,' he said respectfully. 'Save the temple, Deva, is all I begged for.'

Suddenly Ranu realized that people had been praying in silence. His eyes were drawn to the four large bells that hung from the roof. The bhat had swathed the gongs in yards of cloth, rendering them silent. Ranu could sense the worry and tension that filled the shrine – there was no hope or enthusiasm on anyone's face. His eyes filled with tears as he turned towards the deity one last time. His wife sat by his side, immersed in silence.

Ranu Kenkre arrived at a decision after thinking hard all night. If the trees and palms in the orchards, the embankments in the fields, the stock of paddy in the granary, were to be saved; if the meals that were served every day to the workers and their families were to continue, he would have to take this decision.

There was a settlement of Kunbis on the slope just behind his house. The twenty men and women who lived in those shacks worked on Kenkre's estate, they did the household chores and worked in the fields. They were given their midday meal in Kenkre's house. Many of them carried the food home for their children.

That afternoon, twenty-three leaf patravalis were set out in a row on the floor. The bare bodied men and the women who sat before them had been working in the fields since morning and were hungry.

But before they could start eating, Ranu Kenkre arrived there unexpectedly. 'Wait,' he said to them. 'This might be the last meal you will eat here, so I want to say a short prayer. Listen carefully to what I say after that. Only then, may you eat.'

He recited a short Sanskrit sloka, but the workers didn't understand a word. What was the landlord trying to say?

'We've worked together for many years, and we've eaten together too. But I've become a Christian now. I haven't been baptized yet, but I'm a Christian in thought and deed, so if you eat in my house you will be considered as converts. Those of you who choose to be baptized with me, may eat. Those who do not wish to become Christians, may leave. Remember, I am a Christian now.'

An unnatural silence settled over the gathering as all eyes were fixed on Ranu Kenkre's face. Not one hand moved towards the food on the platter, but no one got up to leave the room either. Old man Jugal bent his head at last. He folded his palms reverentially before the food. Dipping his fingers in the rossa that had been poured over the rice, he raised his hand to his mouth and slurped noisily. Seeing him mix his food, the others reached for their patravalis and soon the whole verandah was filled with the noise of people enjoying their meal.

Tears rushed into Kenkre's eyes as he went into the house.

Bhaskar Shenai and Rudra Shenai had assured Durga that they would wait for her, but bad news began trickling into the village over the next couple of days. The Portuguese had destroyed the temple of Lord Mangesh, just across the river. No one knew whether the idol had been saved or whether it too had been destroyed. A boatman who was taking people across from Old Goa noticed the commotion on the other side, and brought his boat back without touching the bank.

This Mangesh temple was a very ancient one and people believed that the deity had very strong powers, so it had become an important place of pilgrimage. Since Adolshi was a remote village it took a long time for news to filter into the village. As the news was relayed by many tongues, it was often exaggerated or had lost touch with what had actually happened. People said that a captain, who looked like a demon, was leading a band of three hundred soldiers, converting people and destroying temples that were on his route. He'd cross the river and arrive in Adolshi in a couple of days and then he'd destroy the temples and force everyone to become Christians.

Subrai Shenai was terrified. 'Let's leave at once. Gather what you have. If we delay any longer, that demon will attack us!' he said. He went to Durga's house and told her that they were leaving that night. Durga didn't know what to do. She could see her husband breaking down, but she also knew that he couldn't take a single step without a support.

'Do you want to go or shall we stay here and become Christians?' she asked him.

'I can't get up from my bed and you want to take me to some unknown land! I'll collapse on the way.'

'Shall we stay here and become Christians, then?'

'If that is in our fate, we can't avoid it. Durga, let us stay here for some time. Let me get a bit stronger. If you are by my side, what does it matter whether we are Hindus or Christians?'

Bhadra, Rudra and Subrai Shenai packed clothes and bedding, copper and brass utensils, money and jewellery, and bags of rice. They discarded the farm implements and set the cattle loose. The farm hands who had worked for them all these years arrived at sunset to carry their belongings and escort them to the river.

'We'll take the gods to a safe site,' they said to everyone they met.

The new converts Mungru and Devrai and their family members stood a little distance away from the temple. Everyone was in tears. 'Deva, forgive us … we have done wrong. Save the others. I shall come to see you some day, Deva, and throw myself at your feet!' old man Mungru sobbed, crouching on the ground. The deity's gold ornaments and the copper vessels that belonged to the temple were stored in Mungru Shenai's house. He was a Christian now, but he offered to keep these articles safely. Who knew what dangers the travellers would have to face.

Krishna Shenai came out of his house spewing vile abuse. 'Let me see which son of a whore dares to touch the Lord! I'll throw his carcass right here,' he screeched, standing at the temple door.

Bhadra Shenai was the eldest of the three. 'What are you up to, Krishna? When they arrive with their sledgehammers and crowbars, will the temple be safe? Will the deity remain intact? They're coming very soon … I beg you, don't stop us. Let us take the deity away.'

Krishna pranced about as if possessed. 'Traitors! Cheats! Want to make off with the Lord! I won't let you. Whatever happens to the village, will happen to the temple, too. Do you think the deity belongs to just the three of you? If the Lord is so powerful, He will save Himself. If we die, our God will die too. I won't let you take Him away!'

Subrai lost control of himself. He grabbed a stout stick and started beating Krishna on his back and shoulders. 'Wretched creature! Sinner! Do you mean to destroy the gods?' he screamed. 'Come. Let us invoke the Lord,' he said, as if he was in a trance.

The members of the three families gathered outside the sanctum and Bhadra Shenai addressed the deity, 'We are taking you out of Goa, Deva, to free you from the clutches of these impure, depraved creatures. Do not be angry with us, do not curse us, Deva! Visit us in a dream and tell us where we should set you down, or we shall, with our limited intelligence, decide on a suitable spot and build a new shrine. Bless us so that we may prosper in a new land and achieve success in our endeavours. Give our families good health and long life. Look after our brothers, who have fallen victim to these people's ploys and been forced to forsake our faith, let them prosper, too!'

There was a loud chorus of 'Hayee Deva, yes, Deva!' from all those assembled there. Subrai Shenai looked possessed. He rushed into the sanctum and hoisted the murti of Ravalnath and set it on a red silken cloth spread on the floor. He placed the five flaming wicks from the oil lamp at the spot where the idol had stood in the sanctum, and placed the lamp on the silk cloth. He ran out of the temple to another tiny shrine and picked up the idol of Siddhanath, one of the lesser gods in the pantheon. He tossed five sone-chafa flowers on to the silk cloth and knotted the ends to make a loose bundle, 'These flowers will not wither and die before we set you down and worship you again, Lord. They will remain fresh and fragrant, by your infinite grace!'

An unmarried youth would have to carry the holy bundle on his head. The image could only be set down on the ground at the spot where a new shrine would be built and consecrated. When the youth needed to rest or perform his ablutions, he could sling the bundle from the branch of a tree. Rudra's elder son who was sixteen years old, was chosen for this task. He hoisted the bundle on his head and the farm hands picked up the other boxes and bundles as they set off for the river bank.

The Brahmin families who had become Christians stood on one side with tears in their eyes. A flood of sorrow swept through people's hearts, yet no one wept. 'The Lord's gold ornaments and copper vessels remain in my care. Let us know where you build a new shrine. I shall bring everything there,' Mungru Shenai assured them yet again.

And so they set out with their earthly possessions loaded on their heads, this little group that knew not which way to go. Behind them were their homes, nestled in cool shady groves, and lush orchards watered by gushing streams – before them lay an unfamiliar, rocky plateau … a stony path without end. It was an umbilical tie that bound them to this soil, pulling out their roots and moving on was such a difficult task. They had tended these coconut palms with such care, now that they were laden with nuts, why were they forsaking them, why did they take such a suicidal step? Man dwells at once in the concrete physical world around him, as well as in the abstract world of faith, thoughts and beliefs. It is this world of the mind that gains precedence when he is forced to make a choice.

They trudged through low-lying fields and cut across hillocks for an hour and a half before they got to the river. They could see three empty boats, but there was no boatman in sight. Bhadra Shenai called out softly and a couple of boatmen emerged with oars and bamboo poles.

'Crossing the river and going out of Goa has become very dangerous these days. They swoop out of the darkness and loot the passengers on the boat. If anyone resists, they kill him and throw him into the river. Sometimes they take everyone away and force them to become Christians, or accuse them falsely,' one of the boatmen said.

'We've set out with our gods. We cannot go back now. If it comes to that, we'll immerse our gods in the water and jump in after them. Just take us across somehow,' Subrai Shenai said.

'It's at your risk. You'll have to pay forty xerafins to get to Dwarbhati.'

'What do you mean? We used to pay five xerafins to go to Dwarbhati and then return with provisions needed for the whole year!' Bhadra Shenai exclaimed.

'Those days are gone, ga.'

'We're Brahmins from Adolshi, the whole village was under our control. Now we have fallen on bad times. We can only give twenty-five xerafins,' Subrai Shenai declared.

'Thirty xerafins. Only for you.'

No one said another word. They threw their belongings into the boat and clambered in as the boatmen struck at the bank with their long poles and pushed the boat away. The boatmen plied their oars and used the bamboo poles to steer the boat, keeping the sail tightly furled. Enveloped by darkness and crouched among their bundles, they could see no horizon, no river bank, no end to the expanse of water on all sides.

It was almost a month since Subrai Shenai and Rudra Shenai left Goa. Within a week of their departure, Krishna Shenai began to encroach on their holdings. He uprooted the stakes and hedges that marked the limits of Rudra's orchards and added them to his own, setting aside only that patch of land on which Rudra's house stood. He smashed the boundary stones that separated his fields from those that belonged to Subrai and claimed ownership of the entire stretch. There were no written records of ownership, nor had the holdings ever been measured. People guarded the boundary stones that marked their own plots, but there was no one to watch over the land that belonged to those who had left the village.

Durga was very upset by this. 'The land belonged to their forefathers. We must guard their property. What if they run into some misfortune and are forced to return?' she asked Krishna Shenai.

'Don't talk of their returning, Durga, why would anyone come back to this wretched place? Those who have gone away are fortunate, they'll prosper in new lands. Who knows what will become of us! Durga, we must safeguard these fields and orchards that belong to the Brahmins. If some low caste Christian convert appropriates this land, he might enter one of these houses and settle in our midst!'

'But you are a Brahmin, Krishna bhaya, you'll have to become a Christian if you want to retain this land. They're targeting the Brahmins now.'

'Do you think I'm going to forsake all this and leave the village? I'll see which way the wind blows. I tell you, Durga, don't leave the village. Let's get together and go to them one of these days. Pour water on our heads, we'll say. Look after your husband, let him get strong soon.'

Durga didn't reply. A strange picture swam up before her eyes. She was leaving the village along with her family and people were grabbing bits of her orchard and fields. Her house had collapsed in the rain. Some strangers were living there now. She shook herself out of that reverie, but knew they would have to leave soon. How could they continue to stay?

One day, Krishna Shenai and his family got baptized and became Christians. He hired labourers and set them to work in his fields. He could usurp other people's land and livestock without fear of punishment now.

Durga's was the only Hindu family left in Raigali. And it was only her field that remained fallow with no sign of activity. Her husband had recovered, but it was too late to sow the autumn crop. Perhaps they could grow the monsoon crop and try to make both ends meet...

The revenue collector arrived in the settlement one day. He was a new convert and known to be a cruel, hard-hearted man. He would take the oxen from the cattle shed or carry away the brass and copper vessels if the taxes were not paid in time. He turned up at Durga's door and demanded thirty xerafins as the first instalment.

'I don't have thirty xerafins. The monsoon crop was destroyed in the floods. We can't make both ends meet, where will we get thirty xerafins from?'

'You will have to pay that amount. All Brahmin landowners must pay a hundred xerafins every year or go to jail.'

'Give me eight days' time. I'll get the money…'

'Or you'll become Christians, no?'

A veil of silence settled over the household. They were all too scared to say anything. They could pay the thirty xerafins required in this instalment, but that would not solve the problem. The demand would be repeated. Why should they pay a hundred xerafins to these people? What if they were forced to leave the village at a later date?

Durga couldn't make up her mind about becoming a Christian. Her husband and father-in-law shook their hands vehemently when she asked them what should be done. 'If we don't convert, what should we do? What will we eat once our savings run out? We'll have to sell the children as slaves,' she snapped.

'Why do you say that, daughter-in-law?' the old man said in a small voice. 'He who has given us life has made arrangements to fill our bellies. So many families have left Goa. We're not destitute, are we?'

'You are almost blind. How will you trudge through unfamiliar forests and strange lands?'

Durga was in tears. They should have left the village along with the others. Who would guide them now? She was a practical woman who had about three hundred xerafins and some gold jewellery hidden away, but she didn't want to draw on those reserves.

Two soldiers stopped by their courtyard that evening.

'What do you want?' Chintaman asked.

'Nothing. This is the only Brahmin household in this settlement. The shef and Padre Colaso sent us to check if you are hiring labourers to work in your fields and orchards.'

'Did you hear what happened in Keloshe? The captain of

the soldiers in Sashti stabbed the members of three Brahmin families and threw the bodies into the river,' one of the soldiers said.

Chintaman's stomach turned cold. 'Why?' he stammered.

'They must have committed some crime against Christianity.'

'Someone threw a pig's carcass into a Brahmin's well at Panel, the other day. The family couldn't use the water from their own well. Since their house was surrounded by the houses of newly converted Christians, they couldn't use their water either,' the other soldier remarked.

'A pig's carcass there. It might be a dead cow here. These are bad times.'

Chintaman broke into a cold sweat at their words. Durga realized that the vultures had started to hover above their roof.

Padre Paulo Colaso summoned all the new converts of Adolshi village to Mass at the Kalapur church on Sunday. Some three hundred and forty villagers gathered in front of the temple. Dugga Mhar and his brother's family were in the throng. As was Ranu Kenkre, now known as Henrik Kaisure, and his family. Ranu and his wife were carried there in a palanquin. They had been forbidden this privilege as Hindus, but now that they were Christians they could continue the practice. The men drew the white shirts that they had been given at their baptism, over their workday clothes. The women wrapped the white lengths of cloth about their bodies.

The settlement at Raigali was deserted and Durga's family realized how isolated they had become. We cannot go to anyone's house, nor can anyone visit our home. We may not partake of food that has been touched by anyone; our neighbours may not touch our foreheads to check if we have fever, they will not lend a shoulder to the bier when we are gone! So many people living in such proximity, yet how distant we have become!

Durga went to Ranu Kenkre's house that evening. She'd come here on various festive occasions and had helped with the arrangements at Puru's wedding. She'd eaten the ritual meal when Ranu's mother passed away. She had often sold her small stock of coconuts and areca nuts to the traders who came to Ranu Kenkre's house to buy what his orchards produced. But today, her legs were trembling as she sent a servant to tell the bhatkar that Durga was here.

Ranu emerged in a little while. He was dressed as usual, but there was no smear of sandalwood paste on his brow. Durga's eyes shifted to the courtyard where the tulsi plant had been uprooted and a wooden cross stuck into the ground.

'What do you want?' Ranu asked. 'You're a very brave woman. The only Brahmin woman left in Raigali.'

'God knows how long that can continue,' Durga's voice was steeped in worry.

'Why? Do you plan to convert too?'

'No. But I have three young children to think about.'

'Durga, you are a brave, capable woman. Your husband is a simpleton, but he is a good man. Your father-in-law has been decent and upright throughout his life. Don't force these people to convert. I'm not saying this because I regret becoming a Christian. But I feel you should leave Goa and set up a new Raigali somewhere far away.'

'I don't know where to go.'

'Don't go to Antruz, there are bands of robbers looting people in those parts. Much of the fertile land has already been occupied. You will have to clear forests if you choose to settle there. You can take the foot tracks to Kusman, Sange or Shinvesar if you like. I hear that boats are sailing down the rivers from Goa to Canara every night. They take people to those parts, and when they return, they are loaded with rice and paddy. People from Kalapur, Raibandar, Chimbal, Bamboli and Palem are taking this route out of Goa. They say there are large tracts of farm land lying fallow in Canara.'

'We have a few oxen, Tato. Let them work in your fields. Give me what you will … the money will be useful on the way.'

'I'm not going to buy your oxen. Let them be in my shed, the cowherds will tend to them, along with our animals. If you return some day, you can sell them or take them away. If you need money, I'll give you some.'

Ranu went into the house and came back with a small bag. 'There are forty xerafins in this. You should be able to reach Honnavar in Canara with this money.'

Durga spent the next day tying whatever they would take with them in small cloth bundles. Her husband, who had gone to check the boats, returned to say that four boats would sail that night and each person would have to pay ten xerafins for the trip.

Durga's innards seemed to be tearing into shreds and her heart was fit to burst in a flood of tears, but she controlled herself. They left their home at sunset but it was dinner time when they reached the river. Her father-in-law trudged along as fast as he could with a hand on his grandson's shoulder, breathing rapidly with the exertion. They were six people in all – the husband, the wife, the father-in-law and three children. Two sons and a daughter.

The boatman set the boat afloat and Durga felt that she was lost. Above her was the crescent moon, on this fifth day in Magh, a tiny sliver in the dark dome of the sky, spangled with countless stars. Below her was this vast expanse of water, an ocean without end. They had set out on what appeared to be their final journey.

They didn't know where they were going, they had no concrete plans. Durga hadn't informed her parents or her siblings so they wouldn't know where she had gone. Would this plant, uprooted from its native soil, find sustenance and take root again on some distant shore, or would it wither and die? Today, there is darkness without end on all four sides. Who knows, the bright light of morning may reveal a new shore where their tiny footprints may eventually leave mighty impressions on the land.

The people of this region had great faith in Lord Ramnath and would often visit the temple in Adolshi to seek His blessings. During the temple festival in Magh, Brahmins and Kunbis, fishermen and agricultural workers from surrounding towns and villages would make their way to Adolshi. Some thirty or forty makeshift stalls selling an assortment of sweetmeats and spices, ornaments and trinkets, toys and articles of daily use would spring up around the temple. But that year, an eclipse seemed to have cast a shadow on the festival.

There was no formal meeting to discuss the arrangements for the festival, no traders from Bardes and Sashti were coming to display their wares, but still a few villagers got together and decided to conduct the jatra as best as they could. Everyone knew that this would probably be the last time they'd celebrate the festival, that it ought to be done on a grand scale yet there was little enthusiasm.

There were only seven stalls at the jatra that year. The sun shone feebly through dark clouds. Fear, worry and regret at their own cowardice were writ large on the faces of the devotees. The thought that it was the last time they would take part in this festival which had been celebrated annually for hundreds of years was more than they could bear. What a great tragedy it was! Like the great flood which had marked the end of an age!

By the evening, the sky had cleared and the bright light of the full moon fell on the earth. The rag that had muffled the gong of one of the temple bells fell away and a devotee began to ring it with all his might. Someone else removed the cover that muffled another bell and began to ring it too. Padre Colaso, heard the bells and became restive, but the shef calmed him down.

'Forgive them, Padre. This is the last time. The final throes of a dying man,' he said.

A huge crowd gathered in front of the temple when it was time to draw the chariot. It was almost like the earlier years. The chariot, which stood tall as a coconut palm, was decorated with flags of multicoloured cloth. Its wheels were as high as a man and the ropes tied to it, as thick as his arm.

Many new converts huddled on the fringes of the crowd, their hands itching to grasp the chariot ropes as they had in the past. Some fifty or sixty young men grasped the rope eagerly, waiting for the gaonkar's permission to draw it forward. Ventu Nayak broke five coconuts, to mark the five settlements that made up Adolshi village. Just then an insane looking young man rushed up and grabbed the rope, but the others shoved him away. Ventu Nayak raised his hand and the chariot trundled forward to cries of '*Har Har Mahadev!*'

The air throbbed with sound and music as the temple dancers twirled about with flaming oil lamps balanced on their heads. The chariot moved around the temple and came to a halt at the door where a pancharati with five-wick lamps was performed. Then the chariot moved towards the little shrine of the Paikdev, after which it would move to the Rudradev shrine.

The air resounded with cries of '*Har Har Mahadev!*', the musicians played without pause, and devotees rushed behind the chariot with their arms upraised. It was as though the people who had been silent and depressed all morning, had suddenly been consumed by an extraordinary frenzy to keep these final moments alive for all time, to atone for their lapses and shortcomings.

The Rudradev shrine stood on an incline and the ropes strained to almost breaking point as the devotees drew the chariot up the slope. People said that Rudradev was angry because Lord Ramnath had defeated him in battle and the groaning and creaking of the chariot wheels was actually Rudradev gnashing his teeth in fury at the indignity he had suffered so many centuries ago!

The rituals were done and it was time for the chariot to return to the temple. The men drawing the chariot began to rush down the slope with the chariot trundling behind them when suddenly a frail, emaciated youth threw himself in its path. The right wheel struck his side, smashing his ribs, and the chariot came to a halt. It was Kantu's son Savlo – Salvador Dias – driven to madness by his love.

Savlo, who was about nineteen years old, was to marry Bhagi, the daughter of one of his mother's cousins. He would often go to his uncle's house to meet Bhagi and they would slip away into the hills. Suddenly, two months before the wedding, Bhagi's family converted to Christianity. Savlo roamed around like a mad man for two months. Then, without saying a word to his family, he went to the church at Nevre and got baptized.

'I'm a Christian now, I can enter your home,' he said to Bhagi's father.

'Come inside. You can't marry Bhagi, though. We've fixed her marriage with Mingel Curreiya of Goapattana. He's a government official. You're just a farmer's son.'

The men who were drawing the chariot dropped the ropes. They set their shoulders to the wheels and freed Savlo's body before drawing the chariot slowly to its resting place beside the temple. The right wheel of the chariot was splattered with blood. The final jatra at Lord Ramnath's temple had come to an end.

Padre Simao Peres lay in profound darkness in the dungeon for three days. There was not a sound to be heard, just this impenetrable darkness and a damp, rotten smell. The guard had said that there was a pot of water in the cell. He'd felt his way around till he found it, and drank a few mouthfuls. Yesterday, or was it the day before? Or perhaps today. He couldn't remember. How long had he been languishing here? Since they nailed Jesus to the cross? Or as soon as he descended the hill after the Last Supper? He had to carry Jesus's teachings to the whole world or the Jews would become drunk on their power!

Strange thoughts whirled about in Padre Simao's head. He suddenly remembered that he hadn't said his prayers, so he sank down on his knees, and chanted, 'Lord Jesus, Son of

God, Protector of the universe! Lead me from darkness into light. Lead me into the world of men, let me hear their voices, fill my heart with love. I will bear no anger, no ill-will towards anyone. Like you, I shall pray to God to forgive them!'

A little window creaked open on the third afternoon and a beam of light, like God Himself, entered the cell, almost blinding the priest. A sense of joy and energy replaced the gloom of death. A long stick with a cloth bundle tied to it was lowered into the cell. The smell of food aroused hunger pangs in the priest's belly and he realized that he didn't want to die so soon. He opened the cloth bundle and found a pot of soup and four pieces of bread.

'How are you, traitor to the faith?' a voice asked.

The priest didn't like to be addressed in this manner, so he remained silent. Yet he was delighted to hear a human voice after such a long time.

'How are you?' the voice persisted and the priest swallowed rapidly, as though testing his vocal chords.

'I'm well,' he finally said.

'The Chief Officer of the Inquisition in Goa is very kind. I ask, on his behalf, is there anything you need?'

'They took away the crucifix I wore. I want it back.'

'You can't get that. You have been divested of your faith. Till such time as you are proved not guilty, you may not get it. Is there anything else?'

'No.'

The voice moved away but the little window remained open. That evening the latch was unfastened and the wooden door as well as the one with iron bars swung open. A guard and a constable beckoned to the priest, and once he had climbed the six narrow steps, they offered him a hand and hauled him out. They fastened a chain about his waist and led him past a series of little cells. Unlike the three or four dungeons they were clean and well lit.

The guard opened the door to a little room, six feet long and six feet broad, with two raised platforms on either side that served as beds. A white-skinned prisoner was lying on one bed, but he didn't open his eyes. The guard gave the priest a water pot, a small earthen tumbler, a broom and a wooden commode. He locked the door, which had iron bars, and moved away.

The priest sat on the reed mat, drawing strength and comfort from the sunshine that he was seeing after three days. And from the fact that a live human being lay on the other bed. There must have been a hundred and seventy five cells housing many prisoners, but everything was quiet and still. It was like the uneasy calm that hangs over the cremation ground once the flaming pyres are stilled.

Suddenly the white-skinned prisoner began to weep and as his wails cut through the still atmosphere, the guard and another soldier rushed into the cell.

They punched and kicked the prisoner till the emaciated creature collapsed face down on his bed. Padre Simao watched this in silence. He was upset that he had witnessed such injustice without protest because he wanted to save his own skin. The prisoner and I are in the same predicament, Simao said to himself. He weeps openly, but I weep deep within. All that I was in the past, all my intelligence, experience and knowledge, everything that made me function as a priest … it is all irrelevant today. I am merely an innocent man accused of committing a crime. I had confronted a hardened criminal and grabbed his sword, preventing him from shedding someone's blood, back in Greece. Where is that strength, now? Where is that confidence? Today, I am just a convict accused by the Inquisition of being a traitor to my faith. I have no other identity.

The prisoner was weeping silently now. Simao Peres went up to him, 'Brother, I feel sorry for you. Your troubles are now mine. Tell me, how did you get to this place?'

In a voice choked with emotion the man, whose name was Timothy, began his tale…

He was born in Pinto, in northern Portugal, and when he was eighteen years old, his father became bed-ridden and the family couldn't make both ends meet. The Portuguese government needed soldiers for their forces in Africa and India, but people were reluctant to join because of the dangers involved. One day Timothy ran away to Lisbon and joined the army. Before setting sail for India, he ensured that his salary would be sent to his family.

The soldiers, who had been promised that they would return to Portugal after five years, remained in Goa even after seventeen years. The officials, including the viceroy, asked them to marry local women and settle down in Goa. They would be given fields and orchards and money and would be discharged from the army if they did so, but Timothy yearned to go back home.

He began to drink and visit the prostitute colony at Brahmapur where he fell in love with a prostitute called Nagi and abducted her from her home. Nagi was baptized and they got married in church the same day. He was discharged from the army and was given money and a house in Goapattana where he set up a bakery.

Nagi was a pretty, affectionate woman who loved him

dearly and bore him a child very soon. Timothy took ill one day and though they tried different medications, there was no relief. Nagi took her husband to Bombo, the medicine man, who tied an amulet about Timothy's arm and made him drink some leaf extract and sure enough, in a week Timothy felt better. Timothy and Nagi knew that it was wrong to consult Hindu priests and medicine men, but the amulet seemed an insignificant matter and so they didn't tell anyone about their visit. That Sunday, when Timothy was at the marketplace, a priest came up to him.

'You are a nobre from Portugal, married to a Goan woman,' he said.

Timothy nodded.

'Your children are mesticos. You've ruined the purity of Portuguese blood.' He stared closely at Timothy for a while. 'I must inform them about what I've seen. It would be a sin to keep silent about this,' he said as he limped away.

The next morning an official of the Inquisition arrived at Timothy's house. Tongues of fire were painted across the front of his official robes. The old priest had complained to the Inquisition about Timothy. He was charged with worshipping an alien god, of wearing an amulet, of going against the tenets of Christianity and of being a traitor to his faith.

As the Shigmo festival drew near, the tension in the village began to mount. People went about their work fearfully and then remained cowering within their homes. Some of them went to Nilu Nayak. 'Nilu bhavo, do something to save our gods,' they pleaded.

Nilu called some of the villagers to his house. There were

twelve gaonkars present, of which Jana Nayak now Joav Dias, Mungru Shenai now Mingel Gracias and Demu Gurav now Dominic Soz were new converts.

'The idol of Lord Ramnath has to be removed from the temple by the third day after the full moon. We will give our support to any brave man who will take the deity out of Goa,' Nilu Nayak said.

Jana Nayak was furious. 'We were tricked and forced to become Christians. Now you want to take our gods away! No. Our gods will not leave Goa. Take the deity to some secluded spot in the forest and worship Him there,' he cried.

'We are Christians now. If you are confident of taking the deity away, do so. Or immerse the gods in some pool. Everything is uncertain these days,' Mungru Shenai said.

Old man Ventu Nayak couldn't control his agitation. 'Shenai, you Brahmins have done nothing for the gods or for the village. You have only worked for your own ends. Now, as Christians, you will curry favour with them and strut about as important people. You don't care whether the idols are destroyed or immersed. You've forsaken your faith … but that doesn't matter. You're important people. You're Brahmins!'

'Yes. We're Brahmins by birth. Not because of our faith. That cannot change.'

Demu Gurav, now Dominic Soz, wiped his tears. 'I've lost everything. I'm a murderer. Killed my son because of my faith. Now I have nothing – no son, no religion. Do whatever you want.'

'What has God done for us that we should try to save these idols? Let's just wait and watch,' Lavu Nayak declared.

'You bastard!' Dattu Nayak grabbed a stout stick. 'Let them destroy the idols, you say! You've sinned so much, that's why the gods have withdrawn their mercy. The Lord is testing us. That's why He is silent. If He gets angry, they will be destroyed. And so will we.'

This was a group of people whose mental faculties were on the verge of collapse. They pounced on each other at every word, writhed in pain and remorse like a serpent in its dying throes. These were a people caught in that troubled half-light between two religions, seeking to quench their spiritual hunger and conquer the fear in their souls.

'There's no point in quarrelling like this. The deity and the village belong to all of us, whether we are Hindus or Christians. Each man must help in taking the gods out of Goa,' Nilu Nayak said at last.

They didn't come to any decision and one by one, the men slipped away.

'The deity will be carried away on the day after the night of the full moon. If you want to come along, be there with your families,' Nilu Nayak called after them.

Adolshi's troupe of dancers and musicians was famous in all the surrounding villages. Their colourful costumes, their songs and rhythmic movements with twirling wooden batons were highly appreciated by the people when they performed at the Shigmo festival.

The origins of this festival are lost in the annals of time. The story goes that Shivnu of Shirvaddo in Adolshi, had a rare penchant for dance. Crops swaying in the breeze, trees in the forest as they burst into bloom, cows as they pranced about, all made him break into a dance and the trilling of birds provided music to his movements.

One afternoon while Shivnu was tending his cattle, he felt thirsty and went to the lake to drink some water. As he cupped his palms to scoop the water, a tiny seed fell into the hollow – red, like mud, elongated, conch-shaped.

'Avo, god has dropped a seed into my palm. Can you tell me what it is?' he asked his mother.

'Go ask the earth. And ask the rain. Let it rest deep in fertile soil and wait for the first showers. The seed will sprout and you will get your answer,' she said.

Shivnu kept constant watch on the tiny seed like the oil lamp that glows steadfastly before the household gods, his hands gently patted down the earth where it was laid, he lavished care and love on the seed and sure enough, a tiny shoot emerged from the ground. He spared no effort in tending the plant which grew bigger and taller with branches sprouting on all sides, and in a few years the tree seemed to touch the sky.

Suddenly one night the Holiye Naas, the spirit that protects the village, as magnificent as a palm laden with nuts, appeared in Shivnu's dream. 'Worship the tree with flowers and sandalwood paste, then cut it down and make musical instruments out of the wood. Fashion pipes with the wood from the lower part of the trunk. Use the wood from the middle portion to make drums. Whittle the wood from the upper part into twelve pairs of batons. Select twelve young men from your village and teach them to dance with these batons in their hands. Take my name and visit ten surrounding villages with your troupe of dancers and musicians,' it said to Shivnu.

'But I don't know this dance' Shivnu protested, in his dream.

'You are a gifted dancer. And I shall extend all support.'

Shivnu's devotion to this powerful spirit led to the birth of a popular new dance form. He took his troupe to village after village every year. As the story about the naas and the baton dance spread people began to believe that the naas had infinite powers.

When a fire was lit at the end of the Shigmo festival, people made offerings of goats and coconuts in thanksgiving. The goat meat curry with coconut was distributed to the people in leaf cup as prasad.

The practice continued through the years.

Padre Paulo Colaso and Shef Camil Ribeir had not been on talking terms for the last three days. The priest would keep insulting the shef and call him a coward. He threatened to request the Archbishop and the viceroy to divest the shef of his duties because of the delay in converting Adolshi into a completely Christian village. Fed up of his taunts and jibes, the shef finally retorted, 'Wait and see if I don't burn their religion in the Holiye fire … I will bring them all to you, and line them up to be baptized.'

The shef summoned Daba Devli, who was now known as Andrew Denes, to the camp on the day before the festival. 'I have a job for you. If you do it, you will get a whole bhaat of land which the Raigali Brahmins have abandoned,' he said.

'Just say what you want me to do, hodda mansha.'

'I have to convert all of Adolshi to Christianity in one night,' the shef said.

'Yes, big man, you must.'

'I want you to fetch a black calf, about the size of a goat. You must cut off its head and throw the carcass into the

Holiye fire. The head must be tossed beneath the banyan tree. I'll handle everything after that. No one will know that you are involved,' he said.

'But that's a sin, hodda mansha, a very grave sin!' Daba was aghast.

'You have to do this. For me. For Christianity.'

'I'm a Christian, sir. The villagers won't let me get near the fire,' Daba's voice was trembling now.

'Your younger brother, Jogi Devli, hasn't become a Christian yet. Get him to do this, or both of you will suffer. Let me know when the calf's carcass has been thrown into the fire. You can be the chief of the village after that.'

Daba, who was now named Andrew Denes, stared at the shef, bewildered. Then he walked away. Dusk had fallen by that time, so instead of going home, he went straight to Jogi's shack which was in a secluded spot. 'Come outside, my brother, listen to me.'

'That wretched shef has put us in a difficult spot. He wants us to cut off the head of a black calf and throw the carcass into the Holiye fire. He'll take away our land and drive us out of the village, or maybe he'll slit our throats, if we don't obey. If the villagers eat the calf's flesh, they'll become outcastes and he can take them to church and have them baptized. No one will know that we are involved. Everything must be done in the dark. We must ensure that the calf's head remains under the banyan tree,' he said.

It took some time for the message to sink in, but when it did, Jogi leapt up in anger. 'How dare you? Do what they want of you and enjoy what they give. Leave me out of this!' he exclaimed.

'I need your help. I'm a Christian. I can't approach the Holiye fire,' Daba wailed.

Jogi stared into the darkness for a long while.

'Dado, I have a plan. They want a calf's head. How will they know what animal has been charred in the fire? When it gets dark, we'll take Sonu Gurav's black calf to the Sinteri slope and cut its head off. We'll throw the body down that slope and put the head under the banyan as they ordered, and then take away one of the goat heads that is already there. We won't commit a sin and the job will be done,' Jogi suggested.

'What if someone sees the calf's carcass on that hill slope?'

'Do you think the jackals and wild dogs will let it be? They'll strip off the flesh in one night.'

'You'll have to manage all this. You'll be going to the Holiye celebration.'

'When I take the calf's head to the banyan tree you go to the soldier's camp and tell them that everything has been done as planned. Just tell them not to take our names. It's not right to kill a calf … but that sin will be on their heads,' Jogi declared.

The brothers went back to their homes, but neither man could sleep that night as the lowing of a calf seemed to resound in their ears.

The next evening the two of them entered Sonu's cowshed as soon as it got dark. The calf was huddled beside its mother. As soon as they laid their hands on it, it lowed so they quickly bound its mouth and carried it away. The cow lunged towards them with her horns lowered, but she was tied to a stake. She mooed loudly, but the piteous sound was drowned in the loud music being played around the festival fire. Jogi passed the knife to his brother and held the calf's head firmly. 'You are a Christian and the cow is not a holy animal for people of your faith. You may kill it and eat its flesh, so you cut off its head,' he said. Daba lifted the knife with both hands and brought it down forcefully. They could still hear the piteous mooing of the cow in her shed.

Jogi tossed the calf's body down the slope and wrapped the head in a piece of cloth. With a thudding heart he made his way to the banyan tree. The moon hadn't risen yet so it was dark at that spot. Jogi left the calf's head in the undergrowth near the Naas stone.

He stood there quietly for a while. Four or five goats were tethered on one side. People were trickling in slowly and joining the large crowd that had already gathered around the pile of logs and branches that would soon be set alight. Some new converts were also present to claim a share in the meat curry since they were residents of the village.

As the moon rose above the horizon, the troupe of dancers and other village youths began to prance around the pile of wood as the musicians played loudly. The Mirashi picked up a flaming palm frond and began to circle the pile of wood, chanting invocation verses. He lowered the frond on to the dry twigs and leaves which caught fire instantly. The leaping flames cast a bright light all around. Jogi quietly melted into the throng as Daba slipped away to the soldier's camp.

People danced exuberantly as though their shackles had suddenly been unbound. Those who had vowed to sacrifice goats to appease the Holiye Naas cut off the animals' heads and tossed the carcasses, along with some coconuts, into the blazing fire. Only the heads lay strewn beneath the tree. Since this was going to be the last time that the festival would be celebrated, there was some amount of confusion and people lost count of the number of animals sacrificed.

Jogi Devli bustled about busily, dragging the roasted carcasses out of the fire, helping others cook the meat curry. By the time the moon was high up in the sky, the curry in the large earthen pot was ready to be distributed amongst the villagers. It was decreed that the curry should be consumed right there and not taken to their homes. Members of all communities and caste groups in the village, except the Brahmins, milled about the bonfire. People ate their fill and started walking back to their homes.

The Nayaks who were returning to Shirvaddo followed a track that took them behind the soldiers' camp. They heard someone whistle softly and a tall figure shrouded in black clothes, loomed up from amongst the bushes.

'Who's that? Who's there?' the men cried.

'So, you Nayaks have eaten the meat of cows, have you?'

'What! Cow flesh?'

'Didn't you see the head under the banyan? A calf, as high as a man's waist. The calf from Sonu Gurav's shed. Daba Devli chopped off its head and his brother tossed the body into the Holiye fire.'

The Nayaks were aghast.

'The calf was roasted in the fire along with the goats. Now it will moo in your bellies!' The shadowy figure melted into the bushes.

The men froze in their tracks. Their stomachs churned and the contents threatened to spill out of their mouths. Shef Camil Ribcir's plan to make Daba and Jogi into scapegoats had succeeded.

The group of thirty or forty men were blinded by rage.

They brandished poles and stakes as though possessed. A few of them started to retch. 'Deva, we have been tricked into eating what we shouldn't have. We are impure. We have polluted the Holiye Naas. We shall not spare Daba Devli or his brother. We'll burn them alive,' they screamed as they rushed back to look for Daba and Jogi.

'Is Jogi Devli there? That demon has tricked us into eating cow flesh. He's made us impure!'

'He polluted the prasad!'

'We won't let him escape!'

'See if there's a calf head under the tree,' someone yelled.

Jogi Devli had picked up the extra goat head and vanished from the scene. The fire was dying and the embers were settling into a pile of ash. Dugga Mhar, as in previous years, was piling the goat heads in his basket when he realized that one of them was that of a calf. He sank to the ground in shock.

Not finding Jogi at the site of the fire, the enraged mob veered off towards Daba's shack. The news flashed through the village and in minutes, men from the different settlements ran out to join the mob.

Some of them peeped into Sonu Gurav's cowshed on the way. Though Sonu insisted that he had tied the cow and the calf in the shed at dusk, the calf was nowhere in sight.

'It is in your bellies. Why are you calling out to it?' Kushta Nayak screamed.

Blood seemed to descend into their eyes, rendering them blind. 'Come out, Daba! We'll cut you into pieces, set fire to your hut,' they threatened.

Daba latched the door and shrank into a corner, terrified. His wife and children began to cry in fear. His paralysed mother heard everything, but not a sound escaped her throat.

'Come out, Daba! Or we'll burn the hut with all of you inside.' They kicked at the door and the walls and tugged at the thatch on the roof. 'Come out, Daba, or you'll roast like that calf!'

Daba staggered out of the door. 'I didn't throw the calf into the fire … Forgive me…' he pleaded, but the mob began to rain blows on him.

They punched and kicked him, turning a deaf ear to his pleas. His wife appeared at the door. The agitated mob dragged her out. They tore off her clothes. The poor woman ran into the darkness to hide her nakedness. Some people dragged Daba's children and tossed them, like bits of wood, on to a pile of stones. Daba continued to mutter disjointed words 'Shef Ribeir … Jogi … Sinteri slope…' but his strength was ebbing away rapidly.

They tossed Daba's battered body into the shack, latched the door from the outside and set the shack alight. Someone uprooted the wooden cross in his courtyard and tossed it into the blaze.

The fifty or sixty men who made up that half-crazed mob then rushed in search of Jogi Devli, but the door of his shack was wide open and Jogi and his wife were nowhere in sight.

'If Jogi Devli is seen in this village again, we'll cut off his legs,' someone shouted as the mob smashed the earthen pots and dragged a mattress into the courtyard and set fire to it. The blood that had rushed into their brains seemed to be draining now. They were beginning to tire. The bamboo poles in Daba's hut exploded in the heat and two human bodies were reduced to embers as the fire raged on.

Soon a crowd had gathered on the ground in front of the

temple. As an enraged mob engaged in a furious dance of hatred, they had not recognized each other, but now, in the clear moonlight, they saw each other's faces and came back to their senses. The man was one of our own!

The silence of a cremation ground seemed to settle about the temple. The oil lamp in the sanctum seemed to be burning in some remote recess and the idol of Lord Ramnath appeared like a faint shadow. The lamp would go out and the shadow would disappear forever. Bands of ghosts would dance in the darkness. This was the last day in the life of this deity, who had existed since time immemorial!

A sense of fear and unease spread through people's hearts as they stared at the deity in the temple. Why did we embark on this senseless dance, why did we set Daba's hut alight? We are powerless and cannot save the deity or the temple from being destroyed, why did we do this then? Instead of rushing to the soldier's camp with sticks and poles in our hands, why did we rush to Daba's house? Wretched cowards that we are, what difference does it make whether we remain Hindus or Christians!

Not one soldier stepped out of the camp though they were aware of the night-long mayhem in the village in which two people had lost their lives. Nothing was achieved through Daba's death, they said to themselves. It was a Hindu, Jogi Devli, who made them eat cow flesh!

The next morning however, some soldiers on horseback with swords in their hands rode through the village. 'You have killed two people. You have thrown a cross, the emblem of Christianity, into the fire. Do you know how grave a crime you have committed by burning a Christian to death? The King of Portugal will send forces to punish you!'

Of the twenty-six Nayak households in Shirvaddo, five had already converted to Christianity while three families were out of the village. When Murari Nayak heard that the soldiers were making their rounds, he took his family and fled into the forest. The soldiers dragged all the men and youths above sixteen years of age from the Nayak community as well as those from the other castes, out of their homes. The soldiers paid no attention to those who claimed they had not left their homes the previous night. They were all equally guilty and would be locked up in jail in Goapattana.

Shef Ribeir was wearing trousers and a long shirt, boots that came up to his knees, and a broad belt with a sword clipped on to it. Beside him was Padre Colaso. Though he too was tall, his narrow waist and sunken chest made it look as though he was stooping forward. His eyes, however, were so sharp that his gaze seemed to pierce whoever it rested upon.

The priest ordered the soldiers to bind the villagers' hands and feet. If anyone resisted, the soldiers whipped them with the supple, leather-enforced canes. There were a hundred and eight men and youths bound together in a long chain.

'You have burnt two persons to death, one of them was a Christian. You have destroyed the cross at his door. You will rot in jail for the rest of your lives. Constable Remet Noronha has gone to Goapattana for more troops. You will be dragged all the way there with your hands and legs tied,' the shef declared.

'We didn't do anything. We were in our houses with the doors shut,' someone screamed.

'Quiet! The crime couldn't have been committed without your support. You didn't stop the criminals, that is your crime. The whole village has to suffer now.'

'Shef Ribeir, I can request the Archbishop to forgive them if they become Christians,' Padre Colaso suggested. He turned to the villagers. 'If you become Christians along with your wives and children, the Archbishop will be compassionate and request the viceroy to forgive you.'

The men looked at each other.

'Will you become Christians?' the priest asked, yet again. The men stood in silence with bowed heads.

'If you wanted to convert the whole village, why didn't you just say so? Why did you make us eat calf flesh?' Ventu Nayak asked.

'We've been saying that for more than a year, Ventu Nayak. Padre Simao Peres said the same thing. Why didn't you become Christians then?'

No one spoke. Their spirit had broken when they realized that they had eaten the flesh of a calf. They knew that becoming Christian was inevitable, now. So they squatted down as though the strength had gone out of their legs.

Gangu, Suba Telu's son, who had fled into the forest before the soldiers arrived, was crouched behind a bush with his family, when he saw a fox run up the Sinteri slope. Soon a vulture swooped down below them. Gangu noticed a dark shape lying in the undergrowth. He made his way down the slope to see that it was a partially eaten carcass of a black calf with its head sliced off. Gangu had seen Sonu Gurav chasing this calf many a time. A wave of relief rushed through him for he had also eaten the meat curry the previous night.

Gangu told his wife and children to go home and rushed towards the soldier's camp. He saw the villagers ranged in a long row, but he didn't realize that they were bound hand and foot.

'Mamo, Sonu Gurav's calf wasn't roasted in the Holiye bonfire. It's dead and the body lies on the Sinteri slope. Saw it with my own eyes! You haven't eaten cow flesh! Someone cut off its head and tossed it under the banyan tree!' he yelled as he ran towards them.

Everyone was stunned for a few seconds and then they began to laugh, forgetting that they had been tied up. The shef ordered Gangu to come up to him. Smacking him with his cane he said, 'Is that true? Have you really seen that black calf?'

'Yes, yes, hodda mansha,' the youth whimpered.

'Tie him up! Bind his hands and feet,' the shef ordered and lapsed into a sullen silence. Obviously Daba Devli had tricked him. One couldn't tell whether he was sorry or very angry, but his plan had succeeded, anyway.

The villagers, however, were making a great noise and some were beginning to protest.

'You force people to convert by treacherous means. What does one call such a religion?' Babli screamed as the shef lashed out at him.

The sun was high up in the sky and everyone was hungry and thirsty. The shef asked some soldiers to bring pots of water. The villagers had their hands tied behind their backs so the soldiers poured water into their mouths. Much of the water splashed on their bodies and trickled on to the ground.

A Tenent accompanied by some more soldiers arrived late that evening. The shef, the priest and the Tenent spoke in low voices for a long while.

'We haven't eaten cow flesh. We're still pure. We're not outcastes,' one of the villagers yelled.

'That's true. You haven't eaten cow flesh. But you have

burnt an innocent Christian and his mother to death. You have destroyed the holy cross. These are very grave crimes and each of you will be imprisoned for thirty or forty years. The Tenent has spoken to the Archbishop and the viceroy and begged for mercy on your behalf. If you will convert, along with your families, you may go free,' the priest declared.

The men were silent for a while.

'I won't become a Christian. I have done no wrong,' Marto Nayak declared.

'I didn't step out of my house. I didn't do anything wrong, so why should I become a Christian?' Abu Mirashi protested.

Ventu Nayak waited to see if anyone else would protest, but no one said a word. 'Who has destroyed your manhood? What weights have buckled your spine? Why don't you all come together and say you won't convert?' he shouted, but no one said anything. 'I won't become a Christian. I'll rot in prison till I die, but I will not convert,' he finally declared.

The shef loosened the ropes that bound Marto Nayak, Abu Mirashi and Ventu Nayak. 'You will be sent to prison in Goapattana,' he declared.

The shef sent four soldiers to Ventu Nayak's house to fetch his two grandsons, one aged fourteen and the other sixteen. He bound them up in the space that Ventu Nayak had vacated and the boys began to scream, 'Ajja! Don't let them take us away. Stay with us!' Tears gushed out of Ventu's eyes. He came back to his spot in the line and stood there silently like an ox waiting to be tied up in its shed.

Marto Nayak and Abu Mirashi still stood on the other side. The shef summoned four soldiers, 'Tie their hands and make them run all the way to Goapattana. Say that the shef of Adolshi village has sent them to jail. I will testify in court that these two men killed Daba Devli and his mother. All the new converts will be witnesses.'

Marto and Abu quietly went back to their place in the line.

'I assume now that all of you will become Christians along with your families. You have worshipped false gods and images. You are sinners. But Jesus will forgive your sins and the gates of Heaven will open before you,' the priest declared.

'Some of our people are hiding in the forest. What will you do about them? And why didn't you bring Nilu Nayak here along with us?' Payak Gaonkar demanded angrily.

'I know Nilu Nayak well. He is a good man who loves the Hindu faith, but bears no ill-will towards Christianity. One day he will come to Jesus of his own will,' the shef declared.

'He will become a Christian. We shall ask him to,' the priest added.

Ventu Nayak, Surya Gurav and Lavu Nayak suddenly remembered that Nilu Nayak had summoned them to the temple to take the deity out of Goa, that evening. But they were standing here, bound by ropes!

Nilu Nayak's anxiety increased as darkness fell. The grace period that had been granted to the villagers had come to an end. A fresh contingent of soldiers had come from Goapattana, perhaps to take control of the temple the next day.

Nilu knew that Murari Nayak's family was hiding in the forest and that Mhablu and Balsu Nayak had returned to their homes earlier that day. He went to the edge of the forest and called out, 'Murari, this is Nilu Nayak. Come out. Don't be afraid. We must decide what we shall do with the gramdev.'

Murari emerged from among the trees and Nilu took him to Mhablu's house. Everyone was so scared that they spoke in whispers.

'Lord Ramnath must be taken out of Adolshi this evening. Let's meet at the temple at dusk,' Nilu Nayak said.

'What happens to us happens to our gods too. Let the gods remain here,' Balsu said quietly as he walked away.

'If someone brings the idol out of the temple, I'll carry it away. But I don't know what I will do with it. I will be lost in those strange lands,' Murari said, his breath caught in his throat, his face dark with worry.

'I'll go with the Lord too. Better than staying here and becoming a Christian. Nilu dado come with us. Be with us till we set the idol down at some new spot,' Mhablu pleaded.

'Let's see. Who wants to come to the temple with me?' Nilu asked, but no one said a word. They were scared that they might be dragged to the camp and tied up with the other villagers. Nilu finally took Mhablu's seventeen-year-old son, Shambhu, by the hand and set off to pick up the ceremonial sword from its shrine.

They could see the oil lamp burning faintly in the sanctum, but its light didn't carry very far and the large temple was quite dark. The priest and his brother, Timanna Bhat, were sitting silently, steeped in worry. 'Who's there?' Rayanna Bhat demanded, startled.

'Nilu Nayak, Bhatto. Come to take the Lord. We'll take Him to some place where there's no danger of sledgehammers and pickaxes,' he said.

'No, no! I won't let you touch the Lord!' The priest rushed to the sanctum and blocked the door.

'Bhatto, the grace period granted to the temple has ended.

They may come here any moment. Then there's no saving the temple, or the Lord.'

The priest seemed to be losing his mind. 'You Nayaks have your fields and your orchards. I have only the Lord. What will I do if I lose Him? I have served this deity since I was an infant. What will I do now, in my old age?' he whined.

Nilu felt sorry for the man as he grasped him by the arms and moved him to one side. Nilu prostrated before the deity and prayed in silence. He spread a length of red silk on the ground before the sanctum and placed the idol on it. He left the flaming wicks on the ground and brought the brass lamp out of the sanctum. He picked up the idol of Paikdev, one of the lesser deities in Lord Ramnath's pantheon, and placed it on the silk cloth before stepping out briskly to fetch the image of Rudradev. Nilu went about his work with no sign of agitation, but the bhat's wails, like drops of water, scattered in all directions.

Suddenly, the priest's wife appeared with a small cloth bundle which she placed beside the idols. 'The Lord's ornaments. No one came to remove them after the festival in Magh,' she said. She was a tall, fair woman, much younger than the priest.

'Why do you weep?' she asked her husband. 'There is a god. Today you serve this god. Tomorrow you can serve that god, if they ask you to.'

Nilu Nayak tied the ends of the cloth together and placed the bundle on Shambhu's head. He hoisted the heavy brass lamp on to his shoulder and picked up the sword, 'Let's go,' he said. They set off with Shambhu in the lead and old man Nilu, with the sword in his hand, following in his wake. They could hear the priest's wails even as they crossed the fields.

The soldiers untied the ropes that bound the villagers once they agreed to become Christians. Some youths were sent home to fetch food for the men, but the cordon of soldiers remained on all sides. They would be baptized, along with their families, at the Kalapur church the next morning.

Some four hundred persons gathered by the camp the next day. The fear and worry of the past months seemed to recede as children laughed and played and women gossiped. It looked like a group of people who were going to attend some temple festival.

Padre Colaso told them how Jesus helped a blind man regain his sight. 'You were blind all this time. You worshipped false gods. You will get new eyes, a new sight … You will be freed from sin and will be led to Heaven,' he declared.

They didn't understand much about the new eyes and the new sight but Payak Gaonkar's squint-eyed wife was delighted. If this wretched squint disappears and I get new eyes, I'll become a Christian as many times as they ask me to!

The next task on Captain Barrett's agenda was to raze the temple and build a church in its place. It was a Christian village now, except for some five or six households that remained Hindu, but he wasn't too bothered about them. How long could they survive without performing their rituals or celebrating their festivals?

In the old days when Portuguese officials came to the village, people remained indoors out of fear. But now the men sat silently on their porches, and the women stared listlessly from behind half-open doors. They were not very excited, but nor were they scared. If a tiger strikes you with his paw and then lets you go, your fear and awe of the animal becomes less. Who knows, as new converts they might have felt these rulers are 'our people' now! Captain Diego Barrett discussed the issue of razing the temple with Shef Ribeir and Padre Colaso. Shef Ribeir would have liked to close up the temple and let the structure decay and collapse on its own, but Captain Barrett and Padre Colaso insisted on bringing it down at once. The viceroy had decreed that whatever material could be salvaged from the destroyed temple should be used in the construction of the church, and the remaining funds should be raised from the village. The church would acquire the gold ornaments, brass and copper vessels and the fields owned by the temple. They would appropriate the funds set aside for temple activities and demand contributions from the villagers for building the church. The senior priest exhorted the Christian gaonkars, telling them that as good Christians they should actively participate in the building of the new church. Every Christian male was expected to go to the temple site armed with pickaxe or crowbar or spade. Those who were not present would be punished.

People huddled in small groups discussing the development. All of them were against going to the site the next morning. None of them could imagine raising their implements on a structure they had worshipped at for generations. The women told their menfolk not to get involved in this task. We don't care whether the church is built or not, we will not touch a single stone in the temple, they said. Just as they used force to convert us, let them destroy the temple themselves.

The next morning, some forty soldiers gathered by the temple. They waited for a long time, but not a single villager turned up. The captain was furious. He wanted the soldiers to start the job at once, but they didn't have enough tools. Nor did they have the skills needed to dismantle beams and tiles and stone slabs.

The soldiers gathered whatever implements they could and set about demolishing the sanctum. And the blows of an evil Satan, the cruel master of a blind, treacherous age began to fall on the sanctum sanctorum walls. The sound reverberated through the village. Harsh, cruel sounds. A temple, a spring, a lake, a peepal … what beautiful surroundings for these gods! No one bothered to ask whether the gods were really present in the temple. It was the innocent faith of people over so many centuries that had turned the idol into a powerful god.

Each stroke of the pickaxe seemed to pierce every eardrum in the village. The sound echoed in every heart. Everyone grieved, as though a near one had died. The blows pounded their heads. An ancient, exquisitely fashioned skull was being crushed.

Rayanna Bhat sat quietly outside the temple while his wife and children watched from their door. His brother Timanna was seated beneath the peepal. Rayanna had been distraught ever since the idol was carried away. He had not spoken a word nor had he eaten anything for four days. He'd been telling everyone over the last few months that if the outsiders dared to touch the deity or the temple, they would be rendered childless, they would take to their beds, the sledgehammers would strike their own heads. But now, the deity had been taken away from the temple, and disaster loomed before him. His brother remained cocooned in silence. His wife tried to reason with him, 'Let's go and live in the holy city, Gokarn' she said, but he refused to listen.

'I've lived in this temple since I was an infant. Forty years have passed here, this is where I shall die.'

When the soldiers entered the temple, Rayanna went up to the captain. 'You are the rulers who have taken over this land, why do you destroy the gods and the temples? Our faith is built around this deity, and it is on Him that we depend for a living. I had believed that the deity would destroy you if you entered the temple, but I know now that nothing of the sort will happen. All the rituals of worship that we conducted here are worthless! What matters now, are our bellies. You are taking away the only means of keeping our bellies filled.'

'Bhatto, you are an ordinary man, and small men like you should have no trouble making a living. You served the temple all these years, serve the church from now on. We will build a large church here, we need people to work in it,' the captain said.

'What work will I do in a church?'

'You were the bhat in the temple, you can be the padre in church.'

'Can I really be a padre?'

'Not you. We were thinking of making your son one,' the captain intervened, signalling Padre Colaso to remain silent. 'Bhatto, become a Christian along with your family. Your son and you can work in the church, we can make your son a priest.'

A trace of a smile appeared on Rayanna Bhat's face. Suddenly the captain asked, 'Where are the deity's ornaments?'

'This wretched woman put the ornaments into the cloth bundle in which they carried the deity away. Didn't listen to anyone,' the bhat snapped.

His wife stepped forward suddenly. 'Can't they make new ornaments for their gods? Why do they need our poor god's ornaments?' she asked.

The captain summoned the villagers for a meeting that afternoon. It was more than a year since the last gaonki had taken place. Kenkre, Mangru Shenai and Krishna Shenai came from Raigali while the Nayaks of Shirvaddo, who were new converts, turned up in full force.

'I had summoned all of you to work on building the church. Why didn't you come?' the captain asked.

'Where was the need to pull down the temple to build a church?' asked Ventu Nayak. 'Just as the temple was built on the people's faith, so will the church one day. What is left in that structure? The deity has been carried away. Hammering at it is like pounding a palm rib thinking it's a snake! Those blows will only land on our hearts! You may have forced us to convert, but that god still resides inside us. Now you go manage the demolition yourselves. We might help in building the church some day, but we'll worship our old gods as well.' The old man was fuming.

'Do you mean that you did not become Christians of your own free will? Do you not consider yourselves as Christians?'

'No! No … No!' There was a chorus of angry voices.

Padre Colaso was beside himself with rage. 'A Christian who goes against his religion commits a grave sin and a heinous crime. The King has set up the Inquisition in Goa to tackle faithless people like you. I shall give your names to those officials and they will throw you in prison and burn you to death,' he threatened.

Restraining the padre, the captain said, 'They have become Christians just now. Very soon they will follow the path of Christianity, they need time.' Turning to the villagers he said, 'Bala Shenai the former kulkarni has left the village so I nominate Andrew Gracias, son of Mungru Gracias, as the new kulkarni. He has brought all the books and papers that I have asked for. You can decide who will be the new mhal gaonkar, but I have a suggestion – Ranu Kaisuro will be a good choice.'

A few members of the Nayak community began to protest. 'No, no, that can't be. There are only three or four Brahmin families left while there are more than forty Nayaks in the village. The Brahmins have used their authority over us all these years, we won't let that happen any more.'

'Yes, the Brahmins wielded their power, so the gaonkari system worked well. Everyone's rights were protected and religious functions were conducted well,' Mungru Gracias declared.

'Forget all that. There are no caste divisions any longer. We are all Christians, now.'

Christa Gracias was most annoyed. 'How can everyone be the same? Brahmins are Brahmins and Kshatriyas are Kshatriyas. We shall remain Brahmins as long as the sun and the moon appear in the sky. We were Brahmins amongst the Hindus, why won't we be Brahmins amongst the Christians? To be a Brahmin is a mark of our caste and our status. We have not sold this status to anyone,' he said.

'We don't care who you are, there are more Nayaks in this village so we are the stronger community. The village headman will be a Nayak. Let Ventu Nayak be the mhal gaonkar,' Babli Dias declared.

'The gaonki system has been disrupted and must be brought back on track. The church must be built and we will need money. The next two years will be very difficult. Padre Colaso and I will accompany the village chief to the viceroy to seek financial help. So he must be a smart and educated person,' the captain said.

'Let Kenkre Bhatkar be the mhal gaonkar,' Ventu Nayak interjected in a small voice.

'The church will replace the temple. Everything else in the village administration will remain the same. The King of Portugal is not interested in village affairs. The temple's wealth belongs to the church now. The land that belonged to the village, which we had taken control of, will not be returned. Some of those fields have been given to new converts. The rest will be sold and the money used for building the church,' the captain declared.

'You had promised land to those who became Christians. Many of the early converts got fields, but new converts have got nothing. Some of us have very little land, we should get fields too,' Surya Gurav said.

'We shall extend full co-operation to all those who have become Christians. No Christian will remain poor and weak. Once the church is built, you will become masters of the village. We will take control of the land that belonged to those who have left the village and distribute it amongst the needy,' the captain promised.

The villagers hadn't come forward to pull down the temple, yet the captain was a happy man. This was a Christian village now, and the system of village administration had been put back in place. 'You are good Christians now, so your names and your clothes must be like other Christians too. You must not wear dhotis or turbans now,' the captain said.

The people looked around and saw that Ranu Kenkre and

the other Brahmin villagers still wore dhotis and had turbans on their heads. The captain was not happy about this.

'You must not use Hindu family names any longer. Use your Christian surnames. You must not hide the Christian names you have been given,' he declared.

The next day a band of workers, skilled in the art of demolishing buildings, arrived in the village. They had been requisitioned by the captains in charge of villages where temples had to be torn down. Some of them had demolished structures in Bardez. One of them, Timothy Moraes, earlier known as Tima Chari, was the son of Narsu Chari of Adolshi. He had worked as a wood cutter until his father-in-law taught him the art of carving beautiful objects out of wood. Skilled craftsmen were paid large sums of money to carve wooden images of Jesus and Mary, crucifixes, ornamental frames and altars for the new churches and chapels that were sprouting all over Goa.

One day Tima went to Goapattana to work on some project and for the next six months there was no news of him. A new law forbidding churches and chapels from using objects created by Hindu craftsmen had been passed. Tima, who was intoxicated by the money he earned and the good life he lived, converted to Christianity to retain his job. He left his wife and married a Christian girl.

Soon Tima, or Timothy, was part of the band that had demolished temples and shrines in Tiswadi, Bardez and Sashti. Soon he was pulling down buildings and setting fire to them without a second thought. Even when it was the temple in his own village, he didn't hesitate for a moment.

The padre and the captain exhorted the workers to be careful since they would use the stones and wooden beams from the temple to build the church. The noise carried all over the village and into people's hearts. Full of fear, they whispered that ghosts and evil spirits would wander through the village, destroying everything in sight. Epidemics would strike and people would vomit blood and die. It is the temple that protects us all, it is the foundation on which the well-being of the village rests. Lured by the promise of tracts of land, these people have tied themselves to the yoke and as a result, everyone must suffer! Their anger was directed at Tima Chari. Traitor! One who had betrayed his clan!

The tiles from the roof were removed and stacked neatly on one side. Bamboo poles and cross beams on the scaffolding of the roof were taken down. Then they started chipping the top of the stone walls. By evening the whole structure stood bare – twelve pillars and six rafters, each one of immense girth, ranged in a row. The first two rafters had ten or twelve large bells suspended from them. With no temple or deity in sight, the bells looked like large cadavers hanging from the beams.

At the end of the day, the workers and soldiers bathed in the temple pool and drank from the large pot of liquor set out for them. The captain, the shef and the priest, ignored the shouts revelry as the men gorged on rice, curry, maize-flour rotis and salted preserves. Satiated, they lay sprawled around in a drunken stupor.

Timothy Moraes hadn't gone home for six years. His first wife lived in the old house with his mother, his younger brother and family, all of whom were Christians now. Timothy was overcome by lust as he thought of his first wife. He got up quietly and set off through the darkness, intoxicated by drink.

The house lay steeped in darkness and everything was still. He banged on the door and his mother's tired voice carried to his ears. 'Ramu! What evil spirit is it that comes through the darkness at this time of night?'

Kasturi, who lay beside her mother-in-law, shivered in fear. Ramu picked up a live coal from the embers and opened the door. He could barely discern the shape of the man standing outside, but as the glow from the coal fell on his face, Ramu recognized his brother and was filled with fear. He had seen him perched on the temple roof that afternoon, prising out bamboo poles from the scaffolding. He shut the door quietly and went inside, 'Vhanni, it's Tima. Your husband,' he said.

Kasturi's heart beat rapidly, like a bell rung without pause, but she was also curious. Why had he come? What would he say? He had forsaken her and taken another wife. She didn't mind that any longer, but the wretch had destroyed the temple today!

Her mother-in-law slowly came to her senses. 'Why has he come here? After destroying the temple, now does he want to destroy the house? Blacken his face and drive him away!' the old woman screamed.

'Ai bodku mhatare, you shaven old widow! Want to blacken my face, do you? This is my house. I have a share in this property. I'll complain to the viceroy and half of it will be mine. I'm the viceroy's man now,' Timothy shouted in a drunken haze.

People emerged from their houses when they heard the loud voices. Those who were guzzling coconut toddy in Shivanna's shack perked up their ears. Though it was dark, everyone knew that it was Tima wandering about in the village, cursing his family and abusing the gods. There was a sudden flurry … a scream … something was struck … someone ran … The noise came from somewhere near the edge of Deulvaddo. And then everything fell silent. The atmosphere was calm for a long while. And then, with a tremendous fluttering of wings a giant vulture swooped towards the Sinteri slope just as the wolves began to howl.

The terrible night came to an end, revealing the row of upright pillars and horizontal beams no longer bearing the weight of the roof they had carried for hundreds of years. They had never buckled under that weight, but now that it had been removed, they seemed broken. But that night, one weight too heavy to bear had attached itself to the cross-beam. Rayanna Bhat's brother, Timanna, had hanged himself on the first cross-beam. His corpse dangled amidst the bells.

Timanna Bhat used to recite prayers in a soft, melodious voice, each word clear and precise, like grains of washed rice. He was a calm, patient man who didn't rush through the rituals in a hurry. He had surrendered himself totally to the acquisition of knowledge and to his gods. But when the temples were gone, what use was his knowledge of the scriptures and the rituals and the prayers? In a state of despair he had grabbed the rope dangling in the well and hanged himself.

A cowherd passing by the temple early in the morning spotted the body. 'Someone has hanged himself in the temple! Come here! Quick!' he screamed. People rushed out of their homes. Rayanna's wife took one look and let out a scream. 'My brother! O my brother!' Rayanna wailed in grief. The soldiers quickly lowered Timanna's body as they would one of the bells, and laid it at Rayanna's feet.

The demolition of the temple continued.

'What should we do with this wretched cross-beam on which that fellow hanged himself? We can't use it in the church. Ask the priest,' a worker called out.

'That young bhat has made sure that at least one beam from the temple will rot and decay…' someone else remarked.

The priest and the captain arrived at the spot. 'He hanged himself right here. We can't build a church at this spot,' the priest said in a low voice.

Shef Ribeir was irritated by the priest's words. 'Hindus go to the temple to seek the deity's blessings before they build their homes. If they get a favourable sign from their gods, they go ahead with their plan. Perhaps we should visit some Hindu temple to check if we should build a church at this spot. They claim that their gods are never wrong,' he said.

Padre Colaso was furious. 'Are you making fun of the church and the Christian religion? You have spoken against our faith by praising their customs. You must be punished. I will go to Goapattana and inform the Inquisition,' he declared.

The shef was terrified. His careless words had got him into this mess! 'Forgive me, Padre, I spoke in jest. I am a devout Christian,' he pleaded.

'You cannot be forgiven. You are an insignificant, local Christian convert from the lower classes. You must be taught a lesson!' The priest stomped off.

The shef sidled up to the captain in remorse. The captain was aware of the influence exercised by the Jesuits. There was no hope of pardon if they lodged a complaint. They drew their authority from the King of Portugal who had decreed that all the captains, the shefs and the viceroy should help them spread the Christian faith. Captain Diego Barrett had come across different types of Jesuits in Goapattana. Some were surrounded by slave women and led hedonistic lives in palatial mansions. Others tramped barefoot through the villages, carrying the teachings of Jesus to the people.

There was a simmering conflict between the faith based on love, compassion and forgiveness that Jesus had taught, and the religion of force propagated by the Jesuits in Goa. This conflict remained hidden under the surface because of the climate of fear generated by the Inquisition. If this had not been the case, the tenets of Christianity would have been discussed and deliberated upon in great detail by the various factions. It would have been purged of much of its dross and emerged as a mature and profound religion that people would willingly embrace and it would have spread beyond the frontiers of Goa. Those who recognized this truth remained slightly withdrawn from the mainstream for they didn't have the strength to combat the Jesuits. They tried to help in whatever way they could, or ordered the shef and police forces to help the Jesuits.

And now Shef Ribeir was trapped in their clutches. The captain went up to the priest, 'Padre, Shef Ribeir and I are always at your service. The King of Portugal wants to spread Christianity in Goa, so it is our job to do so. Shef Ribeir has been doing this very well. Just the other day, he ensured that four hundred and twenty-two people were baptized at the same time. This is a great achievement and he deserves to be forgiven for his lapse.'

Padre Colaso was silent for a while. 'I won't forgive him. But I will not complain to the Inquisition this time. I cannot promise that I will not do so in future, though,' he said.

Shef Ribeir must be shifted out of Adolshi at the earliest, the captain said to himself.

'Padre, decide where you want to build the church, and how big it must be,' said the captain. 'Come with me to Goapattana. Bring the mhal gaonkar with you and we will meet the Archbishop and the Viceroy. This is a poor village. Tell the villagers to ask for a church and for financial help to build it. They can provide the labour, but the engineers and masons will come from Goapattana. The construction of the church can start in a year's time,' he said.

'Can we not sell the land to raise money?'

'No, we cannot. The land belongs to the temple. The revenue officials will transfer the land deeds to the church and church expenses will have to be borne by revenue generated from that land. The King has decreed that the village administration will continue as before. Last year, we forced the mhal gaonkar to sign away some of the village lands to us. Some of it was given to new converts, but there are still large tracts that we can sell.'

'Good.'

'Land prices have fallen in recent times. No one wants land or cattle these days.'

'Whatever happens, we must build the church as soon as possible.'

'Of course, we must, Padre. It will be built at once.' The captain leapt on to his horse and galloped away.

As they began to dig up the foundation of the temple, one of the labourers realized that Timothy Moraes had not come to work. Where was he? Had anyone seen him that morning?

Where did he sleep last night? No one knew anything. Someone had seen him rushing around in a drunken haze, but no one knew where he'd gone. Most of the workers in these demolition bands were Portuguese soldiers and Moors who had converted to Christianity. Very few Hindu converts volunteered to destroy the temples and when one such person appeared on the scene, he was treated with scorn and disdain.

On one side, large stone slabs were being prised out of the temple walls. On the other, a flock of vultures was circling Timothy Moraes's corpse on the Sinteri slope. A few foxes lurked in the shadows sniffing the air, ready to pounce. Who had killed the man? Was he knocked down with a club or did someone stick a knife into him? Did someone bash his head with a rock? No one knew.

People were saying all sorts of things in the village. Some said that the Holiye Naas was enraged and had led Timothy down a crooked path into the Sinteri valley. Others felt that some devotee, distraught on seeing Timothy perched on the temple roof, had killed him. Abu Mirashi insisted that human sacrifice was necessary before a temple could be razed. The deity had extracted what was His due. Sandalwood paste and flowers are offered to the gods when the temple foundation is laid. Human blood must be offered when the structure is destroyed.

'Didn't the young bhat sacrifice himself?'

'The young bhat died because of you, wretched creatures! He was a priest. It was his job to conduct prayers, not to protect the temple. That was the job of the Khatris in the village. When you surrendered meekly, like oxen, what could he do?'

People huddled fearfully in their homes ever since the demolition of the temple began. They felt that some great catastrophe was about to happen … children would die, people would get paralysed and infectious diseases would rage in the village. The crops in the fields would be destroyed and men would attack each other as the Evil Spirit swept into the village which was no longer under the protection of the temple deity. They lit oil lamps furtively as evening fell and prayed to their gods in low voices.

The temple was completely demolished by the fourth day. They had even dug out the foundation stones and piled them up in a heap. On one side lay beams and wooden fixtures. On the other side was a pile of stone slabs. A vibrant temple alive with devotees and rituals was now reduced to a heap of stones. People stared at the rubble in dismay. Where did God vanish, what happened to His power? Did He withdraw His powers and move away quietly because we are all sinners? Or was His presence just an illusion created by this magnificent structure built of stone? No! It was our faith, our devotion, our worship that caused God to be present in every slab.

There was neither a church nor a temple in the village now. They had destroyed many of the little shrines as well as the Ravalnath temple where the Shenai families used to worship. A strange sense of emptiness settled over the village, yet life went on. People felt hungry and thirsty. Dew fell. So did the rain. Mango blossoms appeared, then the trees were laden with fruit. Cows calved. What did one need a God for, then?

It's true the villagers were bathed in holy water and cleansed of all that was old when they were baptized and made Christians. But in their minds and in their behaviour, they remained Hindus. A whole group had been compelled to convert at the same time. Its collective strength was struggling to express itself against Christianity, its sense of being Hindu was rising to the fore. When Sukhdo was the only convert in the area, he'd been quiet and obedient. But now, as part of the larger group he, too, seemed to sprout horns. Turning these new converts into good Christians was the biggest challenge before the Church, the Inquisition and the administration. The new converts were penalized and faced the prospect of being thrown into prison and being burnt to death. On the one hand were the principles of love, compassion and forgiveness as taught by Jesus, on the other was this cruel travesty of faith that was coming to the fore.

Now that they had become Christians the villagers were becoming defiant, and despite several warnings, they grew tulsi plants by their houses and their courtyards were edged by a decorative ridge, typical of Hindu homes. Married women continued to wear the symbols of their status like the Hindus. They didn't invite Hindu priests home, but they sent rice and other gifts at funerals and on death anniversaries, and placed ritual offerings before crows.

The padre was very angry at this and often rebuked the shef. 'Yes, Padre, we must teach them a lesson. They're foolish and ignorant. But how many people can we complain against?' The shef was so afraid of Padre Colaso now that he was quick to nod his head at whatever the padre said.

Sixty-year-old Nilu Nayak, along with Mhablu Nayak and Murari Nayak and their families, were taking their god out of Adolshi. Nilu Nayak marched at the head of the group, the sword firmly in his grasp. Murari's seventeen-year-old son followed carrying Lord Ramnath on his head. They had set out for Antruz, but when they came to the Pilar embankment, they saw a man striding along with a huge bundle on his head, wiping the sweat from his face with the loose end of the cloth hanging down across his shoulder. 'Who are you? From which village? Where are you headed?' the man asked.

'We're from Adolshi, a rich flourishing village, struck now by the evil eye. We're taking our gods with us. We'll drive a stake into the ground and set up new homes at some favourable spot, our gods will be with us,' Nilu Nayak replied.

'Don't step into Antruz,' the man said, 'it's dangerous. Full of Moors and Muslims and people from eighteen different communities who fled the Goan islands. Fights break out, looting takes place. You said you were from Adolshi, didn't you? A Brahmin family from your village had crossed over by boat and was trudging from one village to another when they were attacked. The man was beaten up and the young wife was raped by some Chandals. She was a very religious woman, they say. She jumped into a well and killed herself.'

'Who was she?'

'I don't know her name. She was from some Shenai family of Adolshi.'

Everyone was lost in deep thought. Finally Murari asked, 'Where are you going with that bundle on your head?'

'I was the jalmi at the Khetrapal shrine in Agashe. Three years ago, I uprooted the idol and set it down at a new site in Antruz, where I conduct the rituals as in the past. The Lord's spirit takes possession of my body. We celebrated the jogavani festival just the other day. I'm taking the prasad and Lord Khetrapal's blessings to the Christian devotees in Agashe. They continue to contribute to the temple fund every year even after they became Christians. How will they feel if they don't receive the Lord's blessings and the prasad?' The man set off again. Suddenly he turned back and called out, 'Don't go to Antruz. Take the river route or sail down the coast to Shinvesar instead.'

Murari's son, Shambhu, slung the cloth bundle bearing the gods on a low branch. The others flopped down on the embankment in dismay. A load of worry descended on their heads – they were stuck in the middle – they couldn't move forward and there was no going back. There was fear and worry in the women's expressions. Murari's wife kept mumbling to herself … who could that Brahmin woman be … not Rudra Shenai's wife Sumitra, I hope … Such a pious woman, like a goddess herself!

They put three stones together and placed a pot of rice and water on them. Then they lit a fire under it. They ate the payz with salted mangoes. Just then a man came up to them with a large watermelon and stalks of sugarcane.

'These things cannot be defiled by my touch. Accept them. My elder brother was like a father to me. He took his wife and children and went away without telling anyone, the night before we were to be baptized. They say he crossed the river … who knows where he is.'

The group picked up their gods and set off in the direction of the river at Agashe. Nilu Nayak was familiar with this region and had some idea about which villages could be safe and which direction people who were trying to escape conversion were headed. He had been to Antruz and Sashti in the past and had heard of Shinvesar and Canara.

It was very hot and sunny when they got to the river. The government office on the river bank was closed and there was no one in sight. Because it was low tide, the black mud of the river bed was exposed. The odour of decaying matter hung heavy in the air. Nilu Nayak and his group sat down to wait for the boatmen to arrive.

Sometime later, three men came up to them. One carried a fishing net wrapped about a stick on his shoulder and another, who was quite old, carried a long pole. They seemed used to seeing groups of people carrying their belongings on their heads. 'Which village? Where are you headed? Who's your god?' the old man asked.

'We're from Adolshi village carrying our Ramnath. We don't know where to go. We need to cross the river,' Nilu explained.

'The boatmen and fishermen helped many people in the past. Took them as far as Shinvesar and Canara and Malabar. But it's too dangerous nowadays. A boat that sailed towards Canara two weeks ago hasn't come back yet. The women are all waiting for their men to return. The Arabs loot the boats there and the white-skinned foreigners beat them up here. No one wants to take his boat out any more.'

'What should we do then?'

'There's great unrest in the villages in Sashti, just across the river. Maybe you should cross the river and climb the Sankhval hillock. You can descend into Isorshi village. They say that many boats take the sea route from there.'

'Is it very far?'

'No. You'll get there by evening if you walk fast.'

'Is there a ferry boat to cross the river?'

'Yes. It'll come soon.'

The boatman who ferried them across knew the names of all the villages along the coast, right from Majali and Mirjan to Mangalore. He told them to head for the sea from Isorshi and get back to the coast at Agod. 'Some large-hearted villagers there will certainly help you and give you shelter in their village,' he said.

As they alighted at Kutthal and set off for the Sankhval hillock, they passed the site where the Mangesh temple once stood. Broken stone slabs and wooden beams were scattered on all sides. There was an eerie calm in the village. Everyone spoke in hushed voices, women drew water at the well in silence. The farmers didn't shout at the oxen drawing the plough. A wayfarer they encountered at the foot of the hillock described to them how the temple was destroyed.

Some hundred soldiers gathered on the hillock late one evening. They set fire to a huge kadam tree and the leaping flames cast red shadows all around. The soldiers descended on the village the next morning. Harihar Kosambi, accompanied by some Brahmins and farmhands rushed to the temple, but the sight of that ferocious mob on horseback waving naked swords, was too much for the Brahmins. They ran away.

As the soldiers rode towards the temple, Kosambi picked up the idol and gave it to a farmhand telling him to carry it away. Suddenly he heard Kapil, the sacred cow worshipped through the ages along with the deity, lowing in alarm. Kosambi rushed to the spot and saw a soldier raise his sword to kill the cow. Kosambi brought his club down forcefully on the soldier's head. The other soldiers pounced on Kosambi and struck him dead. They killed the cow and tossed its entrails as well as Kosambi's body into the temple tank.

It was twilight by the time Nilu Nayak and his group reached Isorshi village which lay in the midst of a thick forest. A member of the Nayak community let them stay in his house that night. The other Nayaks gave them rice and set up a hearth where they could cook a meal. Early the next morning they went to the beach carrying a large, ripe jackfruit which had been given to them by their hosts and hired a sail boat for twelve xerafins to take them to Agod.

The sails were unfurled and the boat left the land. Everyone was silent. Even the children seemed overawed by the situation. Suddenly, Murari's wife Kashi burst into tears. Mhablu's wife Dulu stared at her with tears in her own eyes. Murari's eyes were wet, too. Nilu realized that everyone on the boat was on the verge of tears. He didn't know what to say to them. He was taking them to some unknown land, but he planned to return home.

The boatman, Bali, had seen others in similar situations many times, yet the inconsolable grief of a people who were leaving their homeland forever never failed to upset him. He furled the sail and bound it to the mast. Dipping a bamboo pole into the depths of the sea, he said, 'This is the final trip. We will not set out to sea again. The Chaitra month is almost here. Winds and storms are taking root in the ocean. Look over there, black clouds hovering like bees where the sea meets the sky. No more coming, no more going after this. Waves, as high as palm trees will wash away the shore…'

The sun shone down fiercely and steam seemed to rise from the heated ocean. Mothers drew their saris over their children's heads to shield them from the sun. Nilu Nayak had grown old, but he had never exerted himself. He had lived amidst cool orchards and hired labourers to work in his fields, but now his face was flushed and swollen.

They ate the ripe jackfruit that afternoon and drank from a pot of water they had brought along. One of the boatmen advised them to get off at the Agod beach and walk along the shore to a nearby village where they would find Konkani people from the Nayak community.

When the group crossed the sandy strip and climbed the incline, they were met by an angry crowd brandishing sticks and clubs. 'Who are you? Where have you come from? How did you enter our village without permission?' they asked.

'We're Nayaks from Adolshi village in the Tiswadi region. We came by sea and have just stepped into your village. There's great unrest in the area where we lived, we couldn't stay there with our gods. We seek shelter in your village,' Nilu Nayak explained.

'You can't stay here. No outsider will prosper on this land. No outsider might strike a spade into this earth,' one of the villagers declared.

'But we belong to the Nayak community. We're Khatris…'

'A Nayak family came here from the Sashti region last month. They roamed freely in the village and worshipped in our temple. Later, we realized that they were converts, who had fled Goa and were posing as Konkani Nayaks. We beat them up and drove them away.'

'But we are not like them! We've passed through great danger and come to this place.'

'You may not settle in this village. Stay the night on someone's porch. The villagers will give you some rice and you can cook a meal.'

They stayed in the large shed adjoining someone's house. The villagers gathered a measure of rice from each household and they cooked a large pot of payz on a makeshift hearth. They ate the payz with some salted mango. Mhablu's son Shambhu, who had remained hungry in his sister Vitha's home, kept thinking of her all the time. Bai, you asked me to remain faithful to our gods and to our faith ... See, I do so now!

They set off quietly the next morning. Nilu Nayak's knees were aching, his body was heavy and his eyes were bloodshot, yet he tramped along behind them. He yearned to say that he would not come further, that they should proceed without him, but he feared that they might drop the gods and flop down right there in dismay.

The sun was overhead by the time they got to Palolem, and they were very hungry. On one side was a chain of hillocks, on the other was the ocean's roar. In between was a cool, picturesque village with its coconut-laden palms. God has created so much land, these parts are teeming with Nature's abundance, surely we can set down our gods here and rest our bodies. Though they were weighed down with worry, fear and despair, a little spark of hope drew them forward, perhaps the people in the next village would offer support.

They dropped their bundles and sat down to rest. There were four palm trees close by, one of which was short and squat and laden with nuts. They had eaten only payz the previous night, and it was well into the afternoon now. Murari's son, Babuni, slithered up a tree and threw some ten or twelve coconuts down.

'What are you doing? We mustn't rob someone's coconuts like this...' Nilu Nayak called out fearfully.

'There's no sin if we eat the fruit where it has fallen, right under that tree,' Mhablu argued, and Nilu said no more.

They cut open the coconuts and drank the water and ate the kernel, tossing the empty shells under the tree. Just then, a tall, well-built man with a big moustache came up to them.

'I saw you plucking the nuts, but I waited for you to slake your thirst and hunger. You have robbed us and eaten stolen fruit even as you stepped into our village. Pick up your gods and move out at once. If you halt anywhere, I'll cut off your legs!' he thundered.

A few more men stood menacingly on one side. The wayfarers quickly picked up their bundles and trudged along without looking to the left or to the right till, at last, they reached Kolamba. This was a cool, shady region where the earth was moist and water was plentiful. It was the month of Chaitra, yet the furrows in the fields were full of water.

The Nayaks of Adolshi requested permission to settle in these parts. The villagers replied, 'We take no step without consulting our gods. Lord Veerpurus is a powerful deity. We must shower consecrated rice on the jalmi till he is possessed by the spirit of Lord Veerpurus and ask him what we should do'.

That night the spirit of the deity entered the body of Soyru, the temple jalmi. He began to sway as the drums beat softly and then he sprang to his feet. The villagers flung grains of rice on him as he pranced about in a trance. 'Strangers from some unknown regions want to settle here. What do you say?' the villagers asked.

'Who are they? What caste? What is the bloodline that they have descended from? Without all these answers, they may not stay,' the spirit declared.

'We're Nayaks from Adolshi,' Nilu said.

'Where's the proof?'

'Our tongues speak the truth. That's our only proof.'

'Not enough. When they laid the foundation of your village temple, the identification stone was buried on the right side. There are five metal coins under that stone. Fetch them. One of those coins will trace your ancestry.'

'We can't do that, deva,' Mhablu said. 'They've destroyed the temple and forced us to flee.'

'Who is the deity that you bring?'

'Our gramdev. Lord Ramnath.'

'You will have to set up a new village for your gramdev. You can worship two kuldevs in one village, but not two gramdevs. That will lead to violence and bloodshed!'

Soyru began to come out of the trance. The Mirashi sprinkled water on him and broke a coconut at his feet. Everyone was quiet, but the villagers seemed satisfied by what the spirit had decreed.

Nilu Nayak and his party spent the night in a courtyard and set off the next morning for Pansul village. Farmers stopped ploughing their fields and those who had gone into the forest rushed back when they saw this band, with their bundles on their heads, approach their village. People came out of their homes and a large crowd of belligerent villagers blocked their way. 'How did you enter our village without permission? How did you bring your gods into our village? Go back!' They asked the same set of questions.

Nilu Nayak was furious. 'Gods are gods. These are not devils that might attack you! We are wayfarers who have been turned out of our village and our homes. What kind of people are you if you have no sympathy, no kindness for us? You are just showing anger and hostility,' he declared.

'If you came as guests we would welcome you. But you outsiders will strike your spades into the ground and settle on our land. Your plan is to set up a village here for your gods!'

'We're exhausted. Show us the way to some town,' Murari beseeched.

'You can go to Shinvesar. Cut through that grove and you'll reach the Talpan river. Cross it and then move on.'

They set off in the direction of the Talpan river but before long, they were so exhausted that they flopped down in the shade of a tree. They spent the whole evening sprawled amidst their baskets and bundles and the women lit a fire and cooked some rice. The smoke drew the attention of two fishermen who came up to them with a basket of mackerel. 'Apply salt and roast this fish in the embers. We'll try to help you,' they said.

'The village deity is with us … see that red silk bundle. We cannot eat fish till the Lord is set down at some new site,' Nilu Nayak explained.

The fishermen's hearts were filled with devotion. They then returned with a large red pumpkin which the women cooked with the gruel. The fishermen took the group across the river in their boat early the next morning and carried their belongings on their heads.

'We don't want any money from you. We feel that we've lent a shoulder to the Lord's palanquin … helped some deity from some distant land.'

The wayfarers were so tired that they just wanted to collapse on the ground. Yet they trudged on with their load, weeping softly when they were overcome with memories of the land they had left behind. When they got to the temple of Parashuram, they dropped their bundles and sat down. Two men, who noticed the red silk bundle bearing the deity slung on a low branch, came up to them. 'Who are you? Where are you from?' they asked.

'We're Nayaks of the Khatri community of Adolshi village. We've come here with our gods.'

A tall man, with broad shoulders and large arms stood close by. His skin was the colour of wheat, but his eyes were bloodshot and angry. 'Cowards! You have all run away at the slightest hint of danger – that too with your gods on your heads! Couldn't you stand there and fight for your village?'

The group of helpless people cowered silently. Nilu Nayak's gentle personality was at odds with the harsh behaviour of the people they kept meeting every day, so he was a broken man.

'These people won't let you stay in this village,' the stranger said, as he stood leaning against a pillar with his eyes shut. The children, who should have been dancing and playing about, lay quietly in their parents' arms or were sprawled listlessly amidst the baskets and bundles. They must have been hungry and thirsty and tired. Or perhaps they sensed the sheer hopelessness of the situation they were in.

'Where are you from? Which village?' Nilu Nayak asked hesitantly after a while.

The man stared at Nilu intently. 'Majale. Protected by Lord Ramnath. Beyond the slope of the Pavse Ghats,' he said.

'Are there any fields that lie fallow in your village?' Mhablu asked hopefully.

'Are our limbs broken? Why should our fields lie fallow?' the stranger snapped.

'Let us come to your village. All we need is a place to rest, just for some time,' Nilu Nayak pleaded.

The man remained silent for a while.

'Who's your family deity?'

'Lord Ramnath.'

'And your village deity?'

'Lord Ramnath.'

'Toss your gods into some lake and come with me then.'

'Why do you say that? We left our homes and our village to save our gods. That's why we take all this trouble.'

'What use are gods that give so much trouble to their devotees?' he murmured. 'You will have to set up a new village for your gods. Or you'll have to forsake them and settle somewhere.'

'What are you trying to say? We don't understand.'

'You can't have two kings in a kingdom. There cannot be two deities in a temple. Anyway, we'll see what happens when we get to Majale. Come with me.'

The group was enthused by his words. They picked up their belongings and followed him silently. The sunlight had mellowed by the time they walked down the slopes of the Pavsa Ghat and reached Majale.

Seven gaonkars belonging to the Pawar community and six Nayaks formed the thirteen members of the gaonkari system in the village. Nilu, Murari and Mhablu squatted on the ground on one side as the gaonkars debated amongst themselves. Naga Bhat, who performed all the priestly duties in the gramdev temple, was also seated there.

'There's no dearth of farmland in this village. You can till the soil and grow enough to satisfy your needs. The question, you men from a distant village, is, what place will you occupy in our village hierarchy?' Jogi Pawar, the mhal gaonkar asked.

Nilu Nayak folded his hands 'Allow us to take part in your village festivals. Let us have the right to draw the temple chariot and to carry the deity's palanquin like everyone else,' he beseeched.

Naga Bhat turned to the families from Adolshi. 'Ramnath is an incarnation of Ishwar and belongs to the Saiva tradition. He is represented by the black stone pindi or linga. Have you brought that with you? The Ramnath idol without the linga is like a man devoid of masculinity,' he said.

'No. We couldn't carry it. We left it behind. Those wretches must have destroyed it by now,' Nilu Nayak said.

'In that case, you'll have to immerse your deity in the sea.'

The men from Adolshi heard the priest's words in stunned silence. Nilu's eyes filled with tears.

Mhablu, a man of few words, finally spoke. 'We thought our gods were very powerful, the temple in our village was the best. But now we have neither village nor temple. Just this idol without the linga.' In a tone of resignation he declared, 'We'll stay here. We'll do what you want.'

On Monday, the villagers from Adolshi carried their idol around the shrine five times and then placed it in the sanctum of the local Ramnath temple. The priest sent them to bathe in the stream and then guided them through the rituals where they worshipped both the Ramnath idols. They then performed the uttarpuja signifying the withdrawal of sanctity from the idol that they had brought from Adolshi. The three men picked up the idol and moved silently towards the beach.

It seemed to them that the sea had suddenly become calm, not a leaf stirred on the trees and there was no sound from the surrounding hills, even the stream seemed to have stopped flowing. This was a deep stillness, an emptiness, that none of them had ever experienced. Standing waist-deep in water they slowly immersed their beloved deity, allowing the receding waves to carry it into the darkest recesses of the sea. They stared blankly at the white sails of a boat on the horizon. Those sails must be propelled by the wind that blows over Adolshi, they thought.

'What will the people of our village say?' Mhablu exclaimed in despair.

'Which people? Who is left there who has the right to criticize? The white-skinned officer always said that cowards have no god and no religion. He was right,' Nilu remarked.

The next day Appa and Giri Nayak took them to a deserted stretch on the northern fringes of the village. 'You will erect your homes at this site,' Appa said to them. 'May you prosper, may your fortunes increase!'

Eleven days had passed since they left Adolshi. Nilu Nayak was a tired man. His knees ached, his limbs were swollen and he was short of breath. But he hired a boat to take him from Majale to Velsav, 'I'll take the same route back,' he said to his companions.

'Nilu dada, will you be able to trek all that way from Khol?' Mhablu asked.

'I'll have to. Will force myself ... even if I collapse when I get home.'

Everyone stood on the shore staring after him as the boat vanished in the distance. Nilu had felt feverish the previous night, but he hadn't told anyone. As the sun beat down his head began to swim and he slumped to one side. 'I can't bear this,' he said.

The boatman took pity on this tall, fair, aristocratic old man. 'We haven't sailed very far, we're just an hour away from shore. I'll take you back to your people in Majale,' he said.

The boat turned back and his kinsmen carried Nilu into the new shack that they had built. He passed away that night and his kinsmen cremated him under an onvli tree on the beach. Naga Bhat performed the funeral rites.

Who knows what the actual reason for the ill-will between Sukhdo and Jana Nayak was. Was it merely a strip of land, or was it more than that? Jana's pride in his fair skin and his intelligence didn't go down well with Sukhdo, who was quarrelsome by nature and often flew into an abusive rage. Jana believed that Sukhdo had forced him to become a Christian by strewing half-eaten rice in his house and defiling the purity of his home, but for that he would have remained a devout Hindu. This grudge, added to the years of ill-feeling between the two men, only strengthened his resolve to teach Sukhdo a lesson and ruin his family.

Sukhdo and his sons built ridges around the fields they had received and set up marker stones soon after Guna left the village. Two soldiers with swords strapped to their belts stood on guard as they ploughed these fields. The villagers looked on from a distance, but no one came forward to protest.

The three sons were quite cheerful these days, now that everyone was a Christian and the deities had been carried away. But Sukhdo had become morose and silent. He didn't snap at his family nor did he meddle with Jana Nayak. It was as though someone had extracted the venom from his speech and changed his cantankerous nature – he was like a platter of food without salt.

The bhat had once told Sukhdo Nayak that if he didn't offer oblations to his ancestors on certain days in the year their spirits would remain hungry and thirsty and restless forever. This thought kept whirling in his mind so every full moon and new moon, punav and amas, and days of the shraddh, he would tell his older daughter-in-law, 'We must feed my parents' spirits, as well as the spirits of other ancestors today.'

The woman would cook a sweet payas and ladle it on to a plantain leaf. Sukhdo would take that and a tumbler of water to the back of the house. He would place the leaf on the low branch of a mango tree and sprinkle water on it, calling softly to the crows.

That day, however, some strange spirit seemed to take possession of the man and he began to shriek, 'Aaaaaaai … haaaaai…' inviting the crows to partake of the food. The people in the house were beside themselves with fear. His daughter-in-law gesticulated frantically asking him to be quiet. What was wrong with him today!

Jana heard the commotion and rushed to the back door. He saw the food placed on the leaf and called out loudly to his wife, 'See! He's scared that his ancestors will curse him and he'll go to Hell. Haven't we given up all these practices? One must turn the winnowing fan in the direction in which the wind blows, but no! These people will not practise any religion faithfully. Not the old one, nor the new.'

Sukdo saw Jana and his temper rose. 'What are you staring at? The crows will peck out your big wide-open eyes. What happened to the dog that looked down at everyone? He fell flat on his face.' Jana pretended not to have heard or seen anything and quickly went into his house.

The next morning Jana put on a bandi and draped a puduva on his lower body. On his head, he tied a red kerchief and set off clutching a large crucifix in his hand. Hundreds of these crucifixes had been brought from Goapattana and distributed in the village. The villagers had to carry them when they went out on any official work. Sukhdo's younger daughter-in-law saw him and called to the others. Where was he going so early in the morning, they wondered.

The villagers had been hearing frightening stories about the Inquisition over the past year. They knew that Padre Simao Peres had been jailed by the Inquisition officials. When they became Christians they were warned that if they went against the tenets of Christianity they would be thrown into prison and burnt to death. People who returned from Goapattana would talk of the Big House and how people would pass it in silence, not daring to even point it out.

When Jana Nayak approached the soldier's camp his feet seemed to falter, but his hatred for Sukhdo spurred him on. 'I want to meet your leader,' he said, his hands extended in supplication.

'Why have you come here so early today?' the shef asked.

'My neighbour, Sukhdo, is going against our new religion. He clings to the old faith even today. He offers food to the crows and to cows and sends rice to the bhat's house to appease the spirits of his ancestors,' Jana said.

'Did you see Sukhdo Nayak perform those Hindu rituals?' Padre Colaso asked.

'Yes, Father,' Jana said in a low voice.

'You must go to Goapattana and complain to the Inquisition officials.'

Jana nodded in silence.

'Stupid, ignorant fools! They don't know what is right and what is wrong. Everything will fall in place slowly, Padre, shouldn't we forgive them, just this once?' the shef asked.

The priest looked at him strangely. 'Shef, you have worked hard to convert this into a Christian village and to demolish the temple. I consider you a good Christian so I forgive you just as I have forgiven you in the past. Remember, it is a crime to withhold information from the Inquisition. A good Christian must report any acts against Christianity that he has witnessed, or heard of.'

The priest asked two soldiers to accompany Jana Nayak to Goapattana. Sukhdo Nayak has troubled me all his life. He made me an outcaste and caused my ruin. He abuses me… Jana said to himself in a bid to strengthen his resolve, but he was nagged by a desire to withdraw his complaint and return home. However, it was too late for that. He was trapped in their net and his resentment of Sukhdo had sunk deep into his mind.

Padre Simao Peres had brought Annu to St Catherine's Church to be baptized and he'd become Annu's godfather, too. But Annu, who was now called Andrew, couldn't return to Adolshi, as it was still a Hindu village at that time. Caught between his love for the priest and the hostility of the villagers, Annu was miserable when the Fidalgo Castel Branco paid some money to the priest, 'adopted' him at the door of the church and took him home. Annu missed his home, his lame brother and Padre Simao Peres terribly and often he would be in tears thinking of them.

Annu had been adopted by Castel Branco no doubt, but in reality he was no better off than the family's slaves. The only difference was that Annu did all the household chores while the other slaves were sent out to work. They were not paid any money and their wages went directly to their master.

There was a tall, well-built Negro slave who accompanied Branco everywhere. Like a ferocious dog that attacks on its master's command, he often beat up people at Branco's bidding. He would also turn upon the household slaves, but fortunately Annu had never suffered at his hands.

There were four slave women in the household, one of whom was an elderly Negress. She was supposed to do the household chores, keep the other slave women in control and supply Branco and his twenty-two-year-old son with the slave women they desired at night.

There was another slave, a young girl of fifteen or so, who was tall and fair and rather thin. The innocence of childhood was reflected on her face as her delicate lips quivered and her eyes turned moist. Were they wet with tears or were they like that from birth was hard to tell. She was a bit wayward and couldn't understand the language spoken around her, so she was always making mistakes, and getting beaten by Branco's wife and the old Negress.

For the last few days Branco's son Anton had started coming home late. The other slaves told Branco's wife that he was visiting a prostitute much older than himself. Anticipating something like this, Branco's wife had bought this fifteen year old girl, Gorretti, for thirty cruzado at the Lilao market, almost a year ago. The girl had only a strip of cloth around her which barely covered her breasts and hips. An old woman at the market place had stuck a finger into the girl's vagina to certify that she was a virgin. Branco's wife told the old Negress to send Gorretti to Anton's bed.

When Gorretti first came into the household, no one knew her name. She didn't say a word to anyone. Konkani, Kannada, Gujarati and Marathi were the languages in use in Goapattana and most people knew a smattering of these. Gorretti probably spoke a dialect from the Gujarat–Mewar region, but she refused to open her mouth, no matter what language they addressed her in. Even when she was beaten up and blood poured from her mouth, she would remain silent. One day Branco got her baptized in church and she was christened Gorretti. Annu couldn't pronounce the word so he called her Gorey and when he said her name for the first time her eyes lit up and a faint smile appeared on her face.

It was only of late that she had begun to open up a bit and Annu had heard her utter a few words. He felt there was a sweetness to her words, a melody in her voice and he longed to hear her speak. One day when Gorey ran out to the back yard to chase a bird, the cloth covering her upper body fell away and Annu could see her tender, youthful breasts. The girl noticed him and quickly covered herself and ran into the house.

The old Negress pushed Gorretti into Branco's son's room that night. Annu always knew when this happened because Gorey was sullen and brooding the next day. Her eyes would lose their sparkle and her cheeks would be pale and wan. One day, as Gorey was drawing water from the well, the rope slipped out of her grasp shattering the earthen pot. Branco's wife lashed at the girl's bare back with a cane and the girl cried out in pain. Annu saw her sitting by the wood pile a little later, clutching the cloth to her chest. There was a huge blue black welt on her bare back. Annu reached out to touch the flaming mark when Gorey looked at him like a stricken doe and burst into tears.

Although it was more than a year since Gorey had come to the house, she and Annu had rarely spoken to each other openly until now. Everyone kept watch and if a man slave and a woman slave got into a relationship, they could be put to death. Annu had noticed that every time Gorey looked at him, her glance was full of love and entreaty. But they were helpless creatures confined in separate iron cages, the keys to which were with someone else.

One night Annu heard Gorretti shriek as though her heart would burst. There was the sound of a scuffle and then a door slammed. Annu realised what was going on. He felt suffocated with anger and frustration as he could hear sounds of someone being punched and bashed up. Fidalgo Castel Branco, in a drunken fit, had dragged Gorey to his bedroom but the girl had screamed and run out. Outraged that a slave was refusing to sleep with him, Branco kicked and pummelled her till she became a mass of bruised and bleeding flesh. Branco's wife watched, but didn't do anything, she did not even say a word.

A short while later the old Negress led Gorey by the hand to her bed. The girl lay there listlessly till she was overcome by sleep. Branco had emerged from his drunken stupor the next morning so he didn't bother with the girl any more but his wife came to check whether the slave she had bought for thirty cruzados was still alive. She told the other slaves to bathe her body in warm water and to feed her payz and meat soup.

Annu, who had been looking for a chance to see Gorey, came up to her that afternoon. She looked up at him with tenderness... This girl trusts me and hopes I will take care of her, Annu realized. All of a sudden her eyes filled with tears. 'Don't cry, Gorya, God is great. Padre Simao always said that if you have faith in Jesus everything becomes all right.'

'Take me out of this place. Let's run away. Tomorrow, when the first cock crows at dawn, come out here. Together we'll go over that hillock,' she said.

Annu stared at her. 'Have you been beyond that hillock?'

'Yes.'

'What's on the other side?'

'Villages. A river. Fields.'

A broad smile broke out on her face. Her pearly teeth, her rosy cheeks, her eyes that radiated such innocence, all of these added to the beauty of that smile.

'Will you be able to walk through forests and fields?' he asked.

'Yes. If you're with me.'

Annu was by her side very early the next morning as they set off towards the hillock. It was still very dark and they had no idea what the time was. Annu scrambled over a thorny hedge, then helped her across. There was thick vegetation all around. They disentangled themselves from the creepers and thorny undergrowth, and struggled up the slope. All they knew was that they would reach the top of the hill and get to the other side.

Gorey ached all over but she paid no attention to the pain as she clutched Annu's arm and climbed the slope. Their feet were bare, but they didn't pause to remove the thorns that pierced them. When, at last, they reached the top of the hill, they heard cocks crow in the distance. They started running down the slope.

'Can you do it?' Annu asked as Gorey stumbled and crashed into him.

'I will. When I fall, you can help me get up,' she said.

The whole area was awash in sunlight when they got to

the hillock near Adolshi, but nothing seemed to be stirring in the village. Had the whole village moved away? Then it hit Annu: Where was the temple that stood beside that peepal tree? Why was there nothing at that site? Annu held Gorey's hand and led her down the slope silently.

Annu didn't know that Adolshi was now a Christian village. He was very upset when he saw the mound of rubble where the temple once stood. They went to Padre Simao's shack only to find it had been burnt down. The temple had been destroyed, but the villagers were ploughing their fields and urging the oxen on as enthusiastically as they had done in the past. The women were gossiping as they drew water at the well and they could hear the sound of the hammer striking iron at the blacksmith's forge. Annu was amazed. How could the villagers be so indifferent? These were the same people who would not till or sow their fields without seeking the Lord's permission. The temple and the deity were gone, but the people seemed to be managing well enough! What winds of change were these that had struck the village!

Ventu Nayak's grandson, Hari, yelled, 'See! Annu's here! Where have you been, Annu? We've joined their religion. You can come back now!'

Annu's lame brother, Tangan, rushed up to him, 'Where were you, brother? We looked for you everywhere! Come home. No one will drive you away now.'

Some forty people had gathered in the courtyard by now. Annu felt close to all of them, now that they too were Christians. However, some people were getting nervous – the soldiers could come to the village looking for Annu. Branco had never asked Annu which village he belonged to. Most of the Portuguese settlers in Goapattana had no idea that there were myriad villages and settlements beyond the area they were familiar with. If they were to look for Annu, they would probably search the area by the sea and the river thinking that he might have escaped by boat. But Annu had spoken to the other slaves about Adolshi and told them about Padre Simao Peres.

Lavu Nayak's wife, Ubgey, passed a hand lightly over Gorey's back and chest and everyone stared admiringly at her fair skin, smooth as butter, and her small breasts with their rosy nipples. 'Annu, will you marry this girl?'

'I don't know, Mavshi. She asked me to take her away from that house, so we ran away.'

'Marry her. She seems a good girl.'

'If the soldiers come here, they'll create a lot of trouble. Annu should leave the village,' Bablo Nayak said.

'What can they do? We're all Christians now, if they touch us we can complain to the King. He will protect us. Annu, stay right here,' Puttu Nayak declared.

Old man Ventu laughed aloud. 'The King lives beyond the seven seas, we won't even see the nail on his finger or toe. It's his officials who make the rules here. They can chop your legs off or wring your neck and no one will ask any questions!'

Annu knew that it was a grave crime for a slave to run away. He had helped Gorey escape, so the soldiers would be looking for him and could descend on the village at any moment.

'I'm glad that I met all of you, I've been wanting to for a long time,' Annu said. 'But we must leave now. Ventu appa, what route should I take out of Goa?'

Ventu thought for a long while. 'They've taken control of

Sashti too, so don't cross the river and go there. Go towards Marcai, cut through the low-lying marshy areas. Avoid the Agashe port, the soldiers patrol that area,' he said.

Tangan rushed up and clung to Annu, 'Don't go. Don't leave your lame brother,' he cried.

'If the soldiers catch him, he'll be hanged to death. Let him go and find shelter somewhere. If it's possible, he'll come back some day,' Bablo Nayak said as he dragged Tangan away.

'May you complete what you have set out to do!' Ventu Nayak said, as Annu and Gorey took their leave. 'Live on roots and leaves if you must, but don't turn back. Settle down and farm some distant plot of land. Man doesn't die till Death comes looking for him. He can survive on water, if need be.'

Darkness had fallen when they reached Marcai, following the track beaten by the hooves of cows and oxen. A rivulet that had branched off from the main river cut across their path and disappeared into thick forests. There was not a living soul anywhere around. A small wooden raft was moored on the other bank, but no boatman responded to Annu's call.

Annu and Gorey sat down under a tree on the embankment. A strange fear settled coldly in their bellies and they huddled close together without saying a word. Foxes barked. Jackals howled. Swarms of insects buzzed about their heads. There was only the empty dome of the sky overhead and this strange wilderness that stretched boundlessly on all sides. Exhausted after the day's exploits, they soon fell asleep.

It was bright and sunny when they woke up the next morning. Two men, with dark, weather-beaten skins, were prodding at them with a long stick. 'Who are you? Creatures of the forest? How did you get here?' they asked.

Annu was scared. 'We worked as servants in a house in Goapattana. They were going to cut off our heads with a sword, so we ran away,' he blurted.

'Why?'

'They would molest this girl every day. I protested, so they beat me up. Then we ran away.'

The men looked at them pityingly. They took Annu and Gorey across the river and when Annu offered them some money, they refused.

'Go to Antu blacksmith's forge in Marcai and buy a sickle and a spade. If you have these two implements you can rule the earth,' one of them said.

'Brahmins who have fled across the hills from Veling have set up orchards in Pirval. They give a measure of rice and a coconut as payment for working on their land. Build a small shack and stay there,' the other man advised.

The path before them was very steep and full of stones, but Gorey rushed ahead like an excitable calf with the wind whistling in its ears. She looked back at the distance they had travelled and yelled, 'We're free, Annu, we're free! Wherever you go, I'll follow.'

The official of the Inquisition, accompanied by two soldiers, stood at Sukhdo's door the day after Jana Nayak lodged his complaint. He was dressed in formal robes with tongues of fire etched on his chest.

'Sukhdo Nayak has performed evil acts against the Christian faith. The senior officials of the Inquisition have ordered his arrest. He must come with me now. All his fields and orchards, his property and wealth now stand confiscated.

If he is proved innocent, everything will be returned. If he tries to resist or to escape, he will lose everything,' the man announced in loud, ringing tones.

Everyone in the house collapsed in fear. Sukhdo's wife, Mhalkum, wailed loudly, but there was no escape. Sukhdo wound a kerchief about his head and set off with the official. The two soldiers followed close behind.

Jana Nayak came to his door. 'I didn't do anything. I didn't complain. Their spies keep track of everything,' he protested feverishly.

No one lit a lamp in Sukhdo's house that evening. The family remained in darkness as though they had just buried a loved one, so intense was the sorrow and despair that hung over them all. The main root that went deep into the earth had been pulled out.

When it grew very dark, Ramkustha picked up a crowbar and slipped out of the house. He hid himself in the shadows by Jana Nayak's door. Ramkustha could hear Jana Nayak taking the names of Hindu deities and praying in low tones. Jana's son came to the door once, so did Jana's wife. She stood there for a while as though checking on what was happening in the neighbouring house.

Half an hour passed. Jana Nayak opened the door and stepped into the courtyard. Ramkustha brought the crowbar down on his head smashing his skull and the man fell to the ground with a loud thud. His wife ran to the door screaming. So did his sons. There were so many people in that settlement, yet no one rushed up to see what was wrong. They were scared after they saw Sukhdo being led away that afternoon, they didn't want any problems. But they were neighbours and kinsmen of the dead man. How long could they stay away?

Ramkustha flung the crowbar near Jana's courtyard and went home. He poured five measures of rice on to a piece of cloth and tied it up in a bundle. He took some money, tossed a blanket over his shoulder and led his wife Parvati out of the house.

'Tell everyone that I killed Jana Nayak. The crowbar lies somewhere near that courtyard. Blame me for everything, don't take any responsibility. I'm going out of Goa now, if we meet again ... so be it. I'll take a boat and sail along the coast to the Canara region,' he said to his brother.

People were wailing loudly and Jana's relatives were bustling about in the courtyard when Ramkustha set off. He was taking his family and going away forever, but no one in his house had the courage to express their sorrow or to step out and see him off.

It was very dark when they set out. Parvati slung a bundle of clothes on her shoulder and held her infant in her arms. Ramkustha had the bundle of rice on his head, a blanket was tossed over his shoulder and a sickle hung from his waistband. Suddenly they heard footsteps behind them.

'Who is it?'

'It's me, Vasu. Your brother. I'm coming with you.'

'But why? We have a house here. And fields.'

'Bappa has been taken away. None of this will remain. They'll grab everything.'

'What about our mother?'

'She won't live very long. Dado will bury her, she can't be cremated, can she?'

'And what about our Dado?'

'There's poison spreading all over this village. Dado won't stay here after he's buried our mother, he'll also move away.'

Ramkustha was amazed at Vasu's train of thought.

'Let him come along,' Parvati said, and the three set off into the darkness. They would cut through unfamiliar regions, moving to an unfamiliar destination. Home would now be the spot where their boat finally touched the shore.

Rudra Shenai returned to the village with his two young sons, four months after they had left it. His wife, Sumitra, had been with them at that time, but she wasn't with them now. They had left the village hoping to protect their gods and their faith. Why had they returned?

He got home at sunset and squatted on the verandah along with his sons. Rudra, who had always been plump and flushed of face was stooped and emaciated. The skin on his face had turned dark and hung in loose folds, and he had a straggly beard. The boys had become like sticks, and threatened to topple over at the slightest push. The elder boy, sixteen-year-old Sada, and the younger one, twelve-year-old Nanda, had been such robust youngsters. They now looked as though their flesh and blood had melted away.

Devrai Shenai came up to them, dragging his lame foot. 'Rudra, what a state you're in! Where's Sumitri?' he asked.

Rudra's eyes welled with tears.

'Gone. Freed of all troubles. Believed that the flowers she placed on her gods would remain fresh, always. How would she have accepted this?'

Devrai couldn't bear to ask anything more. He realized that Rudra had been duped and deceived and was now in a pathetic state. He'd been cheated there where he had gone, and here in his home as well. During the last four months,

Krishna Shenai on the one hand and Mungru Shenai on the other had shifted the boundary stones of his orchard so that only a narrow strip was left. His fields had also been taken over by others. If he tried to protest, they would fight with him.

'I would get you some food from my house, but I'm a Christian now. My hands and feet are the same, so are the pupils of my eyes. Now that I'm a Christian, has my lame foot become whole, or have those who didn't convert, become lame? Nothing has changed. Yet we've stopped sitting side by side and sharing each other's food. Our touch will defile a Hindu's meal now. Madness!' he exclaimed.

Devrai called his son and asked him to pluck some tender coconuts from the palm near Rudra's house. Rudra's elder son removed the husk from the nuts and made a hole in the shell. The two boys drank the water. Rudra remembered that there was some liquid jaggery in an earthen pot in the house. He opened the door, but it was very dark and the smell of cobwebs and cockroaches filled the air.

'Devrai, will you give me a little light?' he asked.

Devrai sent his son home to fetch a live coal. Rudra lit some palm fronds to make a torch and carried it into the house. The farming tools and implements that they had stored in the house were missing. So were the wicker baskets, storage jars and reed mats, but the earthen pots in the kitchen were in place. Sumitri used to smear dung on the floor and walls and keep the house neat and clean, what a mess it was now. This house would never be the same again.

He picked up the pot of jaggery and returned to the verandah. They scooped out the tender flesh of the coconuts and ate it with the liquid jaggery. Devrai stared at them closely. They are like three hungry ghosts, he thought. He was overcome with pity, but he was angry too.

'Why don't you tell us what happened? You're a Brahmin, from a respected family. How did you get to this miserable state?' he asked.

Rudra looked at Devrai with tears in his eyes, and began his tale—

Rudra Shenai and Subrai Shenai moved from village to village in bullock carts or on foot. Whenever they stopped to rest awhile, they would be confronted by strangers who would silently wave them on.

'Your village is so cool and fertile. Let us have a small patch of land so that we may stay here with our gods,' they pleaded with an old Brahmin when they got to Borye village.

'Why did you bring your gods? You should have immersed them in some river or lake. There's no place for people in these parts, where will you find space for them?'

'Don't say that. We left our village to save our gods.'

'The villagers have decided that no new gods and no strangers will be allowed to settle here. Take pity on a man and offer him a seat and soon enough he picks up the wooden seat and knocks you down! Give a stranger a foot of land, and then he wants a yard and soon he wants to take over the whole village!'

The old man pointed to four houses on the hill. 'Three years ago they came here like beggars. The villagers took pity on them and let them stay. Now they've sprouted horns! The lake dries up in Chaitra and we don't have enough water for our orchards. We tell them not to use this water but they're ready to fight. They refuse to do any work in the village, yet they want to use our facilities!' he ranted.

'We are Saraswat Brahmins from Adolshi village. We enjoyed honour and prestige and owned fertile fields and orchards, but now we're reduced to this state. Who knows, we might be descendants of some common ancestor…' Subrai Shenai suggested.

'These are difficult times. A brother doesn't recognize a brother,' the old man turned away.

Rudra and Subrai Shenai hired two Kunbi porters and the little group set off on foot through the forest towards Shirvade. They spent the night in someone's outhouse where they cooked a meal. It was eighteen days since they'd left home, but they had not found a place to stay. They had a bit of money and some gold ornaments, but they needed a place for their gods, to build a home for themselves, to settle down.

The Kunbi porters took them to Giri Kamat's house in Shirvade. 'People say that Giri Bhatkar has fed so many people and given away so much land that his property, which was as extensive as a kingdom, has disappeared,' the porters told them.

Subrai Shenai and Rudra Shenai told Giri Kamat their story and begged for a plot of land for themselves and their gods.

'You have come here with your gods. I've given so much land to people, how can I refuse the gods? I give you thirty feet of land on the eastern flank, near the mango tree,' he declared.

Suddenly his wife emerged from behind the door. She was a tall, slim and beautiful woman, like a golden goddess. 'I want half that land,' she said.

'But Narmada, I have just given them that stretch.'

'I want half that stretch.'

'But…'

'If you don't give it to me I will go out and beg on the street,' she threatened.

Kamat remained silent for a while. He called a labourer and told him, 'Take these people to the eastern flank of the orchard near the mango tree and measure out thirty feet of land. Let them use fifteen feet and mark out fifteen feet to be given as alms to my wife.'

The worker seemed quite amused as he led the group into the orchard. He was a short man and his hands and legs were like small plantain stems. He cut off a length of stick as long as his arm to serve as a measure of length and marked out thirty feet of land from the mango tree. He turned around at that point and walked back fifteen feet. He stuck a pole into the ground and told them that this strip of land was theirs. He would return the next day and set boundary stones into the ground.

Rudra Shenai looked at the narrow strip with four coconut palms, two mango trees and a bhinna tree with its sweet and sour berries, wondering how they would all live there with their gods.

'We asked for a meal and we've been given such a small portion that no one can fill his stomach. How can two families live here after building a shrine for the gods? We had such large orchards in our village, yet we weren't satisfied. Two families can't stay here,' Subrai declared finally.

Rudra was filled with worry, what was Subrai trying to say? The Kunbi porters cleared the undergrowth and erected a small shack. Subrai Shenai took a dip in the lake and prayed aloud. He turned the idol around so that it faced east and set it down on the ground. But there was no sense of joy in it. Only, a pall of worry and gloom hung over them.

Rudra and Subrai seemed to have fallen out after reaching this spot. They didn't speak freely to each other and when they did, their words were strained and terse. They'd stood by each other during the troubles faced over the last eighteen days, what had happened to them now?

'Let us build two small shacks in the space that remains and get on with our lives. We'll have problems of space. But we can accept that, like oxen who live side by side in their sheds,' Rudra suggested.

'It's such a tiny strip of land. A corpse can't be laid out crosswise and cremated on this patch of land, how can two families live here?' Subrai demanded.

'But Giri Kamat gave the land to both of us.'

'He didn't give it to us. He gave it to the gods. And it isn't enough for the gods, either.'

'Where else can we go? Do we even have the strength to move on?'

'What strength are you talking about? I'm ten years older than you are, yet I travelled all this way. I'll stay here with the gods and perform all the rituals. I'll invite those of you who move on as well as those who've stayed behind in our village to attend the Lord's festivals.'

'What are you talking about, Subrai tato, the deity belongs to both of us. We both have a stake on this land. I'm not going anywhere.'

'Our families and our descendants will fight over this strip of land if you stay here. Move on, Rudra. Settle down somewhere else.'

'Where will I go with my wife and children? This is the last stop. God will solve our problem,' Rudra said.

Subrai raised his voice. 'I tell you, there isn't enough space. We'll be quarrelling over the gods too, at this rate.'

Rudra was taken aback. Subrai tato was a good-natured man, why was he talking like this today? Rudra himself was rather diffident by nature. He took care not to get into arguments or fights. His wife, too, was a soft-hearted, calm and god-fearing woman and he became more mild and quiet in her company.

Rudra went into the forest the next morning and cut four long bamboo poles which he set down on one side of the strip of land. Subrai rushed there in an agitated state and tossed the bamboo poles away, 'Didn't I say two shacks can't be built on this strip? Go away! At once! Or I'll beat you with a stick and drive you away,' he shouted.

Suddenly Rudra's wife, Sumitra, jumped into the fray. She didn't bother about Subrai's age and used the choicest abuses that she could think of as she cursed him and prayed for his death. Subrai responded by casting aspersions on her character and her devotion to her gods. The curses and foul words that flew back and forth filled the air with fear. It was as though the gods had forsaken the world and the great Flood would destroy the earth!

Rudra was overcome with rage. He picked up their belongings and set off with his family. 'May your children die, may you be reduced to ashes,' he cursed. 'I shall never set eyes on your face again. Nor will I pray to the gods you worship!'

Rudra hired a bullock cart and set off with his family for Sange, which lay on the road to Panchvadi. The cart driver was an old man, but he knew all the routes and was familiar with the region.

'Take us to some clearing in the forest where we can find water, and we'll settle there,' Rudra said.

'A man cannot live alone in the forest. These are difficult times and each village guards its borders, no strangers can move in.'

'When your own kinsman turns on you with a stick and drives you away, what can you expect from strangers?' Rudra's voice choked and tears ran down his cheeks.

'We'll look for a clearing amongst the trees. Once you set stakes into the ground and build a shack, the villagers will begin to accept you,' the cart driver said as he listened to Rudra's story.

It was late in the evening when they stopped by a broken temple that lay open to the sky. There was an old well close by. They carried the box and bundles into the temple. Rudra set up a hearth with three stones and lit a fire and Sumitra cooked some payz.

There was an upright stone idol amongst the ruins where the family settled down for the night. The children lay in the middle with their parents on either side. The driver tied the bullocks to a tree and lay down outside. Rudra was full of despair, and worries about the future kept him awake for a long while.

It was almost midnight and the whole area was dark and still except for the drone of insects that cut through the darkness like a saw. A flaming torch appeared in the distance. Footsteps rang out and the bullocks scrambled to their feet, lowing in alarm.

'Who's there? Who is it?' the driver called as four men barged into the temple. 'Stop! Stop! These are travellers from distant places,' he protested, but they shoved him aside. Rudra,

Sumitra and the boys huddled on one side, too terrified to scream. As the men picked up the box and bundles, Rudra shouted, 'Stop! That's all we possess, unfortunate people that we are!' But he didn't move from where he stood.

When Sumitra realized that they were taking the bundle that contained her household deities, she rushed after them, crying in protest. It was then that one of the men picked her up and began to run. 'Let me go! I'm a mother of three children. A mother! Give me my gods!' she screamed. Who knows what passed through the man's mind, for he suddenly flung her down in the undergrowth and ran away.

Rudra came up to where Sumitra lay, bruised and shaken, weeping bitterly about how they'd taken away her gods, how they'd touched her and made her impure. She sat awake all night, refusing to say a word, but as dawn broke she wailed, 'They've taken my gods. They set hands on me! Lord, see how we suffer even as You look on!'

Rudra was a shattered man. 'Who were those vandals, why did they loot us?' he asked the driver.

'Who knows who they were? So many strangers have come here since the unrest began in Goa. The Portuguese drove the Moors and other Muslims out. Some moved on, others remain scattered in these parts. They might be slaves who have run away from Goa. Or people who have fled their homes to escape conversion. They might even be locals hoping to shift the blame on the wayfarers.'

'Were they Moors or Muslims?' Sumitra asked.

'Who knows?'

'What was their caste? Their religion?'

'No one can tell.'

Rudra and the driver fell asleep after a while, but Sumitra

sat there silently. She was a slim, fair woman but the exertions of the last twenty days seemed to have broken her completely. The blood seemed to have drained from her fair skin making her look like a doll of cotton-wool. She got up quietly and walked to the well, which was just a hollow in the ground filled with water. She sat for a while on the edge with her feet touching the water. Overcome by a deep desire for death, she slid in. There was just a plop … like a pot entering the water. No one was jolted awake.

Samba Savke was the chief gaonkar of Talavali village and owned many orchards and fields. The next morning, the driver rushed to him with the sad news. Savke and a few villagers helped to retrieve the body and perform the last rites.

'You are a Brahmin, I am a Khatri, so you will not accept my hospitality. There is a little shack in my orchard where you can stay for some time. I will send some rice, a coconut and some vegetables every day. Your elder son lit the funeral pyre. I will send the priest to the shack. Have him perform the funeral rites. Let me know if you need anything,' he said to Rudra.

Samba Savke had a younger brother who supervised the work in the fields and orchards. He could see with one eye and the white eyeball that seemed to bulge out of the other socket made him look very ugly. One day, he summoned Rudra and the boys and asked them to work in the fields. 'It's been more than a month now. How long will you sit back and enjoy the free food?' he said.

Rudra was feeling uncomfortable about accepting Savke's hospitality, but the thought of working like a labourer upset him deeply. Yet he picked up the spade and built ridges around the coconut palms and shovelled the mud. His sons gathered dry palm fronds and coconuts that had fallen from the trees.

Two months passed in this manner. One day, a servant saw Rudra's sons eating sugarcane in the fields and complained to Savke's brother. It was considered inauspicious to eat the cane before the harvest rituals were performed. The man lashed out at the boys, 'We follow strict rules and rituals here, we will not tolerate thieves!' he yelled.

Rudra Shenai grew very agitated at this. I slog in people's fields even though I am a Brahmin. My sons are beaten up. We cannot stay here and get insulted any longer. We left our village for the sake of our gods and our faith, but God and religion are mere concepts, they don't help us fill our bellies. What difference does it make whether one bathes in a well or in a lake? Why did Sumitra have to die? She worshipped those idols so fervently, did they display any special powers? These gods are responsible for our state, I want no more of them!

He got up early the next morning and went to Samba Savke. 'I cannot repay you for all that you have done, you have saved our lives. But I must go back to my village,' he said.

'You want to return to your village? You can't practise our faith there, I'm told.'

'If we are to suffer more, we'll suffer in our own village. God and religion are important as long as one has food in one's belly. Accepting their religion is better than this life!'

Samba Savke was silent for a while. 'Go. Go back. Each man is a king only in his own village.' He went into the house and came back with twelve xerafins which he gave Rudra Shenai.

It was over a year since the temple had been razed, but no church had been built as yet. Small wood and bamboo shacks with thatched roofs served as churches in the neighbouring villages, but Padre Colaso wanted to build a strong edifice with stone slabs and mortar and a tiled roof. He believed that the church would not have any sanctity if it were built with the wood and stone from the heathen temple. So, he went to meet the Archbishop accompanied by the chief gaonkar, Ranu Kenkre, now Henrik Kaisuro.

'The village will bear half the cost of building the church. With the income from the community fields, the free labour provided by the villagers, and help from you, it can be done,' he told the Archbishop.

'You must get permission from the King of Portugal as well as the viceroy if you want to build a permanent structure,' the Archbishop said. 'The new viceroy, Anton Noronha, is favourably inclined towards us. I will write to him. Take the letter and meet him, along with the chief gaonkar. Say that the villagers of Adolshi want to build a church. Request him to grant some funds.'

They took the letter and went to meet the viceroy. All Ranu Kenkre wanted was to safeguard the interests of the village. Everything had changed so quickly and suddenly he'd become responsible for the village and its welfare.

'You needn't have destroyed the Ramnath temple,' he said to Padre Colaso one day. 'Nilu Nayak had taken the deity away. You could have installed a statue of Jesus and set up a cross right there.'

'You won't understand all that, Kaisuro.'

'What difference would it have made, temple or church? Both are mere structures, four walls and a roof.'

'You won't understand.'

Viceroy Constantin Braganza had returned to Portugal and Anton Noronha had taken his place in Goa. Noronha spoke to them warmly and asked them to sit down. When he heard that Kenkre was the mhal gaonkar, he patted Ranu's shoulder and said, 'The village administration in Goa, and those who conduct it are looked upon with respect all over the world. We have always supported this system, and we shall continue to do so.'

Padre Colaso outlined the proposal for the church and gave him the Archbishop's letter. 'We cannot hope for success without your support. The villagers will do all they can, but we need funds. We request you to carry this plea to the King.'

The viceroy smiled at them. Enthusiastically, he said, 'By the grace of Lord Jesus, the Goan islands, Sashti and Bardez have become Christian localities. Each village needs a church, but this cannot happen so fast. It will take time. We are building large churches in Salgao, Mathgao and Raichur at the moment. Adolshi will get its own church some day. Why don't you use the wooden beams and stone slabs from the old temple to build a temporary structure for now? Thatch the roof with palm fronds. Celebrate Mass and offer prayers. Spread the message of our faith, let it grow strong. Go back to your village and get to work. I'll carry glowing reports about you to the religious assembly and to the King.'

They returned to Adolshi and sent soldiers from door to door asking the villagers to report for work the next day. Those who didn't come of their own accord were threatened and forced to turn up.

Ventu Nayak picked up a stone slab and balanced it on his head. 'If this is all you wanted to do, why did you pull the temple down? You could have placed your gods inside.

Change the ornaments, remove the nath and put on a mokan, but the nose is the same! Utter madness!' he fumed.

The church was ready in eight days. Four walls as high as a man's chest, and a roof of wooden beams thatched with hay and palm fronds. The floor was made of red mud beaten and smoothened. Someone suggested that it be plastered with a coat of dung, but Padre Colaso opposed the idea. 'Those who sing praises of the cow and her urine and dung are heathens. We don't want them here,' he said.

The padre went to Goapattana along with two villagers and brought a large cross and some wooden statues. One was of Jesus nailed to the cross. There was one of infant Jesus, another of Mother Mary and there were a few angels as well. They also bought a table, two bells and a staff. The money was drawn from the village funds. All the temple employees were now employed by the church. This included the musicians who played the drums and the pipes and the devleen who swept and cleaned the place. There were some artisans who made decorations and there were others who tended the oil lamps and carried the flaming torches in processions. Those who had been granted tracts of temple land in lieu of services rendered to the temple were allowed to keep those tracts. They would merely offer their services to the church.

Padre Colaso was looking for a smart, young boy to assist him in his duties and so he thought of Venkat, the bhat's son.

'His father was the priest in the temple,' Kusha Nayak protested, but Padre Colaso merely smiled.

'Rayanna Bhat wanted to make the boy a priest and let him serve as a padre in the church. That's why he became a Christian along with his son. Let's give him some work in the church now.'

Padre Colaso sent a soldier to summon the bhat. His wife came along too. Though the family had become Christians and Rayanna was now Martin Barrett and his son was Vincent Barrett, everyone still referred to him as the bhat.

'I'll give your son a job in the church,' Padre Colaso told the man. 'He'll have to do whatever I ask him to. He must ring a bell and carry information about a Mass or a feast or a death all over the village. He must ring the church bells every morning and evening. He'll be paid from the church funds and it will be enough to keep his belly filled,' the priest said.

'You'll go back to your home across the ocean some day. The temple belonged to us, the church is ours today. It's like dying and being born again, why did we ever resent that death! Let our family be in charge of all the rituals in the church, like we used to be in the temple. We'll manage as best as we can…' the bhat urged.

Padre Colaso smiled. 'The church will certainly be yours some day. The King of Portugal will come and present it to you himself. You will be carried around in a decorated palanquin and eat on golden plates after that. But right now there's only this job that's available. If you don't want it, say so. You can hitch up your loincloth and go and wallow in the muddy fields.'

Padre Colaso gave Vincent a small bell and sent him around the village. 'Go to each settlement and tell the people that the first Mass will be celebrated in the new church on Sunday morning. Everyone must be fully dressed when they come for the ceremony. The padre will not come to your settlement any longer, you must come to the church.'

There were some thirty or forty prison cells in a row. Padre Simao Peres knew that some wretched prisoner was locked up in the cell next to his own, but he couldn't see the man. All he could see were the high walls. When the iron gate of the cell was opened, he could see a bit of the outside world, but there too, he could see only walls. Who built these walls? Who felt the need for these structures that have caused so much sorrow in this world? He yearned to demolish all walls, external and internal – walls that confined him unjustly to a fate like death. How free and beautiful was the life outside!

The prisoner in the adjoining cell had been moaning continuously for the last four days. It sounded like the groans of a dying man though Simao Peres couldn't see him. The attendant who brought the prisoner's meals often yelled at him, but the man said nothing, merely continued to moan … He died one day and his body was taken out of his cell and placed beside the wall. Simao Peres could see it clearly through the iron bars of the gate … a bony ribcage, hip bones sticking out, a skull with two sunken eye sockets … a heap of bones.

A tremor ran through the priest. My body is also turning into a pile of bones. Death approaches me too, he thought, clawing fiercely at his own flesh as he collapsed by the gate of his cell. Why did they arrest that wretched creature, did he refuse to add salt to the rice boiling in the pot or did he water the tulsi plant in the courtyard? Did he celebrate his daughter's engagement with Hindu rituals? Did he refuse to eat cow flesh or did he fast during an eclipse? They will dig out these bones from his grave and burn them, as punishment, on the Day of Judgement.

The last rites for the dead man would be neither Christian nor Hindu nor Jewish, a funeral sanctioned by no known faith. Was this freedom? He would get no Mass, no Christian burial rites because he was a traitor who had betrayed the Christian faith. His soul would remain restless without religious sanction, this death was like the death of an animal!

A wave of hopelessness and profound sorrow washed over Simao Peres when they carried the corpse away and he began to rant, 'Burn me to death! I'll come back to life, like Jesus. I trudged all the way from the Vatican to Adolshi bearing the weight of the cross. Jesus's crown of thorns is embedded in my heart … I'll break out of this prison and carry His teachings all over the world…'

The guard rushed to the cell and smote him with his stick forcing him to be silent. The priest buried his head between his knees and began to weep soundlessly.

In a short while, the door opened and the prison warden appeared. 'It's been three months since you came here. You will appear before the Holy Inquisition for the first hearing now.' Simao Peres dried his eyes and straightened his clothes. The warden marched ahead, followed by Simao Peres with two guards behind him. The priest walked slowly and his footsteps faltered as they moved towards the main hall. He'd been tall and well-built, but now his flesh hung loosely from his bones.

They walked down the long verandah past innumerable little cells till they reached a large door. The warden ushered him into a hall and retreated with the guards. Everything was quiet and peaceful as the sounds from the prison cells did not carry into this place. The grave and solemn atmosphere frightened the priest. He felt as though a naked sword hovered over his head.

There was a large crucifix, ten feet tall, on the wall. In

front of it was a big table around which were several chairs with arms, a few stools and a bench. The Chief Inquisitor and his Deputy sat on the chairs and a secretary sat on a stool nearby. There were two lawyers too, one would advise the officials of the Inquisition while the other would represent the accused. Not a muscle twitched on their faces. They sat there as though carved in stone. The Chief Inquisitor, with his bulging cheeks, broad forehead and clear, dark eyes must have been quite humane and kind-hearted in the past. Perhaps it was his role as the head of this draconian institution that forced him to adopt a cruel, merciless mask. His assistant was a Dominican priest with sagging cheeks and sunken grey eyes.

'You must bow down before the Holy assembly gathered here,' the secretary said, as Simao Peres approached the large table. When Simao made no move to do so, the secretary got up from his seat and said in a louder tone, 'It is your duty to bow down before this Holy assembly.'

The priest raised his eyes to the large crucifix, went down on his knees and made the sign of the cross on his breast. When he identified himself as Padre Simao Peres, the Chief Inquisitor, Padre Alex Dias Falcao, was quick to retort, 'You must not refer to yourself as a Christian priest any longer. You have been stripped of your priesthood for performing acts that go against the faith. You can call yourself a priest only if you are proved innocent.'

The officials asked him the name of the church in which he was baptized. They enquired whether he had received a list of the possessions that had been confiscated from his shack at the time of his arrest.

'I had no possessions. I worked selflessly for the Christian faith. I slept on a length of sack cloth and used a stone as a pillow, like Padre Francis Xavier did,' he said.

The Chief Inquisitor was furious. 'Don't take Francis Xavier's name! You are a sinner and have betrayed our faith.'

Everyone remained quiet for a while.

'Did you resist the officials when they came to arrest you? Did you ask Tomas, the new convert who was deputed to protect you, to attack them with his sword?'

'No. It was his job to protect me. He did what he thought was right. Perhaps he was wrong. I believe he was wrong.'

'Do you know the charges you face and the reason you have been thrown into prison?' the Chief Inquisitor asked.

'No.'

'You have spoken disrespectfully about the Holy Cross, the sacred emblem of Christianity. You have said that the cross on the hill was merely a stone structure, that there was nothing sacred about it. You condoned that vile act. We have examined the witnesses who testified against you.'

'Who are these witnesses? Why don't they appear before me?'

'We are not bound to give you their names. Nor will they appear before you. The onus is on you to prove that you are innocent and have committed no crime. Is there anyone who will testify on your behalf?'

'No. I will speak for myself. They have twisted my words and created this confusion. All I said was that the cross could be erected again.'

The Inquisitor's assistant intervened all of a sudden, 'Did you criticize that act of destruction?' he asked.

Simao Peres remained silent for a long while. 'They are foolish, uneducated people. They know not what they do.

We should have forgiven them and continued with our task of spreading our faith.'

'That doesn't mean that you are innocent,' the Chief Inquisitor declared.

Simao Peres was irritated. 'I'm not a Portuguese citizen. Nor am I a new convert. I belong to the Vatican state and have been sent here by the Pope. Send me back to the Vatican. Let the Pope judge my actions,' he said.

'You have committed the crime within the jurisdiction of this Inquisition and we shall deliver judgement. Do you plead guilty or do you not?'

'No. I have done nothing wrong.'

The lawyer who was appointed on his behalf stood up and spoke in a grave tone. 'I cross-examined the witnesses who testified against you, but I couldn't prove that they were wrong. Take my advice. If you don't want to be burnt at the stake on the Day of Judgement, plead guilty and go free. This Holy assembly will give you another chance to live like a good Christian.'

Simao Peres stared at the man who was supposed to protect his interests. 'I have committed no crime. I am a God-fearing, religious person who tries to keep away from sin. How can I make a false confession?' he asked.

'We don't send Europeans who have been accused of crimes to the special confession rooms. They are wise and educated so we expect them to confess of their own free will. We encourage them to confess and beg pardon and swear that they will be good Christians in future,' the Chief Inquisitor declared.

Simao Peres remained silent, but his eyes filled with tears.

'Think about this. You will get a chance to confess and

plead guilty at the next hearing. If you don't, you will be sent to the special confession room. If you confess and beg pardon you will not be burnt to death. You will get a lighter sentence, but your crime will have to be punished,' the Inquisitor said.

Simao Peres seemed to be talking to himself. 'I have nothing to say about the Inquisition ... but this Christian faith that was taught by Lord Jesus ... is a religion based on love and compassion and forgiveness. Jesus was a sea of compassion. If you believe in the Bible and the teachings of Jesus, how can you condemn people to be burnt to death?' he asked.

The Inquisitor didn't bother to reply. He rang the silver bell violently and ordered the guards to take Simao away.

Simao went down on his knees again and made the sign of the cross. 'Jesus will come down to earth again. Not for my sake, but for yours,' he said as he was led away.

A month passed and Simao was full of despair. He couldn't sleep, nor could he make any sense of this degraded existence. There was such a vast, beautiful universe beyond these walls, but he was confined to this tiny dark cell, condemned to a life without conversation or laughter or tears! He yearned to put an end to his life, but lacked the means to do so. He tried to starve to death by throwing his food into the commode in his cell. When the man who emptied the contents discovered this after three days, he was forced to abandon this plan. The guards began to stand before him threateningly, forcing him to eat.

A stream of gibberish emerged from Simao's mouth these days. Sometimes he'd mutter incoherently as though talking to himself and sometimes his booming voice would attract the attention of the guard. He'd peer through narrowed eyes as the guard rapped on the bars of the cell and asked him to quieten down.

The special confession room, where prisoners were tortured and forced to confess, lay to the west of his cell. The officials of the Inquisition followed a complex set of rules that determined whether the prisoner would be coerced by using fire or water or brutally tugged with ropes to force out their confession. A secretary would record every word that the prisoner uttered, a doctor would monitor the prisoner's health and his capacity to withstand these measures and a priest would oversee all these operations.

The screams of prisoners being tortured in the special confession rooms grew louder as the Day of Judgement approached. Simao Peres's heart grew heavy with sorrow and pity for these unfortunate souls. A woman's heart-rending screams resounded in his ears…

They had tied a woman to a sloping wooden plank so that her head hung down and her legs were above. There was not a scrap of clothing on her body and her forearms had been scratched with red hot nails. As the guards tugged at the rough coir rope that bound her, it bit deep into the gashes on her arms and made her scream in pain…

'Tell the truth!' the priest in the torture chamber barked, as the guard tugged the rope once more through her wounded flesh.

'I can't bear this, Deva! Let me go … I've told you everything … I'll say what you want…'

'Tell the truth!' the priest said again. The guard did what he had to.

'Deva saiba, they're killing me! Let me go … Yes, I've

committed a crime. I've done everything that the witness says I've done … just release me, now…'

'Tell the truth. Say what you've done.'

The guard looped another coil of rope about her body.

'Saiba, tell me what I'm supposed to say. I can't remember anything, tell me and I'll say it. Aavayyy … mother … I'm going to die!'

'Tell the truth! Confess that you fasted on ekadasi and offered food to the cow on a plantain leaf the next day!'

'Saiba, tell them to loosen these ropes … I'm not well … I'll die here … I can't remember anything, if the witness says I did it, it must be true. I have told you all that I know, what more can I say?'

'You must tell the truth. You must confess to everything.'

'I don't know what to say. You tell me, and I'll say that. My father observed the ekadasi fast and I did the same from a young age. Don't know when I stopped doing that … can't remember anything…'

The coir rope dug deep into her wounds and she writhed in agony. 'Lord, release me, I'll tell you everything. I'll bear false witness against myself…'

The priest merely said, 'Tell the truth!' and ordered the guard to tug at the rope.

'Can't bear this, Lord, I haven't done anything wrong … what will I tell you? Take pity on me and my children … Let me go … all right I'll tell the truth. I fasted. I didn't even drink water that day I prayed to the Hindu gods. I offered food to the cow … may that cow die and may I die too!'

'Don't make false confessions. Tell the truth!' The rope passed through the torn flesh once more.

'My head spins. Let me go. I'll tell you everything, I've gone against the law...'

'What law? Tell the truth.'

'Whatever the witness has said. He's my brother-in-law. He wanted me to take my children and go away to my parents' house. He's done the right thing. He's told you the truth. Release me. My arms will be ripped out...'

A doctor, who sat on a stool in one corner, called out for water. A servant brought a small pot of water and poured it over her head. The water splashed into her nose and mouth and she gasped for breath. As the rope cut into her wounds she called out for mercy, 'I'm a sinner. I'm guilty. I'll bear witness against myself. Burn me to death but let me go now!' The woman's voice grew faint and then fell silent as her head hung down from the plank. The doctor examined her and declared that she wouldn't be able to bear any more pain. He told them to put some clothes on her body and to take down what she had said as her final confession. He then smeared some ointment on her wounds.

Padre Simao Peres had been listening to her agonized screams for a long while. He couldn't make out what she said, but the pain in that voice wrenched his heart. When he couldn't bear it any longer, he lay down on his mat clutching his knees close to his chest.

It was four days after this incident that Padre Simao Peres was summoned to the Holy assembly yet again.

'One of the witnesses appearing against you has expressed doubts over your credentials as a Christian priest. Where did you receive your training? Who inducted you formally into priesthood?' the Chief Inquisitor asked.

'I studied at St Paul's Seminary at the Vatican for three

years. I was inducted as a priest at that same church,' Simao Peres replied.

'Who bestowed his blessings on you? Who officiated at that ceremony?'

'I feel insulted that I have to explain all this merely because someone doubts my credentials. But I will tell you. The first Mass was conducted by the Vicar of St Paul's Church, Gabriel Oliver. The Archbishop of the Vatican, James Brodic, delivered the blessings. The secretary of the Holy Pope brought the new robes. Every priest who has studied at the Vatican feels proud that the Holy Father has had a hand in his development.'

'Who were your fellow students at St Paul's seminary?'

'Seven of us received the orders of priesthood at that time. Padre Joshua Paz and Padre Francois Abbe were drowned when their ship sank on the way to Africa. I don't know where the others are.'

'What is the Fifth Commandment that Jesus promulgated so that men would live a life of righteousness?'

'Thou shalt not commit falsehood.'

'And what punishment did He mark out for those who broke this rule?'

'Jesus did not mark any punishment.'

'He didn't. That's why people have begun to betray their religion. They get baptized and swear to be good Christians, and then they commit falsehood and betray the Christian faith. They continue to practise the rituals of the Jewish or the Hindu faith. It is to counter such betrayal that we have established the Inquisition. We propagate the teachings of Jesus, we carry out His holy work.'

Padre Simao Peres said in a low but firm voice, 'Jesus

didn't declare any punishment because He chose to forgive. He believed that love and compassion could win over Satan, too.'

'Are you saying that we don't believe in Jesus, that we don't follow the teachings in the Bible?'

'No. But…'

The Chief Inquisitor didn't let him proceed. 'Do you criticize the Inquisition? Don't you have faith in it?' he asked.

Padre Simao Peres remained silent for a while. 'I agree that you are religious, that you are devoted to the Christian faith … But…'

The Chief Inquisitor raised his hand and cut him off. He rang the silver bell violently and summoned the guards. 'Your punishment will be declared on the Day of Judgement, before the procession sets out. It is up to you to decide whether you will confess to your crime and ask for pardon,' he said.

Padre Simao Peres was very upset that these people had cast aspersions on his priesthood. The dark prison cell and the humiliation he was being subjected to depressed him. To be condemned to death by burning when he had committed no crime … maybe it made sense to throw himself at their feet and beg for pardon.

One day, the prison guard came to his cell along with the lawyer who had been engaged on his behalf. 'Are you aware that I'm supposed to defend you and give you protection according to the law?' he asked.

'Jesus will protect me. I don't trust you. You are on their side. You want to confuse me and have me burnt to death,' Simao Peres said angrily.

'The Inquisition proceeds according to a framework of rules and it delivers justice,' the lawyer replied.

'I'm innocent. Yet they've locked me here to rot in jail. What justice are you talking about?'

'The Holy assembly of the Inquisition can also be merciful. The sixth of December is the Day of Judgement when those who have been found guilty will be burnt to death. If you do not plead guilty and beg pardon, you will also share their fate. But if you confess of your own accord, you will get a lighter sentence,' the lawyer told him.

Simao Peres felt himself shivering violently. 'Yes, yes! I'm guilty. I broke that cross. I said that it was merely a stone structure, I said there was nothing holy about it. I'll throw myself at the Chief Inquisitor's feet and beg his pardon!' he screamed. The priest fell to his knees and raised his arms in supplication, 'Jesus, my Lord! Why should I die when I have committed no crime? You are my witness, I shall ask for pardon in your name,' he cried.

'Jesus will guide you and you will emerge from your troubles,' the lawyer said as he moved away. The prison guard didn't utter a word, he merely stood there like a mute witness to the scene.

They summoned him to the Holy assembly on the third day. The priest was weak and listless, the light had gone out of his eyes. He sank to his knees and made the sign of the cross before taking his place on the bench.

'Do you confess to your crime against your religion?' the Chief Inquisitor asked.

Simao Peres nodded his head but the Inquisitor told him to speak up.

'Do you confess to all the crimes?'

'Yes.'

'Did you commit these crimes consciously?'

'Yes.'

'Do you make this confession of your own free will?'

'Yes.'

'Did you commit these crimes because you have no faith in the Christian religion?'

'I believed in Christianity in the early years. I do so, today. My faith wavered in between.'

'Do you accept the testimony of all the witnesses, and also your own confession, as the truth?'

'Yes.'

'Describe the crimes you have committed against Christianity.'

'I said it was good that the cross was destroyed. I said it was merely a stone structure and not something divine.'

'Do you regret your actions?'

'Yes.'

'Do you beg pardon for your sins? Do you swear that you will be a good Christian henceforth?'

'Yes.'

The secretary noted every word that was uttered in the Holy assembly. He soon came forward with two sheets of paper for the priest to sign. One was his confession and the other was a plea for pardon. The lawyer who had been engaged in his defence was asked to sign as a witness. The priest was told to kneel before the Chief Inquisitor to beg his pardon and was then led back to his cell. The punishment to be meted out to him would be announced later.

Padre Simao Peres sat silent and stony-faced, leaning against the wall in his cell. What had he done! His brain whirled in confusion. If only death would come at this very instant! But death wouldn't come so easily, he knew. If he tried to starve to death, the guards would prod him with their sticks and force him to eat. He had no instrument that could be used to end his life. He'd travelled from Spain to the Vatican, to Greece and then back to the Vatican before crossing the mighty ocean to India. Such a profound journey, and now he'd fallen on his knees before them merely to escape being burnt to death! When the guard brought the afternoon meal the priest stared at him blankly. He didn't touch the food.

'Why didn't you eat your lunch? I'll have to complain to the warden.'

'The smell of food makes me sick. My stomach twists in agony, I'll throw up,' he said, refusing to touch the food despite the guard's threats.

The prison doctor came the next morning and checked his pulse and felt his skin to see if he was feverish. The priest extended his hand and said, 'Slit this vein. Let my blood flow out...'

The doctor stared at him intently. 'There's no fever. The pulse is weak but it hasn't sunk so low that we need to let out blood.' He spooned some white powder into the priest's mouth and made him drink some water. A fire seemed to engulf his stomach in a while and two guards stood by his side forcing him to eat.

He was summoned to the Holy assembly eight days before the Day of Judgement. When he made a move to sit on the bench after kneeling down and making the sign of the cross, they told him to remain standing.

'You have been declared guilty of acting against the Christian religion, so you may not take your seat before the Holy assembly,' the Chief Inquisitor declared. He then pronounced the sentence. 'You are guilty so we condemn you to death by burning on the Day of Judgement. This is the punishment for your crime. But you have begged pardon and sworn that you will be a good Christian henceforth. So the Holy assembly of the Inquisition will be merciful and sentence you to five years of imprisonment at the civil jail during which period you will work in the shipbuilding factory. Further instructions will be given on the Day of Judgement. At the end of five years, you will be free to return to the Vatican or to any other place in Europe.'

Old and wizened, Padre Simao Peres seemed to shrink into himself as he stood there shaking his head. 'The gates of Heaven are opening for me, senor, Jesus is calling out to me. How will I go back to the Vatican now?'

The Chief Inquisitor rang the silver bell. Simao Peres stared at it intently as though it were the bell of death. The guard appeared in the doorway and led him away.

The priest woke up at four in the morning when it was still dark. There was no sound of prisoners coughing or groaning, nor of the guard walking around thumping the ground with his staff. Suddenly the silence was broken by the sound of boots and the low hum of threatening voices cutting through the atmosphere. What was happening, he wondered, when a couple of ghoulish shapes appeared before his cell. The iron door swung open with a grating sound.

Simao Peres stared at the two men. 'Get up! Take these clothes,' they barked, thrusting a bundle at him. 'There will be a procession to mark the Day of Judgement. The guilty will be burnt to death. You are getting these clothes as a sign of mercy.'

'It was the Pope who gave me my priestly robes, so many years ago!' Simao Peres sighed as he took off the short pants and short sleeved vest he was wearing and slipped into the long black trousers and black shirt. Over that he wore a knee-length white smock with a large red cross emblazoned on it.

'Who are you?' Simao Peres asked the man who had remained in the cell. 'You don't look like a guard.'

'I'm your godfather. I've come from the city, of my own free will, to take part in this ceremony. I will be by your side throughout the proceedings.'

'What do the prisoners sentenced to death wear?' he asked the man.

'Their smock bears tongues of fire on one side and a picture of Satan on the other.'

One by one, all the prisoners came out of their cells and stood in a line on the verandah. Simao Peres stared at them in amazement. There were at least a hundred and fifty of them looking like some prehistoric creatures that had emerged from a deep dungeon below the earth. Where had they been all this while? How was it that no one even knew they existed?

Only three of the prisoners wore the smock with the tongues of fire on it. One of them had been pardoned and set free, but he had gone back and criticized the Inquisition. The officials had arrested him again and condemned him to death. The second prisoner had been sent to the torture chamber twice, but he stuck to his stand that he was innocent. However the people who testified against him were thirsting for his blood and persisted with their accusations. The third man said he preferred to be burnt at the stake and would not confess or seek pardon. At one time he must have been tall and well-built, but now he was so emaciated that he seemed even taller, though his neck could barely support the weight of his head that lolled from side to side.

As dawn broke, seven workers trooped in carrying seven boxes in their hands. They each bore a long pole with a man's image attached to the top. The names of the men were inscribed below each image. The boxes contained the bones of those prisoners who had died during the trial or after they had been found guilty. The bones had been exhumed from their graves and were to be burnt to complete the punishment. The Inquisition believed that by doing this the souls of the guilty would be kept out of heaven, forcing them to wander about on earth. It did not let go of the hapless creatures even after death.

Padre Simao Peres read the names. One of them, Sukhdo – Salvador Dias seemed familiar. Only after a while did he realize that it was Sukhdo Nayak of Shirvaddo in Adolshi, who was the first to convert to Christianity along with his three sons, ignoring the mandate of the village. And now his bones lay in that box awaiting judgement! What had happened to his land? Where were his sons now? Who was it who had complained against him and led him to this final resting place, this box?

The procession, of around a hundred and fifty men, about fifty women, and their godfathers, wound out of the building at seven in the morning. After the service at St Catherine's Church, it would make its way to the clearing in the marketplace. Stakes had been set into the ground and wood had been piled at the site. The viceroy and the Archbishop would be present during the proceedings.

Thousands of people had abandoned their homes and fields and livestock as they moved out of Goa. Their cattle roamed about like stray animals, and vast tracts of land remained uncultivated. Rice and paddy were brought to Goa from the Canara region in large boats, and still this was not enough to feed the people. The government coffers were almost empty. The fields belonging to the temple and taken over by the church remained fallow. The viceroy passed a decree that no one was to be driven out of Goa, nor would anyone be allowed to leave of his own free will. Those who had abandoned their homes and land, could return to their villages without fear of prosecution. They could take possession of their fields and orchards if they agreed to become Christians.

But those who had fled their homes did not return. Who knows where the little groups of refugees had reached? It was the ones who had stayed back, the new converts, who were now feeling the heat. It was not enough to be baptized and to become a Christian. They had to learn to live like the Europeans, to wear their clothes and eat their food. They had to forsake all that they had done in the past, and if they committed a mistake, the threat of the Inquisition loomed large. Two people from Adolshi had been ensnared in their web. And everyone knew about Padre Simao Peres.

Difficult times brewed all over Goa. The gaonki system of administration continued to exist, but it was in shambles. In the old days the various Hindu caste groups and classes followed a strict hierarchical pattern, but when the gaonki was held in the church all the Christian villagers were considered equals. Yet, no man was willing to give up the privileges of his caste and class. This led to fights between the new converts who were originally Brahmins, and those who had converted from a lower caste group. The European officials did nothing to erase these class distinctions that were dividing the new converts. They continued to mark the old castes before their new Christian names. They had become Christians, but they couldn't get rid of their caste.

The new converts were a confused lot. They knew nothing about their new religion, they couldn't understand the language and there was no way to gain spiritual succour for they were forbidden to practise the rituals of their old faith. The new culture and language were proving to be major hurdles in their path. They were filled with remorse at having forsaken their old faith; they felt that they were cowards, that they had sinned…

The lesser gods and deities still remained in their tiny shrines, but no one performed any rituals or worshipped them. Many of the new converts were disturbed by this neglect. If someone fell ill or some unfortunate incident occurred in the village they felt that it was because the lesser gods and spirits were angry.

There were three little shrines housing the deities Agyo, Barmo and Vagro at the edge of the village, beyond which was the thick forest. The villagers had a lot of faith in the powers of these deities and took care to ensure that they were not disturbed or enraged.

One day Santan Dias Nayak and Joav Dias Nayak, formerly known as Puttu and Lavu Nayak of Shirvaddo, dropped in at Surya Gurav's house. 'You belong to a family of priests, your father performed the rituals in the village shrines. Conduct the ceremonies in honour of the lesser gods and spirits, we will assist you,' they said.

'What are you saying, Puttu mama? None of that matters today!' Surya Gurav exclaimed.

'The three deities on the border of the village are angry. The annual ceremonies in their honour have not been performed for two years. They must be pacified, or death will stalk this village!'

Surya Gurav, now known as Louis Miranda, was struck with fear. 'They keep a watch on everything. If they get to know this, we'll be thrown into jail,' he said.

On Wednesday afternoon, seven Nayak gaonkars, a Gurav and a Mirashi, assembled furtively at the Vagro shrine. Jiblo Nayak Dias carried a basket on his head. It contained a small pitcher, a new earthen pot, some steamed cakes or sannas, rice, flour and salt. The basket also contained flowers and a cock with its legs bound together. They quickly performed the traditional rituals, sacrificed the cock at the Vagro shrine, offered the sannas to Agyo and also placed the choru and ront in front of Barmo as offerings. They broke the earthen pot right there and tossed the shards to one side, but Jiblo took the pitcher and the basket back and hid them in the loft above Saba Gurav's cowshed.

There were some villagers who tried to prove that they were very good Christians, that they belonged to a class that was on par with the European rulers, so they often visited the soldier's camp. The officials fed them information that was designed to spread fear in people's hearts.

Who knows who turned traitor and carried the news of the religious ceremony to Padre Colaso. The villagers believed that the old faith and gods had a special place in each of their hearts so no one would betray them, but there was a traitor in their midst who gave their names to the priest and to the shef.

'Shef Ribeir, do you see what they've done? What's the point in teaching them anything? I'll complain to the Inquisition and have them locked up!' the priest raged.

'Bad. Very bad!' the shef agreed tiredly. 'But Padre, if all these people are arrested there will be very few left in the village. The officials want us to ensure that people remain here, don't they?'

'Are you suggesting that we ignore these sinful deeds? It's a crime to withold information about acts that go against the Christian faith. The fifty-fifth column in the rule book of the Inquisition states that whoever fails to report what he has seen or heard is guilty of acting against Christianity and must be punished too.'

The next day Padre Colaso and some soldiers went to the edge of the forest. They saw the ashes in the makeshift hearth, the crimson flowers and the cock's blood stained feathers strewn about the Vagro shrine. They noticed the bundle of steamed cakes slung on a stick by the Agyo shrine. There were half-burnt flowers and plantain leaves, shards of a broken mud pot and vermilion powder near the Barmo shrine. The priest told the soldiers to observe everything carefully.

The villagers were beside themselves with fear when they heard this news. The men crouched in their houses while the women went in and out of their houses not knowing what to do. Mad Nanu clutched his stomach and laughed uproariously. 'Those three gods sit there, stripped of their powers. Do you think your cattle will be saved if you rely on them? I tell you, all your cows will die, not a single calf will remain in your shed!'

Ventu Nayak Dias went to Babli's house as soon as it grew dark. 'I'm an old man, worn down by life. I didn't attend the ceremony yesterday, but all of you mustn't sit here as though waiting for the end. They have decreed that no one must leave the village. But they'll arrest all of you tomorrow. So, Babli, leave this village right now. If you wait for daybreak you might be thrown into their dungeons,' he said.

The gravity of the situation slowly sank into their minds. They packed rice, a few clothes and vessels, money and gold ornaments and were ready to leave by ten that night. Surya Gurav and Abu Mirashi arrived with their families as well as the cattle in their cowsheds. The sound of hooves seemed even louder in the stillness of the night.

'We must rush away in whichever direction we can. We might have to cross the river in boats, what will we do with the cattle then?' someone asked.

Their brothers and cousins and other members of their families stood in their doorways and watched in silence as the little group set off. 'Tend to our cows and calves. Who knows if we'll ever return,' they said in low tones. These were people who had once fought over the dung that their animals dropped in the fields. And here they were, leaving sheds full of cattle as they moved away!

It was a group of about fifty people, belonging to nine families, that hurtled through the darkness. Some of them carried infants in their arms, others held on to their bundles. They clenched their teeth and panted with the effort as they hurried towards the river in Shirdone, trying to increase the distance between themselves and disaster and death.

The boatmen were making a lot of money these days taking people across the river as they moved out of Goa for various reasons, the chief one being the fear of the Inquisition. These boatmen loitered on the bank or floated mid-stream posing as fishermen during the day. At night they demanded two gold coins or sixty xerafins to ferry a boat full of people from Shirdone to Karwar. There was not much danger once they crossed the mouth of the Aghnashini river for the soldiers rarely intercepted boats at night. But if they were caught on the river bank or while boarding the boats, they were sure to be killed. It was easier to move out of Goa using the Aghnashini route than it was to sail down the Mandvi. The Mandvi river, with the Adil Shahi palace and the flourishing settlements of Raibandar and Goapattana on its banks, hummed with activity throughout the day and even during night. But once one crossed the Chikhli settlement, one wouldn't encounter any traffic on the Aghnashini river till it reached the sea.

Jiblo Nayak Dias was a tall, slim man, about thirty years old. He wore a brief loincloth, a red kerchief wrapped about his head and a strip of blanket hung from one shoulder. These were the clothes he wore even after he became a Christian. He had an eight-year-old daughter and an infant son who was in Jiblo's elder sister's arms. This sister had returned to her parents' home after being widowed and though Jiblo had asked her to stay back in the village, she had insisted on accompanying them.

'Would the troubles in the Big House have been more than what we're suffering now?' Purso Dias remarked as they rushed along.

'We'd have to leave our homes and the village in any case. But at least we'll die as free men now, under the open sky!' Lavu Dias exclaimed.

They reached the river bank at Shirdone after an hour and a half. There were two boats moored on one side while another one, partly filled with people, was a short distance away.

'Take us somewhere far away. Don't worry about money, what's the use of money if we're not alive? We'll give as much as you want,' Babli addressed the three boatmen huddled in the boat's dark confines. Each boat had a short mast with a tightly furled sail. How will these vessels carry us across this vast expanse of water, they wondered.

'Get in,' a boatman said as two of them moved to the ends of the boat while another grabbed the edge of the sail. 'Get in quickly. We must leave at once. If we're caught, they'll shoot us first of all.'

The people realized that these boatmen spoke a strange language. They were outsiders who had merely come here to earn money. But that didn't matter really, for all they wanted was to get away from Goa as soon as possible. Their legs sank knee-deep into the slush as they waded through the shallow water to get on to the boat. Their hearts fluttered in fear, beneath them was the slush and the swiftly flowing water and all around was an impenetrable darkness.

Each person struggled through the slush and hauled himself on to the boat before looking around for the other members of his family. In the pitch dark they had to guess at their identities since no features were visible. They felt as though a knife would land on their necks if they didn't hurry. The two boats were soon filled with people and only four or five persons remained on the bank. Jiblo was moving up and down helping with other people's sacks and bundles and loading them on to the boats. His wife, Gaura, waited on the bank with their bags. Lavu had come back to collect his last bundle and Surya Gurav's wife, who was unwell, clutched her infant as she waited for her husband to help her wade to the boat.

Suddenly one of the boatmen noticed some ten or fifteen dark shapes rushing down the slope. He could barely see the caps on their heads and weapons sticking out from their bodies. 'They've come! The soldiers … set sail!' he shouted and the boatmen dug their long poles deep into the slush and pushed with all their might to set the boats afloat on the strong tide.

'No one must go forward … stop!' the soldiers screamed but Surya's wife was struggling through the slush with her infant in her arms. Surya was caught with one leg in the boat and the other in the water clinging precariously to its side. 'Bhagi! Come quick!' he screamed but he dared not let go of the boat as it moved away. Bhagi lost her footing and fell into the water. Surya wailed loudly as his wife and child drowned before his eyes.

Lavu rushed forward to grab hold of the boat but the boatmen were moving so fast that he couldn't do so and the air resounded with the wails of his wife and children as he was caught by the soldiers when he scrambled back to the bank. Jiblo, however, grabbed his wife's hand and slipped into the dark shadows of trees and bushes.

The soldiers ordered the boatmen to return but the three boats moved swiftly with the current and were soon lost to sight. Only the wails and cries of the members of the three families could still be heard on the bank. Lavu Nayak's wife threatened to jump into the water along with her four children, Jiblo's sister was beside herself with grief.

Jiblo's wife clung to her husband sobbing inconsolably as he pressed a hand over her mouth to stifle her cries. They crept over an embankment and across a stream before stopping to rest under a tree.

'Tomorrow we'll take some other route, maybe we'll sail down the coast towards Canara ...we'll look for them. I will not rest till I find my sister and my children,' he whispered.

Demu Gurav Ferrao's younger brother, Bamu Gurav Ferrao, had spent his childhood in the temple precincts, playing hide and seek with his friends amidst the trees by the sacred pool. He'd remained immersed in the rituals of worship, the sacred chants and hymns and festivals that were an intrinsic part of the temple routine. He enjoyed all these activities and had great faith in the Lord. He was always taken aback when people questioned the existence of god.

The sight of forty or fifty people demolishing the temple had rendered him speechless with horror and he'd remained withdrawn and silent ever since. His family didn't know what to do. The ghadi and the joish who could drive away evil spirits were too scared to practise their art on him.

When it was time for the Shigmo festival, the sound of cymbals and pipes and the traditional songs began to resound in Bamu's ears and he seemed to stir out of his habitual stupor. He'd set off into the hills every morning and return in the afternoon, exhausted and dirty. His family was quite relieved that he was taking an interest in something, that he was venturing out of the house at least. One day, much to everyone's surprise, he took a crowbar along with his sickle when he set off for the hills. He returned in the afternoon and maintained the same routine for the next eighteen days. And then, one day, he declared, 'Everything will be fine now. All our troubles will pass. The Lord stands again, we'll celebrate the Shigmo this year.'

The next day he bathed early and placed some flowers and vermilion, a piece of sandalwood, a small pot of water and a bell in a basket and set off into the hills. His family was quite alarmed. They informed his brother, Demu Gurav, who followed him into the hills.

Bamu stopped in a clearing deep in the forest where he had built a little temple four feet tall and about three feet wide. It was built on six stakes that had been pushed into the ground and had a thatched roof of golden wild grass. A tiny sanctum made of woven strips of bamboo stood in the centre and within it was a large black stone with a face and eyes etched on its surface. A small peepal sapling had been planted outside the temple and a stone platform erected around its base.

'What have you done, you wretched creature! What sort of madness is this? Imagine building a temple in these troubled times, they'll kill you for this!' Demu hissed. He grabbed his sickle and hacked at the walls prising out one of the stakes so that the whole structure collapsed in a heap. He tossed the basket on to that heap and spread some dry grass over it. The glowing coals in the basket set the grass aflame. Demu hoisted the black stone on his shoulder and tossed it into a ravine.

Bamu Gurav watched all this in silence, his face and eyes seemed carved in stone. That night Bamu Gurav Ferrao hanged himself from a tree in the forest because his own brother had destroyed the temple he had built.

Shabi's grandfather, Devu, had rushed back home when Guna, Raya and Shabi, accompanied by their families, had fled the village. He pottered about the house in a stubborn and eccentric fashion, stoking the fire in the hearth and taking pleasure in the bubbling sounds as the rice boiled in the pot. Sometimes, when no one was around, he'd pluck some ridge gourd or snake gourd or brinjal from someone's vegetable patch and roast it in the embers, to eat with the payz. If some woman caught him in the act, he'd wave his stick angrily and scream, 'You woman of loose morals! Accusing me of theft? Can you declare with your hand on your heart, that all your children have been fathered by your husband?' The poor woman would be forced to retreat, spluttering in anger. This old man, shrivelled of skin and bent at the waist … what a vile tongue he has!

'The whole village is a Christian one. How long can I be isolated, like a pregnant rabbit … I went to the Kalapur church and they sprinkled water on me and made me a Christian too,' he declared one day. But soon enough the villagers saw him pouring pitchers of water over the tulsi plant on its broken pedestal outside his door. One day he hobbled to the Barmo shrine and sat there stroking the idol like a little child.

The roof of Devu's house had not been thatched the previous year so the cross beams were rotten and there were holes in the thatch. He dragged himself about on his haunches, sticking his face out at the door, 'Have those people taken their God-on-the-Cross and gone away?' he asked someone who passed by.

'They won't go without making a Christian of you, Devu ajja,' the passer by retorted.

'But I've converted already!' he said sometimes. At other times he'd get irritated, 'Their fathers will have to come down from the skies to convert me!' he'd snap.

The sound of potters beating the wet clay and the blacksmiths striking iron at the forge could be heard faintly that morning. A herd of stray cattle entered the settlement … someone yelled loudly to drive the cattle away … there was the sound of scampering hooves and the air resounded with the noise … but there was no sound in Devu ajja's house. He didn't emerge leaning on his stick, nor was he seated at the door.

Balsu Nayak's house was close by and Balsu's wife, Mogu, would often ask, 'Devu mam, is your payz ready?' when she spied him at the door.

'The payz is done, but I have nothing to eat with the rice,' he'd say.

Mogu would have liked to give some of the curry she had cooked to the old man, but she was scared that he'd abuse her for being a convert. But there was no sign of the man today. When there was no sign of Devu the next morning too, Mogu grew worried. She went up to his house and called out to him, but there was no response. Where had the old man gone! The door seemed unlatched but she didn't want to step in, it was a Hindu's home, after all. Who knew if he had really become a Christian, despite all that he said? In a matter of minutes, the news spread all over the settlement and some twenty people gathered outside Devu's house.

They called out to him but there was no response. The roof had collapsed in parts so it was dark inside and they couldn't see anything through the windows. Some people climbed on to the verandah and pushed the door open with a stick. Devu ajja was sprawled face-down on the ground, the foam and spit that had emerged from his mouth had dried and was caked about his nose and face. Devu ajja is dead, they declared.

Everyone fell silent, what would happen now? Who would perform the rituals of death? Was this a Hindu corpse or a

Christian one? No one knew. There was no cross at the door, no one had seen a Christian priest blessing the house. How could they believe his child-like rants about having converted to Christianity? If they, who were Christians now, entered a Hindu home and touched a Hindu's corpse, they would be committing a sin. Defiling a Hindu home and turning the family into outcastes when they were alive, was acceptable. But desecrating a Hindu's corpse, was a terrible sin for which no retribution would be great enough!

'What do we do with the corpse? Death is a serious matter, who knows what we'll face when we reach that kingdom of Darkness? We're Christians, so we'll be buried when we die. But this poor wretch, should he be buried or cremated?' Ventu Dias exclaimed.

Everyone stared at Ventu Dias in fear. Finally he said to Puttu Dias and Balsu Dias, 'Go to the soldier's camp and ask the priest if he knows whether Devu had become a Christian. Tell him to check his records.'

The priest scanned the list of new converts in his book. Each person's name, age, caste, the area in which he lived and the new Christian name they received was noted in this book. But Devu Nayak of Shirvaddo didn't feature in this list.

'He's an infidel from another faith. Don't take part in any rituals of death. It's against the law to cremate a corpse in this village,' the priest declared.

'His house is in the middle of the settlement, the corpse will rot and begin to stink. The old man has no family,' Balsu said.

'Drag it away and leave it in the forest.'

'It's not right to let wild animals tear at the corpse.'

'Do whatever you want then. But this is the last time.

Only Christians will be allowed to stay in the village from now on,' the priest declared.

Puttu and Balsu Nayak Dias returned to the settlement and the discussion started all over again.

'Who knows when he died! If we wait till tomorrow the corpse will bloat and the limbs will tear off if we try to drag it away.'

'He is one of our clan after all, someone who has no family to mourn for him. We've forsaken our religion, shall we forsake our duties and the ties of blood too?' Saaton Nayak asked.

Ventu Dias glanced at the wood and logs that Devu's son and grandson had piled beside the house. 'Take these logs and stack them in the clearing in the forest,' he declared. 'Do what I say. Or Devu will turn into a ghost and sit on your doorstep tonight.'

Ten or twelve men carried the logs to the site. Ventu and the others entered the house. They spread a thick blanket on the ground and placed the corpse on it. They bound the blanket with ropes and passed a stout pole through the knots. They performed no rituals as four men hoisted the pole and carried the corpse to the heap of logs that had been stacked under a tree.

'What rituals can we perform? Consider yourself fortunate that we're cremating you,' Ventu said as though he were addressing Devu's spirit.

An uneasy calm settled on the crowd as the corpse was placed on the pyre. Who would set it alight? Whoever did so would be sucked into a sequence of rituals and would have to maintain ritual purity or the soul would not attain freedom. Shiva turned to Ventu Dias hesitantly, 'Who will light the pyre, Ventu bhavo?'

'Will you do it, Shiva?'

'No. I don't want to get involved in all that.'

'All right. So we won't light the pyre. We'll set the wild grass in the forest alight' Ventu declared.

Everyone was amazed, what was this man saying! It was late in the evening and darkness was creeping about the trees and bushes. The dark shadow of death seemed to settle on the site.

'The whole area is overgrown with wild grass. Let us scatter dry grass on the pyre. We'll set the wild grass alight at a distance. If Devu is fortunate the fire will spread up to the pyre and the dry logs will begin to burn,' Ventu explained.

Ventu asked someone to spray some inflammable oil on the pyre. He untied a bundle of hay and dry grass and spread it all around. He walked ten or twelve feet from the pyre scattering dry grass in a long trail. Striking a flint, he set the wild forest grass alight at this point, and everyone walked away without a backward glance.

Ventu Nayak sat by his window all night. He could see the glow of the leaping flames and heard the sound of something exploding in the distance.

At least forty prisoners had pleaded guilty and begged for pardon on the Day of Judgement and had escaped being burnt at the stake. Padre Simao Peres was one of them. Four days later, they were herded into the large hall where the Chief Inquisitor, Castel Mendonca, and the secretary, Gonsal Nunez, sat at the large desk. Each prisoner was summoned up to them and told how he was to behave in the civil jail, what his duties were and what the punishment was if he were to behave in an inappropriate fashion.

The Chief Inquisitor turned to Padre Simao Peres. 'You will serve the five years of your punishment in the civil jail and you will work in the shipbuilding factory. They will not consider your background when they assign duties for all prisoners are treated in the same way. You must follow a few rules. One, you must confess your sins to the priest on the last Sunday of each month and pray for pardon. This must be done without fail for three years. Two, you must attend Mass and listen to the sermon on Sundays and on festivals. Three, you must pray to God, His son Jesus and Holy Mother Mary five times a day and revere the five wounds on the body of Jesus Christ. Four, you will not strike up friendship with anyone who betrays the Christian faith. And five, you will not discuss or criticize what you have seen or heard or experienced during the process of the Inquisition. If you violate any of these rules, the officials of the Inquisition will arrest you and you will be burnt at the stake on the next Day of Judgement. No appeals will be heard and there will be no pardon.'

Padre Simao Peres had to sign on a sheet of paper and swear on the Bible that he would follow the rules carefully.

Once all the prisoners had been taken through this process they were given the items that had been confiscated at the time of their arrest. Each man clutched a bundle under his arm, but Padre Simao Peres had nothing. When his bodyguard, Tomas, reacted violently the officials had merely bound the priest with a rope and dragged him away.

The prisoners were taken out of the Big House and made to walk in a row to the Civil Jail. They were accompanied by two armed guards, but each man laughed and talked delightedly, as though elated by the open sky and sparkling sunshine. After three or four years of confinement, this was their first exposure to the open sky and for the moment, at least, their worries had been pushed aside.

Padre Simao Peres, however, was silent and aloof as he stumbled along with his eyes almost shut. The darkness within his soul seemed to have seeped into his surroundings, the bright sky above still seemed dark. He turned to the prisoner beside him and asked, 'Is it morning now, or is it still night, will you look up and tell me, please?'

The prisoner stared at him closely. This frail, old man has undergone much penance and become a holy ascetic, he thought, but he didn't say a word.

The conditions in the Civil Jail, which was dirty and shabby, were quite different from what they had known in the Big House. Eight prisoners were cooped up in a single cell and there was dirty water and rubbish strewn all around. It was a long, squat building with ten or twelve cells and a large kitchen on one side. There were fifteen earthen ovens on which groups of four prisoners were expected to cook their meals. Each group was given provisions and a mud pot, a saucer and a large spoon. Scraps of leftover food, water and other waste littered the kitchen floor and became a breeding ground for mosquitos that plagued them all night.

The prisoners were herded to the shipbuilding factory at eight in the morning and were brought back at one. They resumed work at three and continued till it was dark. Padre Simao Peres accompanied them, but the other prisoners ensured that he didn't have to work. When the foreman came to check on the work they'd whisper, 'He's a priest. What can he do?' And the foreman would remain silent.

There was a young prisoner called Camil in the padre's group, who insisted that the priest stay away from the cooking duties too. Everyone addressed him as Padre bappa, but they did so in such a low tone that no one heard what they said. One day Simao Peres asked Camil how he had landed in jail.

'I assaulted my father-in-law one day. Broke one of his ribs.'

'But why?'

'My wife kept running off to her parents' house complaining that I had beaten her. When I went to fetch her back, my father-in-law rushed at me with a stick in his hand. I grabbed that stick and turned on him.'

'Why did the Inquisition arrest you then?'

'My father-in-law complained to the authorities that I'd planted a tulsi sapling at my door and asked my wife to water it every day. When she refused I beat her, he said.'

Padre Simao Peres remained silent. These days, his feelings were in a turmoil. He felt insulted when he sensed that the others were taking pity on him. His spirit cried out against the base situation in which he found himself and at the physical, mental and spiritual harassment he had faced throughout his life. He was furious at the injustice of it all, yet he was soft-hearted too and this was the cause of his turmoil. He regretted having begged for pardon and this regret seemed to gnaw at his soul. He craved death at this moment – why, then, had he begged them to spare his life?

There was a foreman called Zaporin at the shipbuilding unit. His mother was a Muslim woman and his father was a Portuguese soldier. This man would constantly yell at the workers and beat them with his stick. One day, Zaporin saw that Simao Peres was lagging behind the others, so he prodded him with his stick. The priest turned around and stared at him with narrowed eyes, 'You should have been an official of the Inquisition. You'd get to pluck people's flesh with a pair of tongs. You'd have enjoyed being on duty in the confession room – you'd have laughed as you dragged the rough rope through people's wounds. You might even have lit the fire on the Day of Judgement,' he said.

The prisoners who witnessed this scene were terrified, so they quickly dragged the priest away. The foreman was quite taken aback too. How did this elderly foreigner dare to speak so openly about such matters?

It was three months since the prisoners had arrived at the Civil Jail. As he lay in the cell, Simao Peres would often get excitable and launch into a disjointed tirade, 'Why should I be bound to the stake? Why should I be burnt to death when I have done no wrong? I tell you again, there was no divinity in that stone structure. The divine cross is embossed on my heart, cut me open and it will burst forth! You burnt Sukhdo Dias's bones. You won't find any of my bones, I assure you. The Pope ordained me as a priest. The King of Portugal can't harm me. That woman kept protesting that she hadn't worshipped the cow, but…'

As Simao Peres's voice grew louder, the prison guards moved towards his cell, but the other prisoners clamped their hands over the priest's mouth and shut him up.

Mass was celebrated in the chapel every Sunday and Padre Timothy Morais would come from the main church to deliver the sermon. The authorities made a note of all the prisoners who skipped Mass. Simao Peres had missed the service for two consecutive weeks because of ill health, but on the next Sunday Mass would be followed by Confession and everyone would have to be present. The other prisoners got him dressed and took him to the chapel where he listened to the sermon with his eyes closed.

'You were not present during the last two weeks. Do you mean to disobey the rules of the Inquisition or don't you have faith in the Christian religion?' Padre Timothy Morais asked, angrily.

Simao Peres shook his head slowly and stared at the priest. 'You are very young, Padre, and your sermon is immature. If I were to deliver a sermon, rays of light would cut through the darkness. The rule book of the Inquisition is your Bible – you have no knowledge of the holy book, the Bible. Did you ever hear the Holy Pope deliver the sermon in the Vatican? Did he give you the priestly robes when you were ordained?'

The priest was standing at the altar with the holy staff in his hand, so he maintained a dignified silence, but his body shook with suppressed rage. The prisoners moved forward and confessed their sins. When it was Simao Peres's turn, he knelt before the priest, 'I am being punished for a crime I did not commit. How can I confess to something I haven't done? Jesus is my witness,' he said.

There was a moment of tense silence as the priest who heard the confession grappled with his rage. Finally, he waved Simao Peres away.

The next day, an Inquisition official in full regalia, with the signs and badges of his office displayed on his chest, arrested Simao Peres and took him away. He would be confined to his cell in the Inquisition prison till the next Day of Judgement when he would be burnt at the stake.

P.S.

Insights
Interviews
& More...

A Saga of Choice and Faith
Vidya Pai

'My Imagination was Fired by Unwritten Stories': In Conversation with Mahabaleshwar Sail
Vidya Pai

Afterword
Vidya Pai

A Saga of Choice and Faith

Vidya Pai

Around twelve years ago when I was doing the rounds of publishers' offices with my translation of a Konkani novel, the first hurdle I encountered was a singular lack of knowledge. Here I was, an unknown translator, trying to place an unknown book by an unknown writer, but the problem was that no one had heard of Konkani. That translation got published eventually (as have three others over the last decade), but the lack of information persists. So, before we look at *Yug Sanvaar* (2004), Mahabaleshwar Sail's historical novel, we need to look at Konkani, the language in which it is written.

Konkani is spoken in Goa and in parts of Maharashtra, Karnataka and Kerala that lie along the western coast. The oppressive linguistic policies of the Portuguese rulers in the sixteenth century ensured that Konkani disappeared from the public sphere in Goa and was spoken only in the privacy of one's home. The exodus of Konkani people from Goa and their subsequent relocation in these southern parts kept the language alive in these pockets. However, the influence of the majority language in each region resulted in the development of widely differing Konkani dialects and the use of the Devanagari, Kannada, Malayalam as well as Roman scripts.

A language thus marginalized by history's tide could hardly boast of any creative literature of note. It was only after Goa was liberated in 1961, after the Sahitya Akademi recognized Konkani as an independent Indian language and it was included in the eighth schedule of the Constitution, that creative writing received impetus with short story and poetry being the most favoured genres. It is against the backdrop of this nascent literary tradition that Mahabaleshwar Sail's *Yug Sanvaar*, perhaps the most ambitious of his five novels, should be viewed.

Yug Sanvaar deals with life in Adolshi village, home to a peaceful agricultural community that lives in accordance with age-old traditions, when the Portuguese arrive in Goa in 1510. The order passed in 1546 to exile Brahmins, ban Hindu religious practices and destroy idolatry in Goa forces entire communities to uproot themselves and move away in a bid to save their religion and their gods. Temples are razed and churches built on those sites. Those who remain behind are forced to convert to Christianity, but they often persist with their old traditions and culture. The Order of the Inquisition (1560–1812) unleashes ruthless, inhuman punishments on the new Christian converts in a bid to retain them within the folds of the Church. This causes a major upheaval in the socio-cultural history of Goa.

'I believe in God but not in any organized religion,' Sail claims in the foreword to the Konkani original. By confining God within the framework of organized religion we breed intolerance of other faiths. By interpreting the teachings of the prophets in a manner that suits our own ends, we create immense havoc...' It is this 'havoc' unleashed by a powerful conqueror with a crucifix in one hand and a naked sword in the other on an ignorant mass of people caught up in rituals and taboos, fragmented by issues of caste and social hierarchies that forms the theme of the novel.

A man's sense of identity is linked to his religion and the culture from which he springs. Faced with an ultimatum from a powerful State to give up his religion or face expulsion, arrest or death, each character in the book is forced to make this difficult choice. While Sukhdo Nayak, the first Christian convert in Adolshi, is tempted by the gold coins and portions of fertile community land being offered to new converts, henpecked Gaja becomes a Christian to spite his cruel, domineering wife.

For Ranu Kenkre, the wealthy Brahmin bhatkar (landlord), conversion is the only way he can retain his orchards and fields and continue to look after the families who work on his land. As for Dugga Mhar and his son Ghungo,'untouchables' who are condemned to haunt the fringes of Hindu society, it is the lure of an existence without barriers of caste or class, where everyone eats at the same table and worships in the same church.

The saga of choice plays out differently with other characters when they choose to safeguard their religious beliefs and move to unknown lands. Guna, the headstrong young man from the Nayak community, tries to instigate the villagers to attack the police camp set up in a local shrine. When no one responds to his call he destroys the large stone cross on the hill and cuts off the legs of two Portuguese soldiers before fleeing from the village in search of a new life. Nilu Nayak and his neighbours, however, choose to abandon their homes and their land so that they can carry their kuldevata (family deity) Ramnath to safer regions and consecrate the idol at a new site.

For Timanna Bhat, the sensitive younger brother of the temple priest, the desecration and destruction of the temple, which has been the centre of his existence, is too much to bear. His lifeless body hanging from a ravaged beam amidst the silent temple bells is an expression of his rebellion, and displays yet another aspect of this choice.

Sail received the Sahitya Akademi Award for his short story collection *Tarangam* in 1993, but his broad, sweeping style eddying into numerous subplots and cul-de-sacs and drawing deeply from dialect and folklore and indigenous religious practices is better suited to the novel as a literary form. *Yug Sanvaar*, with its vast historical canvas, gives Sail the latitude to tackle life in Goan villages revolving around the temple, the orchards and the fields and the upheaval created in this peaceful fabric by 'the white devils from across the seven seas'.

We accompany Sail to distant Spain and Portugal to see what makes the crusader's spirits tick. We are carried into the labyrinthine depths of the 'Big House', the seat of the dreaded Inquisition, 'where Death did not come easily'; where 'solitude and the huge weight of sorrow often killed the inmate long before he was sentenced to death'. We wonder what the future holds for those straggling hordes, forced to uproot their umbilical ties and head into unknown zones. And, like Sail, we hope that though today 'there is darkness without end on all four sides, who knows, the bright light of morning may reveal a new shore where their tiny footprints may eventually leave mighty impressions on the land'.

Much of this breadth of focus is possible because Sail does not follow a linear plot, nor does he confine himself to the fortunes of merely a handful of families during these turbulent times. The novel develops as a series of episodes peopled by a mosaic of characters, many of whom remain mere cameos caught up in the swirl of the narrative for only a couple of pages. But there are notable exceptions like Durga, the spunky Brahmin woman who decides to work in the family's fields challenging the Portuguese order that Brahmin landowners may no longer hire help. Or Camil Ribeir, the local neo-convert who is now a shef (chief official) in the Portuguese police, torn between the need to forcibly convert the villagers and a deep sympathy for the predicament they are in.

It is Padre Simao Peres, the genial Spanish priest who wanders about the village talking of love and compassion and forgiveness, who plays the central role in this novel. 'Some of our people are following the wrong path. They are followers of Jesus, too, but someone has led them astray. The path to Jesus goes through men's hearts. Nothing can be achieved through force,' he laments. He is an effective foil to Padre Paolo Colaso and the other Jesuit priests who clamour for greater use of force and more stringent laws to make Goa a Christian stronghold ruled by the Portuguese king. This Padre bappa's arrest and subsequent trial by the Tribunal of the Inquisition give Sail a chance to flesh out his character and explore the workings of his mind.

While religious conversion, the migration of communities and the excesses of the Inquisition form the three main planks on which the novel rests, Sail is also intrigued by the comparative ease with which a boatload of soldiers and religious practitioners could overrun an entire region. Hindu society, fragmented by divisions of caste and of class, and the Hindu religion, preoccupied with issues like untouchability, ritual purity and taboos of diet were unable to withstand these intruding forces.

The doors of Hinduism opened outwards – people were branded 'outcastes' and expelled from its folds. A hungry child from a Hindu family fed by a kind-hearted Christian woman or unsuspecting Hindus who cooked on a hearth that had been used by a Christian family were therefore tarred with the same brush. Once expelled from its folds they couldn't re-enter Hindu society; they could end their lives or accept the four gold coins offered to each new convert and get baptized, thus swelling the numbers of the Christian faith.

Sail claims that his imagination was fired by the unwritten stories, the drama, the conflict and pain that lurked in this period of Goan history, but he remained hesitant because this was an issue that concerned men's faiths. It called for much research into the historical and sociological accounts of the period. It had to be handled with sensitivity and restraint.

Yug Sanvaar testifies to Sail's mature handling of a turbulent period of Goan history, of interest to Konkani Hindus who flock to the resurrected temples of their kuldevatas even today, and to Konkani Christians in search of their roots.

Social and political upheaval and the resultant migration of communities have been spawning grounds for great literature all over the world. Creative writing born out of such ferment throws light on the collective consciousness of a community and the region it inhabits. *Yug Sanvaar*, if it transcends the boundaries imposed by language, has the potential to do just this.

This essay was published in 50 Writers 50 Books *Eds. Pradeep Sebastian and Chandra Siddan (HarperCollins India, 2013).*

'My Imagination was Fired by Unwritten Stories': In Conversation with Mahabaleshwar Sail

Vidya Pai

Vidya Pai: ***Could you tell us a bit about your background?***

Mahabaleshwar Sail: I hail from a family of farmers in the Karwar region of northern Karnataka, so my early years were spent in tending cows and working in the fields. I started school at the age of six and dropped out in the eighth standard. When I turned eighteen, I joined the Indian Army and served on the battle front during the Indo–Pak war of 1965 and had a stint with the UN Peacekeeping force in Egypt and Israel. I have also served in the police force and worked a supervisor in a project of the Forest Department. I then joined the Post and Telegraph department where I served till my retirement.

How did you start your literary career?

I believe that a writer's ability to create literature is an intrinsic part of his personality, it is a gift that he is born with. My formal education ended in the eighth standard and I had no access to books, nor had I read much literature at that time. But I was very sensitive to all that was happening around me and would try to answer the questions that arose in my mind. The urge to create something new was a constant factor in my life.

The first story I wrote was during a lull in the battle after the Tashkent ceasefire. My literary career took off after my stint in the Army ended and I was transferred to Pune.

I wrote short stories for many years. I used to write in Marathi and my stories were published in leading magazines in Pune and Mumbai. But I always felt that I was translating my experiences into Marathi. It was only after I started writing in Konkani that I could express what I wanted to say in a natural manner. Writing in Marathi and getting published in leading Marathi magazines at that stage of my career gave me a chance to examine my talents, to see where I stood in the larger Marathi literary world. It gave me immense confidence and this proved beneficial in the long run.

Do you see yourself as a short story writer or as a novelist?

I started as a short story writer and have published four collections of Konkani stories. I received the Sahitya Akademi award for my short story collection Tarangam in 1993.

I am more comfortable with the space that a novel offers, because it gives me the freedom to develop my plot and characters. The only problem is that short stories can be published easily while getting a novel published is a difficult task.

My first novel *Kali Ganga*, which dealt with the lives of the farming community on the banks of the Kali River in Karwar, was published in 1996. This was followed by two novellas *Adrusht* and *Aranyakand*. A Konkani film was made on *Adrusht* and it received the Critic's Award at the Toronto International Film Festival. *Yug Sanvar*, *Khol Khol Moolam*, *Vikhar Vilkho* and *Havthan*, which focuses on the lives of a potter's community, are the other novels I have written.

***What made you write* Yug Sanvar?**

I had heard many stories about religious conversion since my childhood, in fact there were a few Christian families in our village who followed the tenets of both religions. It was only after I read Sri Uday Bhembre's article on the Goan Inquisition in the Konkani daily *Sunaparant* in 1991 that my interest was aroused. My imagination was fired by the unwritten stories, the drama and conflict and pain lurking in the gaps in documented history available about that period. I realized that religious conversion, the migration of communities and the Inquisition would provide enough material for a piece of creative writing. But this was an issue that concerned men's faiths, so I was hesitant for a very long time.

What were the reasons for your hesitation? How did you overcome them?

I believe that there are two sides to any conflict, and no one side can be totally right.

I believe in God but not in any organized religion; by confining God within the framework of organized religion we breed intolerance of other faiths. So, my God, who is present in the whole universe, does not need temples or rituals or priests.

But this was a very delicate, sensitive theme. It would have to be handled with maturity and restraint. If the balance were upset in any way religious sentiments would be hurt and that was not my intent.

Besides these moral and ethical issues I would have to study the sociological and historical accounts of the period. Much of this material was available in the Central Library in Panaji, but I lived and worked in Canacona, which was 70 km away.

I thought about these issues for a long time and only then did I start work on the novel.

Could you describe the research that went into the novel?

There are many legends and myths and folk tales dealing with this period of religious conversion but there are few written records. Much of the historical material available is in Portuguese, but I do not know that language. My friend, Vasant Desai, who knows that language well, would accompany me to the Central library and help me take notes. I consulted material written in Konkani and in English too.

It took me two years to gather all the material I would need for my book. Research had to be conducted at the social and cultural level as well the religious and political one. I had to study the social structure of villages, the rituals and superstitions and folk religion that prevailed around that time. I visited the areas where the fictional village Adolshi would be located and where the rest of the action would unfold.

Can* Yug Sanvar *be called a historical novel?

I would prefer to call *Yug Sanvar* a piece of creative writing that is based on historical events. My role is that of a narrator and I have attempted to create a piece of literary fiction based in this historical period drawing upon my imagination, my knowledge of Indian culture and my experience of the agrarian social structure prevalent in this region.

When a writer decides on a theme, he looks at the dramatic potential in the subject, he tries to see if there is any scope for creative writing. He is not interested in merely recording history. History, imagination and creativity appear in varying degrees in this text.

How was* Yug Sanvar *received?

Yug Sanvar was published by Asmitai Prakashan in April 2004. At 424 pages, it was one of the biggest novels published in the

Konkani language, and it received a good response. It was shortlisted for the Saraswati Samman.

Since Konkani readership is very limited, I wanted this novel to reach a wider audience so I translated it into Marathi and *Tandav* was published by Rajhans, a reputed publishing house in Pune. As the author and translator, I have exercised considerable freedom with *Tandav*, editing sections and adding new portions. This translation received many awards, including one from the Maharashtra Sahitya Parishad.

Age of Frenzy, the English translation of Yug Sanvar, was held up for many years because of its length. Every writer believes that what he has written is complete and should not be tampered with. Practical considerations, however, compelled me to edit and condense *Yug Sanvar* for this translation, though I have ensured that no characters have been left out and the flow of the story remains the same.

Afterword

Vidya Pai

When noted Konkani writer Mahabaleshwar Sail sent me a copy of his latest novel *Yug Sanvar* in late 2005, I was pre-occupied with grandmotherly duties and a translation project of this magnitude didn't fit into my schedule. Yet, as I read this moving tale of life in Adolshi, a fictional Goan village in the sixteenth century, I was captivated by Sail's depiction of the social, cultural and religious upheaval after the Portuguese arrived in Goa in 1510.

Here was a novel by a Konkani writer that focused on religious conversion and the severing of umbilical ties as communities moved away from Goa to save their gods. '*Kakkya, tu Goyyan gellolo ve…*', a popular folk ditty, where a young mother asks a crow if it had flown to Goa recently, and if it had met her brother and the family she was forced to leave behind, reflects this sense of yearning and loss. Konkani Hindus flock to the resurrected temples of their kuladevatas, their family deities, in Goa even today and the notion of Goa as a long-lost homeland has been kept alive through myths, rituals and folk lore wherever the community set down roots along the western coast. Not only that, Sail hails from an agrarian family and brings the authenticity of experience in a wealth of detail in the descriptions of folk culture and agricultural traditions. In *Yug Sanvar*, he touches on three sets of religious traditions – the folk religion practiced by the original settlers of the region, Hinduism and Christianity. Yet, *Yug Sanvar*, the novel that dealt with so much personal and political history was virtually unknown.

Creative writing on such a theme should have been of interest to the descendants of those who stayed behind in Goa and embraced the Christian faith as well as to those who moved away. Was it the Goan Konkani dialect used in the book that made it incomprehensible to Goan Christians as well as Konkani speakers in Karnataka, and Kerala? Or was it the Devnagari script, unfamiliar to those attuned to Konkani written in Roman, Kannada, Malayalam scripts that excluded a large chunk of prospective readers? Perhaps an English translation would vault these boundaries, I thought, as I started work on this 424-page tome.

Ten years passed. My translations of Sail's Konkani novellas *Hawthan* (*The Kiln*, 2011) and *Aranyakand* (*Forest Saga*, 2015) were published during this period, but the translation of *Yug Sanvar* found no takers. Mainstream English publishers could publish two translations with these resources, I was told. Could the author be persuaded to bring the book down to a more acceptable size?

Sail, in the meanwhile, translated *Yug Sanvar* into Marathi and the book received critical acclaim. As an author–translator, he was free to adapt, condense or even re-write parts of the book for its Marathi version. This experience of taking a fresh look at the novel finally tilted the scale. He agreed to prune the Konkani book, taking care to preserve the storyline, the theme and spirit of the original. *Age of Frenzy*, therefore, is a 'streamlined' translation of *Yug Sanvar*.

This translation has been 'moth-balled' and then brought out and worked upon many times over the last decade as we swung between hope and despair.

Thank you, Sail *bab*, for having faith.

Thank you, Keerti Ramachandra, for your gentle nit-picking and for the fresh shape you gave to this much-mauled script.

And thank you, Minakshi, and the team at HarperCollins for turning this dream into reality.

HARPERPERENNIAL

Harper Perennial presents special editions of its finest books in translation

Age of Frenzy
Mahabaleshwar Sail
Translated from the Konkani by Vidya Pai

A Life Incomplete
Nanak Singh
Translated from the Punjabi by Navdeep Suri

Mohanaswamy
Vasudhendra
Translated from the Kannada by Rashmi Terdal

The Music of Solitude
Krishna Sobti
Translated from the Hindi by Vasudha Dalmia

No Presents Please: Mumbai Stories
Jayant Kaikini
Translated from the Kannada by Tejaswini Niranjana

A Preface to Man
Subhash Chandran
Translated from the Malayalam by Fathima E.V.

The Secret Garland
Andal
Translated from the Tamil by Archana Venkatesan

Shala
Milind Bokil
Translated from the Marathi by Vikrant Pande

The Weary Generations
Abdullah Hussein
Translated from the Urdu by the author

Written in Tears
Arupa Patangia Kalita
Translated from the Assamese by Ranjita Biswas

HARPER**PERENNIAL**

Bhima: Lone Warrior
M.T. Vasudevan Nair
Translated from the Malayalam by Gita Krishnankutty

Chemmeen
Thakazhi Sivasankara Pillai
Translated from the Malayalam by Anita Nair

Ghachar Ghochar
Vivek Shanbhag
Translated from the Kannada by Srinath Perur

Hindutva or Hind Swaraj
U.R. Ananthamurthy
Translated from the Kannada by Keerti Ramachandra & Vivek Shanbhag

The Liberation of Sita
Volga
Translated from the Telugu by T. Vijay Kumar & C. Vijayasree

A Life Misspent
Suryakant Tripathi Nirala
Translated from the Hindi by Satti Khanna

The Sea Lies Ahead
Intizar Husain
Translated from the Urdu by Rakhshanda Jalil

Selected Poems
Joy Goswami
Translated from the Bengali by Sampurna Chattarji

Wild Animals Prohibited: Stories/Anti-stories
Subimal Misra
Translated from the Bengali by V. Ramaswamy

Wild Words: Four Tamil Poets
Malathi Maithri, Salma, Kutti Revathi and Sukirtharani
Translated from the Tamil by Lakshmi Holmström